OXFORD WORLD'S CLASSICS

THE BOOK OF MARGERY KEMPE

MARGERY KEMPE (née Burnham, b. *c.*1373, d. after 1439) came from the town of Bishop's Lynn (now King's Lynn, Norfolk). She was the daughter of a successful and influential merchant. After her marriage and the birth of her first child, Kempe received her first vision of Christ. Following unsuccessful ventures in brewing and milling, and giving birth to a further thirteen children, Kempe made a vow of chastity and she embarked on a life of prayer, penance, and pilgrimage. *The Book of Margery Kempe* is the account of her spiritual conversion, her travels, and her mystical visions. In Jerusalem she had her first bout of irresistible crying and weeping, which would persist through much of her life. Kempe also visited Rome and all the major shrines of Europe. During the 1420s Kempe was afflicted by an illness that kept her in Lynn, and her husband suffered a serious accident that greatly incapacitated him. Kempe's husband and oldest son died in the early 1430s, after which Kempe made one last difficult journey, to Prussia. She returned home via Wilsnack and Aachen, and then dictated her *Book*. In 1438 she was admitted to the prestigious Guild of the Holy Trinity at Lynn. The precise date of her death is unknown.

ANTHONY BALE is Professor of Medieval Studies at Birkbeck, University of London. He is the author of *The Jew in the Medieval Book: English Antisemitisms 1350–1500* (2006) and *Feeling Persecuted: Christians, Jews, and Images of Violence in the Middle Ages* (2010). In 2011 he was awarded the Philip Leverhulme Prize. For Oxford World's Classics he has also translated Sir John Mandeville's *Book of Marvels and Travels* (2012).

OXFORD WORLD'S CLASSICS

The Book of Margery Kempe

Translated with an Introduction and Notes by

ANTHONY BALE

OXFORD
UNIVERSITY PRESS

OXFORD
UNIVERSITY PRESS

Great Clarendon Street, Oxford, OX2 6DP
United Kingdom

Oxford University Press is a department of the University of Oxford.
It furthers the University's objective of excellence in research, scholarship,
and education by publishing worldwide. Oxford is a registered trade mark of
Oxford University Press in the UK and in certain other countries

First published as an Oxford World's Classics paperback 2015

Impression: 1

Published in the United States of America by Oxford University Press
198 Madison Avenue, New York, NY 10016, United States of America

British Library Cataloguing in Publication Data

Data available

Library of Congress Control Number: 2014949001

ISBN 978-0-19-968664-3

Printed in Great Britain by
Clays Ltd, St Ives plc

ACKNOWLEDGEMENTS

Most of the work on this translation was undertaken during my tenure of the 2012–13 Walter Hines Page Fellowship of the Research Triangle Foundation at the National Humanities Center, North Carolina, USA. I am extremely grateful to the Center for providing such a congenial place to think and work, and to the staff and Fellows for a magical year. I would also like to record my thanks to the Leverhulme Trust which awarded me the Philip Leverhulme Prize, which has allowed me to undertake much of the research for this edition, in particular facilitating visits to East Anglia, Germany, Israel, Italy, Palestine, and Spain. The first fruits of my thinking about Kempe were fostered by an AHRC Research Networking Grant (ref. AH/J002704/1), and the contributors to the network *Remembered Places and Invented Traditions: Thinking about the Holy Land in the Late Medieval West*, in which we explored the travels of Kempe and analogous figures.

For various kinds of input into and support for this project, I would like to thank Jonathan Adams, Sarah Beckwith, Alastair Bennett, Emily Brand, Jeffrey Jerome Cohen, Dyan Elliott, Jess Fenn, Matthew Fisher, Christina M. Fitzgerald, Peter Gibbs, Vincent Gillespie, Caroline Goodson, Cordelia Hess, Bruce Holsinger, Jonathan Hsy, Stephen Kelly, Lisa Lampert-Weissig, Judith Luna, Will Liddle, Dorothy McCarthy, Jake Morrissey, Cath Nall, Timothy Phillips (and Percy), Derrick Pitard, Kyle Reeves, Emily Steiner, and Amanda Walling. I am especially grateful to Sebastian Sobecki for sharing with me his researches on the Kempe family in Gdańsk. I warmly thank those who have informed me about—and accompanied me in Kempe's footsteps around—Bethlehem and Jerusalem, especially John and Ruth Bale, Dana Brueller, Ariel Nura Cohen, Yahel Farag, Maya Lester, Ora Limor, Anna Messner, Mark Pace, and Katharina Palmberger. Isabel Davis, Elliot Kendall, Lara McClure, and Marion Turner gave immensely helpful feedback on drafts of my Introduction. Errors and omissions that remain are, of course, mine to deplore.

I am very grateful to audiences at those institutions where I have presented my work related to Margery Kempe and fifteenth-century pilgrimage, and for the feedback I have received, namely at Birkbeck

College University of London, Duke University, Harvard University, King's College London (Centre for Late Antique and Medieval Studies), University of Tennessee Chattanooga, the Kungliga Vitterhetsakademien Stockholm, and the University of York.

I would also like to record my gratitude to the staff of the British Library, the Custodial Library of the Custodia Terrae Sanctae Jerusalem, the London Library, the National Library of Israel, the exceptional librarians at the National Humanities Center, and the sisters of the Casa di Santa Brigida, Rome.

This book is dedicated to all my friends.

CONTENTS

INTRODUCTION

> The whole book is rich in particular and homely detail of common life; but it is the whole-hearted candour of her self-revelation— set down with the same vigour that sent her tramping in old age through an enemy's country—which gives her self-portrait its power, and will make of MARGERY KEMPE a well-known medieval character.
>
> *The Times*, 30 September 1936

ONE of the most intriguing parts of the story of *The Book of Margery Kempe* happened not in the Middle Ages but at a country-house party, some time in the early 1930s. A group of young people was exuberantly playing ping-pong in the hallway of Southgate House, a Georgian mansion, now a hotel, in the village of Clowne (Derbyshire). The house belonged to the Butler-Bowdons, an old northern English Roman Catholic family. One of the ping-pong players stepped on the ball, and the group set about looking in some cupboards for a new one. There they found 'an entirely undisciplined clutter of smallish leather-bound books'. It so happened that two of the guests then staying at Southgate House were on the staff of the Victoria and Albert Museum in London; they saw that one of these books was of interest, and took it down to London. The little manuscript was intensely studied, and various experts consulted.[1]

Waking up to the world on 27 December 1934, readers of the London *Times* were the first members of the general public to be informed of the rediscovery of *The Book of Margery Kempe*. This news—announced in a letter from the medievalist Hope Emily Allen,[2] who had identified the manuscript—jostled for readers' attention alongside accounts of a fatal train crash in Canada, a Christmas Day prison riot in Glasgow, and, from Berlin, news of Nazi restrictions on German artists and lecturers. Kempe (*c*.1373–after 1439) had long been known of as a medieval mystic, from two early sixteenth-century printings of short excerpts from her visions, but the full account as

---

[1] See Hilton Kelliher, 'The rediscovery of Margery Kempe: a footnote', *British Library Journal* 23 (1997), 259–63; Julie A. Chappell, *Perilous Passages*: The Book of Margery Kempe *1534–1934* (Basingstoke, 2013), 63–6.

[2] *The Times* (London), 27 December 1934, p. 15.

given in this unique manuscript had hitherto been unknown.[3] The rediscovery of Kempe was newsworthy because she was heralded as the author of the earliest autobiography in English, as one of the earliest English women authors, and as a unique personality, whose voice spoke across the centuries. The anecdotal but memorable story of the interrupted house party, the jumbled and messy cupboards, and the *Book*, caught somewhere between esteem and disregard, are all curiously appropriate to the unruly figure of Margery Kempe herself.

In a leader article eighteen months later, *The Times* proclaimed Kempe's *Book*'s 'wide and manifold interest', the 'romance' of its discovery, and 'the strangeness of the whole story'.[4] The *Book*—published first in a modern translation, and then in a Middle English scholarly edition[5]—was widely reviewed, in general media as well as in religious and scholarly publications. Mostly, these reviews valued Kempe's *Book* highly but also passed judgement on the protagonist of the *Book*: Kempe herself. The *Evening Standard* found Kempe 'certainly queer, even in a queer age' whilst the *Daily Telegraph* described Kempe as a 'wet blanket in any company which was innocently enjoying itself'. *The Listener* ventured that 'it would have been wonderful to have met [Kempe] on the bus'. The *Birmingham Post* recommended the book as a Christmas present.[6] Kempe's twentieth-century readers reacted to her with an unusual intimacy, yet they also had widely divergent responses; as R. W. Chambers, in his introduction to the first Modern English translation, said rather patronizingly, '[t]he reader should therefore be warned at the outset that poor Margery is to be classed with those hotels which Baedeker describes as "variously judged"'.[7] In 1980, the Butler-Bowdon family presented the manuscript for sale at auction; it was bought by the British Museum, and is now held at the British Library in London.[8]

[3] On Hope Emily Allen, see the materials listed in the Select Bibliography, 'The reception and rediscovery of Kempe'.

[4] *The Times* (London), 30 September 1936, p. 13.

[5] Respectively, *The Book of Margery Kempe*, trans. W. Butler-Bowdon, with an introduction by R. W. Chambers (Oxford, 1936); *The Book of Margery Kempe*, ed. Sanford Brown Meech and Hope Emily Allen, EETS o.s. 212 (London, 1940), hereafter *BMK*.

[6] These reviews are gathered in George Burns, 'Margery Kempe reviewed', *The Month* 171 (1938), 238–44.

[7] *The Book of Margery Kempe*, trans. Butler-Bowdon, p. 6.

[8] The manuscript is described in the sale catalogue, *Catalogue of Western Manuscripts and Miniatures Comprising . . . the Property of M. E. Butler-Bowdon, O. B. E, Royal Navy,*

The Book of Margery Kempe is a difficult thing to summarize.
It describes the travels and travails of a fifteenth-century Englishwoman, Margery Kempe (née Burnham or Brunham) of Lynn
(Norfolk). The *Book* tells us, in striking detail and lively prose,
about the ways in which its eponymous heroine transformed her life:
from a bourgeois wife and failed businesswoman to serial pilgrim,
exuberant socializer, religious controversialist, and would-be saint.
Kempe travelled far from Norfolk, throughout the Latin Christian
world—around England, through the Baltic, to Spain, Rome, and, via
Venice, to Jerusalem and the Holy Land. The *Book* therefore gives us
a multi-faceted portrait of the world as viewed from pre-Reformation
England. In the *Book* we glimpse Kempe's background as the daughter of the mayor of Lynn, her marital problems, her struggles with
chastity, her various difficulties with important people in power, and
we hear, at length, about her visions of and conversations with Christ,
God, and the Virgin Mary.

The *Book* is in keeping with the emotional and often spectacular
religious sensibility of the later medieval period and also provides us
with a detailed social and cultural history of life as experienced by
one woman. Many episodes in the *Book* are striking and memorable,
as Kempe's disruptive behaviour and down-to-earth wisdom col-
lide with ecclesiastical authorities and vicious detractors. The *Book*
describes many vivid tableaux which foreground Kempe's distinctive
voice and personality: for instance, at Leicester, she pithily rebukes
the Mayor, who had accused her of being a 'strumpet' and a 'deceiver
of the people' (p. 102); in Kempe's account, all the Mayor can do is
insult her, whereas she 'answered intelligently to all that he could say'.
Likewise, at the Archbishop of York's palace Kempe tells a group of
educated and hostile clergy a bold parable about a priest's encounter
with a gluttonous, defecating bear (pp. 115–16). We are told in sur-
prisingly frank language of her sexual desires and temptations (pp. 15,
18, 25, 131), and often the *Book* provides intimate dialogue between
Kempe and her husband, notably the discussion between them
about chastity and sexual desire over a bottle of beer and a cake, one
Midsummer's Eve (pp. 25–7). Elsewhere, inventive and memorable
imagery is used to describe Kempe's mystical religious experiences:
for example, harmonious music (p. 15), dust-motes (p. 81), bellows

(p. 83), the song of a robin redbreast (p. 83), the skin of a stock-fish
(p. 83), a wondrously sweet scent (p. 154). Kempe's *Book* does not
seem to have been widely read in the Middle Ages, yet it is of crucial
importance as a record of popular religion, of women's spirituality,
and of pilgrimage, offering an arrestingly subjective view of medieval
East Anglia, England, and Europe from Galicia to Palestine.

Biography

Kempe was born about 1373, the daughter of John Burnham (d. 1413),
who was a successful merchant in the wealthy town of Bishop's Lynn
(now King's Lynn, Norfolk).[9] At this time, Lynn was an important
trading port in East Anglia, one of the richest areas of provincial
England. Situated just under 100 miles north of London, Lynn was,
before silting in the sixteenth and seventeenth centuries, the port at the
mouth of the River Great Ouse which connected the coast to inland
ports of eastern England, such as Ely, Huntingdon, and Bedford. Lynn
was a main centre for import and export with the Baltic and the Low
Countries,[10] and had at this time a population of approximately 5,000
people, making it amongst the larger towns in England and only slightly
smaller than the nearby county town, Norwich. Anthony Goodman
has stated that, in the late fourteenth century, Lynn 'had one of the
largest concentrations of urban wealth in England'.[11] It was a busy,
cosmopolitan place, and had several large monasteries and friaries (the
Augustinians, Carmelites, Dominicans, and Franciscans, with whom
Kempe dealt, are mentioned at pp. 150, 24, 20, 151 respectively). At the
centre of the town is the grand St Margaret's Church (founded in 1101
by the bishop of Norwich; now known as King's Lynn Minster), the
stage on which some of Kempe's pivotal pious experiences took place,
and there were numerous parish churches and chapels, several of which
dot the landscape described by Kempe.

[9] For a concise biography of Kempe, see Felicity Riddy, 'Kempe, Margery (b. *c.* 1373, *d.*
in or after 1438)', *ODNB*. John Burnham's family probably came from the Burnhams
(Norfolk), a group of villages some 20 miles north-east of Lynn. Kempe's ancestors had
moved to Lynn by 1320 (Anthony Goodman, *Margery Kempe and her World* (Harlow,
2002), 49).

[10] See Dorothy M. Owen, ed., *The Making of King's Lynn: A Documentary Survey*
(London, 1984), giving a documentary portrait of town life in medieval Lynn.

[11] See Goodman, *Margery Kempe*, 15. In comparison, the population of London was
probably in the region of 60,000 people.

John Burnham, Margery Kempe's father, was involved in various commercial activities, including operating a ferry-boat, selling herring, and exporting cloth and lumber; moreover, Burnham was very successful in local government, and held almost every public office in Lynn at one time or another. He was a coroner, a justice of the peace, twice chamberlain, five times mayor, and six times Member of Parliament for Lynn in the later fourteenth century.[12] Kempe herself describes her father's role as alderman of the powerful Holy Trinity Guild in Lynn (p. 13), invoking her elevated social class to defend herself against allegations of heresy. Kempe's father was a well-connected provincial man of means, a member of a mercantile elite.[13] At about the age of 20, Margery Burnham married John Kempe of Lynn. John Kempe seems to have come from local urban merchant stock; his father, a Lynn skinner and merchant also named John (d. 1393), had held local office in Lynn, as a town chamberlain (a kind of town treasurer, responsible for receiving rents on behalf of the town), was involved in trade with Prussia, and owned property on Lynn's quay.[14] John Kempe junior was recorded as a brewer in 1403–5, and by her own account Margery Kempe was briefly and unsuccessfully involved in brewing and milling (see pp. 13–14). John Kempe junior seems to have spent one period as chamberlain of Lynn (1394–5; his older brother Simon (d. *c.*1409) likewise the following year), but did not achieve either wealth or lasting political power. The Burnham and Kempe families owned property throughout Lynn, and Margery and John Kempe probably lived in the centre of the town at Fincham Street or Burghard's Lane (now New Conduit Street), possibly in a house with an attached warehouse.[15] Margery Kempe's disappointment in her husband's status is noted in her *Book*, which sneers that 'he never seemed a likely man to have married her' (p. 13), although John Kempe came from a wealthy and well-connected family.[16] Margery Kempe evidently cared for her husband in his dotage, when

---

[12] The life records of Kempe and her family appear in *BMK* 358–68, and are supplemented by Goodman, *Margery Kempe*.

[13] See Goodman, *Margery Kempe*; Michael D. Myers, 'A fictional true-self: Margery Kempe and the social reality of the merchant elite of King's Lynn', *Albion* 31 (1999), 377–94.

[14] John Kempe's property is recorded in Norwich, Norfolk Record Office KL/C50/514 (*Estate of Margaret Kenynghale, daughter of John Burghard*).

[15] See *BMK* 362–8; Goodman, *Margery Kempe*, 65–6.

[16] See Myers, 'A fictional true-self', 386–7.

he became senile (p. 162), perhaps suggesting that he was somewhat older than her. Kempe's mother is mentioned only once in the *Book* (p. 12); we know very little about her, other than that her name was almost certainly Isabella. A recently revealed document suggests that Kempe's mother was married again, to a man called Geoffrey de Sutton, in the period 1413–18, that period when Kempe was visiting Jerusalem and Santiago and underwent the first bouts of noisy, boisterous crying that would become a hallmark of her behaviour.[17] Kempe had a brother or half-brother, also named John, about whom little is known other than that he was a Lynn guildsman.[18] One of Kempe's kinsmen, possibly an uncle or stepbrother named Robert Burnham, a vintner who was also chamberlain, mayor, and Member of Parliament for Lynn, became very wealthy and was effectively deposed as mayor of Lynn in 1415, although he is not mentioned in the *Book*.[19] It is unclear what became of Kempe's fourteen children, other than the son whose marriage and death are described in the *Book* (pp. 202–4). It is highly unlikely that all of her offspring survived into adulthood.[20] Kempe's oldest son (whose life between Prussia and England features in the *Book*) was almost certainly, like his father and grandfather, called John, and documents have come to light showing that he was active in business in Gdańsk in the early 1430s.[21] Throughout the 1420s and 1430s, Margery Kempe lived in Lynn; her death must have taken place after 1438 when she was admitted to the prestigious and powerful Guild of the Holy Trinity at Lynn.

The *Book* suggests that Kempe could not or did not read and that she could not write, but we should be wary of calling her illiterate. She was clearly educated through aural learning, from being read to and from memorizing texts (e.g. pp. 62, 133).[22] In general, only aristocratic and

[17] William Liddle, *The Virtue of Place in Late Medieval Lynn*, unpublished PhD thesis, Queen's University Belfast (2013), 43. An 'Isabelle Brunham' is mentioned in another document, which states that she had a 'duchman Taylour'—a German tailor—staying in her tenement (Goodman, *Margery Kempe*, 223). This gives a plausible identity to Kempe's first scribe, an alternative to the generally accepted idea that this scribe was Kempe's son (see p. xviii).

[18] Goodman, *Margery Kempe*, 50. On Kempe's social context, see Kate Parker, 'Lynn and the making of a mystic', *CBMK* 55–73.

[19] Goodman, *Margery Kempe*, 42.   [20] Goodman, *Margery Kempe*, 66.

[21] I am very grateful to Sebastian Sobecki for sharing the fruits of his research, publication forthcoming, from the Polish archives.

[22] On the widespread use of 'reading aloud' and active listening in the Middle Ages, see Joyce Coleman, *Public Reading and the Reading Public in Late Medieval England and France* (Cambridge, 1996).

royal women, and some women in nunneries, were formally or exten-
sively educated. However, many women of Kempe's class owned books
and were the patrons of scribes and poets.[23] In the medieval era, those
who *could* read and write often chose to be read to and to use a scribe,
and reading was frequently a social, group activity. As discussed later,
the *Book* is informed by a wide range of written sources, many of
which were known to Kempe through having been read to her, through
preaching, and possibly through other media such as drama, liturgical
processions, church murals, stained glass, and so on. The boundaries
between what we now call literacy and illiteracy were not clearly drawn.
Kempe states that she had little Latin (p. 103) and that she could not
understand spoken Latin, although she quotes Latin from her psalter
to defend herself in an argument with a monk (p. 214), and some of
the Latinate words used in the *Book* suggest a Latin education on the
part of either Kempe or her scribe. The *Book* says that Kempe learned
Scripture 'through sermons and by talking with clerics' (p. 31) and,
like most medieval people, she would have encountered the divine
word most frequently through the oral media of preaching and prayer.
Compellingly, Kempe describes how 'she hungered very severely after
God's word', wishing for her soul to be filled with the divine word for
which 'my soul is always . . . hungry' (p. 129). Women were forbidden from preaching, but they frequently owned prayer-books, poetry
books, historical literature, and they lived in a society that greatly valued the power of the written and spoken word. In the *Book*, Kempe
engages with several figures we might now call 'writers', not least the
renowned mystic Julian of Norwich (1342–1416) and the theological
commentator Alan of Lynn (1347/8–1432), but she seems to be un-
aware of either as an 'author', although they are clearly 'authorities' and
spiritual counsellors. It is then fair to say that Kempe's *Book* displays
an abiding cultural literacy, an ability to engage with a world of signs,
ideas, and other people's words.[24]

[23] For accounts of women's reading at a similar place and time to Kempe's, see
Anthony Bale, 'A Norfolk gentlewoman and Lydgatian patronage: Lady Sibylle Boys
and her cultural environment', *Medium Ævum* 78 (2009), 394–413; Mary Erler, *Women,
Reading, and Piety in Late Medieval England* (Cambridge, 2002); Ralph Hanna, 'Some
Norfolk women and their books', in June Hall McCash, ed., *The Cultural Patronage of
Medieval Women* (Athens, GA, 1996), 288–305; Carol M. Meale, '". . . alle the bokes
that I haue of latyn, englisch, and frensch": laywomen and their books in late medi-
eval England', in Carol M. Meale, ed., *Women and Literature in Britain, 1150–1500*
(Cambridge, 1996), 128–58.

[24] See Jacqueline Jenkins, 'Reading and *The Book of Margery Kempe*', *CBMK* 113–28.

Furthermore, Kempe was not a heretic (or a 'Lollard', to use the pejorative term current in fifteenth-century England): this was a particularly pressing issue in Kempe's times, because of the 'Lollard panic' (as Jacqueline Jenkins has called it) in early fifteenth-century England and because women's literacy was closely related to Lollardy.[25] Norwich and its surrounding area were certainly centres of Lollardy. Prompted by the writings of John Wycliffe (d. 1384), the Lollards—an affiliation of preachers, thinkers, worshippers, and enthusiasts rather than a formal movement—held that the Bible should be translated into the vernacular to make it accessible to the laity; that practices of praying to (and making payments to) saints and going on pilgrimage, and of buying pardons, were corrupt; that the Church's ownership of land and other worldly endowments was immoral; and, most gravely, that the bread and wine of the Eucharist might not have been transformed into the actual body and blood of Christ.[26] It is clear from the *Book* that Kempe did not hold these beliefs; on the contrary, she was avidly devoted to the Eucharist, to the saints, and to pilgrimage. But perhaps because devout women frequently took part in secretive Lollard 'conventicles' (assemblies for prayer and preaching), Kempe is repeatedly accused of being a Lollard.

The response of the Church and the state to the Lollards created a fraught atmosphere of religious censorship and regulation. In 1401, the statute *De heretico comburendo* (*On Burning a Heretic*) had been passed by the English parliament under Henry IV; it threatened Lollards with burning, a warning which resounds several times in the *Book* (pp. 37, 104, 118). Similarly, Archbishop Arundel's Constitutions of Oxford (1408–9) sought to regulate preaching and religious practice. The Constitutions regulated university syllabi, censored vernacular writing, outlawed preaching without a licence, banned preachers' discussion of the clergy's sinfulness, and regulated the discussion of matters of faith outside universities. Especially in the first half of the *Book*, religious authorities appear throughout Kempe's world, looking for signs of illicit activity. Kempe, whilst disruptive and sometimes disrespectful, was always careful to stay on

[25] See Jenkins, 'Reading', 127–8.
[26] For various perspectives on Kempe and Lollardy see John Arnold, 'Margery's trials: heresy, Lollardy and dissent', *CBMK* 75–93, and the materials listed in the Select Bibliography.

the correct side of the line between orthodoxy and heresy and, by her own account, was greeted quite warmly by many of the bishops and clerics she encountered.

Kempe's *Book* aims to show us that the stakes were high for its protagonist: we are to understand that devotion, for Kempe, was a life and death situation. Indeed, Kempe would have heard of her famous contemporary, Joan of Arc (burned at the stake in 1431), who exhibited many similar characteristics to her. Both were renegade women who subverted established gender roles, Kempe through wearing the white clothes of virginity, Joan through cross-dressing; both received the 'gift of tears'; both were publicly abstemious and renounced luxury; both had special reverence for saints Katherine and Margaret; both were pursued by the Duke of Bedford; both record their fear of being raped and were threatened with sexual violence; both had gifts of prophecy; and both worried about the possibility of diabolical inspiration and the difficulties associated with the discernment of spirits.[27] But Joan, canonized as a Catholic saint in 1920, suffered death at the age of 19 for her bringing together of politics and 'heretical' religion, whereas Kempe seems to have lived to an old age, in some comfort and esteem, a guildswoman in a well-to-do provincial town.

Authorship

On one hand, Kempe is often referred to as one of the first English female authors, and her *Book* is known as the earliest English autobiography. On the other hand, Kempe is referred to throughout the *Book* as 'this creature'—in the third person—and the *Book* makes clear that Kempe did not write down the narrative.[28] So who is the author of *The Book of Margery Kempe*?

In order to consider the authorship of *The Book of Margery Kempe*, we need first to reconsider the modern idea of the 'author'. In place

---

[27] On Joan of Arc see Craig Taylor, *Joan of Arc—La Pucelle* (Manchester, 2006). Likewise, Marguerite Porete (d. 1310), whose *Mirror of Simple Souls* was translated into Latin in the fifteenth century at Mount Grace (where the manuscript of Kempe's *Book* was held), was burned as a heretic in Paris.

[28] At one point, the narrative slips into 'we' (p. 35), as if being directly dictated by Kempe, and other scenes are reminiscent of eyewitness. Whilst these instances do not show that the *Book* is a direct copy of Kempe's words, they do suggest that her words directly constitute some of the narrative as we now have it.

of just one 'author' with whom the entire *Book* originated, we must think in terms of the more historically accurate categories of subject, amanuensis (or recorder), and scribe. *The Book of Margery Kempe* is structured by Kempe's life and Kempe is undoubtedly the main subject, protagonist, and source; however, according to its own account, the *Book* was not physically written by Kempe and it is unclear how far she controlled or approved of the *Book* as we now have it.[29] So 'autobiography' is rather a rigid term for such a collaborative way of writing. The introductory proem describes the process of how the book was written: '[t]his book is not written in order, each thing after another as it was done, but just as the story came to the creature in her mind when it was to be written down . . .' (p. 6). At the conclusion of Kempe's *Book* are her prayers to God, foregrounding both Kempe's own voice and her spiritual wellbeing. So the book advertises itself as a faithful, if non-chronological, copy of Kempe's life and visions, and to this extent Kempe is the creator of the narrative; however, these visions, which the *Book* says are divinely ordained, are ultimately 'authored' by God (from Kempe's perspective). Moreover, throughout the *Book* we are challenged to recognize the role of Kempe's scribes and 'listeners', those to whom she had to dictate her account. According to the proem, clerics begged Kempe to have them 'write and make a book of her feelings and her revelations' (p. 5), although she waited more than twenty years, for God's command, to do so. Kempe then approached an acquaintance, an Englishman (possibly her son) who had lived for a long time in German-speaking Europe (pp. 5-6); she narrated to him as much of her account as she could, but this man died.[30] Then, a priest looked at what had been written and saw it was 'so ill-written that he could make little sense of it' (p. 5). This priest promised to attempt to make as much sense of it as he could, but was put off by malicious gossip about Kempe; so he stalled for four years and, eventually, told Kempe to go to another 'good man', who had once received letters from the first scribe and

---

[29] For some important perspectives see the material under 'Authorship' in the Select Bibliography.

[30] This man is often assumed to be Kempe's son based on the circumstantial evidence that Kempe says both her scribe and her son had lived in Germany, both had travelled to England with wife and child, both had stayed with Kempe, and that both had died soon thereafter. The question remains, however, as to why Kempe would not identify her son as such and records from Lynn show that there were many Baltic traders in the town in Kempe's day.

might therefore be able to read the mangled account. This scribe was also unable to make much sense of it. However, the priest was 'vexed in his conscience' (p. 6) that he had delayed work on the book and prayed to be able to understand it: at once it became much easier for him. The priest's sudden literacy mirrors medieval stories of people miraculously being able to see, and gives the *Book* a godly seal of approval (suggesting a kind of divine, rather than human, authorship, echoed in a story, given later in the *Book*, of a German confessor who was miraculously able to understand Kempe, p. 76). So at least four people worked on the original text: Kempe; the Englishman who had lived abroad; this man's friend; and the priest. In the context of medieval authorship, the presence of a clerical writer would add to, rather than diminish, the protagonist's authority. Nicholas Watson has argued that the priest is effectively an editor who rewrote Kempe's material, whilst Lynn Staley has suggested that 'Margery' is a character written by 'Kempe', her scribe also a character designed to enhance the *Book*'s 'bookish quality'.[31]

Other people were involved in composing the *Book* as we have it today. We cannot overlook the role of the scribe, named Salthouse, who composed the surviving manuscript in the fifteenth century and may have made any number of changes to the text with which he was working. Also, at least four sets of annotations have been added to the manuscript (some of these are described in the Explanatory Notes), by various monks, almost certainly Carthusians, in the fifty or so years after Kempe's death. These monks seem to have used the manuscript to trace mystical themes, imagery, and mentions of other mystical writers.

Taken at face value, the difficult genesis of *The Book of Margery Kempe* bears out the requirement on the part of medieval women to rely on educated or ordained men in order to write. The priest's input is implied at many points, referred to as 'the priest who wrote this book' (pp. 52, 56) even as Kempe too is 'occupied in the writing of this treatise' (p. 195). It is unclear how far these roles should be considered 'scribal', compositional, or authorial. This priest clearly acted as a commentator on and editor of Kempe's account (for instance, he writes that 'This creature had many more such revelations in feeling; to write them all down would perhaps be to impede more profitable

---

[31] Lynn Staley, *Margery Kempe's Dissenting Fictions* (University Park, PA, 1994), 4, 36.

things', p. 52), even as Kempe checked the priest's work: 'he read it over in the presence of this creature, and she helped at those times where there was any difficulty' (p. 6). There is, at points, a strong sense of what the critic A. C. Spearing has called 'clerical textuality' and we gravely misunderstand the *Book* if we think it offers Kempe's unmediated voice.[32] Thus, instead of looking for a single 'author' for *The Book of Margery Kempe*, we would do better to acknowledge the collaborative, and sometimes haphazard, way in which medieval writing was produced.

The difficult passage of Kempe's *Book* into the world is in keeping with other medieval works of mysticism. Many mystics strove for a 'negative' or 'apophatic' understanding of God (knowing God through what he is *not*; knowing God by not signifying or representing him); according to such views, it was impossible to represent the goodness and wholeness of God in language. Such a God cannot be confined to words, is not defined by time and space, and cannot be positively described. So, by foregrounding the difficulty of writing about Kempe's experience of God, the *Book* is in keeping with other mystical works which sought to describe the 'cloud of unknowing' which at first obscures and then leads to a perfect understanding of God.[33]

Sources and contexts

The Book of Margery Kempe is at once a biographical record of a provincial woman's religious struggles and a richly allusive, literary document: both Kempe herself and her scribes were familiar with many books, and the *Book* is shot through with references to this reading. In order to be authoritative (i.e. an 'author') in the Middle Ages one had to quote from *auctores*—that is, other writers whose works were considered authoritative.[34] Kempe's *Book* shows a sustained engagement with earlier texts and sheds a great deal of light on the religious reading habits of fifteenth-century England.

[32] A. C. Spearing, 'Margery Kempe', in A. S. G. Edwards, ed., *A Companion to Middle English Prose* (Cambridge, 2004), 83–97. Spearing speculates that Kempe's confessor, Robert Springold, was the priestly scribe and author of much of the *Book*.

[33] For further reading on Kempe and mysticism, see the literature in the Select Bibliography.

[34] See Alastair Minnis, *The Medieval Theory of Authorship: Scholastic Literary Attitudes in the Later Middle Ages* (London, 1984).

Biblical allusions appear frequently throughout the *Book*, and Kempe states that a priest read to her, amongst other books, the Bible with commentary by 'doctors'—that is, a glossed bible, with commentary attributed to the Church Fathers. Elsewhere, Kempe uses language relating to the Virgin Mary to describe herself (p. 202) and, at many points, the saints (especially Katherine, Margaret, and Mary Magdalene) are invoked as powerful models of female wisdom, strength, suffering, and piety, within a framework endorsed by the Church. Kempe would have been intimately acquainted with the saints through everyday culture, including sermons and wall-paintings, often based on Jacobus de Voragine's widely disseminated encyclopaedia of saints' lives, the *Golden Legend* (*c*.1260). In terms of other reading, the *Book* explicitly states (pp. 39, 130) that Kempe and her scribe knew several works of mystical spirituality, all of which would have been available in Latin and English and were staples of any late medieval religious book collection. These are the *Revelations* or *Liber Celestis* of St Bridget [Birgitta] of Sweden (1303–73), including a life of St Bridget; writings by Walter Hilton (*c*.1343–96); the *Stimulus Amoris* attributed to Bonaventure (now known as pseudo-Bonaventure), which was translated into English as the *Pricking of Love* by Hilton; and the *Incendium Amoris* (*Fire of Love*) by Richard Rolle (d. 1349). These books were key influences on the presentation of Kempe's mysticism, piety, prayerfulness, and divinity, and they also inform much of the imagery and diction of the *Book*. Listed twice in the *Book*, they represent a kind of mainstream library of books that informed and supported Kempe's life.

Such a wide range of reading is in keeping with the context of Margery Kempe's Lynn, a highly literate and culturally sophisticated environment. In the 1380s Nicholas of Lynn, a Carmelite in the town, produced the *Kalendarium*, an astronomical work read and referred to by Geoffrey Chaucer.[35] Later, the *Promptorium parvulorum* (*The Children's Store-house*, *c*.1440), an innovative kind of early dictionary, was produced by a Dominican anchorite at Lynn. Dramatic productions and guild performances were also staged in the town.[36] Meanwhile, John Capgrave (1393–1464), the Augustinian prior of Lynn, wrote numerous texts that intersect with Kempe's interests and habits: these include lives of St Norbert of Xanten and

---

[35] Sigmund Eisner, 'Lynn, Nicholas (*fl.* 1386–1411)', *ODNB*.
[36] See Claire Sponsler, 'Drama and piety', *CBMK* 129–43.

St Gilbert of Sempringham, celebrating pious men who had devoted their lives to monasticism; a *Life of St Katherine*, dedicated to the virgin martyr of Alexandria, one of Kempe's favourite saints; and *The Solace of Pilgrims*, a guide to the pilgrimage sites of Rome.[37] The subjects that occupied Capgrave, 'hot topics' of fifteenth-century Lynn, were similar to those that interested Kempe: piety, sanctity, and pilgrimage.

Bridget of Sweden in particular offered to Kempe a role model of a pious and high-born woman visionary who had successfully achieved worldly status *and* ecclesiastical imprimatur (Bridget was a member of the Swedish royal family). Bridget had also been immortalized as the subject of a book of her saintly deeds, albeit one written post-humously. In some simple but important ways, Kempe mapped the contours of Bridget's life onto her own: Bridget had many children (eight to Kempe's fourteen), she successfully persuaded her husband to live with her in chastity for a period, she undertook pilgrimages to Santiago de Compostela, Rome, and Jerusalem, she underwent a mystical marriage with God, and she believed, like Kempe, in the power of the book as a symbol of authority and self-authorization (Bridget's visions include one of a golden, shining book, alive and speaking from a pulpit).[38] There are considerable differences between the two women too—not least that Bridget's sanctity was promoted *after* her death, whereas Kempe had her *Book* made while she was still alive.

Kempe or her scribe also knew of a 'treatise' (p. 139) concerning Elizabeth of Hungary (d. 1338; also known as Elizabeth of Töss), providing a precedent for Kempe's loud crying (p. 139).[39] Elizabeth was a Dominican nun and, like Bridget of Sweden, of royal blood.[40] Yet another holy woman, Marie d'Oignies (d. 1213), is mentioned, her life being read by Kempe's scribe (p. 138), who saw parallels

[37] See Karen Winstead, *John Capgrave's Fifteenth Century* (Philadelphia, 2006).

[38] See *The Revelations of St Birgitta*, ed. William Patterson Cumming, EETS o.s. 178 (London, 1929), 68. On Bridget of Sweden, see Gunnel Cleve, 'Margery Kempe: a Scandinavian influence on medieval England', in Marion Glasscoe, ed., *The Medieval Mystical Tradition in England* (Cambridge, 1992), 163–75; Julia Bolton Holloway, 'Bride, Margery, Julian and Alice: Bridget of Sweden's textual community in medieval England', in Sandra J. McEntire, ed., *Margery Kempe: A Book of Essays* (New York, 1992), 203–22.

[39] Alexandra Barratt, 'Margery Kempe and the king's daughter of Hungary', in Sandra J. McEntire, ed., *Margery Kempe: A Book of Essays* (New York, 1992), 189–201.

[40] A text known as *The Revelations of Elizabeth of Hungary* was associated with her in the Middle Ages, although it is unlikely actually to have been written by her.

between the two women's weeping.[41] These and similar precursors show how Kempe was not behaving 'madly' or unprecedentedly, but rather aping popular and fashionable European models of spirituality.[42] One scholar has gone as far as to describe Kempe's piety as 'pure imitation'.[43]

Other sources, known either to Kempe or her scribes, can be discerned at the level of allusion (referred to in the notes to this edition), although often it is not possible to be sure how much this reflects actual reading of a text or a more general cultural circulation of common mystical imagery. Kempe and/or her scribe were almost certainly familiar with the key work of popular mysticism, the *Meditationes vitae Christi*, then also attributed to Bonaventure but now attributed to John de Caulibus, a Tuscan Franciscan writing in the early fourteenth century. This work, which was widely read and translated into English in the fifteenth century, places great emphasis on the power and efficacy of imagining oneself at scenes of Christ's life and death, not just as a spectator but as an emotional participant. It was particularly suitable for—and, in English translation, aimed at—'unlettered' people, readers who were seen as being fired by enthusiasm and imagination, strong emotions, affective feeling, and the power of prayer. Nicholas Love, who translated the work into English in 1410, said that secular men and women 'need to be fed with the milk of light doctrine and not with the serious meat of great clergy'. The technique of the *Meditationes* assumes an intimate knowledge of biblical stories; from this knowledge came intense personal visions, especially based around Christ's humanity.

As was quite normal for a woman of her class and aspirations, Kempe owned a handful of books. Early on in the *Book* (p. 24), Kempe is holding a book—presumably a book of hours or psalter—in church when a large beam falls on her; miraculously, she is unharmed. Is the

---

[41] Jacques de Vitry (d. 1240) wrote a widely read life of Marie d'Oignies in which he describes how a constant outburst of tears which night and day ran down her cheeks made the church floor all muddy; 'she caught the [tears] in the veil with which she covered her head. She used up so many veils in this manner that she often had to change her wet veil for a dry one' (see Margot H. King, ed. and trans., *Two Lives of Marie d'Oignies*, 4th edn. (Toronto, 1998), 60).

[42] See further Ute Stargardt, 'The Beguines of Belgium, the Dominican nuns of Germany, and Margery Kempe', in Thomas J. Heffernan, ed., *The Popular Literature of Medieval England* (Knoxville, TN, 1985), 277–313.

[43] Barbara Newman, 'What did it mean to say "I saw"? The clash between theory and practice in medieval visionary culture', *Speculum* 80 (2005), 1–42; p. 32.

book here invoked as a protective talisman? Later (p. 214), she cites the psalter in Latin. Such books would likely have been illustrated with images, and possibly highly decorated. An incident involving Kempe's priest-friend (the scribe who wrote the *Book*), in which he is nearly duped over a second-hand book, shows not only the importance of books in Kempe's culture but also their material value, as goods traded and exchanged for their physical as well as moral worth.

Domesticity and intimacy

Kempe made her own interpretations of spiritual life, and the *Book of Margery Kempe* gives a great deal of insight into everyday *things*: the stuff of the life of a devout and well-to-do, but not aristocratic, medieval woman. Many of Kempe's moments of self-validation occur with material objects: not just religious books, but a holy doll, an engraved ring, white clothes, a souvenir replica of Moses' rod, a pietà (an image of Mary cradling Jesus' dead body), even a sheet. Visuality and material culture are crucial elements of Kempe's devotion, as earthly sight is converted into her spiritual vision. In medieval Christianity (or 'sacramental Christianity') every created thing was suffused with divinity: God was everywhere, and the divine made itself felt in the mundane. Moreover, spiritual reward was often discussed in terms of payment, credit, profit.[44] This reflects not only Kempe's mercantile context but also a religious culture in which the divine was interwoven with the everyday.

Kempe's description of the full and resolutely physical humanity of Christ—a handsome man with blood, toes, hands, a beautiful face—is consistent with the religious feelings of other late medieval visionaries. Bathing, cuddling, and kissing the Christ-child were favourite images.[45] Erotic imagery involving the manly, adult Christ was also widespread, seen in the famous vision of Catherine of Siena (1347–80) of Christ as a bridegroom, echoed here in Kempe's mystical marriage with the Godhead in Rome (Chapter 35) and her erotic encounter with Christ, who says to her, 'I must be intimate

[44] See Sarah Beckwith, 'A very material mysticism: the medieval mysticism of Margery Kempe', in David Aers, ed., *Medieval Literature: History, Criticism and Ideology* (New York, 1986), 34–57.

[45] See Mary Dzon and Theresa M. Kenney, eds., *The Christ Child in Medieval Culture: Alpha Es et O!* (Toronto, 2011).

with you and lie in your bed with you' (p. 83).[46] In fact, there was a well-developed popular theology of Jesus as lover, often expressed in frankly erotic terms, that had become widespread in English writing from the twelfth century onwards, in texts like the *Ancrene Wisse* (*Knowledge for Anchoresses*), *Hali Meiðhad* (*Holy Virginity*), and the Middle English lives of saints Juliana, Margaret, and Katherine. A representative example is furnished by a conventional religious tract, *A Talking of the Love of God*, written in the style of Richard Rolle, which repeatedly addresses Christ with intense intimacy, as wooer, lover, and spouse: 'Oh sweet Jesus, sweet life, my dear heart, my life's love, my life, my death, my bliss: for you ordained me your dear lover, between your arms I lay myself, between my arms I embrace you; now give me feeling eternally in you, and hold me in your protection.'[47]

Readers may at first be struck by Kempe's eye for everyday detail and for personalities, but *The Book of Margery Kempe* remains a book about mystical theology. Perhaps the two main subjects, or problems, of the *Book* are the 'mixed life' and the 'discernment of spirits' (also known as *discretio*). The mixed life describes a way of life between action and meditation, combining community life (preaching, nursing, charity) with intense individual contemplation.[48] In other words, how might one combine a worldly life with spiritual growth? The 'discernment of spirits', put simply, concerns the question of how one attempts to tell if messages received through spirits are good or evil, and indeed if they are spiritual messages at all: the problem, as phrased in the *Book*, of how 'that which she understood physically was to be understood spiritually' (p. 196). Are the voices and visions Kempe receives truly from God? As the *Book*

---

[46] See Caroline Walker Bynum, *Holy Feast and Holy Fast* (New York, 1987), 246.

[47] 'A talkyng of the love of God', in C. Horstmann, ed., *Yorkshire Writers* (London, 1896), 366 (my translation). The related 'Wooing group' of medieval texts—probably written for enclosed women in the thirteenth century—includes imagery of Christ as lover-knight and erotic religious language. See Denis Renevey, 'Enclosed desires: a study of the Wooing Group', in W. F. Pollard and R. Boenig, eds., *Mysticism and Spirituality in Medieval England* (Cambridge, 1997), 39–62.

[48] Walter Hilton, whose work was known to Kempe, wrote at length about the mixed life. Kempe's relationship to ideas of the 'mixed life' and the generic problems it presents are discussed in Ruth Summar McIntyre, 'Margery's "mixed life": place, pilgrimage, and the problem of genre in *The Book of Margery Kempe*', *English Studies* 89 (2008), 643–61; see too Hilary M. Carey, 'Devout literate laypeople and the pursuit of the mixed life in later medieval England', *Journal of Religious History* 14 (1987), 361–81.

says, 'this creature much dreaded the illusions and deceits of her spiritual enemies' (p. 4). Is a life lived through divine communication sacred, or profane?

Medieval pilgrimage and travel

The Book of Margery Kempe reflects many kinds of generic conventions—the saint's life, the spiritual biography, the confessional, an extended prayer, a romance—but it is not defined by any one genre. If the *Book* has a structuring principle, it is probably that of pilgrimage, which forms the core of the events described in it (the period from about 1413 to 1419, when Kempe became chaste and undertook many pilgrimages). Kempe's journey to Jerusalem is perhaps her key transformative moment, and her final journey, from Wilsnack via Aachen to Lynn, gives the *Book* a kind of formal completeness, as an old woman struggles to return home; both Kempe's travelling and her *Book* end with a fervent, personal prayer.

Kempe's journeys were sacred pilgrimages—based on intense feeling and moral reformation—rather than travels of curiosity.[49] A pilgrimage was, ideally, a pious journey that culminated—usually at Rome or Jerusalem—with receiving an indulgence, a remission from punishments in Purgatory after death. In the words of Bridget of Sweden, who had such a powerful effect on Kempe, by entering the Church of the Holy Sepulchre in Jerusalem 'one is entirely cleansed of all one's sin . . . [as] all those who come with sincere devotion to this place, Jerusalem, willing to amend themselves and not to return to sin, all their sins are forgiven them.'[50] In practice, pilgrimages in late medieval Europe seem to have been more like package holidays. The pilgrims were organized by guides and supplied by merchants who easily duped their captive market; the pilgrims fell out with each other; they became ill; they often found local customs confusing or hostile; they were subject to thefts, violence, getting lost. Far from travelling alone, Kempe (not unlike Chaucer's Canterbury pilgrims) made journeys which were highly social, busy even, and full of conflict. We see Kempe on established routes, such as from Wilsnack to

---

[49] See Christian Zacher, *Curiosity and Pilgrimage: The Literature of Discovery in Fourteenth-Century England* (Baltimore, MD, 1976).

[50] Bridget of Sweden, *Liber Celestis*, ed. Roger Ellis, EETS, o.s. 297 (Oxford, 1987), 479 (my translation).

Aachen, or from Calais to Dover, struggling along in the company of groups of pilgrims.

A married woman like Kempe would have been expected to get 'spousal permission' to go on pilgrimage (and indeed Kempe is granted permission by her husband, p. 111). In no way was pilgrimage 'reserved' for men only, although many male writers were critical—or satirical—of the motives for women going on pilgrimage (not least Geoffrey Chaucer, whose Wife of Bath, 'who knew much about wandering by the way', seems to be looking out for a new husband on the road to Canterbury).[51] We know that, in the fifteenth century, women pilgrims had their own Franciscan-run dormitories in Bethlehem and Jerusalem, although specific details of daily life for a female Jerusalem pilgrim are lacking.[52] From slightly later in the fifteenth century, the rich records of the English Hospice in Rome (where Kempe stayed *c.*1415) show that Kempe was far from unusual as a British woman travelling there. The records show groups of women travelling together in pairs or in larger groups and women travelling with their husbands. However, many pilgrims seem to have travelled alone, as single women, such as one Marian Haute of Dover (arrived in Rome on 6 June 1479), 'Joanna' without a surname or place of origin (5 November 1479), and Alice Bedleem of London (20 September 1481).[53] As the *Book* makes clear, the mixing of people of different classes and backgrounds was both a pleasure and hazard of pilgrimage. We do not gain a strong sense of the social class of the women admitted to the English Hospice in Rome, though not all of them were wealthy: consider Alice Melton, washerwoman, admitted on 12 June 1483, who died in Rome, far from home and amongst strangers.[54] Unfortunately similarly rich records for fifteenth-century Jerusalem have not come to light, but surviving accounts of the Holy Land pilgrimage show that conditions could be harsh and that many western travellers were dissatisfied with their accommodations and worried for their safety.

[51] See Graciela Daichman, *Wayward Nuns in Medieval Literature* (Syracuse, NY, 1986); Alcuin Blamires, ed., *Woman Defamed and Woman Defended: An Anthology of Medieval Texts* (Oxford, 1992).

[52] See Jonathan Sumption, *Pilgrimage*, rev. edn. (London, 2011), 478–9; Leigh Ann Craig, '"Stronger than men and braver than knights": women and the pilgrimages to Jerusalem and Rome in the later Middle Ages', *Journal of Medieval History* 29 (2003), 153–75; Sylvia Schein, 'Bridget of Sweden, Margery Kempe and women's Jerusalem pilgrimage in the Middle Ages', *Mediterranean Historical Review* 14 (1999), 44–58.

[53] John Allen, ed., *The English Hospice in Rome* (Leominster, 1962), 110; p. 113.

[54] Allen, ed., *English Hospice*, 122.

Pilgrimage was expensive but often funded by generous gifts (like Bishop Repingdon's donation of 26s. 8d. to Kempe, for clothing and prayers, p. 36). An anonymous English pilgrim travelling to Jerusalem in 1344–5 left a list of his expenses: amongst other things, he had to pay tributes to the Sultan and charges to dozens of guards and consuls for entry to different ports, as well as fees for camels and cameleers to cross the desert, for people to look after his luggage and wine, for entering and leaving the Church of the Holy Sepulchre, and even for entering the Holy Sepulchre itself.[55] Most lay pilgrims stayed in the hospices at the now-vanished Mauristan, near the Church of the Holy Sepulchre; conditions there were grim, and fifteenth-century pilgrims frequently complained.[56] Sir Richard Guildford (c.1450–1506), a royal adminis-trator who travelled to the Holy Land, had a spirited, if often rather negative, account of his travels written down by his chaplain. Here, we find angry complaints about the 'great difficulty and outrageous cost' of contracting camels from the Mameluks and gaining safe passage to Jerusalem; we read about the pilgrims' 'very evil' treatment by the local population; we hear about the 'old cave', and its 'bare, stinking stable-ground', in which the pilgrims were held at Jaffa, and the 'bare walls and bare floors' on which they had to sleep in the pilgrim hostels; we are told of the 'sickness' which seems to have afflicted almost all the pilgrims and would claim Guildford's life, before he was able to return home.[57] Likewise, Kempe's experience of travel—including bullying, theft, heatstroke, delays, and many disappointments—evokes both the Christ-like *via crucis* (way of the Cross) she trod for a spiritual reward, and a voyage of practical discomfort, danger, and expense.

Reception and critical approaches

Hope Emily Allen, who identified Kempe's book, looked forward, in her prefatory notes, to 'the professional psychologist who later will doubtless pronounce at length on Margery's type of neuroticism'.[58]

[55] Eugene Hoade, *Western Pilgrims: The Itineraries of Fr. Simon Fitzsimons (1322–23), A Certain Englishman (1344–45), Thomas Brygg (1392)* (Jerusalem, 1952), 84–6.

[56] See *CCKJ* 3. 198–9.

[57] Henry Ellis, ed., *The Pylgrymage of Sir Richard Guylforde*, Camden Society 51 (London, 1851); on Guildford, see Rob Lutton, 'Richard Guldeford's pilgrimage: piety and cultural change in late fifteenth- and early sixteenth-century England', *History* 98 (2012), 41–78.

[58] *BMK*, p. lxv.

An early reviewer of Kempe's *Book*, H. B. Charlton in the *Manchester Guardian*, concluded his brief review with the hope 'that the Freudians will not entirely appropriate these records of abnormal psychology'.[59] In 'diagnosing' Kempe as 'neurotic' and 'abnormal', Allen and Charlton appointed themselves psychiatrists to Kempe's 'patient'; yet both acutely anticipated the dominant mode of much of Kempe's twentieth-century audience, which variously described her as suffering 'post-partum psychosis', as 'quite mad—an incurable hysteric with a large paranoid trend', a depressive woman going through a 'manic-depressive illness', as suffering from '*hysterica compassio*', a 'psychotic', and as suffering from 'frontal lobe epilepsy'.[60] Others have asserted that Kempe was suffering from 'Jerusalem syndrome' (a psychosis occasioned by visiting the city of Jerusalem), or 'Tourette's syndrome' (motor and vocal tics involving socially inappropriate remarks), or have attributed her visions and behaviour to her being menopausal.[61] These readings say much about today's medicalization of society and our reflex resort to popular psychology, but they are neither historically sensitive nor medically sound (in that we cannot use an ancient and partial account like Kempe's *Book* to make any kind of rigorous 'medical' diagnosis). Kempe certainly suffered a crisis after the birth of a child, as she had a 'fever' and she was 'out of her mind' (p. 11). She underwent a period of 'instability', during which she 'lost her reason and her wits', and

[59] H. B. Charlton, 'Three women', *Manchester Guardian*, 24 November 1936, p. 7.

[60] Quoting, respectively, Clarissa W. Atkinson, *Mystic and Pilgrim: The Book and the World of Margery Kempe*, new edn. (Ithaca, 1985), 209; Donald R. Howard, *Writers and Pilgrims: Medieval Pilgrimage Narratives and their Posterity* (Berkeley, CA, 1980), 34–5; Maureen Fries, 'Margery Kempe', in Paul E. Szarmach, ed., *An Introduction to the Medieval Mystics of Europe* (Albany, NY, 1984), 217–36, at note on p. 355; Hope Phyllis Weissman, 'Margery Kempe in Jerusalem: *Hysterica Compassio* in the late Middle Ages', in Mary Carruthers and Elizabeth Kirk, eds., *Acts of Interpretation: The Text in Its Contexts, 700–1600: Essays on Medieval and Renaissance Literature in Honor of E. Talbot Donaldson* (Norman, OK, 1982), 201–17; Mary Hardman Farley, 'Her own creatur: religion, feminist criticism, and the functional eccentricity of Margery Kempe', *Exemplaria* 11 (1999), 1–21; p. 4; Richard Lawes, 'The madness of Margery Kempe', in Marion Glasscoe, ed., *The Medieval Mystical Tradition in England, Wales and Ireland* (Cambridge, 1999), 147–68; p. 160.

[61] Moshe Kalian and Eliezer Witztum, 'Jerusalem Syndrome as reflected in the pilgrimage and biographies of four extraordinary women from the 14th century to the end of the second millennium', *Mental Health, Religion, and Culture* 5 (2002), 1–16; Nancy P. Stork, 'Did Margery Kempe suffer from Tourette's Syndrome?', *Mediaeval Studies* 59 (1997), 261–300; Colleen Donelly, 'Menopausal life as imitation of art: Margery Kempe and the lack of sorority', *Women's Writing* 12 (2005), 419–32.

her recovery from this crisis can be seen as an important stimulus to her self-transformation. Later, she suffers from various ailments for a long time, including 'a severe illness in her head and then in her back, so that she was afraid that she lost her wits' (p. 125). Elsewhere, some people are described in the *Book* as having thought Kempe mad—or epileptic, or drunk—but from Kempe's perspective this shows how people misunderstood her as God's messenger, and their faulty discernment of spirits. Indeed, Kempe's own account sees illness and derangement as positive forces, crises that precede and hasten self-transformation. Madness is repeatedly seen in medieval writing as a pathway to forming an identity and learning to see the truth. Most problematically, for a modern critic to state that Kempe is mad is to regard the writing of Kempe's *Book* as a record of something other than a positive assertion of Kempe's social and spiritual status. The *Book* is not a set of symptoms to be explained and justified, but rather a rhetorical intervention in its culture. By describing somebody as 'mad' or 'eccentric' are we merely trying to discredit and discard someone who challenges our own expectations of what is normal and what is abnormal? The real challenge issued by *The Book of Margery Kempe* is to assess Kempe's behaviour according to her times.

If we judge the *Book* in the harsh terms of hagiography, it is a failure: Kempe was not made a saint and, as far as we know, a formal cult never developed around her. However, the aim of the *Book* was not necessarily to make a saint of Kempe, but to show the power of mystical vision and prayer, and the difficult path of the apostolic life. The *Book* takes pains to show how Kempe is *not* unique, but rather influenced by spirituality known about from books and from other religious people. William Southfield, a friar whom Kempe visits in Norwich, thanks Kempe 'and others like [her]' for her prayers. In people like Southfield himself, Alan of Lynn, Margaret Florentine, Richard of Ireland, Julian of Norwich, Reginald the hermit, Thomas Marshall, Wenceslas of Rome, the *Book* constructs a loose but international community of people who are, in one way or another, similar to Kempe and act as her devout supporters or guides.

There is no evidence of Kempe's grave having become a shrine to followers and believers and it is hard to reconstruct the extent of Kempe's influence. The fact that only one manuscript of the *Book* survives does not mean it was not widely read. There must have been

at least two manuscripts of the *Book* (the lost archetype plus the surviving manuscript), and at least four annotators busily and piously
glossed the extant manuscript. It is clear from these annotations that
Kempe's holy reputation, amongst the Carthusian monks at Mount
Grace in Yorkshire, was alive and well at the end of the fifteenth century (as demonstrated by the annotations referring to late fifteenth-
century preachers at Mount Grace, Richard Methley and John
Norton). Moreover, excerpts from Kempe's *Book* were published in
1501 (by Wynkyn de Worde) and 1521 (by Henry Pepwell), 100 years
after her visions, no mean feat in terms of a text's endurance.[62]

Kempe's reputation soared in the 1980s, and the *Book* has since
become a staple of university curricula in literature, history, theology, and gender studies. The rise of Kempe within contemporary
medieval studies accompanied, and was to some extent enabled by,
the development of feminist and queer literary criticism. Gender is
a very important aspect of the *Book*, as both sexuality and misogyny
appear as major social and personal factors in Kempe's life. Several
important early studies argued that Kempe lent herself to a feminist reading (whilst stopping short of claiming Kempe herself as
a feminist); Karma Lochrie, for example, states that she 'certainly
would not want to argue for [Kempe's] championship of women' but
that Kempe's 'negotiation' of the pressures put on her as a woman
'constitutes a feminist problem for scholarship'.[63] Lochrie suggests
that, by engaging with literary culture and having a book written
that she could not read, Kempe effectively estranged herself from
her own story, symptomatic of a greater marginalization of women
in medieval society. Wendy Harding sees in Kempe an 'alternative
mode of communication', a strategy of 'transgression', which Kempe
used to answer back to male authorities.[64] Liz Herbert McAvoy has
argued that, as a woman, Kempe 'contravened . . . allocated spaces
and reached out through the boundaries with her body and voice to

---

[62] However, Kempe's distinctive personality was largely removed from these versions,
which present her as a visionary and anchoress; see Jennifer Summit, *Lost Property: The
Woman Writer and English Literary History 1380–1589* (Chicago, 2000), 126–40; Allyson
Foster, '*A Shorte Treatyse of Contemplacyon: The Book of Margery Kempe* in its early print
contexts', *CBMK* 95–112.

[63] Karma Lochrie, *Margery Kempe and Translations of the Flesh* (Philadelphia, 1991),
9–10.

[64] Wendy Harding, 'Body into text: *The Book of Margery Kempe*', in Linda Lomperis
and Sarah Stanbury, eds., *Feminist Approaches to the Body in Medieval Literature*
(Philadelphia, 1993), 168–85.

enter the proscribed spaces beyond'.[65] Certainly, Kempe's gender was often invoked by her detractors whilst her experiences as a wife and mother shaped the *Book*.[66] To see Kempe as a proto-feminist remains problematical, not least because of the *Book*'s endorsement by, and Kempe's (possibly strategic) subjection to, male figures, such as her scribes, confessors, priests, a very masculine Jesus, and God.[67] However, the rediscovery of Kempe and her current status, firmly within the canon of medieval English texts, can be seen as a success-ful twentieth-century feminist intervention in literary history. More recently, Kempe has been embraced by queer studies: not because she is thought to have been a 'lesbian', but rather because her boister-ous and disruptive performances of gender subvert the very basis of 'normal' (or heteronormative) behaviour. Carolyn Dinshaw has elo-quently argued that Kempe speaks to 'a queer tradition of answering back', and that her 'acts of sex/gender manipulation' connect her to other kinds of 'social disorder' and disruption.[68]

Many modern readers have identified with the character of Kempe and she has inspired several accomplished and creative works of historical fiction in which her *Book* has been mined for drama and fantasy.[69] However, Kempe remains very much able to frustrate and antagonize her audiences. She may be judged by modern readers as a self-pitying megalomaniac, an egoist, a madwoman, a fraud even. By her own account, this is certainly how she was judged by some of the people she met. Towards the close of the *Book* we learn, in a mor-tifyingly embarrassing episode, how Kempe's hypocrisy became spitefully proverbial in Lynn and London (pp. 220-1). But in terms of medieval ideas of imitating Christ, such antagonism merely con-firms that Kempe is Christ-like—she must suffer shame and mockery

[65] Liz Herbert McAvoy, *Authority and the Female Body in the Writings of Julian of Norwich and Margery Kempe* (Cambridge, 2004), 2.

[66] See Nancy Bradley Warren, 'Feminist approaches to Middle English religious writ-ing: the cases of Margery Kempe and Julian of Norwich', *Literature Compass* 4 (2007), 1378–96; Kim M. Phillips, 'Margery Kempe and the ages of woman', *CBMK* 17–34.

[67] On masculinity and Kempe, see Isabel Davis, 'Men and Margery: negotiating medieval patriarchy', *CBMK* 35–54.

[68] Carolyn Dinshaw, *Getting Medieval: Sexualities and Communities, Pre- and Post-Modern* (Durham, NC, 1999), 181, 152; see too Kathy Lavezzo, 'Sobs and sighs between women: the homoerotics of compassion in *The Book of Margery Kempe*', in Louise Fradenburg and Carla Freccero, eds., *Premodern Sexualities* (New York, 1996), 175–98.

[69] See, for example, Roger Howard, 'Margery Kempe', in *The Tragedy of Mao in the Lin Piao Period and Other Plays* (Colchester, 1989), 41–56; Robert Glück, *Margery Kempe* (London, 1994); Rebecca Barnhouse, *The Book of the Maidservant* (New York, 2009).

as Christ did at Calvary. The *Book* promotes Kempe as an example of holiness: it is, therefore, far from being an impartial document. At the same time, the *Book* needs to show that Kempe had an exceptional religious gift. Kempe should not be dismissed as either ill or eccentric but read as a product of her times.

Kempe's *Book* gives us one of the most penetrating surviving accounts of life as a medieval laywoman, married woman, and urban businesswoman. A human being is never just one thing or another; Kempe might be seen perfectly to encapsulate the paradox of human subjectivity, in her contrariness, her fallibility, her ability both to provoke and inspire, and even her evident lack of self-knowledge at points when she is crafting her own biography. In its jumbled chaos, its eye for detail, its intimate portraits of people and places, its gossipy asides and moments of embarrassment, its hopes and thwarted ambitions, *The Book of Margery Kempe* offers nothing less than an account of what it is truly to be alive. But over and above this, it gives us a portrait of how one medieval woman, transformed from a sinful wretch to a holy pilgrim, wished to be remembered beyond her own times.

NOTE ON THE TEXT AND
TRANSLATION

The Book of Margery Kempe is presented in its unique manuscript (now British Library, Add. MS 61823) in three sections: Book I, the much shorter Book II, and the brief closing section of Kempe's prayers. As the scribe states, the *Book* was rewritten in the period 1436–8, many years after most of the events it describes had taken place. The surviving manuscript is bound with a letter, from Peter de Monte to William Bogy of Soham (Cambridgeshire), dated to *c*.1440, and this suggests that the manuscript could not have been bound before this time; the manuscript is written on paper probably imported to England from Holland in the late 1440s, so it likely dates from something like ten or so years after the *Book* was rewritten by the priest. De Monte's letter suggests too that the manuscript was written in the vicinity of Lynn (Soham is 32 miles from Lynn), corroborated by the name of the scribe of the *Book*, recorded as 'Salthows' (fo. 123r): Salthouse is a Norfolk village, 35 miles from Lynn, and Salthouse was possibly a monk at the Benedictine priory at Norwich, now Norwich cathedral (see note to p. 229). From East Anglia, the manuscript then made its way, at some point in the later fifteenth century, to the Carthusian monastery at Mount Grace (Yorkshire), an isolated religious community in the Yorkshire hills, 160 miles north of Lynn.[1] Julie A. Chappell has recently traced the next stage in the book's journey in detail, suggesting that, in 1533, it was taken from Mount Grace to the London Charterhouse, both to be shared with the highly literate community there and to protect it from the reformist agents of Henry VIII; by 1538 Everard Digby, a former London Carthusian, had acquired the manuscript and it passed into the possession of his family. The Digbys, of Leicestershire and Rutland, were ancestors of the Butler-Bowdon family, in whose country house the manuscript of the *Book* was rediscovered in the 1930s.[2]

[1] Mount Grace also owned Middle English manuscripts of the mystical texts *The Mirror of the Life of Christ* and *The Cloud of Unknowing* (Neil R. Ker, *Medieval Libraries of Great Britain* (London, 1964), 132).

[2] Julie A. Chappell, *Perilous Passages*: The Book of Margery Kempe *1534–1934* (Basingstoke, 2013), 65–7.

The text in the original manuscript is divided into chapters, which have been retained here, although it is not clear that the *Book* was originally put together as presented in the sole surviving manuscript. To some extent, I have followed the rubric of the manuscript for paragraph and sentence breaks, although I have made many editorial interventions too; punctuation and paragraph breaks should be regarded as editorial. I have given some information about the manuscript's marginalia in the Explanatory Notes; to view the manuscript pages, and the full range of marks, notes, illustrations, and erasures, I recommend the online edition with transcription currently in progress, via http://english.selu.edu/humanitiesonline/kempe/ or the British Library's digital facsimile, via http://www.bl.uk/manuscripts/Default.aspx

The Book of Margery Kempe was written in fifteenth-century East Anglian prose.[3] Whilst fairly recognizable to speakers of modern standard English, it nonetheless presents some formidable challenges to the translator. Sentences are long, sometimes with multiple subordinate clauses, parenthetical diversions, or lists of adjectives. The adjectives used are repetitive and can have multiple meanings ('great', 'high', 'worthy', for instance). In general, I have adopted a conservative mode of translation here, seeking to retain as far as possible all the individual elements of the original's full, complex prose style, whilst aiming to present Kempe's *Book* in idiomatic modern English, without archaism, comprehensible to a non-specialist reader. The *Book*'s language is sometimes homely, almost chatty, whilst at other times it is in a high style with many Latinate 'hard words'.[4] There is frequent alliteration in the *Book*, often used to provide rhythmic and memorable pairings of words or to give a more forceful sense of the relationship between two or more concepts, and I have tried to retain such alliteration here.[5] There are points at which I have had to break up Middle English sentences or insert additional pronouns, simply to make good sense to today's reader, but I have also maintained Kempe's complex, and sometimes convoluted, syntax, which often develops the narrative in dynamic, if not always elegant, ways. When the *Book*

[3] See R. K. Stone, *Middle English Prose Style* (The Hague, 1970), 52–4, which includes an account of how the *Book* is sole authority for many Middle English words. See too Sue Niebrzydowski, '"Late hir seye what sche wyl": older women's speech and the *Book of Margery Kempe*', in Sue Niebrzydowski, ed., *Middle-Aged Women in the Middle Ages* (Cambridge, 2011), 101–14, for a reading of Kempe's voice via sociolinguistics.

[4] Stone, *Middle English Prose Style*, 52–88.

[5] Stone, *Middle English Prose Style*, 94–104.

refers to 'this creature' or 'the creature', it almost always refers to Kempe herself. The pronoun 'He', with an editorial upper-case 'H', refers to God or Christ, and proper names have been modernized (e.g. Middle English '*Alnewyk*' becomes 'Alnwick'). Biblical quotations are translated after the sixteenth-century Douay-Rheims Bible (via drbo.org), to give a sense of the difference in register between biblical quotation and reportage, with Latin quotations remaining as given in the manuscript.

Where the *Book* moves into reported speech, between Kempe and her companions and detractors, I have tended towards a more relaxed translation, sometimes using contractions, to reflect the informal, intimate nature of the conversations being represented.

SELECT BIBLIOGRAPHY

Editions of the Middle English text

The Book of Margery Kempe, ed. Sanford Brown Meech and Hope Emily Allen, EETS o.s. 212 (London, 1940). The first scholarly edition of the *Book*; the notes contain a wealth of historical information

The Book of Margery Kempe, facsimile and edition, ed. Joel Fredell et al., via http://english.selu.edu/humanitiesonline/kempe/index.php. Useful online images of the manuscript, with a facing-page transcription in progress.

The Book of Margery Kempe: Annotated Edition, ed. Barry Windeatt (Cambridge: D. S. Brewer, 2000, repr. 2004). Middle English text with notes and an edition of Worde's *Shorte Treatyse* (1501); notes foreground Kempe's sources in medieval mysticism.

The Book of Margery Kempe, ed. Lynn Staley, via http://d.lib.rochester.edu/teams/publication/staley-the-book-of-margery-kempe Online edition of the Middle English text, with notes and glossary.

Lynn, Norfolk, and Kempe's background

Aers, David, 'The making of Margery Kempe: individual and community', in *Community, Gender and Individual Identity: English Writing 1360–1430* (London, 1988), 73–116.

Arnold, John, and Lewis, Katherine, eds., *A Companion to* The Book of Margery Kempe (Cambridge, 2004). Crucial essays on Kempe's historical context and critical approaches to the *Book*.

Ashley, Kathleen, 'Historicizing Margery: *The Book of Margery Kempe* as social text', *Journal of Medieval and Early Modern Studies* 28 (1998), 371–88.

Atkinson, Clarissa W., *Mystic and Pilgrim: The Book and the World of Margery Kempe* (Ithaca, 1983).

Goodman, Anthony, *Margery Kempe and her World* (London, 2002).

McEntire, Sandra J., ed., *Margery Kempe: A Book of Essays* (New York, 1992).

Myers, Michael D., 'A fictional-true self: Margery Kempe and the social reality of the merchant elite of King's Lynn', *Albion* 31 (1999), 377–94.

Nichols, Ann Eljenholm, *The Early Art of Norfolk: A Subject List of Extant and Lost Art including Items Relevant to Early Drama* (Kalamazoo, MI: Medieval Institute Publication, 2002).

Raguin, Virginia, and Stanbury, Sarah, *Mapping Margery Kempe: A Guide* to *Late Medieval Material and Spiritual Life* via http://college.holy-cross.edu/projects/kempe/ Includes images of many of the places and buildings mentioned in the *Book*.

The reception and rediscovery of Kempe

Chappell, Julie A., *Perilous Passages:* The Book of Margery Kempe, *1534–1934* (Basingstoke, 2013).

Dinshaw, Carolyn, *How Soon is Now? Medieval Texts, Amateur Readers* (Durham, NC, 2012), ch. 3.

Foster, Allyson, '*A Short Treatyse of Contemplacyon*: The Book of Margery Kempe in its early print contexts', *CBMK* 95–112.

Hirsh, John C., *Hope Emily Allen: Medieval Scholarship and Feminism* (Norman, OK, 1988).

Hussey, Stanley, 'The rehabilitation of Margery Kempe', *Leeds Studies in English* 32 (2001), 171–94.

Mitchell, Marea, *The Book of Margery Kempe: Scholarship, Community, and Criticism* (New York, 2005).

Questions of authorship and authority

Beckwith, Sarah, 'Problems of authority in late medieval English mysticism: language, agency, and authority in *The Book of Margery Kempe*', *Exemplaria* 4 (1992), 171–99.

Glenn, Cheryl, 'Author, audience and autobiography: rhetorical technique in *The Book of Margery Kempe*', *College English* 54 (1992), 540–53.

Harvey, N. L., 'Margery Kempe: writer as creature', *Philological Quarterly* 71 (1992), 173–84.

Hirsh, John C., 'Author and scribe in *The Book of Margery Kempe*', *Medium Ævum* 44 (1975), 145–50.

Riddy, Felicity, 'Text and self in *The Book of Margery Kempe*', in Linda Olson and Kathryn Kerby-Fulton, eds., *Voices in Dialogue: Reading Women in the Middle Ages* (Notre Dame, IN, 2005), 435–53.

Spearing, A. C., 'Margery Kempe', in A. S. G. Edwards, ed., *A Companion to Middle English Prose* (Cambridge, 2004), 83–98.

Staley, Lynn, *Margery Kempe's Dissenting Fictions* (University Park, PA, 1994), 1–38.

Watson, Nicholas, 'The making of *The Book of Margery Kempe*', in Linda Olson and Kathryn Kerby-Fulton, eds., *Voices in Dialogue: Reading Women in the Middle Ages* (Notre Dame, IN, 2005), 395–434.

Medieval mysticism and Kempe's spirituality

Beckwith, Sarah, *Christ's Body: Identity, Culture, and Society in Late Medieval Writings* (London, 1993).

Bhattacharji, Santha, *God is an Earthquake: The Spirituality of Margery Kempe* (London, 1997).

Dzon, Mary, 'Margery Kempe's ravishment into the childhood of Christ', *Mediaevalia* 27 (2006), 27–57.

Lavinsky, David, "'Speke to me be thowt": affectivity, *Incendium Amoris*, and the *Book of Margery Kempe*', *Journal of English and Germanic Philology* 112 (2013), 340–64.

Powell, Raymond A., 'Margery Kempe: an exemplar of late medieval English piety', *Catholic Historical Review* 89 (2003), 1–23.

Renevey, Denis, 'Margery's performing body: the translation of late medieval discursive religious practices', in Denis Renevey and Christiania Whitehead, eds., *Writing Religious Women: Female Spiritual and Textual Practices in Late Medieval England* (Cardiff, 2000), 197–216.

Uhlman, Diana R., 'The comfort of voice, the solace of script: orality and literacy in *The Book of Margery Kempe*', *Studies in Philology* 91 (1994), 50–69.

Gender, sexuality, and the role of medieval women

Lochrie, Karma, *Margery Kempe and Translations of the Flesh* (Philadelphia, 1991).

Manter, Lisa, 'The savior of her desire: Margery Kempe's passionate gaze', *Exemplaria* 13 (2001), 39–66.

McAvoy, Liz Herbert, *Authority and the Female Body in the Writings of Julian of Norwich and Margery Kempe* (Cambridge, 2004).

Riddy, Felicity, 'Looking closely: authority and intimacy in the late medieval urban home', in Mary C. Erler and Maryanne Kowaleski, eds., *Gendering the Master Narrative: Women and Power in the Middle Ages* (Ithaca, NY, 2003), 212–28.

Summit, Jennifer, *Lost Property: The Woman Writer and English Literary History*, 1380–1589 (Chicago, 2000).

Voaden, Rosalynn, 'God's almighty hand: women co-writing the book', in Lesley Smith and Jane H. M. Taylor, eds., *Women, the Book and the Godly* (Cambridge, 1995), 55–65.

Wallace, David, *Strong Women: Life, Text, and Territory, 1347–1645* (Oxford, 2011), chs. 1 and 2.

Watt, Diane, *Secretaries of God: Women Prophets in Late Medieval and Early Modern England* (Cambridge, 1997).

Williams, Tara, *Inventing Womanhood: Gender and Language in Later Middle English Writings* (Columbus, OH, 2011), ch. 4.

Sainthood, orthodoxy, and heresy

Eberly, Susan, 'Margery Kempe, St Mary Magdalene, and patterns of contemplation', *Downside Review* 107 (1989), 209–23.

Forrest, Ian, *The Detection of Heresy in Late Medieval England* (Oxford, 2005).

Gertz, Genelle, *Heresy Trials and English Women Writers, 1400–1670* (Cambridge, 2012), 48–76.

Gibson, Gail McMurray, *The Theater of Devotion: East Anglian Drama and Society in the Late Middle Ages* (Chicago, 1989), ch. 3, 'St Margery'.

Morse, Mary, ' "Tak and bren her": Lollardy as conversion motif in *The Book of Margery Kempe*', *Mystics Quarterly* 29 (2003), 24–44.

Rees Jones, Sarah, ' "A peler of Holy Cherch": Margery Kempe and the bishops', in Jocelyn Wogan-Browne et al., eds., *Medieval Women: Texts and Contexts in Late Medieval Britain, Essays for Felicity Riddy* (Turnhout, 2000), 377–91.

Shklar, Ruth Nisse, 'Cobham's daughter: *The Book of Margery Kempe* and the power of heterodox thinking', *Modern Language Quarterly* 56 (1995), 277–304.

Varnam, Laura, 'Church', in Marion Turner, ed., *A Handbook of Middle English Studies* (Oxford, 2013), 299–314.

Voaden, Rosalynn, *God's Words, Women's Voices: The Discernment of Spirits in the Writing of Late-Medieval Women Visionaries* (Woodbridge, 1999).

Medieval pilgrimage

Bowers, Terence, 'Margery Kempe as traveler', *Studies in Philology* 97 (2000), 1–28.

Dyas, Dee, *Pilgrimage in Medieval English Literature, 700–1500* (Cambridge, 2001).

Hsy, Jonathan, *Trading Tongues: Merchants, Multilingualism, and Medieval Literature* (Columbus, OH, 2013), ch. 4.

Morris, Colin, 'Pilgrimage to Jerusalem in the late Middle Ages', in Colin Morris and Peter Roberts, eds., *Pilgrimage: The English Experience from Becket to Bunyan* (Cambridge, 2002), 141–63.

Sumption, Jonathan, *Pilgrimage: An Image of Mediaeval Religion*, rev. edn. (London, 2002).

Watt, Diane, 'Margery Kempe's overseas pilgrimages', in Clare A. Lees and Gillian R. Overing, eds., *A Place to Believe In: Locating Medieval Landscapes* (University Park, PA, 2006), 170–87.

Webb, Diana, *Pilgrimage in Medieval England* (London and New York, 2000).

Whalen, Brett, *Pilgrimage in the Middle Ages: A Reader* (Toronto, 2011).

A NOTE ON MONEY

COSTS, prices, and monetary worth appear throughout *The Book of Margery Kempe*. Pilgrimage was an expensive business and there was little currency standardization in medieval Europe and the Mediterranean; many Jerusalem pilgrims took Venetian currency (gold ducats and silver grossi), which became a kind of international currency on the pilgrimage route. In England, currency was based around pounds (£ or *l.*), shillings (*s.*) and pence (*d.*). See further Peter Spufford, *Handbook of Medieval Exchange* (London, 1986).

bolognino: a coin, originally minted in Bologna; in the thirteenth century, the *bolognino piccolo* was worth 1*d.*; the *bolognino grosso* was worth 12*s.* However, the *bolognino* was adopted throughout the Italian peninsula and its value changed depending on local circumstances.

groat: a silver coin worth 4*d.*

ha'penny: a silver coin worth half of 1*d.*

mark: a unit (rather than a coin) of 13*s.* and 4*d.* (160*d.*/two-thirds of a pound).

noble: a gold coin worth 6*s.* 8*d.*

penny: 1*d*, a silver coin. The basis of English currency: a *shilling* comprised 12*d.*; a *pound* comprised 240*d.*

pound: a unit (rather than a coin) of 240*d.* or 20*s.*

shilling: a unit (rather than a coin) worth 12*d.*; 20 shillings made a *pound*.

A CHRONOLOGY OF MARGERY KEMPE

*c.*1373 Margery, daughter of John Burnham of Lynn, born.

1373 (23 July) death of the mystic Bridget [Birgitta] of Sweden.

1384 (31 December) death of John Wycliffe, theologian and dissident whose writings were the basis of the Lollard heresy.

1391 Canonization of Bridget of Sweden by Pope Boniface IX.

*c.*1393 Margery Burnham marries John Kempe of Lynn.

1399 (30 September) deposition of Richard II by Henry IV.

1401 The statute *De heretico comburendo* passed, to punish heretics with burning at the stake; William Sawtry, a priest formerly of Lynn, burned for Lollardy at Smithfield in London.

1408 Promulgation of Thomas Arundel's anti-Lollard Constitutions, regulating orthodoxy and heresy.

*c.*1409 Kempe begins abstinence from eating meat.

*c.*1412 Kempe receives a divine directive to visit Rome, Jerusalem, and Santiago.

1413 (20 March) death of Henry IV; accession of Henry V.

Kempe visits Norwich, probably meeting William Southfield and Julian of Norwich, as well as York and Bridlington. Later in year, leaves Yarmouth for Jerusalem via Zierikzee, Constance, Bologna, and Venice, where she remains for thirteen weeks. Kempe's father, John Burnham, probably died at some point during this year.

1414 Oldcastle's Rebellion, an unsuccessful Lollard conspiracy against the king. Kempe visits Palestine, where, at Calvary, she experiences her first bout of crying; she returns via Assisi and Rome (1414–15).

1415 Council of Constance confirms Bridget of Sweden as a saint. Bridgettine monastery at Syon (Middlesex) founded by Henry V. Kempe returns to England via Middelburg. Visits Norwich. (25 October) English victory over the French at Agincourt.

*c.*1416 Death of Julian of Norwich.

1417 Kempe travels to Santiago de Compostela via Bristol; stays in Santiago for fourteen days. Later in the year she is held and interrogated at Leicester and undergoes subsequent tribulations at York, at the Archbishop of York's Palace at Cawood, and at Hull, Hessle, and

Beverley; also visits London. (4 December) hanging and burning outside London of the prominent Lollard John Oldcastle.

c.1418 Kempe returns to Lynn and starts to suffer from an illness, which will endure for eight years.

1420 Completion by John Lydgate of his *Troy Book*, commenced in 1412, for Henry V. Kempe visits the grave of Richard of Caister at Norwich. (21 May) Treaty of Troyes, promising the French throne to Henry V and his heirs after the death of Charles VI of France.

1421 (23 January) Lynn engulfed by fire.

1422 (31 August) death of Henry V; accession of the infant Henry VI.

1428 Completion of Lynn's Guildhall of the Holy Trinity.

1429 (5 November) Henry VI crowned king of England at Westminster.

1431 (30 May) Joan of Arc, aged 19, burned at the stake in Rouen. (12 June) a John Kempe, possibly Kempe's son, recorded doing business between Gdańsk and Boston. (16 December) Henry VI of England crowned king of France at Notre-Dame, Paris.

c.1432 Probably the approximate date of the first attempts at writing down Kempe's revelations; death of Kempe's husband and of her son.

1433 Kempe boards a ship at Ipswich; sails to Gdańsk via Norway; visits Wilsnack and Aachen, returning to Dover via Calais.

1434 Kempe visits Sheen.

1436 (23 July) priest begins to rewrite Book I.

1437 Henry VI declared of age and assumes government, hoping to end the wars with France.

1438 (February–April) admission of a 'Margeria Kempe' to the Lynn Guild of the Holy Trinity; (28 April) priest begins to write Book II.

1439 (22 May) further mention of 'Margerie Kempe' in the records of the Lynn Guild of the Holy Trinity; this is the last evidence we have to suggest that Kempe was still alive.

1501 Wynkyn de Worde of Fleet Street, London, publishes *A shorte treatyse of contemplacyon taught by our lorde Jhesu cryste, taken out of the boke of Margerie kempe of lyn*.

1521 Henry Pepwell of London publishes extracts from Kempe's *Book* as part of *A veray deuoute treatyse*, a collection of mystical works.

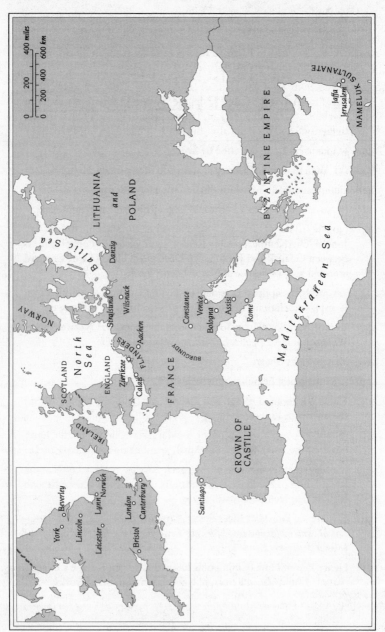

MAP: Major Places visited by Margery Kempe

THE BOOK OF
MARGERY KEMPE

Liber Montis Gracie. This book is from Mount Grace.*

In the name of Jesus Christ.*

HERE begins a short and comforting treatise for sinful wretches, in which they might have great solace and comfort for themselves and understand the high and indescribable mercy of our sovereign Saviour, Lord Jesus Christ—whose name shall be worshipped and magnified without end—who now in our time deigns to exercise His nobility and His goodness to us, the unworthy ones.

All the works of our Saviour are for our example and instruction, and whatever grace He works in any creature is to our profit, if lack of charity be not our hindrance.

So therefore, by the leave of our merciful Lord Christ Jesus, to the magnifying of His holy name, Jesus, this little treatise shall deal somewhat with parts of His wonderful works; how mercifully, how benignly, and how charitably He moved and stirred a sinful wretch towards His love, the which sinful wretch for many years wanted and intended, through the prompting of the Holy Ghost, to follow our Saviour, making great promises of fasts and many other penitential deeds. Yet she was always turned back in times of temptation—like the reed's stalk which bows with every wind and is never unwavering unless no wind blows—until that time that our merciful Lord Jesus Christ, having pity and compassion for His handiwork and His creature,* turned health into sickness, prosperity into adversity, esteem into disgrace, and love into hatred.

Thus with all these things turning upside down, this creature, who for many years had gone astray and always been unstable, was perfectly drawn and stirred to enter upon the way of perfection, the perfect way which Christ our Saviour in His own person exemplified: steadfastly He trod it gravely and duly He took it before. Then this creature (of whom this treatise shall, through the mercy of Jesus, reveal in part the manner of living) was touched by our Lord's hand with great bodily sickness through which she lost her reason and her wits for a long time until our Lord, by grace, returned her to health again, as shall later be shown more openly. Her worldly goods, which in those days were plentiful and abundant, were shortly afterwards utterly barren and bare. Then pomp and pride was cast down and put aside. Those who had previously respected her afterwards rebuked her most sharply; her kinsmen and those who had been her friends were now her utmost enemies. Then she, considering this shocking change, and seeking succour under the wings of her spiritual mother, Holy Church, went and submitted herself to her confessor, accusing herself of her misdeeds and afterwards she did great physical penance. In a short time our merciful Lord visited this creature with profuse tears of contrition day by day, so much so that some people said she could weep whenever she wanted to and in doing so they slandered the work of God.

She was so used to being slandered and disgraced, to being chided and rebuked by the world for the grace and virtue with which she was provided through the strength of the Holy Ghost, that it was a kind of solace and comfort to her when she suffered any distress for the love of God and for the grace that God performed in her. Since the more slander and disgrace that she suffered, the more she increased in grace and in devotion of holy meditation, of high contemplation, and of wonderful speeches and conversation which our Lord spoke and intimated to her soul, teaching her how she should be despised for His love, how she should have patience, setting all her trust, all her love, and all her affection on Him only.

Through the inspiration of the Holy Ghost she knew and understood many secret and private things that would happen afterwards.* Often, whilst she was occupied with such holy speeches and conversation, she would weep and sob so much that people were greatly amazed because they knew very little of how intimate our Lord was in her soul. She herself could never tell of the grace that she felt, it was so heavenly, so high above her reason and her bodily wits, and her body was so feeble in times of the presence of grace that she could never express it with words as she felt it in her soul.

Then this creature much dreaded the illusions and deceits of her spiritual enemies.* Then at the request of the Holy Ghost she went to many honourable clerics, both archbishops and bishops, doctors of divinity and bachelors too. She spoke also with many anchorites* and revealed to them her manner of living and such grace as the Holy Ghost, through His goodness, performed in her mind and in her soul, as her understanding would serve her to express it. And all those to whom she revealed her secrets said she was much obliged to love our Lord for the grace that He revealed to her, and they counselled her to follow her inclinations and promptings, and trustingly believe they were from the Holy Ghost and from no evil spirit. Some of these worthy and honourable clerics accepted, on peril of their souls and as they would answer to God, that this creature was inspired with the Holy Ghost, and begged that she should have them write and make a book of her feelings and her revelations. Some offered to write down her feelings with their own hands, and she would in no way consent to this; for she was commanded in her soul that she should not write so soon. And so it was more than twenty years from that time this creature first had feelings and revelations before she had any of them written.

Afterwards, when it pleased our Lord, He commanded her and tasked her to have her feelings and revelations and her manner of living written down, so that His goodness might be known to the whole world.

Then the creature had no writer who would either fulfil her desire or give credence to her feelings, until such time that a man dwelling in Germany* (who was an Englishman by birth and had since married in Germany and had both a wife and a child there), having good knowledge of this creature and her desire, and moved, I trust, by the Holy Ghost, came to England with his wife and his belongings; and he lived with the aforementioned creature until he had written as much as she would tell him during the time that they were together. But afterwards he died.

Then there was a priest for whom this creature had great affection, and she talked with him about this matter and brought the book to him to read. The book was so ill-written that he could make little sense of it, for it was in neither good English nor German, nor was the handwriting shaped or formed as is other handwriting. Therefore the priest utterly believed that nobody could ever read it, unless it were by special grace. Nevertheless, he promised her that if he could read it he would willingly copy it out and write it better. Then there was so much evil talk about this creature and her weeping that, out of cowardice, the priest dared not speak with her but seldom, and he would not write as he had promised the said creature. And so he avoided and deferred the writing of this book for almost four years or perhaps more, even though this creature often called on him to do it.

In the end he said that he could not read it, for which reason he would not do it. He would not, he said, put himself in peril for it. So he advised her to go to a good man who had been very intimate with he who first wrote the book, supposing that he should know how best to read the book because he had formerly read letters in the other man's handwriting, sent from abroad while he was in Germany. So she went to that man, asking him to write this book and never to reveal it as long as she lived, granting him a great sum of money for his labours. Then this good man wrote about one leaf, and yet it was barely to the purpose for he could not get on well with it as the book was so poorly composed and so unintelligibly written. Then the priest was vexed in his conscience, because he had promised her that he would write this book if he might manage to read it, and he was not doing his part as well as he might have done, and asked this creature to fetch the book again, if she could do so graciously. Then she got the book back and brought it very contentedly to the priest, asking him to do it with good will, and she would pray to God for him and gain grace for him to read it and write it too. The priest, trusting in her prayers, began to read this book and, he thought, it was much easier than it had been before. And so he read it over in the presence of this creature, and she helped at those times where there was any difficulty.

This book is not written in order, each thing after another as it was done, but just as the story came to the creature in her mind when it was to be written down, for it was so long before it was written that she had forgotten the timing and the order of when things happened. Therefore she wrote nothing other than that which she knew full well to be the whole truth.

When the priest first began to write this book his eyesight failed so much that he could not see to form his letters, and he could not see to mend his pen.* He was able to see all other things well enough. He set a pair of spectacles* on his nose but then it was much worse than it was before. He complained to the creature about his illness. She said that his enemy envied his good deed and would hinder him if he could, and she urged him to do as well as God would give him grace and to not leave off. When the priest came back to this book, he could see as well (he thought) as he ever had before, both by daylight and by candlelight. And it is for this reason, when he had written a quire,* he added a leaf to it and then he wrote this proem, to express more openly than the one following does, which was written before this.

Anno Domini 1436.

*

A short treatise of a creature placed in great pomp and pride towards the world, who was later drawn to our Lord through great poverty, sickness, shame, and great disgrace in many different countries and places. Something of these tribulations will be presented hereafter, not in the order in which they happened but as the creature could remember them when this was written. For it was more than twenty years from the time this creature had forsaken the world and eagerly followed our Lord before this book was written (in spite of the fact that this creature received much advice about having her tribulations and feelings written down, and a White Friar* freely offered to write for her if she wished). And she was counselled in her spirit that she should not write so soon. Many years later she was asked in her spirit to write.

And even then it was first written by a man who knew how to write properly neither in English nor in German. So it could not be read except by special grace, as there was so much calumny and infamy about this creature that few people would believe her. And then in the end a priest was powerfully moved to write this treatise, and he could not read it properly for a total of four years. And afterwards, at the request of this creature and compelled by his own conscience, he tried again to read it and it was much easier than it had been before. And so he began to write in year of our Lord 1436, on the day following Mary Magdalene, according to the information of this creature.*

BOOK I

CHAPTER 1

WHEN this creature was twenty years old or somewhat more, she was married to an honourable burgess and was with child within a short time, as nature wished. And after she had conceived she was afflicted with great attacks of fever until the child was born; and then, what with the travails she had in childbirth and the sickness she had beforehand, she despaired for her life, thinking that she might not live. So then she sent for her confessor, for she had something on her conscience that she had never revealed before that time in her whole life.* For she was always hindered by her enemy, the Devil, always saying to her while she was in good health that she need not go to confession but could do penance by herself alone and everything should be forgiven, for God is merciful enough.* Therefore this creature often did great penance through fasting on bread and water, and other deeds of alms with devout prayers, except she would not reveal that one thing in confession.

And, any time when she was sick and troubled, the Devil said in her mind that she would be damned, as she had not been to confession for that fault. For this reason, after her child was born, she, not confident that she would live, sent for her confessor, as said before, fully wishing to be confessed of her whole lifetime, or as close as she could. And when she came to the point of saying that thing which she had concealed for so long, her confessor was a little too hasty and began to scold her sharply before she had fully said what was occupying her mind, and so she would say no more about it no matter what he did. Then afterwards, dreading damnation on the one hand and his sharp rebukes on the other, this creature went out of her mind and was bewilderingly vexed and troubled by spirits for half a year, eight weeks, and odd days.

And at this time she saw, so she thought, devils opening their mouths all inflamed with burning flames of fire, as though they might have swallowed her in, sometimes pawing at her, sometimes threatening her, sometimes pulling her and dragging her around, both night and day during the aforesaid time. And the devils also cried out after her with grave threats, and told her that she should forsake her Christianity, her faith, and deny her God, His mother, and all the saints in Heaven, her good works and all good virtues, her father, her mother, and all her friends. And so she did. She slandered her husband, her friends, and her own self; she spoke many a malicious word and many a wicked word; she knew neither virtue nor goodness; she desired all wickedness; just as the spirits tempted her to say and do, so she said and did. She would have killed herself many a time at their promptings and been damned with them in Hell, and in witness of this she bit her own hand so violently that the scar could be seen afterwards for her whole life. And she also violently tore her skin on her body over her heart with her fingernails, for she had no other instruments and she would have done something worse but that she was bound and forcibly restrained both day and night so that she could not have her way.

Then one time, when she had long laboured with these and many other temptations, such that people thought she could never have escaped alive, as she lay alone and her warders were far from her, our merciful Lord Christ Jesus—ever to be trusted, worshipped be His name, never forsaking His servant in time of need—appeared in the likeness of a man to His creature who had forsaken Him, the most handsome, the most beautiful, and the most affable that could ever be seen with human eye, clad in a purple silk mantle, sitting upon her bedside, looking upon her with so blessed an expression that she was fortified in all her spirits, and He said these words to her:

'Daughter, why have you forsaken me, and I never forsook you?'*

Then at once, as He had said these words, she truly saw the air open up as bright as any lightning, and He stepped up into the air, not very hastily and quickly but elegantly and steadily, so that she could easily behold Him in the air until it closed up again.

And then the creature was steadied in her wits and in her reason as well as she had been before, and pleaded with her husband as soon as he came to her that she might have the keys to the buttery to fetch her food and drink as she had done before. Her servants and her warders counselled him that he should provide no keys to her, as they said that she would only give away such goods as were there, for she did not know what she was saying (so they believed). Nevertheless, her husband, always feeling tenderness and compassion for her, commanded that they should provide her with the keys. And she took her food and drink as her bodily strength would allow her, and again knew her friends and her household and all others who came to her to see how our Lord Jesus Christ had worked His grace in her, so blessed must He be that is ever nearby during tribulation. When people believe that He is far from them, He is very near through His grace. Afterwards this creature undertook all her other responsibilities as fell to her wisely and seriously enough, save that she did not truly know the power of our Lord to draw us to Him.

CHAPTER 2

So when this creature had thus through grace come back to her right mind she thought she was bound to God and that she would be His servant. Nevertheless, she would not put aside either her pride or her pretentious costumes that she had been used to, neither for her husband nor on any other person's advice. And yet she knew full well that they said a great many insulting things about her, for she wore gold piping on her headdress,* and her hoods were dagged with tippets.* Her cloaks were also dagged and lined with many colours between the dags, so that it would be more striking to people's eyes and she herself should be more admired.

But when her husband wanted to speak to her about leaving aside her pride, she answered sharply and shortly, and said that she came from worthy kin—he never seemed a likely man to have married her—for her father had once been mayor of the town of N.* and afterwards he was alderman of the high Guild of the Trinity* in N. And therefore she would uphold the honour of her kin, whatever anybody said.

She was hugely envious of her neighbours, that they were dressed as stylishly as she. Her every desire was that she should be honoured by the people. She would neither learn her lesson from one chastisement nor be content (as her husband was) with the goods that God had sent her but always desired more and more. And then, out of pure covetousness and in order to maintain her pride, she began to brew* and was one of the greatest brewers in the town of N. for three or four years until she lost a lot of money, as she did not have experience of doing this. For, although she had ever such good servants and knowledge of brewing, things would not go successfully for them. For, when the ale had as fine a head on it as could be seen, suddenly the head would fall away, and all the ale would be lost one brew after another, so her servants were ashamed and did not wish to stay with her. Then this creature thought of how God had punished her before, and she could not take heed, and now again through the loss of her money; and then she left off and brewed no more.

And then she asked her husband for mercy that she had not before followed his advice, and she said that her pride and sin was the cause of all her punishment, and she would put right her trespasses most willingly. But she still did not entirely give up the world, for she now thought of a new housewifely job. She had a horse mill. She got herself two good horses and a man to grind people's corn, and so she was sure of making her living. This business did not last long because, a short time after, on the Eve of Corpus Christi,* this marvel happened: this man (being in good physical health) who had two horses (sturdy and pleasing and having pulled at the mill before), now took one of his horses and put him to the mill as he had before, and this horse would not pull the mill for anything the man could do. The man was sad and attempted everything he could think of to get this horse to pull. Sometimes he led him by the head, sometimes he beat him, and at times he pampered him, and to no avail, for the horse would rather go backwards than forwards. Then the man set sharp spurs on his heels and rode on the horse's back to make him pull, and he was no better.

When this man saw that it was of absolutely no use, then he put the horse back in his stable and gave him food, and the horse ate well and eagerly. Afterwards the man took the other horse and put him to the mill. And just as his mate did, so did this horse, for he would not pull anything whatever the man might do. And then this man quit his position and would no longer stay with the aforesaid creature. At once it was rumoured around the town of N. that neither person nor beast would be in service to the said creature, and then some said she was accursed; some said God was openly taking vengeance upon her; some said one thing; and some said another. But some wise people, whose minds were more grounded in the love of our Lord, said it was the high mercy of our Lord Jesus Christ that bade and beckoned her from the pride and vanity of the wretched world. And then this creature, seeing all these adversities coming on every side, thought they were the scourges of our Lord that would chastise her for her sin. Then she asked God for mercy and forsook her pride, her covetousness, and the desire she had for worldly honour, and did great physical penance, and began to enter the way of everlasting life, as shall be told hereafter.

CHAPTER 3

ONE night, as this creature lay in her bed with her husband, she heard the sound of a melody so sweet and delectable that she thought she must have been in Paradise.* And with that she started out of her bed and said, 'Alas that I ever did sin! It is so merry in Heaven!'

This melody was so sweet that it surpassed beyond comparison all the melodies that could ever be heard in this world, and caused this creature, when she afterwards heard any mirth or melody, to have profuse and abundant tears of high devotion, with great sobs and sighs for the bliss of Heaven, without fearing the shame and spite of the wretched world. And ever after being drawn to God like this, she had in her mind the joy and melody that is in Heaven, so much so that she could not very well restrain herself from speaking of it. For when she was in any kind of company she would often say, 'It is so merry in Heaven!'

And those who knew of her previous behaviour and now heard her speaking so much about the bliss of Heaven said to her, 'Why are you speaking so of the joy that's in Heaven? You don't know it, and you haven't been there any more than we have', and they were cross with her as she would neither hear nor speak of worldly things as they did, and as she had beforehand.

Also, after this time she had no desire to have sexual contact with her husband, for the conjugal debt* was so abominable to her that, she thought, she would have rather eaten or drunk the slime, the muck, in the gutter than consent to any sexual contact, except out of obedience. So then she said to her husband, 'I may not deny you my body, but the love and affection in my heart is drawn away from all earthly creatures and fixed only on God.'

He would have his way with her, and she obeyed with great weeping and sorrowing because she could not live in chastity. And often this creature lived chaste, advised her husband to live chaste, and said that they had often (she knew well) displeased God by their inordinate love and the great sensual pleasures that each had in using each other's bodies, so now it would be a good thing if by the will and consent of both they willingly punished and chastised themselves by abstaining from the lusts of their bodies.

Her husband said it would be good to do so, but he might not yet; he should do so when God wished. And so he used her body as he had done before, he would not cease. And all the time she prayed to God that she might live chaste and, three or four years later, when it pleased our Lord, her husband made a vow of chastity, as shall afterwards be written, by Jesus' leave.

And also, after this creature heard this heavenly melody, she did great physical penance. Sometimes she was shriven at confession twice or thrice a day, especially of that sin that she had so long concealed and covered up, as it is written at the beginning of the *Book*.* She gave herself to much fasting and much contemplation; she got up at two or three o'clock in the morning and went to church, and prayed there until noon and also all through the afternoon.

And then she was slandered and disparaged by many people because she kept so strait a lifestyle. Then she got herself a haircloth from a kiln* (the kind that people use for drying malt), and she laid it inside her gown as subtly and privately as she could, so that her husband might not see it; and indeed he did not, even though she lay beside him every night in his bed and wore this haircloth every day, and bore children at the time.

Then she had three years of great travails with temptations that she underwent as meekly as she could, thanking our Lord for all His gifts, and was as merry when she was disgraced, scorned, or teased for our Lord's love, and much merrier than she had been beforehand amongst the dignities of this world. For she knew very well that she had sinned grievously against God and deserved more shame and sorrow than any man could cause her, and contempt of the world was the right path heavenwards, since Christ himself chose that path.

All His apostles, martyrs, confessors, and virgins, and all those who ever came to Heaven, went on the path of tribulation, and she desired nothing so much as Heaven. Then she was glad in her conscience when she believed that she was entering upon the path that would lead her to the place that she most desired. And this creature had contrition and great compunction, with profuse tears and much noisy sobbing, for her sins and for her unkindness against her maker. Very many times she thought about her unkindness since her childhood, as our Lord put it in her mind. And then, beholding her own wickedness, she could only lament and weep and continually pray for mercy and forgiveness.

Her weeping was so profuse and so constant that many people assumed that she could weep and then leave off whenever she wanted, and therefore many people said she was a false hypocrite and that she wept in public for comfort and for worldly profit. And then very many people who had once loved her whilst she was in this world abandoned her and would not acknowledge her, and all the time she thanked God for it all, desiring nothing but mercy and the forgiveness of sin.

CHAPTER 4

FOR the first two years when this creature was thus drawn to our Lord, she had much spiritual peace as far as temptations go. She could easily endure fasting, which did not bother her. She hated the pleasures of the world. She felt no rebellion in her flesh. She was strong (so she thought), so that she dreaded no devil in Hell, for she did so much physical penance.

She thought that she loved God more than He loved her. She was smitten with the deadly wound of vainglory and felt it not, for she many times desired that the crucifix should loosen his hands from the Cross and clasp her in a token of love. Our merciful Lord Christ Jesus, seeing this creature's presumption, sent her, as is written before, three years of great temptations, of which I intend to write about one of the hardest as an example to those who come after so that they should neither trust in themselves nor take joy in themselves as had this creature. For without doubt our spiritual enemy does not sleep, but most busily searches our temperaments and our dispositions and, wherever he finds us most frail, there, by our Lord's indulgence, he lays his snare, which nobody can escape by his own power.

And so he laid the snare of lechery in front of this creature, when she believed that all fleshly lust had been quenched in her. And she was long tempted with the sin of lechery, in spite of anything she might do. Yet she was often shriven at confession, she wore the hair-cloth, and did great physical penance, and wept many a bitter tear, and prayed very often to our Lord that He should preserve her and keep her so that she should not fall into temptation, for she thought that she would rather be dead than consent to that. And all this time she had no wish to have sexual contact with her husband, and it was very painful and horrible for her.

In the second year of her temptations it so happened that a man whom she loved well said to her, before evensong on the Eve of

St Margaret's Day,* that he would do anything to sleep with her and indulge his bodily lusts, and she should not resist him; if he could not have his way that time, he said, he should otherwise have it some other time—it would not be for her to choose. And he did this to test her to see what she would do, but she believed that he had meant it in earnest and she said very little about it to him. So then they parted ways and both went to hear evensong, for her church was St Margaret's Church.* This woman was so troubled with the man's words that she could neither hear evensong nor say her paternoster* nor think any other good thoughts, but was more troubled than she ever had been before.

The Devil put it into her mind that God had forsaken her, or else she would not have been so tempted. She believed the Devil's persuasions and began to consent because she could not think any other good thoughts. Therefore she believed that God had forsaken her. So when evensong was done she went to the aforementioned man and told him that he could indulge his lust, as she believed he desired, but he put on such a pretence that she could not understand his intentions, and so they went their separate ways that night. This creature was so troubled and vexed all that night that she had no idea what she might do. She lay beside her husband, and to have sexual contact with him was so abominable to her that she could not endure it, even though it was a permitted time and permitted for her* to do it if she had wanted. But all the time she was troubled by the other man, to sin with him in the way in which he had said to her. In the end, through the importunity of temptation and a lack of discretion, she was overcome, and consented in her mind, and she went to the man to know if he would then consent to take her. But he said that he would not for all the wealth in this world; he would rather be hacked as small as meat for the pot!*

She went away all ashamed and confused in herself, seeing his steadiness and her own unsteadiness. Then she thought of the grace that God had given her beforehand, how she had two years of great quietness in her soul, of repentance for her sins with many bitter tears of compunction, and a perfect will never to return to her sin, but rather, it seemed to her, to be dead. And now she saw how she had consented in her will to do a sin. Then she half fell into despair. She thought she was in Hell for all the sorrow she had. She thought she was neither worthy of any mercy, for her consent to sin was so wilfully given, nor was she worthy to do service to God, because she was so false to Him.

Nevertheless she was shriven at confession many times and often, and did whatsoever penance her confessor instructed her to do, and she was governed according to the rules of the Church. That grace God gave this creature, may He be blessed, but He did not withdraw her temptation but rather increased it, as it seemed to her. And therefore she believed that He had forsaken her and dared not trust in His mercy, but she was troubled by horrible temptations to lechery and to despair for nearly all the following year, except that our Lord in His mercy, as she told herself, gave her each day the better part of two hours of compunction for her sins, with many bitter tears. And afterwards she was troubled by temptations to despair as she was before, and was as far from feelings of grace as those who had felt none. And she could not bear that, and so she continued to despair. Except for those times that she felt grace, her troubles were so astounding that she could barely cope with them, but always mourned and lamented as though God had forsaken her.

CHAPTER 5

THEN one Friday before Christmas Day, as this creature was kneeling in a chapel of St John* within a church of St Margaret in N., weeping astonishingly bitterly, asking mercy and forgiveness for her sins and her trespass, our merciful Lord Christ Jesus, may He be blessed, ravished her spirit and said to her, 'Daughter, why are you weeping so bitterly? I, Jesus Christ who died on the Cross suffering bitter pains and torments for you, have come to you. I, the same God, forgive you your sins to the utmost point. And you shall never come either to Hell or to Purgatory, but when you pass out of this world, within the twinkling of an eye,* you shall have the bliss of Heaven, for I am the same God who has fetched your sins to your mind and made you be confessed of them. And I grant contrition* to you until your life's end.

'Therefore I bid you and command you to call me Jesus boldly, your love, for I am your love and shall be your love without end. And, daughter, you have a haircloth upon your back. I wish you to take it off, and I shall give you a haircloth in your heart that will please me much more than all the haircloths in the world.

'Also, my dearly esteemed daughter, you must forsake that which you love most in this world, and that is eating meat.* And instead of that meat you shall eat my flesh and my blood, that is the true body of Christ in the sacrament of the altar.* This is my wish, daughter, that you receive my body every Sunday, and I shall fill you with so much grace that the whole world shall marvel at it.

'You shall be consumed and gnawed at by the worldly people like any rat gnaws at stock-fish.* Do not be afraid, daughter, as you shall have the victory over your enemies. I shall give you enough grace to answer every cleric in the love of God. I swear to you by my majesty that I shall never forsake you in good times or bad. I shall help you and support you so that neither devil in Hell nor angel in Heaven nor man on earth shall ever part you from me, for devils in Hell may not, and angels in Heaven will not, and man on earth shall not.

'And daughter, I wish you to leave aside your saying of many prayers and think such thoughts as I put in your mind. I shall give you leave to pray until six o'clock to say whatever you want. Then you shall lie still and speak to me in thought, and I shall give you high meditation and true contemplation. And I ask that you go to the anchorite at the Preaching Friars,* and reveal to him my confidences and my revelations which I reveal to you, and act according to his advice, for my spirit shall speak in him to you.'

Then this creature went forth to the anchorite, as she had been commanded, and revealed to him the revelations such as had been revealed to her.

Then the anchorite said, thanking God, with great reverence and weeping, 'Daughter, you are sucking even at Christ's breast,* and you have got a pledge* of Heaven. I charge you to receive such thoughts (when God will give them) as meekly and as devoutly as you can, and then come to me and tell me what they are, and I shall, with the permission of our Lord Jesus Christ, tell you whether they are from the Holy Ghost or else from your enemy, the Devil.'

CHAPTER 6

ANOTHER day, this creature was giving herself over to meditation, as she had been asked before, and she lay still, not knowing about what she might best think. Then she said to our Lord Jesus Christ,

'Jesus, what shall I think about?'

Our Lord Jesus answered in her mind: 'Daughter, think about my mother, for she is the cause of all the grace that you have.'

And then at once she saw St Anne* pregnant, and then she asked St Anne if she might be her lady-in-waiting and her servant. And forthwith our Lady was born, and then St Anne busied herself taking the child to herself and looking after her until she was twelve years of age, with good food and drink, with fine white clothes and white kerchiefs.

And then she said to the blessed child, 'My Lady, you shall be the mother of God.'

The blessed child answered and said, 'I wish I were worthy to be the handmaiden of her that should conceive the Son of God.'

The creature said, 'I pray, my Lady, that if such grace should befall you, do not relinquish my service.'

The blessed child went away for a certain period, the creature being still in contemplation, and then came back and said, 'Daughter, now I have become the mother of God.'

And then the creature fell down onto her knees with much reverence and much weeping and said, 'I am not worthy, my Lady, to serve you.'

'Yes, daughter,' she said, 'follow me, your service pleases me well.'

Then she went forth with our Lady and with Joseph, carrying with her a half-gallon flask of sweet, spiced wine. Then they went onwards to Elizabeth, St John the Baptist's mother, and when they met together each of them honoured the other, and so they lived together with great grace and gladness for twelve weeks. And then St John was born,* and our Lady took him up from the ground with every kind of reverence and gave him to his mother, saying of him that he should become a holy man, and she blessed him.

Afterwards they took their leave of each other with compassionate tears. And then the creature fell down onto her knees to St Elizabeth and begged her to pray for her to our Lady that she might serve and please her.

'Daughter,' said Elizabeth, 'it seems to me that you do your duties very well.'

And then the creature went on with our Lady to Bethlehem and organized her accommodations every night with great reverence, and our Lady was received most warmly. Also she begged for our Lady

fine white cloths and kerchiefs in which to swaddle her son when
He was born; and when Jesus was born, she organized bedding for
our Lady to lie in with her blessed son. And afterwards she begged
food for our Lady and her blessed child. Afterwards, with bitter tears
of compassion, she swaddled Him, mindful of the harsh death He
would go on to suffer for the love of sinful people, saying to Him,
'Lord, I shall treat you tenderly; I shall not bind you tightly. I beg you
not to be displeased with me.'

CHAPTER 7

AND afterwards, on the twelfth day,* when three kings came with
their gifts and worshipped our Lord Jesus Christ, then in His
mother's lap, this creature, our Lord's handmaiden, watching all
the activity in contemplation, wept astonishingly bitterly. And when
she saw that they wanted to take their leave to go back to their own
region, she could not bear that they might go away from the presence
of our Lord, and, because they wished to go away, in her wonder
she cried astonishingly bitterly. Then soon after an angel came and
instructed our Lady and Joseph to leave the region of Bethlehem
for Egypt.* Then this creature went onwards with our Lady, day
by day organizing her accommodations most reverently, with many
sweet thoughts and high meditations, and also high contemplations,
sometimes lasting, without ceasing, two hours of weeping and often
longer with our Lord's Passion in mind, sometimes because of her
own sin, sometimes because of the sin of the people, sometimes for
the souls in Purgatory, sometimes for those who are in poverty or
in any distress, for she desired to comfort them all. Sometimes she
wept very profusely and very noisily out of desire for the bliss of
Heaven and because that had been withheld from her for so long.
Then this creature really craved to be delivered out of this wretched
world.

Our Lord Jesus Christ said to her mind that she should remain
and languish in love:* 'For I have ordained you to kneel before the
Trinity* in order to pray for the whole world, for many hundreds
of thousands of souls shall be saved by your prayers. And therefore,
daughter, ask whatever you want, and I shall grant your wish.'

This creature said, 'Lord, I ask for mercy and protection from everlasting damnation for me and for the whole world. Chastise us here and in Purgatory however you wish, and in your high mercy keep us from damnation.'

CHAPTER 8

ANOTHER time, as this creature lay down* at prayer, the Mother of Mercy, appearing to her, said, 'Ah, daughter, may you be blessed, your seat is ready in Heaven at my son's knee, and for whoever you wish to have with you.'

Then the blessed son asked, 'Daughter, whom do you wish to have as your companion with you?'

'My most honoured Lord, I ask for my confessor Master N.'*

'Why do you ask for him above your own father or your husband?'

'For I may never repay him the goodness that he has done for me and the generous travails he has had with me in hearing my confessions.'

'I grant you your wish for him, and yet your father shall be saved, and your husband too, and all your children.'

Then this creature said, 'Lord, since you have forgiven me my sins, I make you the executor of all the good works that you work in me. In praying, in thinking, in weeping, in going on pilgrimage, in fasting, or in speaking any good word, it is fully my wish that you give Master N. half of them, to increase his merit, as if he had done these things himself. And the other half, Lord, spread amongst your friends and your enemies and amongst my friends and enemies, for I wish to have only yourself for my reward.'

'Daughter, I shall be a proper executor to you and fulfil all your wishes, and because of your great charity that you have in comforting fellow Christians, you shall have double the reward in Heaven.'

CHAPTER 9

ANOTHER time, as this creature prayed to God that she might live chaste with her husband's permission, Christ said to her mind, 'You must fast on Friday from food and drink, and you shall have your desire before Whitsuntide, for I shall suddenly slay your husband.'*

Then on the Wednesday of Easter Week,* after her husband wanted to have carnal knowledge of her as he had been used to before, and as he began to approach her, she said 'Jesus, help me!' and her husband had no power to touch her in that way at that time, and never afterwards did he have carnal knowledge.

It happened one Friday before Whitsun, as this creature was in a church of St Margaret at N. hearing mass, that she heard a huge and dreadful noise. She was very dismayed, very much dreading public opinion, which said that God should take vengeance upon her. She knelt on her knees, holding her head downwards, with her book* in her hand, praying to our Lord Christ Jesus for grace and for mercy. Suddenly, from the highest part of the church's vaulted ceiling, from under the base of a rafter, a stone weighing three pounds fell down onto her head and her back, and a short end of a wooden beam weighing six pounds, so she thought her back was broken into pieces, and it seemed to her that she would be dead in a little while. Quickly she then cried, 'Jesus, mercy!' and at once her pain was gone.

A good man called John of Wereham,* seeing this marvellous event and supposing that she had been seriously harmed, came and took her by the sleeve and said, 'Madam, how are you feeling?'

The creature, wholly healthy and unharmed, full of wonder and very amazed that she felt no pain yet had felt so much just a little earlier, thanked him for his kindness and his assistance. She did not feel any pain for the following twelve weeks either. Then the spirit of God said to her soul, 'Take this for a great miracle, and if the people will not believe in this, I shall work many more.'

A worshipful doctor of divinity who was named Master Alan, a White Friar,* upon hearing about this marvellous act, enquired of this creature the manner of this sequence of events. He, desiring that the work of God be exalted, got himself that same stone that fell upon her back and weighed it, and then he got the end of the beam that fell upon her head, which one of the stewards of the church had put in the fireplace to burn. And this worshipful doctor said it was a great miracle, and our Lord was to be highly exalted for preserving this creature against the malice of her enemy, and he told many people about it, and many people greatly glorified God in this creature. Yet also many people would not believe in it, but rather believed it to be a token of fury and vengeance than believe it was some token of mercy or graciousness.

Husband is control

CHAPTER 10

SOON after, this creature was moved in her soul to go to visit certain places for spiritual health, inasmuch as she was cured, but she could not go without her husband's consent. She required her husband to give her leave, and he, wholly trusting that it was the will of God, soon consented and they went together to that place as she was prompted. And then our Lord Christ Jesus said to her, 'My servants very much desire to see you.'

Then she was welcomed and made much of in various places.

Because of this she greatly feared vainglory and was very afraid. Our merciful lord Jesus Christ, may His name be worshipped, said to her,

'Don't be afraid, daughter, I shall take vainglory from you. For those who worship you, they worship me; those who despise you, they despise me, and I shall chastise them for it. I am in you, and you in me.* And those who hear you, they hear the voice of God. Daughter, there is no man alive so sinful that, if he will forsake his sin and follow your advice, then such grace as you promise him I will confirm for love of you.'

Then she and her husband went onwards to York* and to various other places.

CHAPTER 11

IT happened one Friday on Midsummer's Eve* in very hot weather, as this creature was coming from York, carrying a bottle of beer in her hand and her husband a cake inside his shirt, that her husband asked his wife this question: 'Margery, if a man came with a sword and wanted to chop off my head unless I had sexual intercourse with you as I used to before, tell me the truth from your conscience—as you say you won't lie—whether you'd allow my head to be chopped off, or else allow me to have sex with you as I previously did?'

'Alas, sir,' she said, 'why are you raising this matter? Haven't we been chaste these eight weeks?'

'Because I want to know your heart's truth.'

And then she said with great sorrow, 'Truthfully I'd rather see you slain than that we should return to our uncleanliness.'

And he said back, 'You're not a good wife.'

And then she asked her husband what had caused him not to have sex with her for the previous eight weeks, since she lay with him every night in his bed. And he said that he had become so frightened when he would have touched her that he dared no longer do it.

'Now, good sir, mend your ways and ask for God's mercy, for I told you nearly three years ago that you would suddenly be slain, and now this is the third year and I am still hoping that I shall have my wish.* Good sir, I pray you grant me that which I shall ask, and I shall pray for you to be saved through the mercy of our Lord Jesus Christ, and you shall have more reward in Heaven than if you wore a haircloth or chain-mail.* I pray you, allow me to make a vow of chastity at the hand of whichever bishop God will have it.'

'No,' he said, 'I won't grant you that, because now I can have sex with you without mortal sin and then I wouldn't be able to do so.'

Then she answered back to him, 'If it be the will of the Holy Ghost to fulfil what I have said, I pray God that you consent to this; and if it be not the will of the Holy Ghost, I pray God that you never consent to it.'

Then they went on towards Bridlington* in very hot weather, the aforementioned creature having great sorrow and great fear for her chastity. And as they came to a cross, her husband sat himself down by the cross, calling his wife to him and saying these words to her: 'Margery, grant me my desire, and I'll grant you your desire. My first desire is that we'll still lie together in one bed, as we've formerly done; the second that you'll pay my debts before you go to Jerusalem; and the third that you'll eat and drink with me on Fridays as you used to do.'

'No, sir,' she said, 'to break the Friday fast is something I'll never grant you as long as I live.'

'Well,' he said, 'then I'll have sex with you again.'

She begged him to allow her to make her prayers, and he granted it good-naturedly. Then she knelt down beside a cross in the field and prayed in this manner, with a great abundance of tears: 'Lord God, you know all things; you know what sorrow I have had in order to be chaste in my body for you all these three years, and now I might have my wish and I dare not, for the love of you. For if I wanted to break that custom of fasting from food or drink which you commanded me to keep on Fridays, I should now have my desire. But, blessed Lord, you know I will not be contrary to your will, and vast is my sorrow now unless I find comfort in you. Now blessed Jesus, make your will known to me, unworthy as I am, then I can follow after it and fulfil it with all my might.'

And then our Lord Jesus Christ spoke with great sweetness to this creature, commanding her to go back to her husband and beg him to grant that which she desired: 'And he shall have that which he desires. For, my dearly esteemed daughter, this was why I commanded you to fast, for you should the sooner obtain and get your desire, and now it is granted to you. I no longer wish you to fast, therefore I order you, in the name of Jesus, to eat and drink as your husband does.'

Then this creature thanked our Lord Jesus Christ for His grace and His goodness, and after that got up and went to her husband, saying to him: 'Sir, if it please you, you shall grant me my desire, and you shall have your desire. Grant me that you'll not come into my bed and I grant you that I'll repay your debts before I go to Jerusalem.* And make my body freely available to God, so that whilst you live you never make any demands of me to ask for the matrimonial debt after this day, and I shall eat and drink on Fridays at your command.'

Then her husband said back to her, 'May your body be as freely available to God as it has been to me.'

This creature thanked God deeply, rejoicing that she had had her desire, pleading with her husband that they should say three pater-nosters in worship of the Trinity for the grand grace that He had granted them. And this they did, kneeling under a cross, and after that they ate and drank together in very high spirits. This was on a Friday, Midsummer's Eve.

Then they went onward to Bridlington, and also to many other regions, and spoke with God's servants, both anchorites and recluses and many other lovers of our Lord, with many praiseworthy clerics, doctors of divinity, and bachelors too, in many different places. So this creature revealed her feelings and her contemplations to various amongst them, as she was commanded to do, to know if there was any deception in her feelings.

CHAPTER 12

THIS creature was sent by our Lord to various religious places, amongst which she came to a monks' place, where she was very much welcomed for our Lord's love, except that there was one monk, who held high office in that place, who despised her and did not value her one bit. Nevertheless, she was sitting at a meal with the abbot, and during the meal she said many good fine words, as God would put them into her mind, this same monk who had so despised her being present with many others to hear what she would say. And through her conversation his feelings began very much to incline towards her and he delighted in her words. So afterwards, she at that time being in church and he also, the aforementioned monk came to her and said, 'Young lady, I hear that God speaks to you. I ask that you tell me whether or not I shall be saved, and for what sins I have most displeased God, for I will not believe in you unless you can tell me what my sins are.'

The creature said to the monk, 'Go to mass, and if I may weep for you, I hope to have grace for you.'

He followed her advice and went to mass. She wept marvellously for his sins. When mass had ended, the creature said to our Lord Jesus Christ, 'Blessed Lord, what answer shall I give to this man?'

'My dearly esteemed daughter, you can say in the name of Jesus that he has sinned in lechery, in despair,* and in the keeping of worldly goods.'

'Oh, gracious Lord, this is hard for me to say. He shall really shame me if I tell him any lies.'

'Do not be afraid, but speak boldly in my name, in the name of Jesus, for these are not lies.'

And then she said back to our Lord Jesus Christ, 'Good Lord, shall he be saved?'

'Yes,' said our Lord Jesus, 'if he will leave his sin and follow your advice. Direct him to leave both his sin (and be confessed and absolved of it) and his external office.'*

Then the monk came back: 'Margery, tell me what my sins are.'

She said, 'I beg you, sir, not to ask about that, for I undertake that your soul shall be saved, if you will follow my advice.'

'Truly, I will not believe you, unless you tell me what my sins are.'

'Sir, I understand that you have sinned in lechery, in despair, and in the keeping of worldly goods.'

Then the monk stood still, somewhat abashed, and then he said, 'Say whether I have sinned with wives or with single women?'

'With wives, sir.'

Then he said, 'Shall I be saved?'

'Yes, sir, if you'll follow my advice. Feel sorrow for your sin, and I shall help you to be sorrowful; be confessed and absolved of your sin and leave it willingly. Leave your external office, and God will give you grace for love of me.'

The monk took her by the hand and led her into a beautiful household room, made her a fine dinner, and after that gave her gold to pray for him. And so she took her leave at that time. Another time, when the creature came back to the same place, the aforementioned monk had given up his office on her advice, and had turned away from his sin, and was made the sub-prior of the place, a well-behaved and well-disposed man, thanks be to God, and he warmly received this creature and mightily blessed God that he had ever seen her.

CHAPTER 13

ONE time, when this creature was at Canterbury* in the church amongst the monks, she was deeply despised and reproached, both by monks and priests, and by secular people, because she wept so much, nearly all day, both morning and afternoon too, and so much that her husband went away from her as if he did not know her and he left her alone amongst them, choose how she might, for she had no more comfort from him that day.

So an old monk, who had been the Queen's treasurer when he was in secular clothes, a rich man,* and greatly feared by many people, took her by the hand, saying to her:

'What can you say of God?'

'Sir,' she said, 'I will both speak of Him and hear of Him', repeating a story from scripture to the monk.

The monk said, 'I would like you to be enclosed in a house of stone, so that nobody might speak with you.'

'Oh, sir,' she said, 'you should look after God's servants but you are the first to side against them. May God help you!'

Then a young monk said to this creature, 'Either you have the Holy Ghost or else you have a devil inside you, for what you are saying here to us is of Holy Writ, and you do not get that from yourself.'

Then this creature said, 'I beg you, sir, give me leave to tell a tale.'

Then the people said to the monk, 'Let her say what she wants.'

And then she said, 'There was once a man who had sinned gravely against God, and when he had confessed and been absolved, his confessor commanded him that as partial penance he should hire people for one year to chide him and rebuke him for his sins, and he would give them silver coins for their labour. So one day he came amongst many people, such as are here now—may God save you all—and he stood amongst them, as I am now doing amongst you, them despising him as you do me, the man laughing and smiling at having good sport at their words. The most important amongst them said to the man, "Why are you laughing, you scoundrel, when you're so deeply despised?"

' "Ah, sir, I have a very good reason to laugh, because for many days I've been taking silver out of my purse and hired people to chide me for remission of my sins, and today I can keep my silver in my purse, thanks to you lot."

'Right so I say to you, worshipful sirs, while I was at home in my own region, with great weeping and mourning day by day, I mourned because I did not have any of the shame, scorn, and spite for which I was worthy. I thank you all very much, sirs, for what I have received today, morning and afternoon, in right measure, may God be blessed for it.'

Then she went out of the monastery, with them following her and shrieking after her, 'You shall be burned, false Lollard!* Here's a cartful of thorns ready for you, and a barrel to burn you with!'

Then the creature stood outside the gates of Canterbury, for it was in the evening, with many people gawking at her.

Then the people said, 'Take her and burn her!'

And the creature stood still, trembling and quaking most dreadfully in her flesh, without any worldly comforts, and did not know what had become of her husband. Then she prayed in her heart to our Lord, thinking in this way: 'I came here, Lord, for your love. Blessed Lord, help me and have mercy on me.'

And then, after she had made her prayers in her heart to our Lord, two handsome young men came and said to her, 'Young lady, are you neither a heretic nor a Lollard?'

And she said, 'No, sirs, I am neither heretic nor Lollard.'

Then they asked her 'where is your inn?' She said she did not know which street it was in, but it was a German man's house.

Then these two young men took her home to her hostel and treated her very kindly, asking her to pray for them, and she found her husband there. Many people in N. had said wicked things about her whilst she was away, and had slandered her about many things she was supposed to have done whilst she was in the region. Then after this she was very much at rest in her soul for a long while, and had high contemplation day by day, and many holy speeches and conversations with our Lord Jesus Christ both morning and afternoon, with many sweet tears of high devotion, so plentifully and constantly that it was a miracle that her eyes endured or that her heart could outlast being consumed with the ardour of love,* the which was kindled with holy conversation with our Lord, when He said to her many times, 'Dearly esteemed daughter, love me with all your heart, for I love you with all my heart and with all the might of my Godhead,* for you were a chosen soul without beginning in my sight and a pillar of Holy Church.* My merciful eyes are forever upon you. It would be impossible for you to suffer the scorn and spite that you shall have if you did not have my grace alone to support you.'

CHAPTER 14

So this creature thought it was a joyful thing to be rebuked for God's love; and it was a great solace and comfort to her when she was chided and taunted for the love of Jesus, for rebuking sin, for speaking of virtue, for talking about scripture which she had learned through sermons and by talking with clerics. She imagined in herself what kind of death she might die for Christ's sake. She thought she might wish to be killed for God's love, but feared the point of death, and therefore she imagined for herself the softest death, so she thought, because of her lack of fortitude: this was to have her head and her feet bound to a stake and her head to be chopped off with a sharp axe, for God's love.* Then our Lord said in her mind, 'I thank you, daughter, that you are willing to suffer death for my love, for as often as you think so, you shall have the same reward in Heaven as though you had suffered that same death. And yet nobody will kill you, or burn you in fire, or drown you in water, or injure you in storms, for I may not forget you, how you are written upon my hands and my feet;* I very much like the pains that I have suffered for you. I shall never be angry with you, but I shall love you without end. Though the whole world is against you, do not be afraid, for they cannot

understand you. I swear to your mind that if it were possible for
me to suffer pain again as I have done before, I would rather suffer
as much pain as I ever did for your soul alone rather than that you
should be separated from me forever. So therefore, daughter, just as
you see the priest take the child at the font and dip it in the water
and wash it clear of original sin so shall I wash you in my precious
blood from all your sin.

'And, although I sometimes withdraw the feeling of grace from
you, either in speaking or in weeping, do not be afraid, for I am a hidden God* in you, so that you have no vainglory, and you should know
well that you may not have tears or such conversations except when
God wishes to send them to you, for they are the free gifts of God,
separate from your merit, and He may give them to whom He wishes
and do you no wrong. Therefore take these gifts meekly and thank-
fully when I wish to send them, and suffer patiently when I withdraw
them, and seek diligently until you can gain them, for tears of compunction, devotion, and compassion are the highest and surest gifts
that I give on earth.

'And what more should I do for you unless I were to take your soul
out of your body and put it in Heaven, and I do not wish to do that
yet. Nevertheless, wherever God is, Heaven is; and God is in your
soul, and many an angel is around your soul, to protect it both night
and day. For whenever you go to church, I go with you; whenever you
sit at your meals, I sit with you; whenever you go to your bed, I go
with you; and whenever you leave your town, I go with you.

'Daughter, there was never a child so humble to its father as I will
be to you, to help you and protect you. With my grace I sometimes
act with you as I do with the sun. Sometimes, as you know well, the
sun shines broadly so that many people can see it, and sometimes it
is hidden under a cloud so that people cannot see it, and yet it is the
sun nevertheless in its heat and in its brightness. And this is how I act
with you and with my chosen souls.

'Although it may be the case that you do not always weep when
you please, nevertheless my grace is in you. Therefore I prove that
you are truly a daughter to me and a mother too, a sister, a wife, and
a spouse, in witness of the Gospel where our Lord says to His disciples, "For whosoever shall do the will of God, he is my brother, and
my sister, and mother."* When you strive to please me, then you are
truly a daughter; when you weep and mourn for my pains and for my

Passion, then you are truly a mother having compassion for her child; when you weep for other men's sins and for difficulties, then you are truly a sister; and when you mourn for being so far from the bliss of Heaven, then you are truly a spouse and wife, for it is fitting for the wife to be with her husband and to have no true joy until she is in his presence.'

CHAPTER 15

THIS creature, when our Lord Jesus Christ had forgiven her for her sin (as is written beforehand), had a desire to see those places where He was born and where He suffered His Passion and where He died, along with other holy places where He was during His life and also after His Resurrection. As she was having these desires, our Lord charged her in her mind, two years before she went,* that she go to Rome, to Jerusalem, and to Santiago, for she would happily have gone but she had no money with which to go.

So then she said to our Lord, 'Where shall I get the money with which to go to all these holy places?'

Our Lord replied to her, 'I shall send you friends enough in the various parts of England to help you. And, daughter, I shall go with you in every region and provide for you; I shall lead you there and bring you back safely and no Englishman shall die in the ship you are in. I shall keep you from all wicked men's power. And, daughter, I say to you, I wish you to wear clothes that are white and of no other colour,* for you shall be dressed according to my wishes.'

'Ah, dear Lord, if I go about attired differently from how other chaste women do, I'm afraid that people will slander me. They will say I'm a hypocrite and mock me.'

'Yes, daughter, the more mockery that you get for my love, the more you please me.'

Then this creature dared not do other than she was commanded in her soul.

And so she went onwards with her husband into the country, for he was always a good man and a kind man to her. Although he some-times (because of baseless fears) left her alone for a while, he always came back to her, and had compassion for her, and spoke up for her as far as he dared for fear of other people. But all the others who had gone with her forsook her, and accused her fully falsely, through the Devil's temptation, of things of which she was never guilty. And thus did one man, in whom she had great trust, and who offered to travel into the country with her, about which she was very glad, trusting that he would really support her and help her when in need, for he had been living for a long time with an anchorite, a master of divinity and a holy man, and that anchorite was this woman's confessor.

So his servant took his leave, through his own initiative, to travel with this creature into the country, and her own maid went with her too, for as long as things went well for them and nobody said anything against them. But as soon as people, through the enticement of our spiritual enemy and with the permission of our Lord, spoke against this creature because she wept so bitterly, and said she was a false hypocrite and falsely deceived the people, and threatened to burn her, then the aforementioned man who had been held to be so holy and whom she so much trusted, utterly reproached her, and grossly despised her, and would go no further with her. Her maid, seeing trouble on all sides, became rowdy against her mistress. She would neither obey her nor follow her advice. She let her mistress go alone into many a good town and would not go with her. And this creature's husband was always ready when all the others failed, he went with her wherever our Lord wished to send her, always trusting that all was for the best and would end up well when God wanted.

And at this time he took her to speak with the Bishop of Lincoln, who was called Philip,* and they waited three weeks before they could speak with him as he was not at home at his palace.

When the Bishop came home and heard how such and such a woman had waited so long to speak with him, he sent for her at once in great haste to know what she wanted. And then she came into his presence and greeted him, and he kindly welcomed her and said he had long desired to speak with her, and he was very glad that she had come. And so she asked him if she might speak with him confidentially and reveal to him the secrets of her soul, and he assigned to her a convenient time to do so.

When the time came she revealed to him her meditations and high contemplations, and other secret things, of both the living and the dead, as our Lord revealed to her soul. He was very glad to hear them, and courteously allowed her to say what she pleased, and very much commended her feelings and her contemplations, saying that they were high matters and very devout matters, inspired by the Ghost, advising her seriously that her feelings should be written down. And she said that it was not God's wish that they should be written down so soon, nor were they written down for twenty years after and more. And then she added: 'My Lord, if it pleases you, I am commanded in my soul that you shall give me the mantle and the ring,* and clothe me all in white clothes. And if you clothe me on earth, our Lord Jesus Christ will clothe you in Heaven, as I understand it through revelation.'

Then the Bishop said to her, 'I will fulfil your desire if your husband consents to it.'

Then she said to the Bishop, 'I beg you to let my husband come into your presence, and you'll hear what he has to say.'

And so her husband came before the Bishop, and the Bishop asked him, 'John, is it your wish that your wife shall take the mantle and the ring and live chaste, the both of you?'

[handwritten margin note: w/ Bishop]

'Yes, my Lord,' he said, 'and as a token that we both vow to live in chastity, I hereby offer my hands into yours.' And he put his hands between the Bishop's hands.

And the Bishop did no more with us that day, except that he treated us very warmly and told us that we were very welcome.* Another day this creature came to dine at the request of the Bishop. And, before he sat down to eat, she saw him give with his own hands thirteen pence and thirteen loaves to thirteen poor men together with some other food. And he did this every day. This creature was stirred to high devotion by this sight, and gave praise and worship to God because He gave the Bishop grace to do these good deeds, and she had such copious weeping that all the Bishop's household wondered what was wrong with her. And after that she sat at table with many praiseworthy clerics and priests and the Bishop's squires, and the Bishop himself very kindly sent her some of his own meal. The clerics asked this creature many hard questions, which she answered, by the grace of Jesus, so that the Bishop liked her answers very much and the clerics wondered at her, how she answered so readily and convincingly.

When the Bishop had eaten, he sent for this creature to come into his chamber, saying to her, 'Margery, you and your husband asked me to give you the mantle and the ring, for which reason I have taken advice and my counsellors will not let me accept your profession of celibacy in such unusual clothing without further consideration. And you say that by the grace of God you will go to Jerusalem. Therefore pray to God that it can wait until you come back from Jerusalem, when you will be the better tried and tested.'

On the next day this creature went to church and prayed to God with all her spirit that she might have knowledge of how she should conduct herself in this matter, and what kind of answers she might give to the Bishop.

Our Lord Jesus Christ answered to her mind in this manner: 'Daughter, tell the Bishop that he is more afraid of the disgraces of the world than the perfect love of God. Tell him, I would have excused him if he fulfilled your wish just as I did the children of Israel when I asked them to borrow the Egyptians' property and leave with it.* Therefore, daughter, tell him, even though he does not wish to do it now, it shall be done another time when God wishes.'

And so she took her message to the Bishop of Lincoln as she had been commanded. Then he wished her to go to the Archbishop of Canterbury—Arundel*—'and pray him to grant leave to me, the Bishop of Lincoln' to give her the mantle and the ring, inasmuch as she was not from his diocese. He invented this reason through the advice of his clerks as they did not love this creature.

She said, 'Sir, I will go to my Lord of Canterbury very willingly for I have other reasons and matters which I need to disclose to his reverence. As far as this reason is concerned, I shall not go, because God does not wish that I ask the Archbishop for it.'

Then she left the Bishop of Lincoln, and he gave her twenty-six shillings and eight pence* to buy her clothes with and to pray for him.

CHAPTER 16

THEN this creature went on to London with her husband, to Lambeth, where the Archbishop was staying at that time.* And as they came into the hall in the afternoon, there were many of the Archbishop's clerics and other thoughtless men, both squires and yeomen, who were swearing many a grave oath and speaking many thoughtless words, and this creature boldly scolded them and said that, unless they left behind their swearing and the other sins that they practised, they would be damned. With that a local woman came forwards who was dressed in a pelisse and who utterly loathed this creature, cursed her, and said most horribly to her, 'I wish you were at Smithfield, and I would carry a faggot to burn you with;* it's a pity that you're alive.'

This creature stood still and did not answer, and her husband endured it with immense pain and was very sorry to hear his wife rebuked in this way.

Then the Archbishop sent for this creature to come to him in his garden.

When she entered into his presence she greeted him as best she could, begging him in his gracious lordship to grant her the authority to choose her confessor and to receive communion every Sunday,* if God would dispose her to this, under his letter and seal through all his province. He granted her all her desires most benevolently without taking any silver or gold for it, and he would not let his clerks take anything for writing and sealing the letter.

When this creature found this grace in his sight, she was very much comforted and strengthened in her soul, and so she revealed to this honourable lord her manner of living, and such grace as God performed it in her mind and in her soul, so that she might know what he would say about this, if he found any fault either in her contemplation or in her weeping. And she told him too of the cause of her weeping and the manner of conversation when our Lord conversed with her soul. He found no fault with this, but approved of her manner of living, and was very glad that our merciful Lord Christ Jesus revealed such grace in our time, blessed may He be!

Then this creature spoke boldly to him about rectifying his household, saying with respect, 'My lord, the Lord of all, God almighty, has not given you your benefice and worldly wealth to sustain those who are traitors to Him and those who kill Him every day through the swearing of grievous oaths. You shall have to answer for them unless you correct them or else put them out of your service.'

Very agreeably and meekly he allowed her to say what was on her mind and he gave a decent answer, she supposing that it would then be better. And so their conversation continued until stars appeared in the heavens. Then she took her leave and her husband did too.

After that they came back to London, and many worthy people wanted to hear her communication and her conversation, for her conversation was so much to do with the love of God that those who heard it were often moved to weep very gravely. So they had a warm welcome there—and her husband too because of her—as long as they wished to stay in that city.

Afterwards they came back to Lynn, and then this creature went to the anchorite at the Preaching Friars' in Lynn and told him how warmly she had been welcomed and how she had fared while she was going about the country. And he was really pleased by her coming home and held it to be a great miracle, her coming and going to and fro.

And he said to her, 'I've heard so much wicked talk about you since you went away, and I've been strongly advised to desert you and not mix with you any more, and many excellent friendships have been promised to me on condition that I desert you. And I answered for you thus: "If you were still in the same condition as you were when you left, I would certainly say you are a good woman, a lover of God, and greatly inspired by the Holy Ghost." And I would say, "I will not forsake her for any lady in this realm, if speaking with the lady means leaving her, for I should rather leave the lady and speak with this lady [i.e. Margery Kempe], if I am unable to do both, than do the contrary."' (Read the twenty-first chapter first, and then this chapter after that).*

CHAPTER 17

ONE day long before this time, while this creature was bearing children and she was recently delivered of a child, our Lord Christ Jesus said to her that she should bear no more children, and therefore he charged that she go to Norwich.

So she said, 'Ah, dear Lord, how should I go? I'm feeling both faint and feeble.'

'Do not be afraid, I shall make you strong enough. I charge that you go to the Vicar of St Stephen's* and say that I greet him warmly, and that he is a high, chosen soul of mine, and tell him that he pleases me greatly with his preaching and reveal to him your secrets and my confidences such as I have revealed to you.'

Then she took herself to Norwich and went into his church on a Thursday a little before noon. And the Vicar was walking up and down with another priest who was his confessor, who was alive when this book was made. At that time this creature was clad in black clothing.* She greeted the Vicar, begging him that she might speak with him about the love of God for an hour or maybe two hours that afternoon, after he had eaten.

He, lifting up his hands and blessing himself, said '*Benedicite!** How could a woman occupy an hour or two hours with the love of our Lord? I won't eat a single thing until I see what you can say of our Lord's love in the space of an hour.'

Then he sat himself down in the church. She, sitting a little to one side, told him all the words that God had revealed to her in her soul. After that she told him all her manner of living from her childhood as closely as it would come to her mind: how unkind she had been towards our Lord Jesus Christ, how proud and vain she had been in her deportment, how obstinate against the laws of God, and how envious towards her fellow Christians; and, later, when it pleased our Lord Christ Jesus, how chastised she was with many tribulations and horrible temptations and how afterwards she was fed and comforted with holy meditations and was especially mindful of our Lord's Passion.

And, while she conversed on the Passion of our Lord Jesus Christ, she heard so hideous a melody that she could not bear it. Then this creature fell down, as if she had lost her physical strength, and lay still for a long while, desiring to be rid of this noise but unable to be so. Then she knew surely by her faith that there was great joy in Heaven, where the smallest speck of bliss surpasses without comparison all the joy that might ever be thought or felt in this life. She was greatly strengthened in her faith and emboldened to tell the Vicar her feelings, which she had from revelations about both the living and the dead, and about his own self.

She told him how sometimes the Heavenly Father conversed with her soul as plainly and as truly as one friend speaks to another in bodily speech. Sometimes the Second Person of the Trinity,* sometimes all Three Persons of the Trinity and one substance of the Godhead, conversed with her soul and instructed her in her faith and in His love how she should love Him, worship Him, and dread Him, so excellently that she never heard any book: neither Hilton's book, nor Bridget's book, nor *Stimulus Amoris*, nor *Incendium Amoris*,* nor any other that she ever heard being read, that spoke so highly of the love of God as she felt working greatly in her soul, if she could have communicated what she felt.

Sometimes our Lady spoke to her mind; sometimes St Peter,

sometimes St Paul, sometimes St Katherine, or whatever saint in Heaven she was devoted to appeared to her soul and taught her how she should love our Lord and how she should please Him. Such conversations were so sweet, so holy, and so devout that this creature could often hardly bear it, but fell down and twisted her body, and behaved in a marvellous way, with noisy sobbing and a great many tears, sometimes saying 'Jesus, mercy', sometimes 'I'm dying!'

Therefore many people slandered her, not believing it was the work of God but that some evil spirit had vexed her in her body, or else that she had some physical sickness. Notwithstanding the rumours and grumbling of the people against her, this holy man, the vicar of St Stephen's Church in Norwich, whom God has exalted and through marvellous works revealed and proved to be holy, stood by her and supported her against her enemies inasmuch as he was able, after the time that she, by God's command, had revealed to him her manner of behaviour and living, for he assuredly believed that she was very learned in the law of God and provided with the grace of the Holy Ghost, to whom it belongs to inspire wherever He will. And even though His voice is heard, the world does not know from whence it comes or whither it goes.

After this time this holy Vicar was always confessor to this creature when she came to Norwich and gave her communion with his own hands. And, one time when she was ordered to appear before certain of the Bishop's officers, to answer certain allegations which were made against her by the agitation of envious people, the good Vicar, putting the love of God before the shame of the world, went with her to her examination and rescued her from the malice of her enemies. And then it was revealed to this creature that the good Vicar should live for seven years more, and then he would pass hence with great grace, and so he did as she . . .*

CHAPTER 18

THIS creature was charged and commanded in her soul to go to a White Friar, who was called William Southfield,* in that same city of Norwich, a good man and one who lived righteously, to reveal to him the grace that God had performed in her soul, as she had done to the good Vicar beforehand. She did as she was commanded, and came to the friar one morning, and was with him in a chapel for a long time, and revealed to him her meditations and what God had performed in her soul, so she could know if she was deceived by any delusions or not.

This good man, the White Friar, held up his hands for the whole time she was telling him of her feelings, and said, 'Jesus, mercy, and thanks! Sister,' he said, 'do not be afraid of your manner of living, for it is the Holy Ghost working His grace bountifully in your soul. Thank Him highly for His goodness, for we are all bound to thank Him for you, who now in our days inspires you with His grace, to the help and comfort of all of us who are supported by your prayers and by others like you. And we are preserved from many mishaps and ailments that we would deservedly suffer for our trespasses if it were not for having such good creatures amongst us. Blessed be almighty God for His goodness!

'And therefore, sister, I counsel you to prepare yourself to receive the gifts of God as humbly and meekly as you can, and to put no obstacle or objection against the goodness of the Holy Ghost, for He may give His gifts wherever He wishes, and He makes the unworthy worthy, He makes the sinful righteous. His mercy is always ready for us, unless the fault be in ourselves, for He will not dwell in a body subject to sins. The Holy Spirit flees from all falseness and fakery;* He asks of us a humble, meek, and contrite heart, with a good will.* Our Lord says Himself, "My spirit shall rest upon a meek man, a contrite man, who fears my words."*

'Sister, I trust in our Lord that you have these conditions either in your will or in your affections or else in both, and I do not consider that our Lord allows those who put their trust in Him to be endlessly deceived and who seek and desire nothing but Him only, as I hope that you do. And therefore fully believe that our Lord loves you and works His grace in you. I pray that God may increase it and continue it to His everlasting worship, for His mercy.'

The aforementioned creature was much comforted both in body and in soul by this good man's words and greatly strengthened in her faith. So then she was charged by our Lord to go to an anchoress in the same city, who was called Dame Julian.* And so this she did, and revealed to her the grace that God had put in her soul, of compunction, contrition, sweetness and devotion, compassion with holy meditation and lofty contemplation, and very many holy speeches and conversations that our Lord spoke to her soul, and many wonderful revelations which she revealed to the anchoress to know whether there was any deceit in them, for the anchoress was an expert in such things and could give good advice. The anchoress, hearing about the marvellous goodness of our Lord, highly thanked God with all her heart for His visitation, advising this creature to be obedient to the wishes of our Lord God and to fulfil with all her might whatever He put in her soul, if it were not against the worship of God or the profit of fellow Christians; for, if it were, then it was not the guidance of a good spirit, but rather an evil spirit.

'The Holy Ghost never urges anything against charity, and, if he did, He would be contrary to His own self, for He is all charity. Also, He moves a soul to chastity, for those who live chaste are called to the temple of the Holy Ghost,* and the Holy Ghost makes a soul stable and steadfast in the right faith and the right belief.

'And a double-minded man is inconstant and unstable in all his ways.* He who is always doubting is like a wave on the sea, which is moved and carried about by the wind, and such a man is not likely to receive any of the Lord's gifts.* Whatever creature has these tokens must steadfastly believe that the Holy Ghost lives in his soul. Much more so, when God visits a creature with tears of contrition, devotion, or compassion, the creature can and ought to believe that the Holy Ghost is in their soul. St Paul says that the Holy Ghost asks for us with lamentations and unspeakable groaning;* that is to say, he makes us ask and pray with lamentations and weeping so plentifully that the tears may not be counted. No evil spirit can give these tokens, as Jerome says that tears torment the Devil more than do the pains of Hell.* God and the Devil are always contrary to each other, and they shall never live together in one place, and the Devil has no power in a person's soul.

'Holy Writ says that the soul of a righteous man is the seat of God,* and so I trust, sister, that you are. I pray that God grants perseverance to you. Place all your trust in God and do not fear what the world says, because the more spite, shame, and rebuking that you have in the world, the more merit is yours in the sight of God. Patience is necessary for you, because in that you shall preserve your soul.'*

The anchoress and this creature had much holy conversation in talking about the love of our Lord Jesus Christ for the many days that they were together.

This creature revealed her manner of living to many a worthy cleric, to honourable doctors of divinity, both religious men and those in secular dress, and they said that God performed great grace in her and charged her not to be afraid—there was no deception in her manner of living. They advised her to persevere, for their biggest fear was that she might turn away and not keep her perfection. She had so many enemies and so much slander that it seemed to them that she might not bear it without great grace and a mighty faith.

Others who had no knowledge of her manner of self-conduct except by outward appearances, through the tattling of other people, through the perverting of true opinion, said really wicked things about her and caused her to have much enmity and much distress, more than she should otherwise have had if they had not spoken so wickedly about her. Nevertheless, the anchorite at the Preaching Friars' in Lynn—who was the principal confessor to this creature, as is written earlier—took responsibility, on his soul, that her feelings were good and secure and that there was no deceit in them. He, by the spirit of prophecy, told her how, when she went on her way to Jerusalem, she should have many troubles with her maidservant and how our Lord would try her strictly and test her very severely.

Then she replied to him, 'Ah, good sir, what shall I do when I am far from home and in strange lands, and my maidservant is against me? Then my physical comfort will be gone and spiritual comfort from a confessor like you, well I don't know where I'll find that.'

'Daughter, don't be afraid, for our Lord shall comfort you in His own self, He whose comfort surpasses all others, and when all your friends have forsaken you, our Lord shall provide a hunchbacked man to guide you wherever you're going.'

And so it happened in every detail as the anchorite had prophesied and, as I trust, shall be written about more clearly afterwards.

Then this creature said to the anchorite, in a complaining kind of way, 'Good sir, what shall I do? He who is my confessor in your absence* is very strict to me. He will not believe in my feelings; he sets no store by them; he thinks they are just fripperies and jokes. And this is really painful to me for I do love him and I would happily follow his advice.'

The anchorite, answering back to her, said, 'It is no wonder, daughter, if he cannot believe in your feelings so soon. He knows full well that you have been a sinful woman and therefore he thinks that God would not be intimate with you in such a short time. After your conversion I would not, for the whole world, have been as strict with you as he is. God, because of your deservingness, has appointed him to be your scourge and behave with you as a blacksmith with a file,* making the iron bright and clear to the sight that before appeared rusty, dark, and debased in colour. The stricter he is with you, the more clearly your soul shines in God's sight, and God has appointed me to be your nurse and your comfort. Be humble and meek and thank God for both one and the other.'

*

One time beforehand, this creature went to her prayers in order to learn what answer she should give to the widow.* She was commanded in her spirit to charge the widow, if she wished to please God, to leave her confessor at that time, and go to the anchorite at the Preaching Friars' in Lynn and reveal everything about her life to him. When this creature gave this message, neither the widow nor her confessor would believe in her words, unless God would give the widow the same grace that He gave this creature, and she ordered this creature no longer to come to her house. And because this creature told the widow that she had to feel love and affection for her confessor, therefore the widow said it would have been good if this creature's love and affection was directed as hers was.

Then our Lord charged this creature that she have a letter written and send it to the widow. A master of divinity wrote a letter at the request of this creature and sent it to the widow with the following clauses: one clause was that the widow should never have the grace that this creature had. Another was: although this creature would never come inside the widow's house, this pleased God very much.

Our Lord said afterwards to this creature, 'It would be better than the whole world for her if her love was as directed as yours is. And I charge you to go to her confessor and tell him, because he will not believe your words, that they will be separated before he knows it, and those who are not confided in by her shall know this before he does, whether he likes it or not. See, daughter, you will realize how hard it is to separate a man from his own will.'

All this story was truly fulfilled, as the creature had said before, twelve years afterwards. Then this creature suffered much tribulation and great sadness for she said these words as our Lord charged her to say. And she always increased in the love of God and was bolder than she had been before.

CHAPTER 19

BEFORE this creature went to Jerusalem our Lord sent her to an admirable lady so that she could speak with her confidentially and do His errand to her. The lady would not speak with her unless her confessor were present and she said she was happy with this. Then when the lady's confessor had come, all three went into a chapel together, and then this creature said with great reverence and many tears, 'Madam, our Lord Jesus Christ commanded me to tell you that your husband is in Purgatory,* and that you shall be saved, but it shall be a long time before you reach Heaven.'

So then the lady was displeased and said that her husband had been a good man—she did not believe that he was in Purgatory. Her confessor stood by this creature, and said it might well be as she had said and validated her words with many holy tales.

And then this lady sent her daughter, accompanied by many others of her household, to the anchorite who was this creature's principal confessor, so that he should forsake her, and else he would lose her friendship. The anchorite said to these messengers that he would not forsake the creature for anybody on earth, for to such people as would enquire of him about her manner of self-conduct and his thoughts about her he would say that she was God's own servant and also that he said she was the tabernacle of God.

And the anchorite said to her to strengthen her in her faith, 'Though God should take all tears and conversations from you, believe nevertheless that God loves you and that you shall be sure of Heaven for what you have had beforehand, for tears with love are the greatest gift that God can give on earth, and all people who love God should thank Him for you.' There was also a widow who begged this creature to pray for her husband and find out if he had any need of help. And, as this creature prayed for him, she was answered that his soul should spend thirty years in Purgatory unless he had better friends on earth. She told the widow this and said, 'If you will do charitable deeds for him, giving three or four pounds in masses and alms to poor folk, you shall greatly please God and very much ease his soul.'

This widow paid little attention to her words and let it pass. Then this creature went to the anchorite and told him how she had felt, and he said that the feeling was from God and the deed in itself was good, even though the soul had no need of it, and he advised that it should be fulfilled. Then this creature told this matter to her confessor in order that he should speak to the widow, and then for a long time this creature heard no more of this matter.

Afterwards, our Lord Jesus Christ said to this creature: 'That thing I asked to be done for the soul has not been done. Now ask your confessor.'

And so she did, and he said it was not done.

She said back to him, 'My Lord Jesus Christ told me as much just now.'

CHAPTER 20

ONE day, as this creature was hearing her mass, a young man, a good priest, held up the sacrament in his hands over his head, and the sacrament shook and fluttered to and fro as a dove flutters its wings. And when he held up the chalice with the precious sacrament, the chalice moved to and fro as if it should fall out of his hands. When the consecration had been done, this creature greatly marvelled at the stirring and moving of the blessed sacrament, desiring to see more consecrations and looking to see if it would do it again.

Then our Lord Jesus Christ said to the creature, 'You will not see it any more in this manner; therefore thank God that you have seen it. My daughter, Bridget, never saw me in this way.'*

Then the creature said in her thought, 'Lord, what does this betoken?'

'It betokens vengeance.'

'Ah, good Lord, what vengeance?'

Then our Lord said back to her, 'There shall be an earthquake.* Tell it to whoever you like, in the name of Jesus. For I tell you honestly, I spoke to St Bridget exactly as I spoke to you, daughter, I tell you that every word written in Bridget's book is true, and through you it shall be known for the absolute truth. And you shall have success, daughter, in spite of all your enemies; the more they envy you for my grace, the better I shall love you. I would not be a righteous God unless I loved you, for I know you better than you do yourself, whatever people say about you. You say that I have great patience for the people's sins, and you speak the truth, but if you saw the people's sins as I do, you would marvel much more at my patience and have much more grief for the people's sins than you have.'

Then the creature said, 'Alas, praiseworthy Lord, what shall I do for the people?'

Our Lord answered, 'It is enough for you to do as you do.'

Then she prayed: 'Merciful Lord Christ Jesus, all mercy and grace and goodness is in you. Have mercy, pity, and compassion on them. Show your mercy and your goodness to them, help them, send them true contrition, and never let them die in their sin.'*

Our merciful Lord said, 'I may do no more righteousness, daughter, than I do. I send preaching and teaching to them, plagues and battles, hunger and famines, loss of their property, great sickness, and many other tribulations, and neither will they believe my words nor will they recognize my visitations. So therefore I shall say to them that "I made my servants to pray for you, and you despised their deeds and their way of life."'

CHAPTER 21

AT the time* this creature had revelations, our Lord said to her, 'Daughter, you are pregnant.'

She replied, 'Oh, Lord, how shall I arrange for my child to be looked after?'

Our Lord said, 'Daughter, do not be afraid, I shall arrange for someone to look after your child.'

'Lord, I am not worthy to hear you speak and then have sex with my husband, even though it greatly pains and distresses me.'

'Therefore it is no sin for you, daughter, because it is instead more reward and merit for you, and nevertheless you will have grace because I wish you to bring forth more fruit to me.'

Then the creature said, 'Lord Jesus, this manner of living belongs to your holy virgins.'

'Yes, daughter, but rest assured that I love wives too, and especially those wives who want to live chastely (if they might have their wish), and busy themselves to please me as you do; because, although the state of virginity is more perfect and more holy than the state of widowhood, and the state of widowhood is more perfect than the state of wedlock, yet, daughter, I love you as much as any virgin in the world. Nobody can prevent me from loving who I wish and as much as I wish, because, daughter, love douses all sin. And therefore ask of me the gifts of love. There is neither a gift as holy as is the gift of love nor is there anything to be desired as much as love, because love can acquire whatever it desires. So therefore, daughter, you cannot please God better than to think continually on His love.'

Then this creature asked our Lord Jesus how she should best love Him. And our Lord said, 'Be mindful of your wickedness and think of my goodness.'

She replied, 'I am the most unworthy creature that you ever showed your grace to on this earth.'

'Oh, daughter', said our Lord, 'fear not, I take no notice what a man has been, but I take notice of what he will be. Daughter, you have despised yourself, therefore you shall never be despised by God. Be mindful, daughter, of what Mary Magdalene was, St Mary the Egyptian, St Paul,* and many other saints who are now in Heaven, for I make worthy the unworthy, righteous the sinful. And so I have made you worthy to me, once loved and forever loved by me. There is no saint in Heaven that you wish to speak with, but he shall come to you. The saints love those whom God loves. When you please God, you please His mother and all the saints in Heaven. Daughter, I take witness of my mother, and of all the angels in Heaven, and of all the saints in Heaven, that I love you with my heart and I may not forgo your love.'

Then our Lord said to His blessed mother, 'Blessed mother, tell my daughter about the greatness of love I have for her.'

Then this creature lay still, all weeping and sobbing as if her heart should burst for the sweetness of the speech that our Lord spoke to her soul. Very soon afterwards the Queen of Mercy, God's mother, conversed with this creature's soul, saying, 'My esteemed daughter, I bring you sure tidings, bearing witness for my sweet son Jesus, with all angels and all saints in Heaven who love you most highly. Daughter, I am your mother, your lady, and your mistress, to teach you in every way how you shall best please God.'

She taught this creature and educated her so marvellously, the subjects were so high and holy, that this creature was embarrassed to talk of it or tell anybody about it except the anchorite who was her principal confessor, for he was very well-informed in such things. And he charged this creature, by virtue of obedience, to tell him whatever she felt, and this she did.

CHAPTER 22

As this creature lay in contemplation, weeping bitterly in her spirit, she said to our Lord Jesus Christ, 'Oh Lord, virgins are now dancing merrily in Heaven. Shall I not do so? Because I am not a virgin, lack of virginity is really a great sorrow to me; I think I wish I had been slaughtered when I was taken from the baptismal font so that I could never have displeased you and then you, blessed Lord, could have had my virginity without end. Oh dear God, I have not loved you all the days of my life and I regret that so bitterly! I have run away from you, and you have run after me; I would fall into despair, and you would not let me.'

'Oh, daughter, how often have I told you that your sins are forgiven and that we have been united together without end? You are to me a unique love, daughter, and therefore I promise that you shall have a unique grace in Heaven, daughter, and I promise you that I shall come to your life's end, at your death, with my blessed mother and my holy angels and twelve apostles, and St Katherine, St Margaret, St Mary Magdalene, and many other saints that are in Heaven, who greatly worship me for the grace that I give to you, your God, your Lord Jesus. You need not fear dreadful pains at your death, for you shall have your desire, that is, to be more mindful of my Passion than of your own pain. You shall not dread the Devil of Hell because he has no power over you. He dreads you more than you do him. He is angry with you because you torment him more with your weeping than does all the fire in Hell; you win many souls from him with your weeping. And I have promised you that you should have no other Purgatory than the slander and slurs of this world for I have chastised you myself as I wished to, by many fears and torments that you have had from evil spirits, both during sleeping and waking, for many years. And therefore I shall preserve you at the end of your life through my mercy, so that they shall have no power over you either in body or in soul; it is a great grace and a miracle that you have your wits, considering the vexation you have had with them in the past.

'Also, daughter, I have chastised you with the fear of my Godhead, and many times I have made you afraid with vast gusty gales, so that you thought that vengeance should fall on you for your sins. I have tested you with many tribulations, many great disappointments, and many grave illnesses, so much so that you have been anointed for death,* and these you have escaped entirely through my grace. Therefore do not be afraid, daughter, for with my own hands, which were nailed to the Cross, I shall take your soul from your body with much merriment and melody, with sweet smells and good fragrances, and offer it to my Father in Heaven, and there you shall see Him face to face, living with Him without end.

'Daughter, you shall be very welcome to my father and to my mother and to all my saints in Heaven, for you have very many times given them the tears of your eyes to drink. All my holy saints shall rejoice at your homecoming. You shall be fulfilled with the kind of love that you crave. Then you shall bless the time that you were made and the body that has redeemed you. He shall rejoice in you and you in Him without end.

'Daughter, I promise you the same grace that I promised St Katherine, St Margaret, St Barbara,* and St Paul, in that if any creature on earth until Judgement Day asks any wish of you and believes that God loves you he shall have his wish or else something better. Therefore those who believe that God loves you shall be blessed without end. The souls in Purgatory shall rejoice at your homecoming, for they know well that God loves you especially. People on earth shall rejoice in God because of you, for He shall work much grace for you and make known to the whole world that God loves you. You have been despised because of my love, and therefore you shall be honoured because of my love.

'Daughter, when you are in Heaven, you may ask for whatever you wish and I shall grant you all your desires. I have told you before that you are a unique lover, and therefore you shall have a unique love in Heaven, a unique reward, and a unique worship. And, because you are a virgin in your soul, I shall take you by the hand in Heaven and take my mother by the other hand, and so you shall dance in Heaven with other holy maidens and virgins, for I can call you dearly bought and my own dearly-prized darling. I shall say to you, my own blessed spouse, "Welcome to me, with all kinds of joy and gladness, to live here with me and never, without end, to depart from me, but to live forever in joy and bliss, which neither eye can see nor ear hear nor tongue speak, nor no heart think, that I have appointed for you and for all my servants who desire to love me and please me as you do." '

CHAPTER 23

A vicar once came to this creature, pleading with her to pray for him and learn whether he would please God more by leaving aside his curing of souls and his benefice or by keeping it, because he thought he was of little profit amongst his parishioners. The creature being in her prayers and having this matter in her mind, Christ said to her spirit, 'Tell the vicar to keep with his curing of souls and his benefice and to be diligent in preaching and teaching to them in person, and sometimes procuring others to teach my laws and my commandments to them, so that there is no fault on his part and, if they do not do any better, his reward shall be no smaller for it.'

And so she took her message as she was commanded and the vicar kept with his curing of souls.

As this creature was in a church of St Margaret, in the choir, where a corpse was present, and he who was the husband of the corpse (when she had been alive) was there in good health to make an offering of a mass-penny,* as was the custom of the place, our Lord said to the aforementioned creature, 'Lo, daughter, this corpse's soul is in Purgatory, and he who was her husband is now in good health, and yet he shall be dead in a short while.'

And so it happened, as she felt through revelation.

Also, as this creature lay in the choir at her prayers, a priest came to her and pleaded with her to pray for a woman who lay at the point of death. As this creature began to pray for her, our Lord said to her, 'Daughter, it is very necessary to pray for her, because she has been a wicked woman and she shall die.'

And she said back, 'Lord, as you love me, save her soul from damnation', and then she wept with plentiful tears for that soul. And our Lord granted her mercy for the soul, commanding her to pray for her.

This creature's spiritual confessor came to her, pressing her to pray for a woman who lay at the point of death, as far as people could see. And then our Lord said she should live and thrive, and so she did.

A good man, who was a close friend to this creature and a helpful person to the poor, was extremely sick for many weeks. A great deal of lamenting was made for him, because the people believed he would not live, the pain was so tremendous in all his joints and all throughout his body.

Our Lord Jesus said to her spirit, 'Daughter, do not be downcast about this man, because he will live and greatly thrive.'

And thus he lived for many years after in good health and in prosperity. Another good man, who read and expounded Scripture,* also lay sick and, when this creature prayed for him, it was answered to her mind that he should languish in poor health for a while and after that he would be dead of the same illness. And so he was a short time after. Also a decent woman and (so people believed) a holy woman, who was a special friend to this creature, was really sick, and many people believed she would die. Then, as this creature was praying for her, our Lord said, 'She shall not die for ten years, as after this you will make merry together and have excellent conversations as you had before.'

And so it was in truth: this holy woman lived for many years after.

This creature had many more such revelations in feeling; to write them all down would perhaps be to impede more profitable things. These ones are written down to show the familiarity and goodness of our merciful Lord Christ Jesus rather than as a commendation of this creature.

These feelings and similar ones, many more than can be written down, both about living and about dying, of some who will be saved, of some who will be damned, were a great pain and punishment to this creature. She would rather have suffered any physical penance than have these feelings, and she might have put them aside as she was so afraid of the illusions and deceptions of her spiritual enemies. She sometimes had such bad trouble with these feelings when they did not seem quite accurate to her understanding, that her confessor worried that she should fall into despair over them. And then, after her trouble and her grave fears, it would be shown to her soul how the feeling should be understood.

CHAPTER 24

THE priest who wrote this book, in order to test this creature's feelings, asked her questions and enquired of her many times and at different times about things that were to come—things about which the conclusion was at that time unsure and uncertain to any creature— asking her, though she was averse and unwilling to doing such things, to pray to God and know, when our Lord wished to visit her with devotion, what the conclusion would be, and to tell him truly and without any pretending how she felt, or else he would not have gladly written the book.

And so this creature, somewhat compelled by the fear that he would not otherwise have followed her intention to write this book, did as he asked her and told him her feelings about what should happen in such matters as he asked her about, if her feelings were true. Thus he tested them for the real truth. And yet he would not always give credence to her words and that hindered him the following way:

It happened once upon a time that a young man came to this priest, the which young man this priest had never seen before, complaining to the priest about the poverty and trouble which had befallen him through misfortune, explaining the cause of the misfortune, saying too that he had taken holy orders in order to be a priest. Because of a little over-hastiness in defending himself (as he had no choice, unless he wanted to be pursued by his enemies and killed), he struck a man (or maybe two), as a result of which, as he said, they were dead or were likely to die. And so he had fallen into violating religious rules and could not perform the functions of his holy orders without a dispensation from the papal court at Rome, and because of this he fled from his friends and dared not go to his own region for fear of being arrested for their deaths. Giving credence to the young man's words, in so far as he was a likeable person, fine looking, well-favoured in his bearing and in his conduct, serious in his speech and conversation, priestly in his deportment and attire, the aforementioned priest had compassion for the man's troubles. The priest, intending to get friends to relieve and comfort the young man, went to a respected burgess in Lynn, a mayor's equal and a compassionate man, who lay with a serious illness and had done so for a long time. He bewailed to him and to his wife (a very good woman) the young man's misadventure, believing he would receive generous donations, as he often had for others on whose behalf he had asked.

It so happened that the creature about whom this book is written was present there and heard how the priest bewailed the young man's story and how the priest praised the young man. She was grievously moved in her spirit against that young man, and said they had many poor neighbours whom they knew to be in great need of help and relief, and it was more charitable to help those whom they knew well to be well-behaved people and her own neighbours rather than other strangers whom they did not know, because superficially many people speak and appear very attractively when they are seen by other people—God knows what they are in their souls!

The good man and his wife thought that she spoke very well, and therefore they wished to give him no charitable donation. At that time the priest was very displeased with this creature, and when he met her alone he repeated how she had hindered him in getting a donation for the young man, whom he thought a well-disposed man and he much commended his conduct.

The creature said, 'Sir, God knows what his conduct is because, as far as I know, I've never seen him before. And yet I have an understanding what his conduct might be and therefore, sir, if you will follow my advice and my feelings, let him choose and help himself as well as he's able and don't you meddle with him, as he'll deceive you in the end.'

The young man was always returning to the priest, flattering him, and saying that he had good friends in other places who would help him if they knew where he was (and in a short time too), and also that they would thank those people who had supported him during his troubles.

The priest, trusting that it was as this young man told him, willingly lent him money to help him out. The young man asked the priest to excuse him if he did not see him for two or three days, as he said he needed to travel a little distance and return again in a short time and bring him back his money, fully and truly. The priest, having confidence in the young man's promise, was utterly content, granting him good love and leave until the day on which he had promised to come back.

When he was gone, the aforementioned creature, having an understanding through feeling in her soul that our Lord wished to show that the young man was unfaithful and would never come back, she, in order to prove whether her feeling was true or false, asked the priest where the young man, whom he had praised so much, was. The priest said that he had gone a little way away and he trusted that he would come back. She said she supposed that he would never see him again, and he never did ever again. And then he regretted to himself that he had not followed her advice.

A short time after this had happened, another deceitful rogue, an elderly man, came to the same priest and offered to sell him a breviary,* a good little book. The priest went to the aforementioned creature, asking her to pray for him and to know whether God wished that he buy the book or not and, while she prayed, he indulged the man as well as he could, and after that he came back to this creature and asked her how she felt.

'Sir,' she said, 'don't buy any book from him, for he's not to be trusted and you will know that if you meddle with him.'

Then the priest asked the man if he might see this book. The man said he did not have it on him. The priest asked how he had come by it. The old man said he was the executor to a priest in his family, and he had charged him to sell it and to dispose of it for him.

'Father,' said the priest, respectfully, 'why are you offering me this book rather than other men or other priests, when there are many more prosperous, richer priests in this church than me, and I know full well that you had no knowledge of me before now?'

'In truth, sir,' he said, 'I had no knowledge of you, but I feel well-inclined towards you, and also it was his will, he who owned it before, that if I knew of any young priest who I thought was sober and well-disposed, he should have this book before any other man, and for a lower price than any other man, so that he might pray for him. And these reasons move me to approach you rather than another man.'

The priest asked him where he was living.

'Sir,' he said, 'just five miles from here, in Pentney Abbey.'*

'I've been there,' said the priest, 'and I haven't seen you.'

'No, sir,' he replied, 'I have been there only a little while, and now I've got dining rights there, thank God.'

The priest asked him if he might have a look at the book and see if they could come to an agreement.

He said, 'Sir, I hope to be back here next week and bring it with me and, sir, I promise you that, if you like it, you'll have it before any other man.'

The priest thanked him for his good intentions, and they went their separate ways, but the man never came to the priest afterwards and then the priest knew full well that the aforementioned creature's feeling was true.

CHAPTER 25

FURTHERMORE, here follows a very significant matter concerning the creature's feeling, and it is written down here because of its appropriateness inasmuch as it is similar in feeling to the matters that have been written down before, notwithstanding that it happened long after the matters that follow.

It happened in a renowned town where there was one parish church and two chapels annexed to it, the chapels having and administering all the sacraments except christening and purifications, as permitted by the parson, who was a monk of the Benedictine order sent from the abbey in Norwich, residing with three of his brethren in the renowned town already cited.*

Through the wishes of some parishioners to make the chapels like the parish church, suing for a bull from the papal Court* of Rome, many lawsuits and much strife happened between the Prior* (who was their parson and curate) and the said parishioners who wished to have baptismal fonts and purifications in the chapels like there were in the parish church. And especially in one chapel, which was the larger and the prettier, they wanted to have a font.

A papal bull was sued for, in which a font was granted to the chapel, as long as it was of no detriment to the parish church. The bull was put in plea, and various days were spent in litigation to test whether the font, if they had it, would be detrimental to the parish church or not. The parishioners who were suing were really well-placed and had much help from people of high rank, and also, above all, they were rich men, respectable merchants, and had lots of money, 'which benefits every necessity'—and it is a shame that the power of money should be of greater benefit than truth.

Nevertheless, the Prior, who was their parson, although he was poor, withstood them manfully through the help of some of his parishioners who were his friends and loved the honour of their parish church.

This matter was in litigation for so long that it began to irk those on both sides, and it was still no nearer an end. Then the matter was put to my Lord Bishop of Norwich—that is, Alnwick*—to see if he might be able to bring it to an end, through a truce. He diligently laboured in this matter, and in order to establish peace and quiet he offered the aforementioned parishioners much of what they wished for, with certain conditions, in so much as those who held with the parson and with their parish were very sorry, really dreading that those who sued for a font should obtain and gain their objective and thus make the chapel equal to the parish church.

Then the priest who afterwards wrote this book went to the creature of whom this treatise makes mention, as he had done before at times of litigation, and asked her how she felt in her soul about this matter, as to whether they should have a font in the chapel or not.

'Sir,' said the creature, 'don't be afraid, for I understand in my soul that, even though they are willing to give a bushel of nobles,* they shan't have it.'

'Oh, mother,' said the priest, 'my Lord Bishop of Norwich has offered it to them with certain conditions, and they have a period of deliberation to say "nay" or "yea" as to whether they want it, and therefore I am afraid they will not rebuff it but be really glad to have it.'

This creature prayed to God that His will might be fulfilled. And inasmuch as she had known by revelation that they should not have it, she was all the more bold to ask our Lord to counter their intentions and deflate their boasting. And so as our Lord wished, they neither obeyed nor liked the terms that were offered them, because they were utterly sure that they would gain their objective through lordly patronage and through the legal process; and, as God wished, they were prevented from gaining their objective, and because they wanted to have everything, they lost everything. And so, may God be blessed, the parish church continued to stand in all its dignity and prestige as it had for the previous two hundred years and more, and by experience the inspiration of our Lord was proved most true and sure in the aforementioned creature.

CHAPTER 26

WHEN the time came* that this creature should visit those holy places where our Lord lived and died, as she understood through revelation years beforehand, she asked the parish priest of the town where she was living to say in the pulpit for her that, if any man or woman claimed any debt of her husband or her, they should come and speak with her before she went; and she, with God's help, would settle the debt with each of them so they could consider themselves content. And so she did.

After that she took her leave of her husband and the holy anchorite, who had told beforehand of the sequence of her leaving and the many troubles that she would suffer on the way, and how all her companions would forsake her, and how a hunchbacked man should guide her on in safety, through the help of our Lord. And so indeed it happened, as it shall be written hereafter.

Then she took her leave of Master Robert* and asked him for his blessing, and likewise took her leave of other friends. And then she went on to Norwich and made an offering at the Trinity,* and after that she went to Yarmouth* and made an offering at an image of our Lady, and there she boarded her ship.

And the next day they came to a large town called Zierikzee,* where our Lord in his high goodness visited this creature with abundant tears of contrition for her own sins and sometimes for other people's sins too. She especially had tears of compassion in thinking of our Lord's Passion. And she received communion each Sunday, wherever there was time and a convenient place for it, with keen weeping and extravagant sobbing, so that many people marvelled and wondered at the great grace that God had performed in this creature.

This creature had neither eaten meat nor drunk wine for four years before she left England. And as now her spiritual confessor ordered her, by virtue of obedience, that she should both eat meat and drink wine, and so she did for a little while. After that she asked her confessor if he would excuse her if she ate no meat, and he allowed her to do so for what time he pleased.

And soon after, through the prompting of some of her companions, her confessor was displeased because she ate no meat, and so were many of the company. They were also most displeased because she wept so much and was always talking about the love and goodness of our Lord, at table as well as in other places. Therefore, shamefully, they rebuked her and downright chided her and said they would not endure her as her husband did when she was at home and in England.

So she meekly replied to them, 'Our Lord, Almighty God, is as great a lord here as in England and I have as much cause to love Him here as I have there, may He be blessed.'

Because of these words her companions were angrier than they were before, and their anger and unkindness was a matter of great unhappiness to this creature, as they were held to be very good people and she really wanted their love, if she might have had it to the pleasure of God. And then she said to one of them in particular, 'You are doing me much shame and a great grievance.'

He then answered back to her, 'I pray to God that the Devil's death may overtake you, and soon', and he said many more cruel words to her than she could repeat.

Then soon after, some of the companions in whom she most trusted, and her own maidservant as well, said she should no longer travel in their company, and they said they wanted to take her maid-servant away from her so that she would not be a loose woman in her company. And then one of them, who was looking after her gold for her, with great anger and crossness left her one gold noble to do with as she liked and help herself as well as she could because, they said, she could no longer stay with them, and they abandoned her that night.

Then, on the next morning, one of her company came to her, a man who loved her well, asking her to go to his fellow-travellers and humble herself to them and plead with them to let her go on in their company until she arrived at Constance.* And so she did, and went on with them until she arrived at Constance with much distress and in great turmoil, as they really shamed her and greatly reproved her as they went through different places. They cut her gown so short that it came only a little below her knees, and made her wear a white can-vas made of shaggy sackcloth,* so she would be taken for a fool and the people should not have regard for her or esteem her. They made her sit at the end of the table below everyone else, so that she hardly dared speak a word.

Notwithstanding all their malice, she was held in more respect than they were, wherever they went. And the good man of the house in which they were lodging would (as far as he was able) always treat her more hospitably than the others, even though she sat at the lowest end of the table, and he sent her what he could from his own meal, and that aggravated the fellowship very bitterly.

As they went on the road towards Constance, it was said to them that they should be harmed and be in terrible distress unless they had great grace. Then this creature came by a church and went in to make her prayers, and she prayed with all her heart, with great weeping and many tears, for help and assistance against her enemies.

Then our Lord said to her mind, 'Do not be afraid, daughter, your fellowship shall come to no harm whilst you are in their company.'

And so, may our Lord be blessed in all His works, they went forth in safety to Constance.

CHAPTER 27

WHEN this creature and her companions came to Constance, she heard tell of an English friar, a master of divinity and the papal legate, who was in that city. Then she went to that honourable man and revealed her life to him from the beginning up to that moment, as near as she could in confession because he was the papal legate and an honourable cleric.

And afterwards she told him what troubles she had had with her companions. She told him what grace God gave her of contrition and compunction, of sweetness and devotion, and of many different revelations our Lord had revealed to her, and the dread that she had of illusions and deceits of her spiritual enemies, of which she lived in great fear, desiring to put them aside and not to feel them, if she were able to resist them.

And when she had said this, the honourable cleric gave her words of great comfort and said it was the work of the Holy Ghost, commanding and charging her to obey them and receive them when God would give them and to have no doubt, for the Devil has no power to work such grace in a soul. And also he said that he would support her against the ill will of her fellowship.

Afterwards, when it suited her companions, they asked this worthy doctor of divinity to dinner. And the doctor told the aforementioned creature, forewarning her to sit during the meal in his presence as she did in his absence and to conduct herself in the same way that she did when he was not there. When time came that they should sit down to eat, each person took their place as they wished; the honourable legate and doctor sitting at the head, and then others, and at last, at the table end, sat the aforementioned creature and she spoke no words (as she was used to doing when the legate was not there).

Then the legate said to her, 'Why are you not merrier?'

She sat still and did not answer, as he himself had commanded her to do.

When they had eaten, the party really complained to the legate about this creature, and said that she absolutely could no longer be in their company unless he would order her to eat meat like they did and put aside her weeping and that she not talk of holiness so much.

Then the honourable doctor said, 'No, sirs, I won't have her eat meat while she can abstain and be the better disposed to loving our Lord. Whichever of you made a vow to walk to Rome barefoot, I wouldn't absolve him of his vow whilst he might fulfil it, nor will I ask her to eat meat whilst our Lord gives her the strength to abstain. As for her weeping, it is not in my power to restrain it, because it's the gift of the Holy Ghost. As for her speech, I will ask her to cease until she reaches a place where people are happier to hear her than you are.'

The party was furious and very irate. They handed her over to the legate and said that they wanted absolutely no more involvement with her. He very benevolently and kindly received her as if she were his mother, and he looked after her money—about twenty pounds—and still one of them wrongfully kept hold of about sixteen pounds.* And they also kept hold of her maidservant and would not let her go with her mistress, even though she had promised her mistress and assured her that she would not abandon her for any necessity. And the legate arranged things for this creature and had her money exchanged for her as if she were his mother.

Then this creature went into a church and asked our Lord to arrange a guide for her. And then our Lord spoke to her and said, 'You shall have very good assistance and a good guide.'

And very soon afterwards an old man with a white beard came to her. He was from Devon, and he said, 'Madam, will you ask me for God's love and for our Lady's, to walk with you and be your guide, as your compatriots have abandoned you?'

She asked him what his name was.

He said, 'My name is William Weaver.'*

She asked him, out of reverence of God and of our Lady, to help her in her need, and she would reward him well for his work. And so they were agreed.

Then she went to the legate and told him how well our Lord had arranged things for her, and she took her leave of him and of her company that had so unpleasantly rejected her, and also of her maidservant who had been duty-bound to go with her. She took her leave with a very long and rueful face, inasmuch as she was in a foreign country and knew neither the language nor the man who was going to guide her. And so she and the man went onwards together in great fear and gloominess. As they went on together, the man said to her, 'I'm afraid you shall be taken from me and I shall be beaten up because of you and lose my jacket.'

She said, 'William, don't be afraid; God shall guard us very well.'

And every day this creature was mindful of the Gospel that tells of the woman who was taken in adultery and brought before our Lord.* And then she prayed: 'Lord, as you drove away her enemies, so drive away my enemies, and guard well my chastity that I vowed to you, and never let me be defiled, and if I am, Lord, I will make a vow that I will never come back to England as long as I live.'

Then they went onwards day by day and met with many excellent people. And they said no evil words to this creature but rather gave her and her man food and drink, and in many places that they went to, the good wives who were at their inn had her lie down in their own beds for God's love. And our Lord visited her with great grace of spiritual comfort as she went on her way.

And so God carried her onwards until she came to Bologna the Rich.* And after she had got there, her other companions, who had abandoned her before, arrived. They were absolutely astonished when they heard tell of how she had arrived in Bologna before they had, and one of their party came to her, asking her to join his party and to try to see if they would receive her again into their party. And so she did.

'If you will join our party, you must make a new promise, and that is this: you shall not talk of the Gospels wherever we go, but shall sit still and make merry, as we do, at all mealtimes.'

She agreed, and was received back into their party. Then they went onwards to Venice and they stayed there for thirteen weeks. And there this creature received communion in a large nunnery—and she was warmly welcomed amongst them—where our merciful Lord Christ Jesus visited this creature with great devotion and plentiful tears, which really amazed the good ladies of the place.

Later, it happened, as this creature sat dining with her companions, that she repeated a text of the Gospel that she had learned beforehand along with other good sentences. So then her companions said that she had broken the agreement.

And she said, 'Yes, sirs, in truth I can no longer keep the agreement, for I really must speak of my Lord Jesus Christ, even though the whole world has forbidden me to do so.'

Then she took herself to her room and ate alone for six weeks, until the time that our Lord made her so sick that she thought she was going to die, and after that He suddenly made her well again. And all the time her maidservant left her alone and made the party's food and washed their clothes yet she would not attend whatsoever to her mistress, whom she had promised to serve.

CHAPTER 28

ALSO, this party (which had put this creature away from their table so that she could no longer eat amongst them) arranged for themselves a ship in which to sail.* They bought vessels for their wine and arranged bedding for themselves, but nothing for her. Then she, seeing their unkindness, went to the same man whom they had visited, and provided herself with bedding as they had done, then she went to where they were and showed them what she had done, intending to sail with them in that ship that they had arranged.

After that, as this creature was in contemplation, our Lord warned her in her mind that she should not sail in that ship, and he assigned to her another ship, a galley, that she should sail in. Then she told this to some of the fellow-travellers, and they told it to their companions, and then they dared not sail in the ship which they had arranged. And so they sold off their vessels that they had organized for their wines and were very pleased to come to the galley where she was, and so, though it was against her will, she went on with them in their party, for they dared not do otherwise.

When it was time to make their beds, they locked up their bed-clothes, and a priest who was in their party took away a sheet from the aforementioned creature and he said it was his. She took God as her witness that it was her sheet. Then the priest swore a grave oath, by the book in his hand, that she was as false as could be. And he derided her and thoroughly rebuked her.

And so she continued to have such tribulations until she got to Jerusalem. And before she got there, she said to those whom she believed to be aggrieved with her, 'I ask you, sirs, to be charitable towards me, for I'm charitable towards you, and forgive me if I have upset you along the way. And if any of you have committed any trespasses against me, God forgive you for it, as do I.'

And so they went on to the Holy Land until they could see Jerusalem.* And when this creature, riding on an ass, saw Jerusalem, she thanked God with all her heart, asking Him for His mercy that, just as He had brought her to see this earthly city of Jerusalem, He would grant her the grace to see Jerusalem the blissful city above, the city of heaven.* Our Lord Jesus Christ, answering to her thought, granted her her desire. Then, for the joy that she had and the sweetness she felt in conversing with our Lord, she was on the verge of falling off her ass, for she could not bear the sweetness and grace that God performed in her soul. Then two German pilgrims went to her and kept her from falling off. One of them was a priest, and he put spices in her mouth to comfort her, believing her to have been ill. And so they helped her onwards to Jerusalem. And when she got there, she said, 'Sirs, I ask you both not to be offended though I weep bitterly in this holy place where our Lord Jesus Christ lived and died.'

Then they went to the Temple in Jerusalem,* and they were let in one day at the time of evensong and they waited therein until the next day at evensong.* Then the friars* lifted up a cross and led the pilgrims around from one place to another where our Lord had suffered His pains and His Passion, every man and woman bearing a wax candle in their hand. And, as they went around, at all times the friars told them what our Lord suffered in every place. And the aforementioned creature wept and sobbed so plentifully as though she had seen our Lord with her physical eye, suffering His Passion at that time. Before her, in her soul, she saw Him truly by contemplation, and that caused her to have compassion. And when they came up on to the Mount of Calvary,* she fell down because she could not stand or kneel, but rather writhed and wrestled with her body, spreading out her arms widely, and crying with a loud voice as though her heart should burst apart, for in the city of her soul she saw truly and freshly how our Lord was crucified. Before her face she heard and saw in her spiritual sight the mourning of our Lady, of St John* and Mary Magdalene, and of many others who had loved our Lord.

So she had such great compassion and such great pain to see our Lord's pain that she could not keep herself from crying and roaring, though she could have died from it. And this was the first cry that she ever cried in any contemplation.* And this kind of crying endured for many years after this time, whatever anybody might do, and she suffered much spitefulness and rebuking for it. The crying was so loud and so wonderful that it astonished the people, unless they had heard it before or else if they knew the cause of her crying. And she had this crying so often that it made her really weak in her physical strength, especially if she heard about our Lord's Passion.*

And sometimes, when she saw the crucifix, or if she saw a person or a beast, whichever it was, who was wounded, or if a man beat a child in front of her, or struck a horse or another beast with a whip, if she could see it or hear it, in her thought she saw our Lord being beaten or wounded, just as she saw it in the man or the beast, either in the fields or in town, and alone by herself as well as amongst people.

When she first had her cryings in Jerusalem, she had them often, and she had them in Rome too. And when she came home to England, at first her crying came only seldom, maybe only once a month, then after that once a week, afterwards daily, and once she had fourteen cryings in one day, and another day she had seven, just as God would visit her: sometimes in the church, sometimes in the street, sometimes in the chamber, sometimes in the fields, whenever God wished to send them, for she never knew either the time or hour when they should come. And they never came without unsurpassed sweetness of devotion and high contemplation.

As soon as she perceived that she was going to cry, she would hold it in as far as she could, so that the people should not hear it, to keep from annoying them. Because some people said that it was a wicked spirit that vexed her; some said it was a sickness; some said she had drunk too much wine; some cursed her; some wished that she were thrown in the harbour; some wished she were put out to sea in a bottomless boat; and so on, each person as he or she thought. Others—spiritual people—loved her and esteemed her all the more. Some important clerics said that neither our Lady nor any saint in Heaven cried so, but they knew very little about what she felt, nor would they believe that she could not desist from crying if she wanted.

So therefore, when she knew that she was going to cry, she held it in for as long as she could and did all that she could to withstand it or put it aside, until her complexion turned as bruised as lead, and all the time it would be working away more and more in her mind until the time that it burst out. And when the body could no longer endure the spiritual labours, but was overcome with the indescribable love that was performed so fervently in her soul, then she fell down and cried wondrously loudly. And the more that she laboured to keep it in or to put it aside, so much the more did she cry and then all the more loudly. And so she did on the Mount of Calvary, as it is written beforehand.

She had such true contemplation in the sight of her soul as if Christ hung before her in His manhood before her physical eye. And when, through dispensation of the high mercy of our Sovereign Saviour Christ Jesus, it was granted to this creature to behold His precious tender body so truly—all slashed and torn with scourges, more full of holes than any dove-cote* ever was, hanging on the Cross with the Crown of Thorns upon His head, His blissful hands, His tender feet nailed to the hard tree, the rivers of blood flowing out plentifully from every limb, the grisly and grievous wound in His precious side shedding forth blood and water* for her love and for her salvation—then she fell down and cried out with a loud voice, marvellously twisting and writhing in her body on every side, spreading out her arms wide as if she should have died, and could not keep herself from crying and from these physical movements, due to the fire of love* that burned so fervently in her soul with pure pity and compassion.

It is not to be wondered at if this creature cried and made astonishing poses and faces, when we can see each day with our own eyes how both men and women will cry and roar and wring their hands—some for loss of worldly goods, some out of affection for their family or for worldly friendships, through too much study or earthly affection, and most of all through inordinate love and physical affections if their friends are parted from them—as if they were out of their wits and minds, and yet they know well enough that they displease God.

And if a person counsels them to leave aside or cease their weeping and crying, they will say that they cannot; they loved their friend so much, and he was so gentle and kind to them, that they can in no way forget him. How much more might they weep, cry, and roar, if their most beloved friends were violently grabbed in front of their eyes and brought with every kind of reprimand before the judge, wrongfully condemned to death, and especially so shameful a death as our merciful Lord suffered for our sake? How would they endure it? No doubt they would both cry and roar and avenge themselves if they could, or else people would say they were not friends.

Alas, alas, for sorrow, that the death of a creature who has often sinned and trespassed against their maker should be so immoderately mourned and sorrowed over. And it is an offence to God and a hindrance to other souls. And the compassionate death of our Saviour, by which we are all restored to life, is not kept in mind by us unworthy and unkind wretches, nor will we support those whom our Lord has entrusted with His secrets and provided with love, but rather deride and hinder them as much as we can.

CHAPTER 29

WHEN this creature with her companions came to the grave where our Lord was buried,* as she entered that holy place she fell down with her candle in her hand, as if she should die of sorrow. And after that she got up again with great weeping and sobbing, as though she had seen our Lord buried right in front of her. Then she thought she saw our Lady in her soul, how she mourned and how she wept for her son's death, and then our Lady's sorrow was her sorrow.

Thus wherever the friars led them in that holy place, she wept and sobbed marvellously all the time, and especially when she came to where our Lord was nailed to the Cross.* There, she cried and wept without measure, for she could not restrain herself. Also, they came to a marble stone* that our Lord was laid on when He was taken down off the Cross, and there she wept with great compassion, remembering our Lord's Passion.

Afterwards, she received communion on the Mount of Calvary* and then she wept, she sobbed, she cried out so loudly that it was a marvel to hear it. She was so full of holy thoughts and meditations and holy contemplations in the Passion of our Lord Jesus Christ, and holy conversations that our Lord Jesus Christ intimated to her soul, that she could never express them afterwards, they were so holy and high. Our Lord showed much grace to this creature for the three weeks she was in Jerusalem.

Another day, early in the morning, they went out to the high hills. Her guides told of where our Lord carried the Cross on His back, and where His mother met with Him, and how she swooned, and how she fell down and He fell down too.* And so they went onwards, all afternoon, until they came to Mount Zion.* And all the time this creature wept abundantly all the way out of compassion for our Lord's Passion. On Mount Zion is a place where our Lord washed His disciples' feet, and a little way from there He celebrated the Last Supper with His disciples.*

And therefore this creature had a great desire to receive communion in that holy place where our merciful Lord Christ Jesus first consecrated His precious body in the form of bread and gave it to His disciples. And so she did, with great devotion, with plentiful tears, and with noisy sobbing, for in this place is plenary remission from sin.* Likewise in four places in the Temple: one is at the Mount of

Calvary; another is at the grave where our Lord was buried; the third at the marble stone on which His precious body was laid when it was taken off the Cross; the fourth is where the Holy Cross was buried,* and in many other places in Jerusalem.

And when this creature came into the place where the apostles received the Holy Ghost,* our Lord gave her great devotion. Afterwards she went to the place where our Lady was buried,* and as she knelt on her knees for the time it took to hear two masses our Lord Jesus Christ said to her, 'You do not come here, daughter, for any need except merit and reward, as your sins were forgiven before you came here, and therefore you come here to increase your merit and your reward. And I am well pleased with you, daughter, for you stand obediently before Holy Church, and you obey your confessor and follow his advice, who, by authority of Holy Church, has absolved you of your sins and given you dispensation, so that you need not go to Rome or Santiago de Compostela, unless you yourself wish to. All this notwithstanding, I command you in the name of Jesus, daughter, that you should visit these holy places and do as I ask you, for I am above all Holy Church and I shall go with you and keep you very safe.'

Then our Lady spoke to her soul in this way, saying, 'Daughter, you are well blessed, for my son Jesus will flow such grace through you that the whole world will marvel at you. Do not be ashamed, my highly esteemed daughter, to receive the gifts that my son shall give you, as I tell you truly that they shall be great gifts that He shall give you. And therefore, my highly esteemed daughter, do not be ashamed of Him that is your God, your Lord, your love, any more than I was when I saw Him hanging on the Cross—my sweet son, Jesus!—to cry and to weep for the pain of my sweet son, Jesus Christ; and Mary Magdalene was not ashamed to cry and weep for my son's love. Therefore, daughter, if you will partake of our joy, you must partake of our sorrow.'

This creature had these sweet speeches and conversations at our Lady's grave, and much more besides than she could ever repeat.

Afterwards, she rode by ass to Bethlehem,* and when she came to the temple and to the crib where our Lord was born,* she had great devotion, much speech, and conversation in her soul, and high spiritual comfort with much weeping and sobbing, so that her fellow pilgrims would not let her eat in their company. And therefore she ate her food alone by herself.

And then the Grey Friars who had led her from place to place received her amongst them and placed her with them at mealtimes, so that she should not eat alone. And one of the friars asked one of her party if that was the Englishwoman who, they had heard it said, spoke with God. And when this came to her knowledge, she knew well that it was the truth that our Lord had said to her, before she left England: 'Daughter, I shall make all the world marvel at you, and many men and many women shall speak of me out of love for you, and worship me in you.'

CHAPTER 30

ANOTHER time, this creature's party wanted to go to the River Jordan* and would not let her go with them. Then this creature pleaded with our Lord that she might go with them, and he charged that she should go with them whether they wanted it or not. And then she set out by the grace of God and did not ask their permission. When she came to the River Jordan, the weather was so hot that she believed her feet should burn for the heat that she felt.

After that she went on with her companions to Mount Quarantine,* where our Lord fasted for forty days. There she asked her companions to help her up the mountain. And they said 'no', because they could barely help themselves up. Then she had much sorrow, for she could not get up the hill. And then a Saracen, a good-looking man, chanced to come upon her, and she put a groat into his hand, making signs to him to take her up the mountain. And swiftly the Saracen took her under his arm and led her up the high mountain where our Lord fasted for forty days. Then she was terribly thirsty and had no sympathy from her party. Then God, in His high goodness, moved the Grey Friars with compassion and they comforted her when her own compatriots would not even acknowledge her.

And so she was ever strengthened in the love of our Lord and all the more bold to suffer shames and rebukes for His sake in every place she went, for the grace that God performed in her in weeping, sobbing, and crying, the which grace she could not resist when God wished to send it. And she always proved her feelings were true and those promises that God had made to her while she was in England, and in other places too, came to her in actuality just as she had sensed before, and therefore she dared the better receive such speeches and conversations, and act all the more boldly thereafter.

After that, when this creature had come down from the Mount, as God wished, she went onwards to the place where St John the Baptist was born.* And after that she went to Bethany, where Mary and Martha lived,* and to the grave where Lazarus* was buried and raised from death to life. She also went to the chapel where our blessed Lord appeared to His blissful mother before all others on Easter Day in the morning.* And she stood in the same place where Mary Magdalene first stood when Christ said to her, 'Mary, why weepest thou?'* And so she was in many more places than are written, for she was in Jerusalem for three weeks and in the regions thereabouts. And she was always very devout while she was in that region.

And the friars of the Temple made her very welcome and gave her many fine relics, wishing that she might stay with them,* if she wanted, as they had such faith in her. Also, the Saracens made much of her and escorted her and led her around the region, wherever she wished to go. And she found all the people to be good and gentle towards her, except her own compatriots.

And as she came from Jerusalem to Ramlah,* she wanted to return to Jerusalem for the great grace and spiritual comfort that she had felt when she was there, and to purchase more pardons for herself.* And then our Lord commanded her to go to Rome, and from there home to England, and said to her: 'Daughter, as often as you say or think, "Worshipped be all those holy places in Jerusalem in which Christ suffered bitter pain and Passion" you shall have the same pardon as if you were physically present there,* both for yourself and for all those to whom you wish to give it.'

And as she went on to Venice, many of her companions were really sick, and our Lord always said to her, 'Do not be afraid, daughter, no person shall die in the ship you are in.'

And she found her feelings to be really true. And when our Lord had brought them back to Venice in safety, her compatriots forsook her and went away from her, leaving her alone. And some of them said that they would not travel with her for a hundred pounds.

When they had gone away from her, then our Lord Jesus Christ, who always helps in times of need and never forsakes His servant who truly trusts to His mercy, said to His creature, 'Do not be afraid, daughter, for I shall provide for you really well, and bring you to

Rome in safety and home again to England without any sexual abuse of your body, if you will be clad in white clothes, and wear them as I said to you when you were in England.'

Then this creature, being in great woe and great bewilderment, answered back in her mind, 'If you are the spirit of God who speaks in my soul, and I may prove you to be a true spirit through the church's counsel, I shall obey your will, and, if you bring me to Rome in safety I shall, for your love, wear white clothes, even though the whole world will wonder at me.'

'Go forth, daughter, in the name of Jesus, for I am the spirit of God, the which shall help you in all your needs, and shall go with you and support you in every place, and therefore do not distrust me. You have never found me deceitful, and I have never asked you to do anything but that which, if you will do it afterwards, is the worship of God and a profit to your soul, and I shall flow into you with a great plenty of grace.'

Then, as she looked to one side, she saw a poor man, sitting down, who had a great hunch on his back. His clothes were all patched up, and he seemed to be a man of fifty years of age. Then she went to him and said, 'Good man, what's wrong with your back?'

He said, 'Madam, it was broken during an illness.'

She asked what was his name and of what nationality he was. He said his name was Richard and that he was from Ireland. Then she thought of the words of her confessor, who was a holy anchorite, as is written before, who had said the following to her while she was in England: 'Daughter, when your own party has forsaken you, God shall arrange a hunchbacked man to guide you wherever you want to go.'

Then, with a glad spirit, she said to him, 'Good Richard, guide me to Rome, and you shall be rewarded for your labour.'

'No, madam,' he said, 'I know full well that your compatriots have forsaken you, and therefore it would be hard for me to guide you. For your compatriots have both bows and arrows, with which they might defend both you and themselves, and I have no weapon except a cloak full of clouts. And so I fear that my enemies should rob me, and per- haps take you away from me and rape you, and therefore I dare not escort you, as I would not, for a hundred pounds, have you suffer some indignity in my company.'

Then she replied, 'Richard, don't be afraid; God shall look after both of us very well, and I'll give you two nobles for your labours.'

Then he consented and set off with her. Soon afterwards two Grey Friars came along, with a woman who had come with them from Jerusalem and she had an ass with her that carried a chest and an image in it made in our Lord's likeness.*

Then Richard said to the aforementioned creature, 'You shall go onwards with these two men and this woman, and I shall meet you in the morning and in the evening, for I must go on with my occupation and beg for my living.'

And so she did as he advised and went on with the friars and the woman. And none of them could understand her language, and yet every day they arranged for her food, drink, and lodgings as well, if not somewhat better, as they did for themselves, so that she was always obliged to pray for them. And every evening and morning hunchbacked Richard came and comforted her as he had promised.

And the woman who had the image in the chest, when they came to fine cities, she took the image out of her chest and set it in the laps of honourable women. Then they would clothe it in shirts and kiss it as if it were God Himself. And when the creature saw the worship and the reverence that they made to this image, she was moved with sweet devotion and sweet meditations so that she wept with immense sobbing and loud crying. And she was all the more moved because when she had been in England she had lofty meditations of Christ's birth and childhood, and she thanked God because she saw these creatures having as great a faith in what they saw with their physical eye as she had beforehand with her spiritual eye.

When these good women saw the creature weep, sob, and cry so marvellously and powerfully that she was nearly overcome by it, then they arranged a fine soft bed and laid her upon it, and comforted her as much as they were able for our Lord's love, may He be blessed!

CHAPTER 31

THE aforementioned creature had a ring, which our Lord had commanded her to have made while she was at home in England and to have engraved upon it '*Jhesus est amor meus*'.* She gave much thought to how she should keep this ring from thieves and from being stolen on her travels as she made her way through different regions, for she thought she would not have lost the ring for £1,000 and much more, because she had it made at God's wish. And also she wore it at His command, as she had earlier intended, before she had it by revelation, never to wear a ring.

And as it happened, she was in lodgings in a good man's house, and many neighbours came in to encourage her in her perfection and her holiness—and she gave them the measurement of Christ's grave,* which they received very piously, taking great joy in it and thanking her very much for it—and after that this creature went to her room and let her ring hang from her purse-strings, which she carried at her breast. On the morning of the next day, when she went to get her ring, it had gone—she could not find it! Then she was greatly downcast and complained to the landlady of the house in this way: 'Madam, what I call "my precious wedding-ring to Jesus Christ" is gone!'

The landlady, understanding what she meant, asked her to pray for her, and she changed her attitude and her countenance peculiarly, as though she were guilty. Then this creature took a candle in her hand and looked all around her bed where she had been lying all night, and the landlady of the house took another candle in her hand and busied herself also in searching around the bed. And at last she found the ring under the bed on the floorboards, and with great joy she told the landlady that she had found her ring. Then the landlady, meekly, begged this creature for forgiveness as best she could: '*Bone Cristian, prey pur me!*'*

Afterwards this creature came to Assisi, and there she met with a Friar Minor,* an Englishman, and he was held to be a serious cleric. She told him about her manner of living, of her feelings, of her revelations, and of the grace that God performed in her soul through holy inspiration and high contemplation, and how our Lord spoke with her soul in a kind of conversation. Then the honourable cleric said that she was much beholden to God, as he said that he had never heard of anyone living in this world who was so intimate with God, through love and homely conversation, as was she, God be thanked for His gifts, for it is His goodness and no man's merit.

Once upon a time, as this creature was in church at Assisi, our Lady's veil* that she had worn on earth was presented there, with many candles and much reverence. Then this creature had much devotion. She wept, she sobbed, she cried with many tears and many holy thoughts. She was also there on Lammas Day,* when there is a huge pardon with plenary remission, to obtain grace, mercy, and forgiveness for herself, for all her friends, for all her enemies, and for all the souls in Purgatory.

And a lady was there who had come from Rome to obtain her pardon. Her name was Margaret Florentine.* She had with her many Knights of Rhodes,* many gentlewomen, and much fine luggage. Then Richard, the hunchbacked man, went to her, asking her if this creature might go with her to Rome, and himself too, to be kept safe from the peril of thieves. And then that respectable lady received them into her party and let them go with her to Rome, as God wished. When the aforementioned creature reached Rome, those who were her companions beforehand and had put her out of their party were in Rome too and heard tell of such a woman who had arrived there, and they were really astonished at how she had reached there safely.

And then she went and arranged white clothes for herself and was clothed all in white, as she had been commanded to do years before by revelation in her soul, and now it had been achieved.

Then this creature was received into the hospital of St Thomas of Canterbury in Rome,* and she received communion there every Sunday, with great weeping, violent sobbing, and loud crying, and was highly beloved by the master of the hospital and by all his brethren.

And then, through the guidance of her spiritual enemy, a priest arrived there who was held to be a holy man in the hospital and also in other places around Rome, and he was one of her party and one of her compatriots. And notwithstanding his holiness, he spoke so evilly about this creature and slandered her name so much in the hospital that, because of his evil language, she was sent out of the hospital, so that she could no longer be shriven or take communion there.

CHAPTER 32

WHEN this creature saw that she had been abandoned and cast out from the good men, she was very woeful, most of all because she had no confessor, and she could not be shriven as she wished. Then, with a great many tears, she prayed to our Lord, of His mercy, that He would arrange for her as was most pleasing to Him. And after that she called the aforementioned hunchbacked Richard to her, asking him to go over to a church opposite the Hospital* and inform the church's parson of her mode of behaviour, and the sorrow she had, and how she wept because she could not be shriven or take communion, and what compunction and contrition she had for her sins.

Then Richard went to the parson and told him about this creature, and how our Lord gave her contrition and compunction with a great many tears, and how she desired to receive communion every Sunday if she could, and she had no priest to confess to. And then the parson, hearing of her contrition and compunction, was very glad and asked that she should come to him in the name of Jesus and say her *Confiteor*,* and he should give her communion himself, for he could not understand any English.

Then our Lord sent St John the Evangelist* to hear her confession, and she said '*Benedicite*'.* And he said '*Dominus*'* truly in her soul, so that she saw him and heard him in her spiritual understanding, as she might have done another priest in her bodily senses. Then she told him all her sins and all her grievances with many sorrowful tears, and he heard her most meekly and generously. And after that he enjoined on her the penance she should do for her trespasses, and absolved her of her sins with sweet words and meek words, heartily strengthening her to trust in the mercy of our Lord Jesus Christ, and asked her that she should receive the sacrament of the altar in the name of Jesus. And after that he passed away from her.

When he had gone, she prayed with all her heart all the time, as she heard mass, 'Lord, as surely as you are not angry with me, grant me a well of tears* through which I may receive your precious body with all kinds of tears of devotion to your worship and for the increase of my merit; for you are my joy, Lord, my bliss, my comfort, and all the treasure I have in this world, as I covet no other worldly joy, but only you. Therefore, my highly esteemed Lord and my God, do not forsake me.'

Then our blissful Lord Christ Jesus answered to her soul and said, 'My highly esteemed daughter, I swear by my high majesty that I shall never forsake you. And daughter, the more shame, spites, and disgrace that you suffer for my love, the better I love you, because I act like a man who loves his wife well: the more that men envy her, the better he will adorn her to spite his enemies. And just so, daughter, shall I act towards you. In nothing that you either do, daughter, or say, you can please God no better than to believe that He loves you; for if it were possible that I might weep with you, I would weep with you, daughter, for that compassion that I have for you. The time shall come when you shall think yourself well pleased, for in you the common proverb* that people say shall be proved true: "He who can sit in his seat of blessedness and talk about his seat of sadness is blessed indeed." And so shall you do, daughter, and all your weeping and your sorrow shall turn to joy and bliss, the which you shall never lack.'

CHAPTER 33

ANOTHER time, as this creature was at the Church of St John Lateran,* in front of the altar, hearing mass, she thought that the priest who said mass seemed like a good and devout man. She was painfully moved in her spirit to speak with him. Then she asked her hunchbacked man to go to the priest and ask him to speak with her. Then the priest did not understand English and did not know what she was saying, and therefore they spoke through an interpreter, a man who told each what the other said. Then she asked the priest in the name of Jesus to make his prayers to the blessed Trinity, to our Lady, and to all the blessed saints in heaven, and also guiding others who loved our Lord to pray for this priest, that he might have grace to understand her language and her speaking of such things as she, through the grace of God, wished to say and show to him.

The priest was a good man, a German by birth, a good cleric, and a most learned man, extremely beloved, much cherished, and widely trusted in Rome, and he had one of the greatest offices of any priest in Rome. Desiring to please God, he followed this creature's advice, and every day made his prayers to God as devoutly as he could, so that he might have the grace to understand what the aforementioned creature wished to say to him, and also he made other lovers of our Lord pray for him. They prayed thus for thirteen days. And after thirteen days the priest came back to her to test the effect of their prayers, and then he understood what she said to him in English, and she understood what he said. And yet he did not understand the English that other men spoke; although they spoke the same words that she spoke, he still did not understand them, unless she herself spoke.

Then she was confessed to this priest of all her sins, as best as her memory would serve her, from her childhood until that time, and she received her penance very joyfully. And after that she showed him the secret things of her revelations and high contemplations, and how she gave so much thought to His Passion, and had such great compassion when God would give it that she fell down because of it and could not bear it. Then she wept bitterly, she sobbed violently, and she cried very loudly and horribly, so that the people were often afraid and really astonished, judging that she was vexed by some evil spirit, or a sudden sickness, not believing that it was the work of God but rather some evil spirit, or a sudden sickness, or else dissimulation and hypocrisy, an illusory imitation by her own self.

The priest very much trusted that this was the work of God, and when he lacked faith, our Lord sent him such signs via the aforementioned creature of his own misconduct and manner of living—the which nobody knew except God and himself, as our Lord showed to her through revelation and asked her to tell him—that he knew very well because of them that her feelings were true.

And then this priest received her very meekly and reverently, as he would his mother or his sister, and he said he would support her against her enemies. And he did so for as long as she was in Rome and suffered many evil words and much tribulation. And, also, he left his office, because he wanted to support her in her sobbing and in her crying when all her compatriots had forsaken her, for they were her worst enemies and caused her much misery wherever they went, for they wished that she would neither sob nor cry. She could not choose this, but they would not believe her. And they were always against her there and against the good man who supported her.

And then this good man, seeing this woman sobbing and crying so wonderfully, and especially on Sundays when she should receive communion amongst all the people, undertook to test whether it was the gift of God, as she said, or else her own pretence through hypocrisy, as the people said. So another Sunday he took her alone to another church after mass had been done and all the people were at home, and nobody knew about this apart from only himself and the cleric. And when he came to give her communion, she wept so abundantly, and sobbed and cried so loudly, that he was himself astonished, for it seemed to his hearing that she had never cried so loudly before. And then he fully believed that it was the working of the Holy Ghost and neither pretence nor hypocrisy by her own self. So afterwards he was not embarrassed to side with her and to speak against those who would defame her and speak ill of her until he was defamed by the enemies of virtue almost as much as her, and he very much liked to suffer tribulations for God's cause. Many people in Rome who were virtuously disposed loved him all the more, and her too, and often they asked her to dinner and gave her a very warm welcome, asking her to pray for them.

And her own compatriots were always obstinate, and especially a priest who was amongst them. He led many people against her and spoke ill of her, for she wore white clothing more than did others who were holier and better than she ever was, so he thought. The cause of his malice was that she would not obey him. And she knew full well it was against her soul's health to obey him as he wished her to do.

CHAPTER 34

THEN the good man, the German priest to whom she had confessed, asked her, through the agitation of the English priest who was her enemy, whether or not she would be obedient to him?

So she said, 'Yes, sir.'

'Then will you do as I shall ask you to do?'

'Very willingly, sir.'

'Then I charge you to put aside your white clothes, and wear your black clothes again.'

So she did as he commanded. And then she had the feeling that she pleased God with her obedience. Then she suffered much mockery from the women of Rome. They asked her if highwaymen had robbed her, and she said, 'No, madam.'

After that, as she went on pilgrimage, it happened that she met with the priest who was her enemy, and he greatly rejoiced that she had been side-tracked from her intentions and he said to her, 'I am glad that you go about in black clothing like you used to do.'

And she replied, 'Sir, our Lord would not be displeased even though I wore white clothes, as he wishes that I do so.'

Then the priest said to her, 'Now I know full well that you have a devil within you, as I can hear him speak in you to me.'

'Ah, good sir, I ask that you drive him away from me, as God knows I would very gladly do well and please Him if I could.'

And then he was really angry and said very many wicked words; and she said to him, 'Sir, I hope I've no devil within me, for if I had a devil within me, rest assured that I'd be angry with you. And, sir,

I don't think that I'm at all angry with you for anything that you can do to me.'

And then the priest went away from her with a grim expression. And then our Lord spoke to this creature in her soul and said, 'Daughter, do not be afraid, whatsoever he says to you, because even though he hurries to Jerusalem every year, I have no liking for him because, for as long as he speaks against you, he speaks against me, for I am in you and you are in me. And hereby may you know that I suffer many wicked words, for I have often said to you that I should be crucified anew in you by wicked words, as you shall be killed in no other way than by suffering wicked words. As for this priest who is your enemy, he is just a hypocrite.'

Then the good priest, her confessor, charged her, by virtue of obedience, and also in part out of penance, to serve an old woman of Rome, a poor creature. And she did so for six weeks. She served her as she would have done our Lady. And she had no bed to lie in, and no bedclothes to be covered with, except her own cloak. And then she was full of parasites and suffered much pain from them. Also, she fetched home water and sticks on her shoulders for the poor woman, and begged for both food and wine for her. And when the poor woman's wine was sour, this creature drank that sour wine herself, and gave the poor woman good wine that she had bought for her own self.

CHAPTER 35

As this creature was in the Apostles' Church in Rome* on St Lateran's Day,* the Father of Heaven said to her, 'Daughter, I am very pleased with you, inasmuch as you believe in all the sacraments of Holy Church and in all the beliefs that relate to them, and especially because you believe in the manhood of my Son and for the great compassion you have for His bitter Passion.'

The Father also said to this creature, 'Daughter, I will have you married to my Godhead, because I shall show you my secrets and my schemes, for you shall dwell with me without end.'

Then the creature kept silent in her soul and did not answer this, for she was so dreadfully afraid of the Godhead; and she had no knowledge of conversation with the Godhead, as all her love and all her affection was placed in Christ's manhood, and she had much knowledge of that and would not be parted from that for anything. She had so much affection for Christ's manhood that when she saw women of Rome carrying children in their arms, if she knew for a fact that any of them were little boys, she would cry out, roar, and weep, as if she had seen Christ in His childhood. And if she could have had her way, she often wanted to take the children out of their mothers' arms and kiss them in place of Christ. And if she saw a handsome man, it caused her great pain to look at him, in case she might see He who is both God and man. Therefore she often cried many times when she met a handsome man, and wept and sobbed most dreadfully for Christ's manhood as she went about the streets of Rome, so that those who saw her were really astonished by her, because they did not know the cause of this.

Therefore it was no surprise that she was silent and did not answer the Father of Heaven, when He told her that she should be married to His Godhead. Then the Second Person, Jesus Christ, whose manhood she loved so much, said to her, 'What do you say, Margery, daughter, to my Father about these words that He speaks to you? Are you really pleased that it is so?'

And then she would not answer the Second Person, but wept marvellously bitterly, desiring still to have Him and in no way to be separated from Him. Then the Second Person of the Trinity answered to His Father for her and said, 'Father, excuse her, for she is just young and has not fully learned how she should answer.'

And then, in her soul, the Father took her by the hand, before the Son and the Holy Ghost, and the Mother of Jesus, and all the Twelve Apostles, and St Katherine and St Margaret and many other saints and holy virgins, with a great multitude of angels, saying to her soul, 'I take you, Margery to be my wedded wife, for better, for worse, for richer, for poorer,* so that you dutifully and submissively do what I ask you to do. Because, daughter, there was never a child so obedient to its mother as I shall be to you, both in good times and bad, to help you and comfort you. And that is what I pledge to you.'

And then the Mother of God and all the saints who were present in her soul prayed that they might have much joy together. And then the creature, with high devotion and a great many tears, thanked God for this spiritual comfort, holding herself in her own feeling to be most unworthy of any such grace as she felt, for she felt many deep comforts, both spiritual comforts and physical comforts. Sometimes she felt sweet smells in her nose; it was sweeter, she thought, than any sweet earthly thing she had smelled before, and she could not describe how sweet it was, as she thought she could have lived on those smells if they had lasted. Sometimes she heard with her physical ears such sounds and melodies that she could not hear at that time what people said to her unless they spoke louder. She had heard these sounds and melodies nearly every day for twenty-five years when this book was written, and especially when she was at devout prayer, and also many times while she was in both Rome and England.

She saw with her physical eye many white things flying all around her on every side, as thick as motes in the sunlight; they were really delicate and comforting, and the brighter the sun shined the better she could see them. She saw them at many different times and in many different places, both in church and in her room, at her food and at her prayers, in the country and in town, both whilst walking and whilst sitting. Many times she was afraid of what they might be, for she saw them as well at night in darkness as in daylight. Then, when she was afraid of them, our Lord said to her, 'By this sign, daughter, believe God that speaks in you, for wherever God is, there are many angels, and God is in you and you are in Him. And therefore do not be afraid, daughter, for these signify that you have many angels around you, to watch you both day and night so that no devil can have power over you, and no evil man can harm you.'*

Then from that time onwards she used to say when she saw them coming, '*Benedictus qui venit in nomine Domini.*'*

Also, our Lord gave her another sign, which lasted about sixteen years, and it always increased more and more, and that was a flame of the fire of love,* marvellously hot and delicious and very comforting, not lessening but always increasing as, even if the weather was never so cold, she felt the heat burning in her breast and at her heart, as truly as if a person should feel an actual fire if he put his hand or his finger into it. When she first felt the fire of love burning in her breast, she was afraid of it, and then our Lord answered her in her mind, and said, 'Daughter, do not be afraid, for this heat is the heat of the Holy Ghost, the which shall burn away all your sins, for the fire of love smothers all sins. And you shall understand through this sign that the Holy Ghost is in you, and you know well how wherever the Holy Ghost is, the Father is there, and where the Father is, the Son is there, and so you have the whole of the Holy Trinity in your soul. Therefore you have great cause to love me really well, and yet you shall have greater cause than you have ever had to love me, for you shall hear that which you have never heard, and you shall see that which you have never seen, and you shall feel that which you have never felt.

'For, daughter, you are as secure in God's love as God is God. Your soul is more secure in God's love than you are in your own body, for your soul shall be separated from your body, but God shall never be separated from your soul, for they are united together without end. Therefore, daughter, you have as great a reason to be merry as any lady in this world. And if you knew, daughter, how much you pleased me when you allow me willingly to speak in you, you would never do otherwise, for this is a holy life, and the time is very well spent. For, daughter, this life pleases me more than wearing chainmail or a hair-cloth next to the skin, or fasting on bread and water. For if you said 1,000 paternosters every day, you should not please me as well as you do when you are silent and allow me to speak in your soul.'

CHAPTER 36

'Fasting, daughter, is good for young beginners or an inconspicuous penance, specifically if a spiritual confessor gives it to them or enjoins them to do it. And to pray many prayers is good for those who know no better, but it is still not perfect. It is, however, a good way towards perfection. For I tell you, daughter, those who are great fasters and penitents, they would hold that to be the best life; also, those who give themselves to saying many prayers, they would consider that to be the best life; and those who give a lot of alms, they would consider that to be the best life. And I have often, daughter, told you that thinking, weeping, and high contemplation is the best life on earth. And you shall have more merit in Heaven for one year of thinking in your mind than for a hundred years of praying with your mouth; and still you will not believe me, as you pray many prayers whether or not I want it. Yet, daughter, I will not be displeased with you, whether you think, say, or speak, for I am always pleased with you. And if I was physically on earth as I was before I died on the Cross, I should not be ashamed of you, as many other people are, for I should take you by the hand amongst the people and make much of you, so that they would know really well that I love you very much.

'For it is appropriate that the wife is intimate with her husband. Be he ever such an important lord and she just a poor woman when he married her, yet they must sleep together and rest together in joy and peace. Just so it must be between you and me, as I pay no attention to what you have been but rather to what you will be. I have often told you that I have wholly forgiven you for all your sins. Therefore I must be intimate with you and lie in your bed with you.* Daughter, you really desire to see me, and boldly you can: when you are in your bed take me to yourself as your wedded husband, as your dear darling, as your sweet son, for I wish to be loved as a son should be loved by the mother, and wish that you love me, daughter, as a good wife ought to love her husband. And therefore you may boldly take me in your soul's arms and kiss my mouth, my head, and my feet as sweetly as you wish. And as often as you think of me, or when you would do some good deed for me, you shall have the same reward in Heaven as if you did it to my own precious body which is in Heaven. For I ask no more of you but that your heart loves me who loves you, for my love is always ready for you.'

Then she gave thanks and praise to our Lord Jesus Christ for the lofty grace and mercy that He showed to her, an unworthy wretch.

This creature had various signs in her physical hearing. One was a kind of sound, as if a pair of bellows* was blowing in her ear. She, being ashamed of this, was warned in her soul to have no fear of it, for it was the sound of the Holy Ghost. And then our Lord turned that sound into the voice of a dove,* and after that he turned it into the voice of a little bird called a redbreast* that often sang really gaily in her right ear. And then she always had great grace after she heard such a sign. And, at the time of writing this book, she had become used to such signs for about twenty-five years.

Then our Lord Jesus Christ said to His creature, 'By these signs you may be sure that I love you, for you are like a true mother to me and to all the world, for the great charity that is within you; and yet I am myself the cause of that charity, and you shall have a great reward for it in Heaven.'

CHAPTER 37

'DAUGHTER, you are so obedient to my will and cleave as tightly to me as the skin of stock-fish cleaves to a man's hands when it is boiled, and you will not forsake me for any shame that people can do to you.

You say too that even though I stood in front of you in my own person and said to you that you should never have my love or ever come to Heaven or ever see my face, you still say, daughter, that you will never forsake me on earth, and never love me the less, and never labour any the less to please me, though you should lie in Hell without end, as you may neither forgo my love on earth nor can you have any other comfort but me alone, who am I, your God, and I am all joy and all bliss to you. Therefore I say to you, dearly-esteemed daughter, it is impossible that any such soul which has such great meekness and charity towards me should be damned or separated from me. And therefore, daughter, never be afraid, for all the large promises that I have made to you and yours, and to all your spiritual confessors, shall always be true and truly fulfilled when the time comes. Have no doubt about it.'

Another time, when she was in Rome, a little before Christmas,* our Lord Jesus Christ commanded her to go to her spiritual confessor, Wenceslas* was his name, and asked him to give her leave to wear her white clothes again, as he had taken her from them by virtue of her obedience, as was written before. And when she told him about the will of our Lord, he dared not once say 'no'. And so she wore white clothes ever after.

Then our Lord charged that she should, at Christmas, go back home to her host's house where she had been lodged beforehand. And then she went to a poor woman whom she served at that time at the request of her confessor, as is written before, and told the poor woman how she must go away from her. And then the poor woman was really remorseful and really complained about her departure. And then this creature told her how it was God's will that it should be so, and then she took it somewhat better.

Afterwards, as this creature was in Rome, our Lord asked her to give away all her money and make herself penniless for His love. And then at once she, with a fervent desire to please God, gave away the money that she had and that which she had borrowed too from the hunchbacked man who went around with her. When he found out how she had given away his money, he was extremely upset and most displeased as she had given away his money, and he spoke very sharply to her. And then she said to him, 'Richard, by the grace of God we'll get home to England soundly. And you'll come with me to Bristol in Whitsun week, and there I shall pay you in full and honestly by the grace of God, for I trust very well that He who charged that I give it away for His love will help me to pay it back.'

And so He did.*

CHAPTER 38

AFTER this creature had thus given away her money, and had neither a penny nor a ha'penny with which to help herself, as she lay in St Marcellus's church in Rome,* thinking and pondering how she might have enough to live on (inasmuch as she had no coins to keep herself) our Lord answered to her mind and said, 'Daughter, you are not as poor as I was when I hung naked on the Cross for your love, for you have clothes on your body and I had none. And you have counselled other people to be poor for my sake, and therefore you must follow your own advice. But do not be afraid, daughter, for there is gold coming your way, and I have promised you before that I will never let you down. And I shall ask my own mother to beg for you, for you have begged for me and also for my mother many times. Therefore do not be afraid. I have friends in every region and I shall make my friends comfort you.'

When our Lord had sweetly conversed thus with her soul, she thanked Him for this great comfort, trusting utterly that it should be as He said. After that she got up and went forth into the street and happened to meet a gentleman. And then they fell into conversation as they went on their way together, and she told him many good tales and fine exhortations until God visited him with tears of devotion and compunction so he had great comfort and consolation. And then he gave her money, by which she was very relieved and comforted for a good while.

Then one night she saw in a vision how our Lady, she thought, sat at dinner with many worshipful people and asked for food for her. And then this creature thought that our Lord's words were fulfilled spiritually in this vision, for a little earlier He had promised this creature that He should ask His mother to beg for her.

And a short while after this vision she met a respectable lady, Dame Margaret Florentine, the same lady who had brought her from Assisi to Rome. And neither of them could understand the other very well except by signs and gestures and a few common words. So then the lady said to her, '*Margerya in poverte?*' She, understanding what the lady meant, said back to her, 'Yes, *grawnt poverte*, madam.'*

Then the lady requested her to eat with her every Sunday and placed her at her own table above herself, and served her food to her with her own hands. Then this creature sat and wept most bitterly, thanking our Lord that she was so prized and cherished, for His love, by those who could not understand her language. When they had eaten, the good lady used to take her a hamper with other stuff to make a soup from, enough for her to serve herself two days' food, and filled her bottle with good wine. And sometimes she added eight bolognino coins to it.

And then another man in Rome, who was called Marcello, asked her to dine two days each week, and his wife was pregnant, and she very much desired to have this creature act as godmother to the child when it was born, but she did not stay in Rome for that long. And also there was a pious young woman who gave this creature her food on Wednesdays. On other days, when she was not provided for, she begged for food from door to door.

CHAPTER 39

ANOTHER time, just as she went past a poor woman's house, the poor woman called her inside and had her sit down by the little fire, giving her wine to drink from a stone cup. And she had a little baby boy sucking on her breast for some of the time; at other times it ran to this creature, as the mother sat full of sorrow and sadness. Then this creature burst into tears, as though she had seen our Lady and her son at the time of His Passion, and she had so many holy thoughts that she could never tell the half of them, but always sat and wept plenteously for a long time, so that the poor woman, having compassion for her weeping, pleaded with her to stop, not knowing why she wept.

Then our Lord Jesus Christ said to the creature, 'This place is holy.'

And then she got up and went out into Rome and saw much poverty amongst the people; and then she thanked God highly for the poverty that she was in, trusting to partake in merit with them.

Then there was a fine gentlewoman in Rome asking this creature to be the godmother of her child and she named it after St Bridget, for they had known her during her lifetime. And so she did. After that, God gave her grace to be greatly loved in Rome, both by men and by women, and to find favour amongst the people.

When the Master and brothers of the Hospital of St Thomas,* from which she had been refused beforehand, as is written earlier, heard tell what love and what favour she had in the city, they asked her if she would come back to them, and she would be more welcome than she ever was before, for they were really sorry that they had sent her away from them. And she thanked them for their charity and did their bidding. And when she came back to them, they made her very welcome and were really glad that she had come.

Then there she found the one who had been her maidservant beforehand, and who by right should still have been so, living in the Hospital in much wealth and prosperity, for she looked after their wine-cellar. And this creature sometimes went to her, out of humility, and asked her for food and drink, and the maidservant gave it to her willingly, and sometimes added a groat too. Then she complained to her maidservant, and said that she felt a lot of despair about her departure, and the slander and wicked words that people had said about why they had parted ways—but the maidservant never wanted to go back to her.

Afterwards, this creature spoke with St Bridget's maidservant in Rome,* but she could not understand what she said. Then she got a man who could understand her language, and that man told St Bridget's maidservant what this creature said and how she asked after St Bridget, her mistress. Then the maidservant said that her mistress, St Bridget, was kind and meek to every creature, and that she had a smiling face. And also, the good man where this creature had been lodging told her that he had known St Bridget herself, but he little knew that she had been as holy a woman as she was, as she was always intimate with and kind to all creatures that wished to speak with her.

She was in the room in which St Bridget died,* and heard there a German priest preaching about her, about her revelations and her manner of living. And she also knelt on the stone on which our Lord appeared to St Bridget and told her on what day she should die.* And it was on one of St Bridget's days* that this creature was in her chapel, which before had been the room in which she died. Our Lord sent such storms, of wind and rain, and different atmospheric forces, that those who were in the fields and at work outdoors were forced to enter houses to protect their bodies, to avoid various dangers. Through such signs, this creature supposed that our Lord wanted His holy saints' days to be held sacred, and that the saint was to be worshipped more than she was at that time.*

And sometimes, when this creature would go to the Stations of Rome,* our Lord warned her during the night, when she was in her bed, that she should not leave her hostel, for that day He should send great storms of thunder and lightning. And indeed so it was. There were such great storms that year of thunder and lightning, of heavy rains and different gales, that very old men then living in Rome said that they had never seen the like before; the lightning was so frequent and shone so bright into their houses that they really thought it would burn their houses down along with the contents. Then they cried out to the aforementioned creature to pray for them, entirely trusting that she was the servant of almighty God and that through her prayers they would be helped and relieved. This creature prayed at their request to our Lord of mercy, and he answered in her soul, saying, 'Daughter, do not be afraid, for neither weather nor storm shall harm you, and therefore do not distrust me, for I shall never deceive you.'

And our merciful Lord Christ Jesus, as it pleased Him, put aside the storms, protecting the people from all afflictions.

CHAPTER 40

THEN, through the provision of our merciful Lord Christ Jesus, a priest came along, a good man, from England to Rome with other companions, searching and asking carefully after the said creature, whom he had never seen before nor she him. But while he was in England he heard tell of such a woman who was in Rome, with whom he longed to speak, if God would grant him grace to do so. So, while he was in his own country, intending to see this creature when (through the Lord's permission) he might reach where she was, he provided himself with gold coins to bring her relief if she needed it. Then, through enquiries, he reached the place where she was, and very humbly and meekly he called her 'mother', asking her out of charity to receive him as her son. She said that he was as welcome to God and to her as if by his own mother.

So, through holy conversation and communication she really felt sure that he was a good man. And then she, divulging the secrets of her heart, revealed what grace God performed in her soul through His holy inspiration and something of her manner of living. Then he would no longer allow her to beg for her food from door to door, but asked her to eat with him and his companions, unless good men and women asked her to eat with them through charity and for spiritual comfort; then he wished her to accept in the name of the Lord; otherwise she ate with him and with his companions every day, and he gave her sufficient gold coins to return home to England. And in this was fulfilled what our Lord had said to her a little beforehand: 'Gold is coming your way.' And so indeed it was, almighty God be thanked!

Then some of her companions, with whom she had been at Jerusalem, came to this good priest, newly arrived in Rome, complaining about her, and said that she had confessed to a priest who could understand neither her language nor her confession. Then this good priest, trusting her as he would trust his mother, desiring the health of her soul, asked her whether or not her confessor understood her when she spoke to him.

'Good son, I implore you, ask him to dine with you and your companions, and let me be present, and then you'll know the truth.'

Her confessor was asked to dinner and, when the time came, was seated and served with this good priest, and his companions (the said creature being present) and the good English priest chatted and conversed in their own language, English. The German priest, a worthy cleric, as is described earlier, confessor to the said creature, sat silently in a kind of despair, because he did not understand what they said in English, only when they spoke in Latin. And they did it on purpose, unbeknownst to him, to test whether he understood English or not.

In the end, the said creature saw and understood well that her confessor did not understand their language, and that was tedious to him; so, partly to comfort him and partly (or, rather, mainly) to prove God's working, she told a story from Holy Writ in her own language, in English, which she had learned from clerics when she was at home in England, for she would speak neither of vanities nor of fantasies. Then they asked her confessor if he understood what she had said, and then in Latin he told them the same words that she had just said in English, for he knew neither how to speak English nor how to understand English except from her speech. And then they really marvelled, for they knew well that he understood what she had said, and she understood what he said, and he could understand no other English people. So may God be blessed, who made a foreigner understand her when her own compatriots had forsaken her and would not hear her confession unless she put aside her weeping and her talking of holiness.

And still she could not weep except when God gave it to her; and often he gave it so copiously that she could not resist it. But the more that she tried to resist it or put it aside, the more strongly it worked in her soul with such holy thoughts that she could not stop it. She would sob and cry very loudly, utterly against her will, so that many men and women were amazed at her.

CHAPTER 41

SOMETIMES, when the aforementioned creature was at sermons which Germans and other people preached, teaching God's laws, a sudden sorrow and dejection occupied her heart and caused her to complain with mournful expressions at her lack of understanding, as she desired to be refreshed with some crumb of spiritual understanding of her most trusted and entirely beloved sovereign, Christ Jesus, whose melodious voice, the sweetest of all sweetnesses, sounding softly in her soul, said, 'I shall preach to you and teach you myself, for your will and your desire is acceptable to me.'

Then her soul was so deliciously fed with the sweet conversation of our Lord and so filled with His love, that, like a drunkard, she turned herself first to one side and then to the other, with much weeping and loud sobbing, unable to keep herself steady because of the unquenchable fire of love which burned very fiercely in her soul. Then many people gawped at her, asking what was wrong with her, to whom she, like a creature wounded with love and that had lost its mind, cried with a loud voice, 'The Passion of Christ is killing me!'

The good women, having compassion for her sorrow and very much marvelling at her weeping and her crying, loved her all the more. And therefore they, desiring to give her solace and to comfort her spiritual labours—by signs and gestures, as she did not understand their speech—pleaded with her, and in a way compelled her, to come home with them, wishing her not to leave them.

Then our Lord sent her grace to have much love and great favour from many people in Rome, both religious men and others. Some religious people came to some of her compatriots who loved her and said, 'This woman has sown much good seed in Rome since she came here;* that is to say, she has shown a good example to the people, through which they love God more than they did before.'

One time, as this creature was in a church in Rome where the body of St Jerome* lies buried (which was miraculously translated from Bethlehem to that place, and is now very much worshipped there, next to the place where St Laurence* lies buried), St Jerome appeared to this creature's spiritual sight, saying to her soul, 'You are blessed, daughter, in the weeping that you weep for the people's sins, for many people shall be saved by it. And, daughter, do not be afraid, for it is a singular and special gift that God has given you—a well of tears, the which shall any person never take from you.'

With such words as these he greatly comforted her spirits. And he also very much praised and thanked God for the grace that he worked in her soul, for if she had not had such spiritual comforts it would have been impossible for her to bear the shame and gawping which she suffered patiently and meekly for the grace that God showed in her.

CHAPTER 42

WHEN Easter, or Passover, had come and gone,* this creature and her companions, intending to go back to their native country, were told that there were many thieves on the route who would strip them of their possessions and perhaps kill them.

Then the said creature, with many a bitter tear in her eye, prayed to our Lord Jesus Christ, saying, 'Christ Jesus, in whom I have placed all my trust, as you have promised me many times before that no person in my company should be harmed, and I was never deceived or defrauded in your promises as long as I fully and truly trusted in you, so hear the prayers of your unworthy servant who is entirely trusting in your mercy. And grant that me and my companions may go back home, for your love, without hindrance to our bodies or our property (as for our souls, Lord, they have no power over those!), and never let our enemies have power over us, Lord, if it pleases you. As you wish it, so must it be.'

Then our Lord said to her mind, 'Do not be afraid, daughter, for you and everybody in your company shall go forth as safe as if you were in St Peter's Church.'*

Then she thanked God with all her spirits, and was bold enough to go where God wished, and she took her leave of her friends in Rome and in particular of her spiritual confessor who, for our Lord's love, had supported her and assisted her very tenderly against the wicked winds of her envious enemies; her parting from him was very sad, as was witnessed well by the pure tear-drops running down their cheeks. She, falling on her knees, received the benefit of his blessing, and so they parted ways, whom charity had joined in one, and through which they trusted to meet again, when our Lord wished, in their common homeland, when they had passed through this wretched worldly exile.

And thus she and her companions set off towards England. And when they were a little way out of Rome, the good priest (the one who, as was written before, had been received by this creature as if he was her own son) had a great fear of enemies. Because of this he said to her, 'Mother, I'm afraid of dying, of being killed by enemies.'

She said, 'No, son, you'll go on your way very well and you'll be safe, by the grace of God.'

And he was greatly comforted by her words, as he very much trusted in her feelings, and he treated her as warmly on the road as if he had been her own son, born of her body.

And so they reached Middelburg,* and then her companions wanted to start their journey towards England on the Sunday.* Then the good priest came to her, saying, 'Mother, will you go with your companions or not on this noble day?'

And she said, 'No, son, it is not my Lord's will that I should go there so soon.'

And so she waited there with the good priest and some other members of the party until the Sunday after. And many of her companions took a ship on the Sunday. On the Friday after, as this creature went to enjoy herself in the countryside, with people from her own country with her whom she instructed in God's laws as well as she could— and she spoke back to them sharply for they swore grave oaths and broke our Lord God's commandments—and as she went on conversing with them, our Lord Jesus Christ charged her to go home in haste to her hostel, as a huge and dangerous storm was coming. Then she went on her way homewards with her party and as soon as they got to their hostel the storm broke as she had felt through revelation. And many times, as she was on the road and in the countryside, there was strong lightning with hideous thunder, horrible and harmful, such that she was afraid it would strike her to death, and there was a lot of rain, which caused her much fear and anguish.

Then our Lord Jesus Christ said to her, 'Why are you afraid while I am with you? I am powerful enough to look after you here in the countryside as much as in the sturdiest church in the world.'

And after that time she was not so much afraid as she was before, for she always placed great trust in His mercy, blessed may He be who comforted her in every sorrow!

And after that it happened that an Englishman came to this creature and swore a great oath. She, upon hearing that oath, wept, mourned, and sorrowed beyond measure, with no power to restrain herself from weeping and sorrowing, inasmuch as she saw that her brother, who would pay little attention to his own fault, offended our Lord God almighty.

CHAPTER 43

EARLY on the next day,* the good priest, who was like a son to this creature, came to her and said, 'Mother, there's good news! We have a good wind, thanks be to God!'

And at once she gave praise to our Lord, and asked Him for His mercy to grant them continuing good wind and weather, so that they could get home safely. And it was answered and commanded in her soul that they should go on their way in the name of Jesus.

When the priest knew that she would at any rate set off, he said, 'Mother, there's no ship here; there's only a little boat.'

She answered back, 'Son, God's as mighty in a little ship as in a large ship, for I will travel in that boat, by God's leave.'

And when they were in the little boat, great gales and filthy weather started to develop. Then they cried out to God for grace and mercy, and then the gale ceased, and they had fine weather and sailed all through the night and through the next day until evensong, and then they reached land. And when they were on land, the said creature fell down on her knees, kissing the ground, highly praising God who had brought them home safely.

Then this creature had neither a penny nor a ha'penny in her purse. And so they happened to meet other pilgrims who gave her three ha'pennies on account of her having told them some godly stories in conversation. And then she was very cheerful and merry, for she had some money that she might offer in worship of the Trinity when she reached Norwich, as she had when she had left England.*

And so when she got there, she made an offering with a very good will, and after that she went with her companions to the vicar of St Stephen's, Master Richard Caister,* who was then still alive. And he led them with him to the place where he ate his meals and made them very welcome indeed; and he said to the aforementioned creature, 'Margery, I marvel at how you can be so merry when you have had such great labours and have travelled so far from here.'

'Sir, it's because I have great reason to be merry and to rejoice in our Lord, who has helped me and assisted me and brought me back safely, blessed and worshipped may He be!'

And so they talked about our Lord for a good while and it was all very pleasant. And then they took their leave, and she went to an anchorite, who was a monk from a distant region and lived in the Chapel in the Fields.* He had a name for his great perfection and had, previously, loved this creature very much. And after that, through the wicked talk he heard about her, he utterly turned against her. And therefore she went to him with the purpose of humbling herself and drawing him to charity, if she could. When she had come to him, he welcomed her curtly and asked her what she had done with her child, the which was conceived and born whilst she had been away, as he had heard tell. And she said, 'Sir, I have brought home the same child that God has sent me, for God knows that since I went away I never did anything through which I might have a child.'

And yet he would not believe her for anything that she could say. And nevertheless she still humbly and meekly told him, because of the trust she had in him, how it had been our Lord's will that she should be dressed in white clothing.

And he said, 'God forbids it', for she would then make the whole world wonder at her.

And she replied, 'Sir, I do not care, so long as God is pleased with it.'

Then he asked her to come back to him and be overseen by him and by a good priest called Sir Edward.* And she said she should first learn whether it was God's will or not, and with that she then took her leave of him. And as she went on her way away from him, our Lord said to her soul, 'I do not wish you to be overseen by him.'

And she sent him word of the answer she had from God.

CHAPTER 44

AND then she prayed to God, saying, 'As surely, Lord, as it is your will that I should be dressed in white, as surely grant me a sign of lightning, thunder, and rain—in such a way that neither hinders nor harms me—so that I, unworthy, may the sooner fulfil your will.'

Then our Lord answered and said to His unworthy servant, 'Daughter, do not doubt it, you shall have that sign within three days.'

And so it was. On the following Friday, early in the morning, as she lay in her bed, she saw great lightning, she heard great thunder, and great rain followed, and just as quickly it passed over and the weather was fair again. And then she fully intended to wear white clothes, except she had neither gold nor silver with which to buy her clothing.

And then our Lord said to her soul, 'I shall provide for you.'

Then she went to an honourable man in Norwich, by whom she was warmly welcomed, and was received very kindly. And as they sat together telling godly stories, our Lord kept on saying to her soul, 'Speak to this man! Speak to this man!'

Then she said to that honourable man, 'God wishes, sir, that I might find a good man who will lend me two nobles until I can pay him back, to buy myself clothes with.'

And he said, 'I will happily do that, madam. What clothes do you wish to wear?'

'Sir,' she said, 'white clothes, with God's permission.'

So this good man bought white cloth, and made her a gown from it, and a hood, a kirtle, and a cloak. On the Saturday, that is the next day, in the evening he brought her this clothing and gave it to her for God's love, and he did many other good deeds to her for our Lord's love—may Christ Jesus be his reward and have mercy upon his soul and on all Christians! And on the Trinity Sunday* following thereafter, she received communion all in white, and after that she suffered much spitefulness and much shame in many different regions, cities, and towns, thanks be to God for all of it.

Soon afterwards her husband came from Lynn to Norwich to

see how she was getting on and how she had thrived, and then they went home together to Lynn. Then she, after a short while, fell into a grave sickness, so much so that she received extreme unction* because she was expected to die. And she desired, if it were God's will, that she might visit Santiago* before she died, and that she might suffer all the more shame for His love, as He had promised beforehand that she should. And then our Lord said to her in her soul that she should not yet die, and she herself had thought that she should not live because her pain was so great. And shortly afterwards she was hale and hearty.

And when winter was approaching she was so cold that she did not know what she might do because she was poor and had no money, and she was also in great debt. Then she suffered the shames and disgrace of wearing her white clothes, and because she cried so loud when our Lord brought His Passion to her mind. And for the compassion that she had for our Lord's Passion she cried so amazingly loudly, and they had never heard her cry beforehand, and it was all the more marvellous to them. The first time she cried was at Jerusalem, as is written before.

Many people said that there was never a saint in heaven who cried like she did, from which they concluded that she had a devil inside her which caused her crying. And they said this openly, and many more wicked things besides. And she took it all patiently for our Lord's love, for she knew well that the Jews said much worse of His own person than people did of her. And therefore she took it all the more meekly.

Some people said that she had epilepsy as she, with her crying, twisted her body,* turning from one side to the other, and she went all black and blue, like the colour of lead. And then folk spat at her in horror of the illness, and some of them scorned her and said that she howled like a dog, and chided her, and cursed her, and said that she did much harm amongst the people. And then those that beforehand had given her both meat and drink for God's love, now they cast her aside and asked her not to come near them, because of the roguish tales that they had heard about her.

And afterwards, when the time came for her to go to Santiago, she went to the best friends she had in Lynn and told them about her intentions, how she proposed to go to Santiago, if she had the money to travel, she was poor and owed many debts. And her friends said to her, 'Why have you given away your money, and other people's too? Where will you get as much money as you owe?'

And she said back, 'Our Lord God shall be a great help, for He never failed me in any region, and for that I trust Him very much.'

Then suddenly a good man came along and gave her forty pence, and with this sum she bought herself a fur pelisse.

And all the time our Lord said to her, 'Daughter, pay no attention to money, as I shall provide for you, but always give your attention to loving me and keep your mind on me, for I shall go with you wherever you go,* as I have before promised you.'

Then afterwards a woman came along, a good friend to this creature, and gave her seven marks so she should pray for her when she reached Santiago. And then she took her leave of her friends in Lynn, intending to progress as quickly as she could. And then it was said in Lynn that there were many thieves on the route. She was very afraid then that they should rob her and take her gold away from her. And our merciful Lord, comforting her, said to her, 'Go forth, daughter, in the name of Jesus, no thief shall have power over you.'

Then she went forth and came to Bristol* on the Wednesday in Whit Week,* and there she found the hunchbacked man ready who had been with her in Rome, whom she had left in Rome when she came to England two years earlier. And while they were in Rome, she borrowed a sum of gold from him and, at God's bidding, she gave all the money that she had (and that she had borrowed from him too) away to poor people, as is written before. And then while she was in Rome, she promised him that she would pay him back in Bristol at this time, and so he had come there for his repayment. And our Lord Jesus Christ so arranged it for her, as she went towards Bristol, that so much money was given to her that she could easily pay the aforesaid man all that she owed him. And so she did, for which may our Lord be blessed.

And then she stopped in Bristol at the bidding of God to wait six weeks for a ship, on account of there being no English ships that might sail from there as they had been detained and requisitioned for the King.* And other pilgrims who were at Bristol, wishing to hurry on their journey, went about from port to port but had no more success; and so they came back to Bristol, while she stopped there and progressed better than them for all their efforts.

And while she had thus stopped in Bristol at the request of God, our merciful Lord Christ Jesus visited His creature with many holy meditations, and much high contemplation, and many sweet comforts. And she received communion there every Sunday with plentiful tears and violent sobbing, with loud crying and shrill shrieking. And therefore many men and many women wondered at her, scorned her, and despised her, banished her and cursed her, said many evil things of her, slandered her, and asserted that she had said things that she had never said. And then she wept very bitterly for her sins, praying God for mercy and forgiveness for them, saying to our Lord, 'Lord, as you said, hanging on the Cross, for your crucifiers, "Father, forgive them, for they know not what they do",* so I beseech you, forgive the people all the scorn and slander and all that they have trespassed, if it is your will, for I have deserved much more and I am much more worthy.'

CHAPTER 45

On the following Corpus Christi Day,* as the priests carried the sacrament around the town in solemn procession with many candles and great solemnity (as it was appropriate to do), the aforesaid creature followed, full of tears and devotion, with holy thoughts and meditation, painful weeping and noisy sobbing. And then a good woman came to this creature and said, 'Madam, God give us grace to follow the footsteps of our Lord Jesus Christ.'

Then those words worked so sharply in her heart and in her mind that she could not bear it, she was glad to go into a house. And there she cried, 'I'm dying! I'm dying!', and roared so astonishingly that the people gawped at her, wondering at what was ailing her. Yet our Lord made some of them love and cherish her very much, and they took her home for both food and drink and were very glad to hear her converse about our Lord.

So, there was a man from Newcastle*—his name was Thomas Marshall*—who often invited this creature to dine with him, in order to hear her conversation. And he was so drawn by the good words that God put in her to say of contrition and compunction, of sweetness and of devotion, that he was all altered as if he were a new man, with tears of contrition and compunction, both day and night, as our Lord wished to visited his heart with grace that sometimes, when he went into the countryside, he wept so bitterly for his sins and his trespasses that he fell down and could not bear it, and he told the said creature that he had been a very foolhardy and disobedient man and that he bitterly repented, thanks to God. And then he blessed the day that he had met this creature and fully intended to be a good man. And he said to the said creature, 'Mother, I've got ten marks here. I beg you that it be yours, as your own, for I will help you on your way to Santiago with God's grace. And whatever you ask me to give to any poor man or woman, I will do what you ask—always one penny for you, another for myself.'

Then, as it pleased our Lord, he sent a ship from Brittany to Bristol, the which ship was readied and equipped to sail to Santiago. And then the said Thomas Marshall went and paid the ship's master for himself and the said creature.

Then there was a rich man from Bristol who would not let the said creature sail in that ship, as he considered her to be no good woman. And then she said to that rich man, 'Sir, if you banish me from the ship, my Lord Jesus shall banish you from Heaven, for I tell you, sir, our Lord Jesus has no liking for a rich man unless he is a good man and a meek man.'

And so she said many severe words to him without any cajoling or flattering; and then our Lord said to her in her soul, 'You shall have your way and go to Santiago at your desire.'

And then afterwards she was called before the Bishop of Worcester,* who lodged three miles away from Bristol,* and ordered to appear before him as he lodged there. She got up early the next day and went to the place where the Bishop lodged and, whilst he was still in bed, she happened to meet one of his most illustrious men in the town, and so they conversed about God. And when he had heard her talking for a good while, he asked her to dine and after that he brought her into the Bishop's hall. And when she came into the hall, she saw many of the Bishop's men with their clothes all modishly striped and cut.* Lifting up her hand, she blessed herself. And then they said to her, 'What the devil's wrong with you?'

She spoke back, 'Whose men are you?'

They answered, 'The Bishop's men.'

And then she said, 'No, in truth, you're more like the Devil's men.'

Then they were angry, and they rebuked her and spoke angrily to her, and she withstood them well and meekly. Then after that she spoke so gravely against sin and against their misconduct that they went silent, and found themselves very pleased with her conversation—thank God—before she left.

And then she went into the church and awaited the arrival of the Bishop. And when he came, she knelt down and asked him what it was he wanted, and why she had been summoned to come before him; it was a great nuisance and hindrance to her, on account of her being a pilgrim and heading, by the grace of God, towards Santiago.

Then the Bishop said, 'Margery, I have not summoned you, for I know full well that you are the daughter of John Burnham of Lynn. I beg you not to be angry, but behave pleasantly towards me and I'll behave pleasantly with you, for you shall dine with me today.'

'Sir,'* she said, 'I beg you to excuse me, but I have promised a good man in town that I shall eat with him today.'

And then he said, 'You shall both eat with me.'

And so she waited with him until God sent wind so that she might sail, and was made most welcome by him and by his household too. And after that she made her confession to the Bishop. And then he asked her to pray for him so that he might die in charity, as he had been warned by a holy man who had a revelation that this Bishop should be dead within two years. And indeed so it happened. And he lamented this to this creature and asked her to pray for him, so that he might die in charity. In the end she took her leave of him, and he gave her gold coins and his blessing, and instructed his household to lead her forth on her route. And also he asked her, when she came back from Santiago, to visit him.

So on she went to her ship. Before she embarked on the ship, she made her prayers that God should watch them and preserve them from affliction, storms, and peril at sea, so that they might leave and return in safety, as she had been told that if there was a storm she would be thrown into the sea, because they said it was because of her; and they said that the ship was the worse because she was on it. And therefore she said her prayers in this manner: 'Almighty God Christ Jesus, I beseech you for your mercy, if you wish to chastise me, spare me until I come back to England. And when I come back, chastise me just as you wish.'

And then our Lord granted her wish. So she embarked on her ship in the name of Jesus and sailed off with her party, whom God sent fair wind and weather, so they reached Santiago in seven days. And then those who were against her when they were in Bristol were now very friendly towards her. And so they stayed there in that country for fourteen days* and she had a very pleasant time there, both physically and spiritually, and high devotion, and many great cryings in having our Lord's Passion in mind, with plentiful tears of compassion.

After that they came back home to Bristol in five days. She did not stay there long, but went on to the Blood of Hailes,* and there she was shriven at confession and had loud crying and noisy weeping. And then the religious men had her amongst them and made her very welcome, except they swore many grave and horrible oaths. And she reprimanded them for it in accordance with the Gospel, and they were astonished at that. Nevertheless, some were well pleased with it, thanked be God in His goodness.

CHAPTER 46

AFTER that she went on to Leicester,* with a good man too, Thomas Marshall, about whom it is written before. And there she went into a fair church where she regarded a crucifix that was stirringly painted and harrowing to regard, and, through regarding it, the Passion of Our Lord entered her mind, whereupon she began to melt and utterly dissolve in tears of pity and compassion. Then the fire of love* was kindled so smartly in her heart that she could not keep it private, whether she wished to or not, it caused her to break out in a loud voice and she cried astonishingly, and wept and sobbed most hideously, so that many men and women gawped at her because of it.

When it had passed over, she was going out of the church door when a man took her by the sleeve and said, 'Madam, why are you weeping so bitterly?'

'Sir,' she said, 'you are not to be told.'

And so she and the good man, Thomas Marshall, went on and procured their hostel and ate their dinner there. When they had eaten, she asked Thomas Marshall to write a letter and send it to her husband, so that he could fetch her home. And while the letter was being written, the innkeeper came up to her chamber in great haste and took away her purse and asked her to come quickly and speak with the Mayor.* And so she did. Then the Mayor asked her from what region she came and whose daughter she was.

'Sir,' she said, 'I am from Lynn in Norfolk, a good man's daughter of the same Lynn, who has five times been mayor of that honourable borough, and alderman too for many years, and I have a good man, also a burgess of the said town, Lynn, for my husband.'

'Ah,' said the Mayor, 'St Katherine* described what kin she came of, and yet you're not like her, because you're a false strumpet, a false Lollard,* and a false deceiver of the people, and therefore I shall have you imprisoned.'

So she replied, 'I am as ready, sir, to go to prison for God's love as you are ready to go to church.'

After the Mayor had long chided her and said many wicked and horrible words to her and she, by the grace of Jesus, had answered intelligently to all that he could say, then he commanded the jailer's helper to lead her to prison. The jailer's helper, feeling compassion for her, with tears streaming, said to the Mayor, 'Sir, I have no room to put her in, unless I put her amongst men.'

Then she, moved with compassion for the man who had compassion for her, praying for grace and mercy to that man as if for her own soul, said to the Mayor, 'I beg you, sir, not to put me amongst men, so that I can keep my chastity and my bond of wedlock to my husband, as I am bound to do.'

And then the jailer himself said to the Mayor, 'Sir, I will be duty bound to guard this woman in safe-keeping until you want her back.'

Then there was a man from Boston,* and he said to the landlady where she was lodging, 'Truth to tell', he said, 'in Boston this woman is regarded as a holy woman and a blessed woman.'

Then the jailer took her under his watch, and led her home to his own house and put her in a fair chamber, shutting the door with a key and entrusting his wife to guard the key. Nevertheless he let the creature go to church whenever she wished, and let her eat at his own table, and made her very welcome for our Lord's love, may almighty God be thanked for it!

CHAPTER 47

THEN the Steward of Leicester,* a handsome man, sent to the jailer's wife for the said creature, but the jailer's wife—as her husband was not at home—would not let her go to any man, steward or otherwise. When the jailer knew of this, he came in person and brought this creature before the Steward. Then the Steward, when he saw her, spoke Latin to her, with many priests and other people too standing around to hear what she might say. She said to the Steward, 'Speak English, if you please, as I don't understand what you're saying.'

The Steward said to her, 'You lie falsely, in plain English.'

Then she said back to him, 'Sir, ask whatever question you want in English and, through the grace of my Lord Jesus Christ, I shall answer it intelligently.'

So then he asked many questions, which she answered eagerly and intelligently, so that he could not make a cause against her. Then the Steward took her by the hand and led her into his chamber and spoke many foul lewd words to her, intending and desiring (as it seemed to her) to violate her and rape her. And then she was very afraid and very distressed; crying out at him for mercy, she said, 'Sir, out of reverence for almighty God, spare me, for I am a man's wife.'

And then the Steward said, 'You'll tell me whether you get your speech from God or from the Devil, or else you'll go to prison.'

'Sir,' she said, 'I am not afraid to go to prison for my Lord's love, who suffered more for my love than I can for His. I ask that you do as you think best.'

The Steward, seeing her boldness, that she was unafraid of imprisonment, grappled with her, making dirty gestures and making wicked faces at her, through which he frightened her so much that she told him how she had her speech and her communication from the Holy Ghost and not from her own knowledge. And then he, utterly astounded by her words, put aside his actions and his lewdness, and said to her, as many a man had done before, 'Either you're a really good woman or else you're a really wicked woman', and he delivered her again to her jailer. And he led her back home with him.

After that they took two of her fellows who had been on pilgrimage with her—one was the aforementioned Thomas Marshall, the other was a man from Wisbech*—and put them both in prison because of her. Then she was downcast and sorry for their distress, and prayed to God for their deliverance. And then our merciful Lord Christ Jesus said to His creature, 'Daughter, for your love, I shall so dispose for them that the people will be very pleased to let them go and not detain them for long.'

And on the next day, our Lord sent such weather, of lightning, thunder, and constant rain, that all the people in the town were so afraid they did not know what to do. They feared that it was because they had put the pilgrims in prison. And then the town authorities went in great haste and took out the two pilgrims, who had lain in prison all the night before, and led them to the Guildhall* to be examined there in front of the Mayor and the town's respectable men, requiring them to swear whether the aforementioned creature was a woman of the correct faith and correct belief, chaste and clean in her body, or not. As far as they knew, they swore, as surely as God should help them at Judgement Day, that she was a good woman of the correct faith and correct belief, clean and chaste in all her conduct, as far as they could know, in manner, bearing, in word and in deed.

And then the Mayor let them go wherever they wished. And then the storm subsided, and it was fair weather, may our Lord God be worshipped. The pilgrims, who were glad that they had been discharged, dared stay in Leicester no longer but went ten miles from there and waited there until they knew what they should do with the said creature, as when they were both put in prison they had themselves told her that they supposed that if the Mayor might have his way, he would have her burned.

CHAPTER 48

ONE Wednesday the said creature was brought into the Church of All Hallows at Leicester,* where the Abbot of Leicester* was sitting in front of the high altar with some of his canons and the Dean of Leicester,* a worthy cleric. There were also many friars and priests, and the Mayor of the same town too, with many other lay people. There were so many people that they stood on stools to look at her and marvel at her. The said creature went down onto her knees, making her prayers to Almighty God that she might have the grace, wit, and wisdom to answer that day in such a way as would be most gratifying and respectful to Him, most profitable to her soul, and the best example to the people.

Then a priest came to her and took her by the hand and brought her before the Abbot and his advisers, sitting by the altar, who had her swear on a book that she should answer truly to the Articles of the Faith just as she felt about them. And first they repeated the blessed sacrament of the altar, charging her with saying precisely how she believed in it.*

Then she said, 'Sirs, I believe in the sacrament of the altar in this way: that whatever man has taken the order of priesthood, however wicked a man he is in his way of life, if he duly say those words over the bread that our Lord Jesus Christ said when He celebrated His Last Supper amongst His disciples, I believe that it is His true flesh and His blood and not ordinary bread,* and it cannot be unsaid if it is once said.'

And so she went on to answer about all the Articles, as many as they would ask her, so that they were very pleased. The Mayor, who was her deadly enemy, said, 'Truly, she doesn't mean with her heart what she says with her mouth!'

And the clerics said to him, 'Sir, she answers us very well.'

Then the Mayor utterly rebuked her and repeated many insulting and unpleasant words, which it would be more expedient to conceal than to express.

'Sir,' she said, 'I take as witness my Lord Jesus Christ, whose body is present here in the sacrament of the altar, that I have never actually had any part of a man's body in this world by way of sin, except my husband's body, to whom I am bound by the law of matrimony, and by whom I have borne fourteen children.* For I'll have you know, sir, that there's no man in this world that I love as much as God, for I love Him above all things, and, sir, I tell you truly that I love all men in God and for God.'

And furthermore she said openly to his face, 'Sir, you are not worthy to be a mayor, and I shall prove that through Holy Writ, for our Lord God said Himself, before He would take vengeance on the cities, "I will go down and see",* and yet He knew all things. And, sir, that was for nothing other than to show men like you that you should implement no punishment, unless you know beforehand that it's fitting. And, sir, you have done quite the opposite to me today for, sir, you have caused me much humiliation for things that I am not guilty of. I pray God forgives you for it.'

Then the Mayor said to her, 'I want to know why you go about in white clothes, as I believe that you have come here to take our wives away from us and lead them off with you.'

'Sir,' she said, 'you shall not know from my mouth why I go about in white clothes; you're not worthy enough to know it. But, sir, I will tell these worthy clerics, most willingly, through the form of confession. Let them consider whether they will tell it to you.'

Then the clerics asked the Mayor to go down from them, along with other people. And when they had gone, she knelt down on her knees in front of the Abbot, and the Dean of Leicester, and a Preaching Friar, a respected cleric, and told these three clerics how our Lord warned her through revelation and asked her to wear white clothes before she got to Jerusalem.

'And I have told my spiritual confessors just so. And therefore they have charged me that I should go about like this, as they daren't go against my feelings for fear of God, and if they dared, they would do so most happily. Therefore, sirs, if the Mayor wants to know why I go about in white, you may say, if you like, that my spiritual confessors have asked me to go about like this, and then you will tell no lies but he will not know the truth.'

So the clerics called back the Mayor and told him in confidence that her spiritual confessors had charged that she wear white clothes and she had bound herself to obedience to them. Then the Mayor called her to him, saying, 'I will not let you go away from here in spite of anything you say unless you will go to my Lord, the Bishop of Lincoln, for a letter, in as much as you are in his jurisdiction, so I can be rid of you.'

She said, 'Sir, I am very happy to speak to my Lord, the Bishop of Lincoln, for I have been made most welcome by him before this time.'

And then the other men asked her if she felt charitable towards the Mayor, and she said, 'Yes, and with all creatures.'

And then she, with tears falling, making a low bow to the Mayor, asked him to be charitable towards her, and forgive her for any thing she may have done to displease him. And he gave her some fine words for a while, so that she believed all was well and that he was her good friend, but afterwards she knew well that it was not so. And so she left the Mayor to go to my Lord, the Bishop of Lincoln, and to fetch a letter by which the Mayor might be discharged of his responsibility for her.

CHAPTER 49

So she went first to the Abbey at Leicester,* into the church and, as soon as the Abbot had spotted her he, in his goodness, with many of his brethren, came to welcome her. When she saw them coming, in her soul she then beheld our Lord coming with His apostles, and she was so enraptured with the sweetness and devotion of contemplation that she could not stand up as they approached, as courtesy

demanded, but leant against a pillar in the church and held it tightly
for fear of falling over, as she wished to stand but could not for the
abundance of devotion, which caused her to cry and weep very bitterly. When her crying had passed over, the Abbot asked his brother
to have her brought in to them and to comfort her, and so they gave
her very good wine and made her very welcome.

Then she got herself a letter from the Abbot to my Lord, the
Bishop of Lincoln, as an attestation of the conversations she had had
during the time she was in Leicester. And the Dean of Leicester was
ready to attest and bear witness for her too, as he had great confidence
that our Lord loved her, and therefore he welcomed her very warmly
into his own palace.

And so she took her leave of her aforementioned son,* intending
to go towards Lincoln with a man called Patrick,* who had been with
her in Santiago beforehand. At this time he was sent to Leicester by
the aforementioned Thomas Marshall from Melton Mowbray,* to
enquire after and find out how things stood with that creature; as the
said Thomas Marshall very much feared that she should be burned,
and therefore he sent this man called Patrick to learn the truth.

So she and Patrick, with many good Leicester folk who came to greet
her, thanking God who had protected her and given her victory over
her enemies, went out to the edge of the town and were warmly wished
goodbye. They promised her that if she ever came back she would be
more warmly welcomed amongst them than she ever had been before.

Then she realized that she had forgotten and left in the town
a staff like Moses' rod* that she had brought from Jerusalem, and
she would not have lost it for forty shillings. Then Patrick went back
into the town for her staff and her purse and happened to meet with
the Mayor, and the Mayor wanted to put him in prison. In the end he
escaped with difficulty and left her purse there.

The aforementioned creature waited for this man in a blind
woman's house in severe depression, dreading what had happened to
him, as he took so long. In the end this man came riding up to where
she was. When she saw him she cried, 'Patrick, son, where have you
been away from me for so long?'

'Yes, yes, mother,' he said, 'I've been in great peril for you. I was
on the point of being put in prison for you, and the Mayor has very
much persecuted me because of you, and he has taken away your
purse from me.'

'Oh, good Patrick,' she said, 'don't be displeased, for I shall pray for you, and God shall reward your labours well; it will all be for the best.'

Then Patrick set her on his horse and brought her home to Melton Mowbray, into his own house, where the aforementioned Thomas Marshall was, who took her down from the horse greatly giving thanks to God that she had not been burnt. So they rejoiced in our Lord all that night.

Afterwards she went on to the Bishop of Lincoln, where he was lodging at that time. She, not really knowing where he was, met a respectable man with a furred hood, a decent officer of the Bishop's, who said to her, 'Madam, don't you know me?'

'No, sir,' she said, 'truly.'

'And yet you're beholden to me,' he said, 'as I've previously made much of you.'

'Sir, I trust that what you did you did for God's love, and therefore I hope that he shall reward you very well now. And I beg that you excuse me, as I take little notice of a man's beauty or of his face, and therefore I forget him all the more quickly.'

And then he kindly told her where she should find the Bishop. And so she got herself a letter from the Bishop to the Mayor of Leicester, admonishing him that he should neither vex her nor stop her from coming and going as she pleased.

Then there was great thunder and lightning and much rain, so that the people thought that it was in vengeance for the said creature, and they really wanted her to leave that region. And she in no way wanted to leave until she had her purse back.

When the said Mayor received the aforementioned letter, he sent her purse to her and let her go about in safety wherever she wished. She was delayed in her journey for three weeks by the Mayor of Leicester, before he would let her leave that area. Then she hired the aforementioned man, Patrick, to go into the regions, and so they went on to York.

CHAPTER 50

WHEN she had got to York, she went to an anchoress whom she had really loved before she went to Jerusalem, in order to have knowledge of her spiritual growth and desiring more spiritual communication too, and that day to eat with the anchoress nothing but bread and water, for it was on Our Lady's Eve.* And the anchoress would not receive her as she had heard so much evil said about her. So she went on to other people, strangers, and they made her welcome for our Lord's love.

One day, as she sat in a church in York,* our Lord Jesus Christ said in her soul, 'Daughter, there is much tribulation coming your way.'

She was somewhat sad and dismayed at this, and therefore she, sitting silent, did not answer.

Then our blessed Lord said back to her, 'What, daughter, are you displeased by suffering more tribulation for my love? If you wish to suffer no more, I shall take it away from you.'

And then she replied, 'No, good Lord, let me be at your will, and make me mighty and strong always to suffer what you wish me to suffer, and grant me meekness and patience with it.'

And so, from that time forward, she knew it was our Lord's will that she should suffer more tribulation, she received it well when our Lord would send it, and thanked him highly for it, being very glad and happy on those days when she suffered some hardship. In due course, on any day on which she suffered no tribulation she was not as cheerful and glad as a day on which she suffered tribulation.

After that, as she was in the said York Minster, a cleric came to her, saying, 'Madam, how long will you be staying here?'

'Sir,' she said, 'I intend to stay for fourteen days.'

And so she did. And in that time many good men and women asked her to dine and made her very welcome, and were very glad to hear her conversation, greatly marvelling at her speech, for it was spiritually fruitful.

And also she had many enemies who slandered her, scorned her, and despised her, and one priest came to her, while she was in the said Minster, and, taking her by the collar of her gown, said, 'You wolf, what is that clothing you're wearing?'

She stood silently and did not wish to answer in her own defence. Children of the monastery,* passing by, said to the priest, 'Sir, it's wool!'

The priest was annoyed because she would not answer and he began to swear many grave oaths. Then she began in God's defence; she was not afraid. She said, 'Sir, you should keep God's commandments and not swear as thoughtlessly as you do.'

The priest asked her who kept the commandments.

She said, 'Sir, those who keep them.'

Then he said, 'Do you keep them?'

She said back to him, 'Sir, it is my will to keep them, for I am bound to, and so are you and every person who will be saved in the end.'

When he had long sparred with her, he quietly went away before she noticed, and she did not know what became of him.

CHAPTER 51

ANOTHER time, an important cleric came up to her, asking how the words *Crescite et multiplicamini** should be understood. She, answering, said, 'Sir, these words are not understood only in terms of producing children physically but also in terms of the attainment of virtue, which is spiritual fruit, such as through the hearing of God's words, through setting a good example, through meekness and patience, charity and chastity, and other such things, for patience is more praiseworthy than miracle-working.'

And she, through the grace of God, answered so that cleric was very pleased. And our Lord, in His mercy, always made it so some men loved and supported her. And so in this city of York there was a doctor of divinity, Master John Acomb,* and also a canon from the Minster, Sir John Kendal,* and another priest who sang by the Bishop's tomb; these were her good friends at the church court.

So she stayed put in that city for fourteen days, as she had said before, and somewhat more, and on the Sundays she received communion in the Minster with much weeping, noisy sobbing, and loud crying, so that many people really wondered what was wrong with her. So afterwards a priest came along, he seemed like a respectable cleric, and he said to her, 'Madam, you said when you first came here that you'd stay here for only fourteen days.'

'Yes, sir, with your leave, I said that I would stay here for fourteen days, but I did not say that I would stay here for either more or less. But right now, sir, I truly tell you, I'm not leaving yet.'

Then he set a day, commanding her to appear in front of him in the Chapter House.* And she said that she would willingly obey his command. She then went to Master John Acomb, the aforesaid doctor, pleading with him to be there on her side. And so he was, and he found great favour amongst all of them. Also, another master of divinity had promised her that he would be there with her, but he held back until he knew how the case would proceed, whether with her or against her.

That day there were so many people in the Minster's Chapter House who had come to hear and to see what would be said or done to the aforementioned creature. When the day came, she was in the Minster all ready to come to her own defence. Then her friends came to her and urged her to have a cheery manner. She, thanking them, said that she would do so. And a very good priest came at once and kindly took her by the arm to help her through the crowd of people and he brought her before a venerable doctor, the one who had commanded her to appear before him in the York Minster Chapter House on this day. Many other clerics sat with this doctor, all honourable and venerable, and some of these clerics loved the said creature very much. Then the venerable doctor said to her, 'Woman, what are you doing here in this region?'

'Sir, I came here on pilgrimage to make an offering at the shrine of St William.'*

He said back to her, 'Have you got a husband?'

She said, 'Yes.'

'Have you got an affidavit from your husband?'*

'Sir,' she said, 'my husband gave me leave with his own mouth. Why are you carrying on with me more than you do other pilgrims who are here, who have no more affidavits than have I? Sir, you let them go about in peace and quiet and in rest, and I'm not allowed any rest amongst you. And, sir, if there is any cleric here amongst all of you who can prove that I have said any word that I ought not to have said, I am ready to make amends for it willingly. I will support neither error nor heresy, as it's my full intention to hold as Holy Church holds and to please God fully.'

Then the clerics examined her in the Articles of the Faith and in many other topics as they liked, to which she answered well and truly, so that they found in her words no occasion to harm her, thanks be to God. And then the doctor, who sat there like a judge, summoned her to appear before the Archbishop of York, and told her on what day, at a town called Cawood,* commanding that she be held in prison until the day of her appearance came around.

Then the laypeople answered for her, and said she should not be taken to prison, as they themselves would vouch for her and go to the Archbishop with her. And so, at that time, the clerics said no more to her, as they rose and went away as they wished, and let her go wherever she wished, worship be to Jesus!

Then soon after a cleric came to her—one of the same ones who had sat against her—and said, 'Madam, I ask you not to be displeased with me, though I sat with the doctor against you. He berated me so that I dared not do otherwise.'

And she said, 'Sir, I am not displeased with you for this.'

Then he said, 'I ask you then, pray for me.'

'Sir,' she said, 'I will very gladly do so.'

CHAPTER 52

THERE was a monk who preached in York, and had heard many slanders and many evil things about the said creature. And, when he went to preach, there was a great crowd of people to hear him, and she was present amongst them. So, during his sermon, he repeated many matters so openly that the people fully understood that it was because of her, at which her friends who really loved her were very distressed and dejected, and she was much the merrier, because these circumstances tested her patience and her charity, by way of which she confidently expected to please our Lord Jesus Christ.

After the sermon, a doctor of divinity who, along with many others, loved her very much, came to her and said, 'Margery, how did you get on today?'

'Sir,' she said, 'very well indeed, God be blessed! I've reason to be very happy and glad in my soul that I may suffer anything for His love, for He suffered much more for me.'

Soon after, a man who held her in great affection came along, with his wife and some others, and accompanied her seven miles from there to the Archbishop of York,* and brought her into a beautiful room into which a good cleric came, saying to the good man who had brought her there, 'Sir, why have you and your wife brought this woman here? She'll sneak away from you, and then she'll have brought disgrace on you.' The good man said, 'I dare well say she will stay here and answer for herself most willingly.'

On the next day she was led into the Archbishop's chapel, and many of the Archbishop's household came in, looking down on her, calling her 'Lollard' and 'heretic', and swearing many awful oaths that she should be burned. So she, through the strength of Jesus, said back to them, 'Gentlemen, I'm afraid that you shall be burned in eternal Hell unless you correct yourselves for swearing oaths, as you do not keep God's commandments. I would not swear as you do for all the money in the world.' Then they turned away, as if they were ashamed.

Then, saying a prayer in her mind, she asked for grace to conduct herself that day as was most pleasing to God and most profitable to her own soul and as an example to her fellow Christians. Our Lord, in answer to her, said that all would go very well. Eventually the said Archbishop entered the chapel with his clerics, and brusquely said to her, 'Why are you going about in white? Are you a virgin?' Kneeling on her knees in front of him, she said, 'No, sir, I am no virgin; I am a wife.' He ordered his followers to fetch a pair of shackles and ordered that she should be fettered, because she was a faithless heretic. She then said, 'I am no heretic, and you shall not prove me one.' The Archbishop went away and left her standing alone.

Then for a while she composed her prayers to our Lord God Almighty, that He might help her and assist her against all her enemies, spiritual and physical, and her body trembled and shook so amazingly that she was forced to put her hands under her clothes so that it couldn't be seen.

Later, the Archbishop returned to the chapel with many important clerics, amongst whom was the same doctor who had examined her before and the monk who had preached against her a little earlier in York. Some of the people asked whether she were a Christian woman or a Jew; some said she was a good woman, and some said not. Then the Archbishop took his seat, and his clerics too, each according to his rank, many people being present. So during the time the people were gathering themselves and the Archbishop taking his seat, the said creature stood at the back, composing her prayers with great devotion for help and assistance against her enemies, and for so long that she utterly melted into tears. In the end, she cried out loudly, so that the Archbishop and his clerics and many people were utterly astonished by her, because they had not heard such crying before.

When her crying had passed, she approached the Archbishop and fell down on her knees, as the Archbishop said most rudely* to her, 'Why are you weeping like this, woman?' She, in answer, said, 'Sir, some day you shall wish that you had wept as bitterly as I have.' And then, after the Archbishop had put to her the Articles of our Faith, to which God gave her grace to answer well and faithfully and instantly without having to think, so she could not be blamed, then he said to the clerics, 'She knows her religion well enough. What shall I do with her?'

The clerics said, 'We know full well that she knows the Articles of our Faith, but we will not allow her to live amongst us, because the people put great faith in her chatter, and perhaps she will pervert some of them.'

Then the Archbishop said to her, 'I have been told very evil things about you; I have heard tell that you're an utterly wicked woman.' And she answered, 'Sir, likewise, I hear tell that you are a wicked man. And if you are as wicked as people say, then you will never get to Heaven unless you mend your ways while you are here.' Then he said most coarsely, 'Why, you! What do people say about me?' She replied, 'Other people, sir, can tell you well enough.' Then a highly-regarded cleric wearing a furred hood said, 'Quiet! You just talk about yourself, and let him be!'

Then the Archbishop said to her, 'Place your hand on the book in front of me and swear that you shall leave my diocese as soon as you can.'

'No, sir,' she replied. 'I pray you, please permit me to return to York to say goodbye to my friends.' So he gave her leave for one or two days. She thought that this was too short a time, and so she said again, 'Sir, I cannot leave this diocese so hastily, because I need to stay and speak with good people before I leave, and I must, sir, with your permission, travel to Bridlington and speak to my confessor,* a good man, who was the confessor to the good prior who has now been canonized.'

Then the Archbishop said to her, 'You shall swear that you shall neither teach nor censure people in my diocese.'

'No, sir, I shall not swear this,' she said, 'for wherever I go I shall speak of God and censure those who swear grave oaths, until such time that the Pope and Holy Church have ordained that no person should be so bold to speak of God, for God Almighty does not forbid, sir, that we should speak of Him. Moreover, the Gospel mentions that, when the woman had heard our Lord preaching, she approached Him with a loud voice and said, "Blessed is the womb that bore thee, and the paps that gave thee suck."* Then our Lord said again to her, "Yea rather, blessed are they who hear the word of God, and keep it."* Therefore, sir, I think that the Gospel permits me to speak of God.'

'Ah, sir,' said the clerics, 'by this we truly know that she has a devil inside her, as she speaks of the Gospel.'

At once a powerful cleric produced a book and quoted St Paul to support his position, against her, that no woman should preach.* She, answering this, said, 'I don't preach, sir, I enter no pulpit. I use only discussion and good words, and I'll do so as long as I live.'

Then a doctor who had previously examined her said, 'Sir, she told me the worst tale about priests that I have ever heard.' The Archbishop commanded her to tell that tale.

'Sir, by your reverence, I spoke about only one priest by way of example, who, as I have learned, went astray in a wood (through the punishment of God, for the profit of his soul) until night-time came upon him. He, lacking any shelter, found a pretty garden in which he rested that night, with a fair pear-tree in the middle of it, flourishing and ornamented with flowers and blossoms which he found delectable to look at. Then a large and vicious bear came, an ugly sight, shaking the pear-tree and causing all the blossoms to fall. This lawless beast ate and gobbled down all those pretty blossoms. Then, when he had eaten them, he turned his rear-end towards the priest and voided them all out of his nether regions.

'The next day the priest, feeling truly disgusted by this appalling sight, and becoming very miserable about what it might mean, wandered onwards, dejected and pensive. It happened that he encountered a handsome old man,* like a palmer or a pilgrim, who asked the priest why he was so downcast. The priest, repeating the narrative written before, said that he felt great dread and dejection when he had seen that horrible beast defile and devour such fair flowers and blossoms and then afterwards void them so horribly in front of him from his rear-end, and he did not understand what this might mean.

'Then the pilgrim, revealing himself to be the messenger of God, addressed him thus: "Priest, you yourself are the pear-tree, partly flourishing and flowering through your saying of services and administering of the sacraments, though you do so irreverently, as you pay little attention to how you say your matins and your service, as if you're babbling just to reach the end. You go to Mass without devotion, and you are barely contrite for your sins. In this way you receive the fruit of everlasting life, the sacrament of the altar, in a very base frame-of-mind. All day long afterwards you misspend your time, giving yourself over to buying and selling, bargaining and exchanging, just like a man of the world. You sit with your ale, giving yourself over to gluttony and excess, to the lusts of your body, through lechery and impurity. You break God's commandments through swearing, lying, slanders and back-biting, and the practice of other such sins. So, by your wrongdoing, just like the ugly bear, you devour and destroy the flowers and blossoms of virtuous living, causing your eternal damnation and damage to many other people unless you receive the grace of repentance and correction." '

Then the Archbishop, having greatly enjoyed this tale, commended it, saying it was a fine story. Then the cleric who had examined her beforehand in the absence of the Archbishop said, 'Sir, this tale cuts me to the heart.'

The aforementioned creature said to the cleric, 'Ah, honourable doctor, sir, there is a cleric in the place where I mostly live, a good preacher, who boldly speaks against the misconduct of the people and will flatter nobody. He has said many times in the pulpit, "If anybody is displeased by my preaching, note him well, because he is guilty." And you, sir, behave just like this towards me,' she said to the cleric, 'may God forgive you for it.'

This cleric did not know what he could say to her. Afterwards, this same cleric came to her and prayed for her forgiveness for having so opposed her. Also he requested that she pray especially for him. And then some time later the Archbishop said, 'Where shall I find a man who might conduct this woman away from me?'

Many young men suddenly jumped up and every one of them said, 'My Lord, I will go with her.' The Archbishop replied, 'You are too young; I will not have you doing it.'

Then a good, sensible man from the Archbishop's retinue asked his lord what he would give him should he conduct her. The Archbishop proffered five shillings and the man asked for a noble. The Archbishop, in answer, said, 'I don't want to spend so much on her body.'

'Yes, good sir,' said the aforementioned creature, 'our Lord shall reward you very well for it.'

Then the Archbishop said to the man, 'Look, here's five shillings, conduct her quickly out of this region.' She, kneeling down on her knees, asked his blessing. He, requesting her to pray for him, blessed her and released her. Then, returning again to York, she was received by many people and by very important clerics, who rejoiced in our Lord, who had given to her, illiterate though she was, the wit and wisdom to answer so many educated men without shame or criticism, thanks be to God.

CHAPTER 53

AFTERWARDS, that good man who was her escort led her out of the town, and then they went on to her confessor (who was named Sleightholme) at Bridlington,* and spoke with him and with many other good men who had previously welcomed her and done much for her. But she would not stay there, and took her leave to walk onwards on her journey. And then her confessor asked her if she dared not stay because of the Archbishop of York. And she said, 'No, indeed.'

Then the good man gave her silver coins, asking her to pray for him. And so she went on to Hull.* And there, one time, as they went in procession, a fine woman behaved with utter contempt for her, and she said not a word in reply. Many other people said that she should be put in prison and made grave threats. But notwithstanding all their malice, a good man still came and asked her to dine with him and really made her very welcome. Then the malicious people, who had really despised her before, came to this good man and asked him that he should not show her any kindness as they believed her not to be a good woman. The next day, at morning, her host escorted her out to the edge of town, as he dared to put her up no longer.

And so she went to Hessle* and wished to cross the water of the Humber. Then she happened to find there two Preaching Friars and two of the Duke of Bedford's yeomen.* The friars told the yeomen what kind of woman she was, and the yeomen arrested her as she was boarding her boat, and they arrested a man with her too.

'Our lord, the Duke of Bedford, has sent for you,' they said. 'And you are held to be the greatest Lollard in this whole region, and around London too. And we've been looking for you in many regions, and we'll get a hundred pounds for bringing you before our lord.'

She said to them, 'Sirs, I shall go with good will wherever you'll lead me.'

Then they brought her back to Hessle, and men there called her 'Lollard', and women came running out of their houses with their distaffs, crying out, 'Burn this false heretic!'

So, as she went towards Beverley* with the aforementioned yeomen and friars, they many times met with local people, who said to her, 'Madam, abandon this life you have, and go and spin and card wool as other women do, and do not suffer so much shame and so much woe. We would not suffer so much for any money on earth.'

Then she said to them, 'I do not suffer as much sorrow as I would for our Lord's love, as I only endure spiteful words, and our merciful Lord Christ Jesus, worshipped be His name, suffered hard strokes, bitter scourges, and shameful death at the last, for me and for all mankind, blessed may He be. And therefore I'm not suffering at all compared to what He suffered.'

And so, as she went on with the aforementioned men, she told them good tales, until one of the Duke's men who had arrested her said to her, 'I rather regret that I met you, as it seems to me that you speak very fine words.'

Then she said to him, 'Sir, don't regret that you met me. Do your lord's bidding, and I trust that all will be for the best, as I'm really pleased that you met me.'

He replied, 'Madam, if ever you're a saint in Heaven, pray for me!'

She answered, saying back to him, 'Sir, I hope you'll be a saint yourself, and every person who shall come to Heaven.'

So they went onwards until they came into Beverley, where the wife of one of the men who had arrested her lived. And they escorted her there and took her purse and her ring away from her. They arranged a nice room and a decent bed for her, with all the necessaries, locking the door with the key and taking the key away with them.

After that they took the man whom they had arrested with her, who was the Archbishop of York's man, and put him in prison. And soon after, that same day, came reports that the Archbishop had come into the town where his man had been put in prison. The Archbishop had been told about his man's imprisonment, and then he had him let out. Then that man went to the said creature in an angry mood, saying, 'Alas that I ever knew you! I've been imprisoned because of you.'

She, comforting him, replied, 'Have meekness and patience, and you shall have a great reward in Heaven for it.'

So he went away from her. Then she stood looking out from a window, telling many good tales to those who would listen to her, so much so that women wept bitterly and said with much heaviness in their hearts, 'Alas, woman, why should you be burned?'

Then she asked the good woman of the house to give her a drink, as she was terribly thirsty. The good woman said that her husband had taken away the key, and so she could neither come to her nor give her a drink. And then the women took a ladder and set it up at the window, and gave her a pint of wine in a pot, and a cup too, begging her to secrete the pot and cup somewhere, so that when the husband came he should not see it.

CHAPTER 54

THE said creature, lying in her bed the following night, heard with her physical ears a loud voice calling 'Margery.' With that voice she woke, very much afraid, and, lying still and in silence, she made her prayers as devoutly as she could at that moment. And soon our merciful Lord, present everywhere, said to her, comforting His unworthy servant, 'Daughter, it is more pleasing to me that you suffer humiliation and scorn, injustice and distresses, than if your head was chopped off three times a day, every day for seven years. And therefore, daughter, do not be afraid of what any man can say to you. But in my goodness, and in your sorrow that you have suffered for it, you have great reason to be joyful for, when you come home to Heaven, then every sorrow shall be turned to joy for you.'

The next day she was brought into the Chapter House* at Beverley, and the Archbishop of York was there and many important clerics with him—priests, canons, and secular men. Then the Archbishop said to the aforementioned creature, 'What, woman, have you come back? I would happily be rid of you!'

And then a priest brought her before him, and the Archbishop said, in the hearing of all those present, 'Sirs, I had this woman in front of me at Cawood, and there I, with my clerics, examined her in her faith and found no fault in her. Furthermore, sirs, I have since that time spoken with good people who believe her to be a perfect woman* and a good woman. All this notwithstanding, I gave one of my men five shillings to lead her out of this region, to quieten down the local people. And, as they were going on their journey, they were taken and arrested, and my man was put in prison on account of her, and also her gold and her silver was taken away from her, with her beads and her ring, and now she's brought back in front of me. Is there anybody here who can say anything against her?'

Then other people said, 'Here's a friar who knows many things against her.'

The friar came forwards and said that she derided all people of Holy Church, and then he uttered much harsh language against her. Also he said that she should have been burnt at Lynn if it had not been for his order, the Preaching Friars, being there. 'And, sir, she says that she can weep and have contrition whenever she wants.'

Then the two men came there who had arrested her, saying to the friar that she was Cobham's daughter and had been sent to bear letters around the region.* Then they said that she had not been in Jerusalem, or in the Holy Land, or on any other pilgrimage, as she had been in truth.* They denied all true things and maintained lies, as many others had done before. When they had said enough for a long while and a long time, they were quiet.

Then the Archbishop said to her, 'Woman, what do you say to this?'

She said, 'My Lord, saving your reverence, all the words that they're saying are lies.'

Then the Archbishop said to the friar, 'Friar, the words are not heresy; they are slanderous and erroneous words.'

'My Lord,' said the friar, 'she knows her faith well enough. Nevertheless, my Lord Bedford is angry with her, and he will have her.'

'Well, friar,' said the Archbishop, 'you shall escort her to him.'

'No, sir,' said the friar, 'it's not fitting for a friar to go escorting a woman around.'

'But I do not wish', said the Archbishop, 'that the Duke of Bedford should be angry with me because of her.'

Then the Archbishop said to his men, 'Keep watch of the friar until I want to have him back', and he commanded another man to guard the aforementioned creature too, until he would have her back another time as he pleased. The said creature begged him, of his lordship, that she should not be put amongst men, as she was a man's wife. And the Archbishop said, 'No, you shall come to no harm.'

Then he who was charged with looking after her took her by the hand and led her home to his house, and had her sit with him to eat and drink, showing her a warm welcome. Many priests and other men came there to see her and speak with her, and many people had great compassion that she had been so badly treated.

In a short time afterwards, the Archbishop sent for her, and she came into his hall. His retinue was eating, and she was led into his chamber right to his bedside.* Then she, obeying, thanked him for his gracious lordship that he had showed towards her beforehand.

'Yes, yes,' said the Archbishop, 'I have been informed of worse things about you than I ever was before.'

She said, 'My Lord, if it would please you to examine me, I shall acknowledge the truth and if I am found guilty, I will obey your correction.'

Then a Preaching Friar came forwards, who was Suffragan* to the Archbishop, to whom the Archbishop said, 'Now, sir, say now while she is present what you said to me when she wasn't present.'

'Should I?' said the Suffragan.

'Yes,' said the Archbishop.

Then the Suffragan said to the said creature, 'Madam, you were at my Lady Westmoreland's.'*

'When, sir?' she said.

'At Easter,' said the Suffragan.

She, not replying, said, 'Well, sir?'

Then he said, 'My Lady herself was well pleased with you and liked your words well, but you advised my Lady Greystoke,* who is a baron's wife and my Lady Westmoreland's daughter, to leave her husband, and now you've said enough to be burned.'

And so he reiterated many nasty words in front of the Archbishop—it is not expedient to repeat them. In the end she said to the Archbishop, 'My Lord, if it is your wish, I haven't seen my Lady Westmoreland for two years and more. Sir, she sent for me before I went to Jerusalem and, if you please, I will go back to her to get a testimony that I pressed no such matter.'

'No,' said those who were standing around, 'let her be put in prison, and we shall send a letter to the noble Lady, and if what she says is true, let her go quietly without being peevish.'

And she said she was very satisfied that it was so.

Then a great cleric who was standing a little to the side of the Archbishop said, 'Put her in prison for forty days and she shall love God all the better for the rest of her life.'

The Archbishop asked her what tale it was that she had told Lady Westmoreland when she had spoken with her. She said, 'I told her a good tale of a lady who was damned because she would not love her enemies, and of a bailiff who was saved because he loved his enemies and forgave those who had trespassed against him, and still he was held to be an evil man.'

The Archbishop said it was a good tale. Then his steward and many more with him said, crying in loud voices to the Archbishop, 'Lord, we beg you, let her go from here now but if she ever comes back, we shall burn her ourselves.'

The Archbishop said, 'I believe there was never a woman in England who was treated as she is and has been.'

Then he said to the aforementioned creature, 'I do not know what I shall do with you.'

She said, 'My Lord, I ask that you let me have your letter and your seal as a testimonial that I have vindicated myself against my enemies, and that nothing is alleged against me, neither error nor heresy, that can be proved against me, thanks be to our Lord, and let John, your man, bring me back over the water.'

And the Archbishop very happily granted her all her wishes, may our Lord reward him, and delivered her purse with her ring and her beads which the Duke of Bedford's men had taken from her before. The Archbishop was very astonished at how she had money with which to travel about the region, and she said good people gave it to her so that she would pray for them.

Then she, kneeling down, received his blessing and took her leave in a very happy mood, leaving his chamber. And the Archbishop's retinue asked her to pray for them, but the steward was angry, because she laughed and was in good form, and he said to her, 'Holy folk shouldn't laugh.'

She said, 'Sir, I've a great reason to laugh, because the more shame and spite that I suffer, the merrier I may be in our Lord Jesus Christ.'

Then she came down into the hall, and there stood the Preaching Friar who had caused her all that woe. And so she carried on with one of the Archbishop's men, bearing the letter which the Archbishop had granted her as a testimonial, and he brought her to the River Humber,* and there he took his leave of her, returning to his lord and bearing the said letter back with him—so she was left alone, without the people knowing.

All the aforesaid trouble happened to her on Friday, thanks be to God for all.

CHAPTER 55

WHEN she had crossed the River Humber, then she was arrested at once as a Lollard and led towards prison. There happened to be a person there who had seen her before the Archbishop of York and got permission for her to go wherever she wanted, and excused her to the bailiff, witnessing for her that she was no Lollard. And so, in the name of Jesus, she escaped.

Then she met with a London man who had his wife with him. And so she went on her way with them until she came to Lincoln, and there she suffered much scorn and many harmful words, answering back in God's cause without any hindrance, wisely and discreetly, so that many people were astonished by her knowledge. Lawyers there said to her, 'We've been schooled for many years, and yet we're not competent to answer as you do. From whom did you get this knowledge?'

And she said, 'From the Holy Ghost.'

Then they asked, 'Do you have the Holy Ghost?'

'Yes, sirs,' she said, 'nobody can say a good word without the gift of the Holy Ghost, for our Lord Jesus Christ said to His disciples, "Take no thought how or what to speak: for it shall be given you in that hour what to speak. For it is not you that speak, but the spirit of your Father that speaketh in you." '*

And thus our Lord gave His grace to answer them, may He be worshipped!

Another time a great lord's retinue came to her, and they swore many great oaths, saying, 'It's been made known to us that you can tell whether we'll be saved or damned.'

She said, 'Yes, truly I can, for as long as you swear such horrible oaths and break God's commandments as knowingly as you do, and won't put aside your sins, I dare well say that you'll be damned. And if you'll be contrite and shriven for your sins, willingly doing penance and leaving your sin while you can, with the intention of never turning back to it, then I dare well say that you shall be saved.'

'What, can't you tell us anything but this?'

'Sirs,' she said, 'I think this is very good.'

And then they went away from her. After this she went back towards home until she got to West Lynn.* When she got there, she sent into Bishop's Lynn for her husband, and for Master Robert (her confessor) and Master Alan (a doctor of divinity), and she told them, in part, of her tribulations. After that she told them that she could not come home to Bishop's Lynn until she had been to the Archbishop of Canterbury for his letter and his seal.

'For when I was in front of the Archbishop of York,' she said, 'he would give no credence to my words, inasmuch as I didn't have my lord of Canterbury's letter and seal.'

And then she took her leave of the said clerics, asking their blessing, and travelled onwards with her husband to London.* When she got there, she was soon successful in getting her letter from the Archbishop of Canterbury.* And so she stayed in the city of London for a long time and had a very warm welcome from many fine people.

After that she went towards Ely* in order to come home to Lynn, and she was three miles from Ely when a man came riding at great speed and arrested her husband and her too, intending to lead them both to prison. He cruelly rebuked them and reviled them, repeating many insulting words. So in the end she asked her husband to show him my Lord of Canterbury's letter. When the man had read the letter, then he spoke pleasantly and well to them, saying, 'Why didn't you show me your letter before?'

And so they left him, and then they came into Ely and from there home to Lynn, where she suffered many spitefulnesses, many reprimands, many scorns, many slanders, many profanities, and many curses.

And one time a thoughtless man, with little care for his own shame but with willingness and purpose, cast a bowlful of water on her head, as she came down the street. She, totally unmoved by this, said, 'May God make you a good man', highly thanking God for it, as she did about many more occasions.*

CHAPTER 56

AFTERWARDS God punished her with many great and various illnesses. She had dysentery for a long time until she was given extreme unction, thinking she was going to die. She was so feeble that she could not even hold a spoon in her hand. Then our Lord Jesus Christ spoke to her in her soul and said that she should not yet die. Then she recovered again for a little while. And then afterwards she had a severe illness in her head and then in her back, so that she was afraid that she had lost her wits through it. Afterwards, when she had recovered from all this sickness, in a short time another sickness followed, which settled in her right side, lasting over a period of eight years (apart from eight weeks), at different times.

Sometimes she had it once a week, sometimes for thirty hours, sometimes twenty, sometimes ten, sometimes eight, sometimes four, and sometimes two, so hard and so sharp that she had to void everything that was in her stomach, as bitter as if it was gall, neither eating nor drinking while the illness endured, but always groaning until it had gone. Then she would say to our Lord, 'Oh blissful Lord, why did you wish to become a man and suffer so much pain for my sins and for all men's sins that shall be saved, and we are so unkind, Lord, to you, and I, the most unworthy, cannot suffer this little pain? Oh, Lord, for your great pain, have mercy on my little pain; for the great pain that you suffered, do not give me as much as I am worthy of, because I cannot bear as much as I am worthy of. And if it is your will, Lord, that I must bear it, send me patience, or else I may not endure it.

'Oh, blissful Lord, I'd rather suffer all the nasty words that people say about me, and that all clerics should preach against me for your love (so long as it would not be a hindrance to anybody's soul) than to have this pain that I have. It does not hurt me at all to suffer nasty words for your love, Lord, and the world can take nothing from me but esteem and worldly goods, and I set no store at all by the world's esteem.

'And, I pray to you, Lord, to forbid me all kinds of goods and esteem, and kinds of earthly love, namely all those loves and possessions of any earthly thing which might decrease my love towards you, or lessen my merit in Heaven; and all kinds of loves and goods which you know in your Godhead should increase my love for you, I pray to you, grant me to your mercy to your everlasting worship.'

Sometimes, even though the said creature had great bodily sickness, still the Passion of our merciful Lord Christ Jesus was performed in her soul so that for that time she did not feel her own illness but wept and sobbed at the thought of our Lord's Passion, as though she saw Him with her physical eye suffering pain and Passion in front of her.

After that, when eight years had passed, her sickness went away, so that it no longer came week by week as it did before, but her crying and her weeping then increased so much that priests dared not give her communion openly in the church, but rather privately in the Prior's Chapel at Lynn,* out of the people's hearing. In that chapel she had such high contemplation and so much communication with our Lord, so much so that she was put out of the church for His love, so that she cried whenever she should take communion as if her soul and her body should have been taken apart, so that two men held her in their arms until her crying ceased, as she could not bear the abundance of love that she felt in the precious sacrament, which she steadfastly believed to be the true God and man in the form of bread. Then our blissful Lord said to her mind, 'Daughter, I will not have my grace that I give to you hidden, for the more assiduous the people are at hiding and hindering it, the more shall I announce it and make it known to all the world.'

CHAPTER 57

THEN it so happened that another monk came to Lynn at the time of removing* (as was the custom amongst them) and he did not love the aforementioned creature, and would not allow her to come into their chapel, as she had done before he arrived there. Then the Prior of Lynn, Master Thomas Hevingham,* met with the said creature and Master Robert Springold (who was her confessor at the time) and asked them to excuse him if she could no longer take communion in his chapel.

'For there has come,' he said, 'a new brother of mine, who will not come into our chapel as long as she is in it. And therefore provide yourself with another place, please.'

Master Robert answered, 'Sir, then we must have her take communion in the church. We cannot choose, as she has the letter and seal of my Lord of Canterbury, in which we are commanded, by virtue of obedience, to hear her confession and administer the sacrament to her as often as we are required.'

Then she took communion after this time at the high altar in St Margaret's Church, and our Lord visited her with such great grace when she should take communion that she cried so loudly that it could be heard all around the church and outside the church, as if she should have died from it, so that she could not receive the sacrament from the priest's hands, the priest turning back to the altar with the precious sacrament, until her crying had ceased. And then he, turning back to her, would administer the sacrament to her as he ought to do. And so it happened many times when she should receive communion. And sometimes she would weep very quietly and peacefully when receiving the precious sacrament, without any violence, as our Lord would visit her with His grace.

One Good Friday, as the said creature saw priests kneeling on their knees and other dignified people with torches burning in their hands in front of the sepulchre,* devoutly representing the lamentable death and doleful burial of our Lord Jesus Christ according to the good customs of Holy Church, the memory of our Lady's sorrows, which she suffered when she beheld His precious body hanging on the Cross and afterwards buried in front of her sight, suddenly occupied the heart of this creature, drawing her mind entirely into the Passion of our Lord Christ Jesus, whom she beheld with her spiritual eye in the sight of her soul as truly as if she had seen His precious body beaten, scourged, and crucified with her physical eye; the which vision and spiritual observation performed by grace so fervently in her mind, wounding her with pity and compassion, so that she sobbed, roared, and cried and, spreading her arms wide, said with a loud voice, 'I'm dying! I'm dying!' so that many people were astonished by her and wondered what was wrong with her. The more she tried to stop herself from crying, the louder she cried, as it was not in her power to take it or leave it, but only to receive it as God would send it. Then a priest took her in his arms and carried her into the Prior's Cloister in order to give her some air, supposing that she would not be able to sustain it, her travails were so great. Then she went all purple as if she was made of lead and she sweated very profusely.

So this way of crying lasted for a period of ten years, as has been written before.* And every Good Friday in all the aforesaid years she was weeping and sobbing for five or six hours together, and with it she was crying very loudly many times, so that she could not restrain herself, which made her utterly weak and feeble in her physical powers. Sometimes she wept for an hour on Good Friday for the sinfulness of the people, having more sorrow for their sins than for her own, inasmuch as our Lord forgave her her own sins before she went to Jerusalem.

Nevertheless, she wept for her own sins very abundantly whenever it pleased our Lord to visit her with His grace. Sometimes she wept for another hour for the souls in Purgatory; or another hour for those who had suffered misfortune, poverty, or some distress; or another hour for Jews, Saracens, and all false heretics, that God might in His great goodness put aside their blindness, so that they might be turned through His grace to the faith of Holy Church and be children of salvation.

Many times, when this creature went to make her prayers, our Lord said to her, 'Daughter, ask whatever you will, and you shall have it.'*

She said, 'I ask for nothing at all, Lord, except that which you can well give me, and that is mercy, which I ask for the people's sinfulness. You have often said to me during the year that you have forgiven me my sins. Therefore I ask now for mercy for the sinfulness of the people as I would do for my own, because, Lord, you are all charity and charity brought you into this wretched world and caused you to suffer very hard pains for our sins. Why should I not then have charity for the people and desire forgiveness of their sins?

'Blessed Lord, I think that you have shown very great charity towards me, an unworthy wretch. You are as gracious to me as though I was as clean a virgin as any in this world, as though I had never sinned. Therefore, Lord, I wish I had a well of tears with which to constrain you,* so that you should not take total vengeance on man's soul, to separate him from you forever, for it is a hard thing to think that any earthly man should ever do any sin through which he should be separated from your glorious face forever.

'If I might, Lord, also give the people contrition and weeping as you give me for my own sins and other people's sins too, and as easily as I might give a penny from my purse, soon I should fill people's hearts with contrition, so that they can cease their sinfulness. I greatly marvel in my heart, Lord, that I, who have been so sinful a woman and the most unworthy creature that you ever showed your mercy to in the whole world, that I have such great charity to my fellow-Christians' souls that I think, even though they had arranged for me the most shameful death that anybody might suffer on this earth yet I would forgive them for it for your love, Lord, and have their souls saved from everlasting damnation.

'And therefore, Lord, I shall not cease, when I can weep, to weep for them plentifully, if I may succeed. And if you wish, Lord, that I should cease weeping, I ask you to take me out of this world. What should I do here unless I can be of profit to others? For, even if it were possible that the whole world could be saved by the tears of my eyes, I would not be worthy of any thanks. Therefore, all praising, all honour, all reverence must be to you, Lord. If it were your will, Lord, I would, for your love and for amplifying your name, be chopped as small as meat for the pot.'*

CHAPTER 58

ONE time, as the aforementioned creature was in her contemplation, she hungered very severely for God's word and said, 'Alas, Lord, whilst you have so many clerics in this world, you have not wished to send me one of them who might fill my soul with your word and with the reading of holy scripture! All the clerics who preach may not fill it, for it seems to me that my soul is always similarly hungry. If I had money enough, every day I would give a noble to have a sermon every day, because your word is worth more to me than all the money in this world. And therefore, blessed Lord, pity me, for you have taken the anchorite away from me,* who was a unique solace and comfort to me and many times refreshed me with your holy word.'

Then our Lord Jesus Christ answered in her soul, saying, 'One shall come from afar who shall fulfil your desire.'

So, many days after this answer,* a priest came, new to Lynn, who had never known this creature before, and when he saw her going through the streets he was very much moved to speak with her, and enquired of other people what kind of woman she was. They said they trusted to God that she was a very good woman. Afterwards, the priest sent for her, asking her to come and speak with him and with his mother, for he had hired a room for his mother and for him, and so they lived together. Then the said creature came to know what he wanted, and spoke with his mother and with him, and had a really warm welcome from both of them.

Then the priest took a book and read in it how our Lord, seeing the city of Jerusalem, wept thereupon,* repeating the misfortunes and sorrows that should befall it, for she, Jerusalem,* did not know the time of her visitation. When the said creature heard it read how our Lord wept, then she wept bitterly and cried loudly, neither the priest nor his mother knowing the cause of her weeping. When her crying and her weeping had ceased, they rejoiced and were very merry in our Lord. After that she took her leave and left them at that time. When she had gone,* the priest said to his mother, 'I am very astonished at this woman, why she weeps and cries so. Nevertheless, I think she's a good woman, and I very much desire to speak more with her.'

His mother was well pleased, and advised that he should do so. And afterwards the same priest loved her and trusted her very much, and blessed the time since he had known her, for he found great spiritual comfort in her and caused him to examine good scripture and many a good doctor, which he would not have looked at, if she had not been there.

He read many a good book to her about high contemplation and other books too, such as the Bible with commentary by doctors, St Bridget's book, Hilton's book, Bonaventure's *Stimulus Amoris*, the *Incendium Amoris*, and other such books.* And then she knew that it was a spirit sent from God that said to her, as was written a little earlier, when she had complained about a lack of reading material, these words: 'One shall come from afar to fulfil your desire.' And thus she knew from experience that it was a very true spirit.

The aforementioned priest read books to her for the greater part of seven or eight years, very much increasing his understanding and his merit, and he suffered many a spiteful word for his love of her, inasmuch as he read so many books to her and supported her in her weeping and in her crying. Afterwards he was given a benefice and had a large cure of souls, and then he was well pleased that he had read so much beforehand.

CHAPTER 59

THUS, through hearing holy books and through hearing holy sermons, she kept on increasing in contemplation and holy meditation. It would be an impossible thing to write down all the holy thoughts, holy speeches, and the high revelations which our Lord showed to her, both of herself and of other men and women, also of many souls, some to be saved and some to be damned, and this was to her a great punishment and a sharp chastisement; for to know about who should be saved she was really glad and joyful, as she desired (as far as she dared) that all people should be saved, and when our Lord showed to her any that should be damned she felt great pain. She would neither hear nor believe that it was God who showed her such things, and put it out of her mind as far as she might. Our Lord blamed her for this and asked her to believe that it was His high mercy and His goodness to show her His private counsel, saying to her mind, 'Daughter, you must hear about the damned as well as the saved.'

She would give no credence to the counsel of God, but rather she believed that it was some evil spirit sent to deceive her. Then because of her disobedience and her unbelief, our Lord withdrew from her all her good thoughts and all good memories of holy speech and conversation, and the high contemplation that she had been used to beforehand, and He allowed her to have as many evil thoughts as she had before had good thoughts. And this affliction lasted for twelve days altogether, and just as beforehand she had four hours of the morning in holy speeches and dalliance with our Lord, so she now had as many hours of foul thoughts and foul memories of lechery and all dirtiness, as though she should have offered herself in public to all kinds of people.

And so the Devil had led her astray, conversing with her through accursed thoughts, just as our Lord conversed with her beforehand with holy thoughts. And, exactly as she before had many glorious visions and high contemplation in the manhood of our Lord, in our Lady, and in many other holy saints, so now she had horrible and abominable sights, which she could not do anything about, of visions of men's genitals, and other such abominations. She saw, as she truly thought, various religious men, priests and many others, both heathen and Christian, coming before her eyes, so that she could not avoid them or put them out of her view, showing their bare genitals to her. And with this the Devil asked her in her mind to choose which she would have first of all, and she must offer herself in public to all of them. And he said that she liked some of them better than the others. She thought that he spoke the truth: she could not say no; and she had to do his bidding, and yet she would not have done it for the whole world. But yet she thought that it should be done, and she thought that these horrible sights and cursed memories were delightful to her against her will. Wherever she went and whatever she did, these cursed thoughts stayed with her. Whenever she should see the sacrament, or make her prayers, or do any other good deed, such outrage was always put into her mind. She was shriven and did all that she might, but she found no release, until she was nearly at the point of despair. It is impossible to describe in words the pain that she felt and the sorry state she was in.

Then she said, 'Alas, Lord, you have said beforehand that you should never forsake me. Where is the truthfulness of your word now?'

And then straight afterwards a good angel came to her, saying, 'Daughter, God has neither forsaken you nor shall He ever forsake you, as He has promised you. But, because you do not believe that it is the spirit of God that speaks in your soul and shows you His private counsel, of some who shall be saved and some who shall be damned, therefore God chastises you in this way. And this chastising shall last for twelve days until you will believe it is God and no devil who speaks to you.'

Then she said to her angel, 'Ah, I ask you, pray for me to my Lord Jesus Christ that He will vouchsafe to take from me these cursed thoughts and speak to me as He did beforehand, and I shall make a promise to God that I shall believe that it is God who has spoken to me beforehand, as I can no longer endure this great pain.'

Her angel said back to her, 'Daughter, my Lord Jesus will not take it away from you until you have suffered it for twelve days, for He wishes that you should know thereby whether it is better that God speaks to you or the Devil. And my Lord Christ Jesus is never any angrier with you, although he allows you to feel this pain.'

So she suffered that pain until twelve days had passed, and she had as holy thoughts, as holy memories, as holy desires, as holy speeches and conversations from our Lord Jesus Christ as she had ever had before, our Lord saying to her, 'Daughter, now you well believe that I am no devil.'

Then she was filled with joy, for she heard our Lord speak to her as He was used to do. Therefore she said, 'I shall believe that every good thought is the speech of God, blessed must the Lord be, that you do not disdain to comfort me again! Lord, I would not wish for the whole world to suffer such a pain again as I have suffered for these twelve days, as I thought that I was in Hell, blessed may you be that it has passed! Therefore, Lord, now I wish to lie still and be obedient to your will; I ask you, Lord, speak in me what is most pleasant to you.'

CHAPTER 60

THE good priest, about whom it has been written beforehand, who was her reader, fell very ill, and she was moved in her soul to look after him, on God's behalf. And when she lacked any such thing as was necessary for him, she went around to good men and good women and got such things as were necessary for him. He was so sick that people had no confidence that he would live, and his sickness continued for a long time. Then one time, as she was in the church hearing her mass and praying for the same priest, our Lord said to her that he should live and fare very well.

Then she was stirred to go to Norwich, to St Stephen's Church, where the good vicar is buried,* he who died just a little before that time, for whom God showed high mercy to His people, and she thanked Him for the recovery of this priest. She took leave of her confessor, setting off for Norwich. When she came to the churchyard at St Stephen's, she cried, she roared, she wept, she fell down to the ground, so fervently did the fire of love burn in her heart. After that she got up again and went on, weeping, into the church to the high altar, and, all ravished with spiritual comfort in the goodness of our Lord, there she fell down with violent sobs, weeping, and loud cries beside the grave of the good vicar, who performed such great grace for His servant who had been her confessor, and had many times heard her confession of all her way of life, and administered to her the precious sacrament of the altar at various times. And in this way her devotion was increased, so that she saw our Lord work such special grace for such a creature as she had been conversant with during his lifetime. She had such holy thoughts and such holy memories that she had control over neither her weeping nor her crying. And therefore the people were greatly astonished at her, supposing that she wept out of some physical or earthly affection, and said to her, 'What's wrong with you, woman? Why are you conducting yourself like this? We knew him as well as you did.'

Then some priests who knew about her way of behaving were in the same place, and they very charitably led her to a tavern and made her take a drink, and gave her a very grand and good welcome. Also, there was a lady there who wished to have the said creature to a meal. And therefore, as manners required, she went to the church where the lady heard services, where this creature saw a pretty image of our Lady called a 'pity'.* And through beholding that 'pity' her mind was fully occupied in our Lord Jesus Christ's Passion and in the compassion of our Lady, St Mary, by which she was compelled to cry very loudly and weep very bitterly, as though she were going to die. Then the lady's priest came to her, saying, 'Madam, Jesus is long since dead.'

When her crying had ceased, she said to the priest, 'Sir, His death is as fresh to me as though He had died this very day, and I think it ought to be so to you and to all Christian people. We ought always to have in mind His kindness and always think about the doleful death that He died for us.'

Then the good lady, hearing their conversation, said, 'Sir, it's a good example to me, and to other people too, of the grace that God works in her soul.'

And so the good lady was her advocate and answered for her. After that she had her home with her to dine and she welcomed her gladly and with good cheer for as long as she wanted to stay there. And soon afterwards she came back home to Lynn, and the aforesaid priest, for whom she went especially to Norwich, and who had read to her for about seven years, recovered and went about wherever he liked, thanked be almighty God for His goodness!

CHAPTER 61

THEN a friar,* who was held to be a holy man and a good preacher, came to Lynn. His name and his accomplishment in preaching were wonderfully well-known over a wide area. Other good men came to the said creature, in good charity, and said, 'Margery, now you'll have preaching enough, for one of the most famous friars in England has come to this town, to be in the convent here.'

Then she was merry and glad and thanked God with all her heart that such a good man had come to live amongst them. Shortly afterwards, he said a sermon in a chapel of St James at Lynn,* where many people had gathered to hear the sermon. And before the friar went to the pulpit, the parish priest of the place where he was going to preach went to him and said, 'Sir, I beg you, don't be displeased. A woman shall come here to your sermon who very often, when she hears about the Passion of our Lord, or of any high devotion, weeps, sobs, and cries, but it doesn't last long. And therefore, good sir, if she makes any noise at your sermon, endure it patiently and don't be embarrassed by it.'

The good friar proceeded to say the sermon, and said it very piously and very devoutly, and spoke a good deal about our Lord's Passion, so that the said creature could no longer bear it. She kept herself from crying for as long as she might, and then in the end she burst out with a great cry and cried marvellously bitterly. The good friar endured it patiently and said not a word about it at that time.

Shortly afterwards he preached again in the same place. The said creature was present and, seeing how quickly the people came running to hear the sermon, she had great joy in her soul, thinking in her mind: 'Ah, Lord Jesus, I believe that if you yourself were here to preach in person, the people would have great joy in hearing you. I ask you, Lord, make your holy word settle in their souls as I wish it should in mine, and may as many be turned by his voice, as they would be by your voice if you preached yourself.'

And with such holy thoughts and holy memories she asked grace for the people at that time. And after that, whether through the holy sermon or whether through her meditation, grace of devotion had such a strong effect in her mind that she fell into a fit of noisy weeping. Then the good friar said, 'I want this woman out of the church; she's annoying people.'

Some people who were her friends answered back, 'Sir, do excuse her. She can't stop it.'

Then many people turned against her and were really glad that the good friar had taken against her. Then some people said that she had a devil within her. And they had said so many times before, but now they were bolder, as they thought that their opinion was well strengthened or else fortified by this good friar. He would not let her hear his sermon, unless she would leave off her sobbing and her crying.

There was then a good priest who had read much good scripture to her and knew the cause of her crying. He spoke to another good priest, who had known her for many years, and told him his idea: how he intended to go to the good friar and try, if he might, to humble his heart. The other good priest said he would willingly go with him to obtain grace, if he could. So they went, both priests together, and asked the good friar as earnestly as they could, that he would allow the said creature to come quietly to his sermon, and to endure her patiently if she happened to sob or cry, as other good people had endured her before. He replied shortly that if she came into any church where he was going to preach, and she made any noise as she was wont to do, he should speak out sharply against her; he would not allow her to cry in any way.

After that, a worshipful doctor of divinity, a White Friar, a solemn cleric and elderly doctor (and a very experienced one), who had known the said creature for many years of her life and believed in the grace that God performed in her, took with him a worthy man, a bachelor of law, a man well-educated in scripture and an expert of many years' standing.* This worthy man was confessor to the said creature, and went to the said friar as the good priests had before, and sent for wine with which to entertain him, asking him of his charity to look favourably on the works of our Lord in the said creature, and to grant her his benevolence in support of her, if it happened that she should cry or sob while he was giving his sermon. And these worthy clerics told him that it was a gift of God, and that she could not have it except when God wished to give it, nor might she withstand it when God wanted to send it, and God could withdraw it whenever He wished to; as that she had through revelation, and that was unknown to the friar.

Then he, giving credence neither to the doctor's words nor to those of the bachelor, and very much trusting in the opinion of the people, said he would not look favourably on her crying—not for anything that anybody could say or do—for he would not believe that it was a gift of God. But, he said, if she could not withstand it when it came, he believed it was a cardiac arrest, or some other illness, and if she could acknowledge that this was the case he would, he said, have compassion for her and direct the people to pray for her, and on these conditions he would have patience with her and allow her to cry somewhat, if she would say that it was a physical illness.

She herself knew well, by revelation and by experience, that it was no illness and therefore she would not, for the whole world, say otherwise. And therefore she could not agree. Then the honourable doctor and her confessor advised her that she should not come to his sermon, and that was a great pain to her.

Then another man, an honourable burgess who would become the Mayor of Lynn a few years later, went and asked him as the worthy clerics had done before, and he received the same answer that they had.

Then she was commanded by her confessor that she should not come to where he preached, and when he preached in one church she should go to another. She felt so much sorrow that she did not know what to do, for she was banished from hearing the sermon, which had been the greatest comfort on earth to her; and indeed the contrary, when she could not hear it, was the greatest pain on earth to her. When she was alone by herself in one church, and he was preaching to the people in another, she had as loud and as astonishing cries as when she was amongst the people.

For years she was not allowed to come to his sermon, because she cried so much when it pleased our Lord to give her the memory and the true beholding of His bitter Passion. But she was not excluded from any other cleric's preaching, but only from the good friar's, as it is said before, notwithstanding that in the meantime many honour-able doctors and other worthy clerics preached there, both religious and secular, at whose sermons she cried really loudly and sobbed most violently many times and often. And yet they endured it very patiently, and some who had spoken with her before and knew of her manner of living excused her to the people when they heard any rumour or grumbling against her.

CHAPTER 62

AFTERWARDS, on St James's Day,* the good friar preached in St James's churchyard at Lynn—he was at that time neither a bachelor nor doctor of divinity—where there were many people and a great audience, for he had a holy name and was very well-regarded by the people, so much so that some people, if they knew that he would be preaching in the region, they would go with him or follow him from town to town, because they delighted so much in hearing him; and so, may God be blessed, he preached very piously and very devoutly.

Nevertheless, on this day he preached strongly against the said creature, not uttering her name but explaining his thoughts in such a way that people knew that he meant her. Then there was such a stir amongst the people, for many men and many women trusted her and loved her very well, and were really dejected and sorrowful that he spoke so much against her in the way he did, and they wished that they had not heard him that day.

When he heard the murmuring and grumbling of the people, supposing he would be contradicted another day by those who were her friends, he said, whilst striking the pulpit with his hand, 'If I hear these matters repeated, I shall hit the nail on the head so hard', he said, 'that it shall shame her supporters!'

And then many of those who pretended to be her friends drew away from her just because of their vain fear of his words and then they dared not speak with her; the same priest was one of these people, who afterwards wrote this book and he had resolved never to believe in her feelings again.

And still our Lord drew him back in a short time, blessed may He be, so that he loved her more and trusted her weeping and her crying more than he did before. For afterwards he read of a woman called Marie d'Oignies,* and of her way of life, and of the wonderful sweetness that she had in hearing the word of God, of the wonderful compassion that she had in thinking of His Passion, and of the plentiful tears that she wept, which made her so feeble and so weak that she could not endure seeing the Cross, or to hear our Lord's Passion repeated, so she dissolved into tears of pity and compassion.

Of the plentiful grace of her tears, he* writes especially in the book mentioned above in the twenty-eighth chapter, which begins '*Bonus es, domine, sperantibus in te . . .*',* and also in the nineteenth chapter, where it tells how she, at the request of a priest that he should not be troubled or distracted in his mass by her weeping and her sobbing, went out of the church door, crying with a loud voice that she could not restrain herself from it.

So our Lord also visited Marie's priest, during Mass, with such grace and with such devotion when he read the holy Gospel, so that he wept wondrously so much so that he got his vestments and altar ornaments wet and could control neither his weeping nor his sobbing, it was so abundant; he could not restrain it either, or stand very well at the altar with it.

Then he well believed that the good woman (for whom he had before had little affection) could not restrain her weeping, her sobbing, or her crying, she who felt much more abundance of grace than he ever did, beyond any comparison. Then he knew well that God gave His grace to whom He wished.

Then the priest who wrote this treatise, through the direction of an honourable cleric, a bachelor of divinity, had seen and read the matter previously described much more seriously and more fully than it is written in this treatise (because here there is just a little of the purpose of it, as he did not have a very clear memory of the said matter when he wrote this treatise, and therefore he wrote rather the less of it). Then he drew back and inclined more earnestly towards the said creature, from whom he had fled and avoided through the friar's preaching, as is written before.

Also, the same priest afterwards read in a treatise called the *Prick of Love*,* in the second chapter, that Bonaventure himself wrote the following words: 'Oh, Lord, what more shall I utter or cry? You delay and do not come and I, weary and overcome with desire, begin to go mad, for love and not reason governs me. I run with a hasty course wherever you wish, Lord. I submit, Lord, that those who see me are irked and pitying, not knowing that I am drunk with your love. "Lord," they say, "look at that mad man over there, crying in the streets!" But they do not perceive the extent of the desire of my heart' (*Et capitulo Stimulo Amoris et capitulo ut supra*).*

He also read of Richard of Hampole, hermit, in the *Incendio Amoris*,* similar material that moved him to give credence to the said creature. Also, Elizabeth of Hungary cried with a loud voice, as it is written in her treatise.*

Also many others, who had forsaken her through the friar's preaching, repented and turned back to her in the course of time, even though the friar kept his opinion. And he would always in his sermon have a section against her, whether she was there or not, and caused many people to judge her most evilly for many and long days.

For some said that she had a devil within her, and some said to her own face that the friar should have driven those devils out of her. Thus was she slandered, eaten away at, gnawed at, by the people, for the grace that God performed in her of contrition, of devotion, and of compassion, through the gift of which graces she wept, sobbed, and cried most grievously against her will—she could not choose, for she would rather have wept softly and privately than openly, if it had been in her power.

CHAPTER 63

THEN some of her friends came to her and said it would be easier for her to leave the town than to stay there, so many people were against her. And she said she should stay there for as long as God wished.

'For here,' she said, 'in this town I have sinned. Therefore it is fitting that I suffer sorrow in this town because of it. And yet I have not so much sorrow or shame as I deserve, for I have trespassed against God. I thank almighty God for whatever he sends me, and I ask God that all kinds of wickedness that any person shall say about me in this world may count towards remission of my sins, and any goodness that any person shall say about the grace that God works in me may turn God to the worship and praise and magnifying of His Holy Name, without end. For all kinds of worship pertain to Him, and all spitefulness, shame, and reproof belongs to me, and those I have well deserved.'

Another time, her confessor came to her in a chapel dedicated to our Lady, called the Gesine,* saying, 'Margery, what are you going to do now? Everything is against you except the moon and the seven stars. There's hardly one person who sticks with you but me alone.'

She said to her confessor, 'Sir, don't worry, because it will all be well in the end. And I tell you truly that my Lord Jesus gives me great comfort in my soul, or else I'd fall into despair. My blissful Lord Christ Jesus will not let me despair for any holy name that the good friar has, as my Lord tells me that he is angry with him, and he says to me that it would be better if he'd never been born as he hates His works in me.'

Also our Lord said to her, 'Daughter, if he's a priest who despises you, knowing full well why you weep and cry, he is cursed.'

One time, as she was in the Prior's Cloister and dared not abide in the church, in case she disturbed the people with her crying, our Lord said to her, as she was feeling very cast down, 'Daughter, I request that you go back into the church, for I shall take the crying away from you, so that you shall no longer cry so loudly or in the way that you have before, even if you want to.'

She obeyed the Lord's commandment and told her confessor how she felt, and it happened truly as she felt. Afterwards she no longer cried so loudly, or in the manner that she had before, but later she sobbed marvellously and wept as terribly as she had before, sometimes loud and sometimes quiet, as God would determine it Himself.

Then many people believed that she dared cry no longer because the good friar had so preached against her and would not endure her in any way. Then they believed him to be a holy man and her to be a false hypocrite. And just as some of them before spoke wickedly about her because she cried, so some now spoke evilly of her because she did not cry. And so slander and physical anguish came to her on every side, and all to the increase of her spiritual comfort.

Then our merciful Lord said to His unworthy servant, 'Daughter, I must needs comfort you, as you now have the right way to Heaven. By this way I and all my disciples came to Heaven, for now you shall better know what sorrow and shame I suffered for your love, and you shall have the more compassion when you think on my Passion. Daughter, I have told you many times that the friar said evil things of you. Therefore I warn you that you should not tell him of the private counsel I have shown to you, as I do not wish that he should hear it out of your mouth. And indeed, daughter, I tell you that he shall be chastised sharply. As his name is now, it shall be thrown down, and yours shall be raised up. And I shall make as many people love you for my love as have despised you for my love. Daughter, you shall be in church when he shall be outside it. In this church you have suffered much shame and reproof for the gifts that I have given you, and for the grace and goodness that I have performed in you, and therefore in this church and in this place I shall be worshipped in you. Many a man and woman shall say, "It is easy to see that God loved her well." Daughter, I shall work so much grace for you, that the whole world shall wonder and marvel at my goodness.'

Then the said creature said to our Lord, with great reverence, 'I am not worthy for you to show such grace on my account. Lord, it is enough to me that you save my soul from endless damnation by your great mercy.'

'It is my worship, daughter, that I shall perform, and therefore I wish that you have no will but my will. The less value you set on yourself, the more value I set on you, and all the better will I love you, daughter. See that you do not sorrow after earthly goods. I have tested you in poverty, and I have chastised you as I would chastise myself, both inwardly in your soul and outwardly through the people's slander. Look, daughter, I have granted you your own desire: for you should have no other purgatory except in this world alone.

'Daughter, you often say to me in your mind that rich people have a great reason to love me well, and you speak very truthfully, as you say that I have given them much money through which they can serve me and love me. But, good daughter, I ask you, love me with all your heart, and I shall give you money enough with which to love me, for Heaven and earth should fall before I would fail you. And even if other people fail, you shall not fail. And, even though all your friends forsake you, I shall never forsake you. You once made me steward of your household and executor of all your good deeds,* and I shall be a faithful steward and a faithful executor in fulfilment of all your wishes and all your desire. And I shall arrange for you, daughter, as for my own mother and as for my own wife.'

CHAPTER 64

THE creature said to her Lord Christ Jesus, 'Oh, blissful Lord, I wish I knew how I might best love you and please you, and that my love were as sweet to you as I think your love is to me.'

Then our sweet Lord Jesus, answering His creature, said, 'Daughter, if you knew how sweet your love is to me, you would never do anything but love me with all your heart. And therefore believe well, daughter, that my love is not so sweet to you as your love is to me. Daughter, you do not know how much I love you, as it cannot be known in this world how much it is, nor felt as it is, for you would fail and burst and never endure it for the joy that you would feel. And therefore I allot it as I wish to your greatest relief and comfort. But, daughter, you shall know well in another world how much I love you on earth, for there you shall have much cause to thank me. There you shall eternally see every good day that ever I gave you on earth, of contemplation, of devotion, and of all the great charity that I have given to you, to the profit of your fellow Christians. For this shall be your reward when you enter Heaven.

'There is no cleric in the whole world, daughter, who can teach you better than I can, and if you will be obedient to my will I shall be obedient to your will. What better token of love is there than to weep for your Lord's love? You know well, daughter, that the Devil has no charity, for he is very angry with you and he might somewhat hurt you, but he shall not harm you (except slightly, to make you afraid sometimes) in this world, so that you should pray all the more strongly to me for grace, and steer your charity all the more towards me. There is no cleric who speaks against the way of life which I am teaching you; and if he does, he is not God's cleric, he is the Devil's cleric. I tell you very truthfully that there is nobody in this world—if they would suffer as much slander for my love as willingly as you have done, and cleave to me as steadfastly, not willing, for anything that may be done or said against them, to forsake me—whom I should not treat fairly and be very graceful towards, both in this world and in the other.'

Then the creature said, 'Oh, my highly esteemed Lord, you should show this life to religious people and to priests.'

Our Lord replied to her, 'No, no, daughter, for that thing that I love best, they love not, and that is shame, humiliation, scorn, and the people's reproofs, and therefore they shall not have this grace. For, daughter, I tell you, he who dreads the shames of the world may not love God perfectly. And daughter, under the habit of holiness much wickedness is covered. Daughter, if you saw the wickedness that is performed in this world as I do, you would be astonished that I do not take total vengeance on them. But, daughter, I hold back because of your love. You weep so much every day for mercy that I must grant it to you, and the people shall not believe the goodness that I work in you for them. Nevertheless, daughter, the time will come when they shall be very glad to believe the grace that I have given you for them. And I shall say to them when they have passed out of this world, "See, I arranged for her to weep for her sins, and you held her in utter contempt, but her charity for you would never cease." And therefore, daughter, those who are good souls shall thank me highly for the grace and goodness that I have given you, and those who are wicked shall grumble and find it very painful to endure the grace that I show to you. And therefore I shall chastise them as it were for myself.'

She prayed: 'No, highly esteemed Lord Jesus, chastise no creature for me. You know well, Lord, that I do not desire vengeance, but I ask for mercy and grace for all men, if it be your will to grant it. Nevertheless, Lord, rather than eternally separating them from you, chastise them as you yourself wish. It seems, Lord, in my soul, that you are full of charity, for you say that you do not wish for the death of a sinful man. And you say also that you wish for all people to be saved. Then, Lord, since you wish for all people to be saved, I must wish for the same, and you yourself say that I must love my fellow Christians as my own self.* And, Lord, you know that I have wept and sorrowed many years for I wish to be saved, and so I must do this for my fellow-Christians.'

CHAPTER 65

OUR Lord Jesus Christ said to the said creature, 'Daughter, you shall see full well when you are in Heaven with me that nobody is damned except he who is well worth being damned, and you shall hold yourself well pleased with all my works. And therefore, daughter, thank me highly for this great charity that I work in your heart, for it is myself, almighty God, that makes you weep every day for your own sins, for the great compassion that I give you for my bitter Passion, and for the sorrows that my mother had on earth, for the anguish that she suffered and for the tears that she wept. Also, daughter, for the holy martyrs in Heaven (when you hear about them, you give thanks to me with crying and weeping for the grace that I have showed to them, and when you see any lepers, you have great compassion for them, giving me thanks and praise that I favour you more than I do them); and also, daughter, for the great sorrow that you have for the whole world, that you might help them as well as you would help yourself both spiritual and physical; and furthermore, for the sorrows that you have for the souls in Purgatory, that you would so happily see out of their pain, so that they might praise me eternally.

'And all this is my own goodness that I have given to you, for which you are very much bound to thank me. And nevertheless I still thank you for the great love you have for me, and because you have such great will and such great desire that all men and women should love me very well; for, as you think, all of them, holy and unholy, want money with which to live, as is lawful for them, but they will not busy themselves to love me as they do to get themselves temporal goods.

'Also, daughter, I thank you because of thinking for so long that you are out of my blessed presence. Furthermore, I thank you especially, daughter, because you suffer no man to break my commandments, or to swear by me, without it being a great pain to you, and you are always ready for my love to reprove them for their swearing. And for this you have suffered many a spiteful word and many an insult, and you shall therefore have many a joy in Heaven.

'Daughter, I once sent St Paul to you, to strengthen you and to comfort you, so that you should speak boldly in my name from that day forwards. And St Paul said to you that you had suffered much tribulation because of his writings, and because of this he promised that you should have as much grace for his love as you had shame or insults for his love. He also told you about the many joys of Heaven and of the great love that I had for you. And, daughter, I have often said to you that there is no saint in Heaven who, if you wish to speak with him, is not ready to comfort you and speak to you in my name. My angels are ready to offer holy thoughts to you and your prayers to me and the tears of your eyes too, for your tears are angels' drink, like spiced wine to them.

'Therefore, my highly esteemed daughter, do not be irked by me on earth, sitting alone all by yourself thinking of my love, for I am not irked by you and my merciful eye is always on you. Daughter, you may boldly say to me, "*Ihesus est amor meus*", that means, "Jesus is my love."* Therefore, daughter, let me be all your love and all the joy of your heart.

'Daughter, if you will think hard about this, you have a really good reason to love me above all things for the great gifts that I have given to you beforehand. And yet you have another good reason to love me, for you have had your will of chastity as if you are a widow, even though your husband is alive and in good health.'

'Daughter, I have drawn the love of your heart from everybody's hearts into my heart. Once, daughter, you thought it was an impossible thing for it to be so, and at that time you suffered terrible pain in your heart with bodily feelings. And then you could well cry to me, saying, "Lord, for all your wounds smart, draw all the love of my heart into your heart."*

'Daughter, for all these reasons and many other reasons and benefits, which I have shown you on this side of the world and on the other half of the world, you have good reason to love me.'

CHAPTER 66

'Now, daughter, I wish you to eat meat again like you used to, and that you are submissive and supple to my will and to my bidding, and put aside your own will, and ask your spiritual fathers that they let you act according to my wish. And you will never have the less grace, but so much the more, as you shall have the same reward in Heaven as though you still fasted according to your own will. Daughter, I asked you first that you should put aside meat and not to eat it, and you have obeyed my will for many years and you have abstained, following my advice. Therefore, now I ask you to take up meat-eating again.'

The said creature said, with reverent fear, 'Oh, blissful Lord, the people—who have known of my abstinence for so many years—will see me now returning to meat-eating, they will be utterly astonished and, I suppose, they'll insult me and scorn me for it.'

Our Lord said to her again, 'You shall not take heed of their scorn, just let every person say as they wish.'

Then she went to her confessors and told them what our Lord had said to her. When her confessors knew the will of God, they charged her by virtue of obedience that she eat meat as she had done many years before. Then she had many an insult and much reproof for eating meat again.

Also, she had made a vow to fast one day each week as long as she lived, in honour of our Lady, the which vow she kept for many years. Our Lady, appearing to her soul, asked her to go to her confessor and say that she would have her released from her vow, that she should be stronger for bearing her spiritual labours, for without bodily strength it could not be endured. Then her confessor, seeing by the eye of discretion that it was expedient that this should be done, commanded her by virtue of obedience to eat moderately like other creatures did, when God wished her to have her food. And her grace was not decreased but rather increased, for she would rather have fasted than have eaten, if it had been God's will.

Furthermore, our Lady said to her, 'Daughter, you are weak enough from weeping and crying, as both these make you feeble and weak enough. And I can thank you more for eating your meat for my love than fasting, so that you can endure your perfection of weeping.'

CHAPTER 67

ONE time, there happened to be a great fire in Bishop's Lynn,* and this fire burned down the Guildhall of the Trinity, and the same hideous and grievous fire looked likely to burn the parish church dedicated to St Margaret (a dignified and richly honoured place) and the whole town too, if there had been no grace or miracle.

The said creature being present there, seeing the town imperilled and injured, cried very loudly many times that day and she wept most abundantly, praying for grace and mercy for all the people. And notwithstanding that at other times they could not tolerate her crying and weeping for the plentiful grace that our Lord performed in her, on this day, in order to evade their physical peril, they allowed her to cry and weep as much as she liked, and nobody would ask her to stop but instead they asked her to continue, fully trusting and believing that through her crying and weeping our Lord would have mercy on them.

Then her confessor came to her and asked if it were best to carry the sacrament towards the fire or not?

She said, 'Yes! Sir, yes! For our Lord Jesus Christ told me that it shall be very well.'

So her confessor, the parish priest of St Margaret's Church, took the precious sacrament and went in front of the fire as devoutly as he could and afterwards brought it back into the church—and the sparks of the fire were flying around the church! The said creature, desiring to follow the precious sacrament to the fire, went out of the church door, and as soon as she saw the hideous flames of the fire she cried out with a loud voice and immense weeping: 'Good Lord, make it all right!'

These words occupied her mind, in as much as our Lord had said to her beforehand that he should make it all right, and therefore she cried, 'Good Lord, make it all right, and send some rain down or some weather, through your mercy, that may quench this fire and ease my heart!'

Then she went back into the church, and then she saw how the sparks came into the choir through the church's lantern. Then she had a new sorrow, and she cried really loudly again for grace and mercy, with plenty of tears. Soon after, three honourable men came to her, with white snow on their clothes, saying to her, 'Look, Margery, God has performed great grace for us and sent us a fair snowstorm with which to quench the fire! Be in good spirits now and thank God for it!'

Then with a great cry she gave praise and thanks to God for His great mercy and His goodness, and especially that He had said to her before that it should all be well, when it was very unlikely to be well, except through a miracle and special grace. And now she saw that indeed it all was well, she thought that she had great cause to thank our Lord.

Then her confessor came to her and said he believed that, because of her prayers, God granted them to be delivered out of their great peril, as it could not happen, without devout prayers, that the air—being bright and clear—should have changed so suddenly into clouds and darkness and sent down great snowflakes, through which the fire was impeded in its natural functioning, blessed may our Lord be!

Yet, notwithstanding the grace that he showed for her, when the peril had ceased, some people slandered her because she cried, and some said to her that our Lady never cried; 'Why are you crying like this?' And she said that she could not do otherwise.

Then she fled from the people to the Prior's Cloister, so that she gave them no more occasion to insult her. When she was there, she had such a strong memory of the Passion of our Lord Jesus Christ, and of His precious wounds, and how dearly He redeemed her, that she cried and roared amazingly, so that she could be heard a great way away and she could not restrain herself from it.

Then she was really amazed at how our Lady could not bear or endure to see His precious body being scourged and hanging on the Cross. Also it came to her mind how people had said to her before that our Lady, Christ's own dear mother, had not cried as she did, and that caused her to say in her crying, 'Lord, I am not your mother. Take away this pain from me, for I cannot bear it! Your Passion will kill me!'

So then an honourable cleric came past her, a doctor of divinity, saying, 'I'd rather have such a sorrow for our Lord's Passion than twenty pounds!'

Then the said doctor sent for her to come and speak to him, and she willingly went to him, with tearful weeping, to his chamber. The worthy and honourable cleric gave her a drink and really made her very welcome. Then he led her to an altar and asked her what the reason was for her crying and weeping so bitterly. Then she told him very many reasons for her weeping, and yet she told him of no revelation. And he said that she was very much bound to love our Lord for the tokens of love that He showed to her in various ways.

And afterwards a parson came who had taken a university degree, who wanted to preach both morning and afternoon. And as he preached with great holiness and devotion, the said creature was moved by devotion during his sermon, and in the end she burst out with a cry. And the people began to grumble about her crying, as it was at that time that the good friar preached against her (as was written before) and also before our Lord took her crying away from her (for although the matter was written before this, nevertheless it happened after this). Then the parson paused a little in his preaching and said to the people, 'Friends, be quiet and do not grumble about this woman, for each of you may sin mortally in her, and she is not the cause, but rather your own judgement. For although this kind of behaviour may seem both good and bad, you should still judge for the best in your hearts, and I do not doubt that it is very fine. Also I dare well say it is a most gracious gift of God, blessed may He be!'

Then the people blessed him for his good words and were the more moved to believe his holy deeds. Afterwards, when the sermon had ended, a good friend of the said creature met with the friar who had preached so bitterly against her, and asked how he thought of her. The friar, responding sharply, said, 'She has a devil within her!'—not shifting at all in his opinion, but rather defending his error.

CHAPTER 68

SOON after, the General Chapter of the Preaching Friars was held at Lynn, and many honourable clerics came there from that holy order, one of whom wished to preach a sermon in the parish church. And to the said Chapter there came, amongst others, an honourable doctor who was called Master Constance,* and he had known the aforementioned creature many years previously. When the creature heard that he had come there, she went to him and showed him why she cried and wept so bitterly to find out if he could find fault in her crying and in her weeping. The honourable doctor said to her, 'Margery, I've read about a holy woman to whom God had given great grace in weeping and crying as He has done to you. In the church where she lived there was a priest who did not approve of her weeping and caused her, through his direction, to go outside the church. When she was in the churchyard, she asked God that the priest might feel the grace that she felt, as it certainly was not in her power to cry or weep except when God wished. And so suddenly our Lord sent him devotion during his mass, so that he could not control himself, and then he did not despise her afterwards but rather comforted her.'*

Thus the said doctor, confirming her crying and weeping, said it was a gracious and special gift from God, and God was very much to be commended for His gift. And then the same doctor went to another doctor of divinity, who was assigned to preach in the parish church in front of all the people, asking him that if the said creature should cry or weep during his sermon, that he would endure it meekly, and not at all to be embarrassed by it or speak against it. So afterwards, when the worshipful doctor went to preach and was brought appropriately to the pulpit, as he began to preach very piously and devoutly of the Assumption of our Lady, the said creature, lifted up in her mind by high sweetness and devotion, burst out with a loud voice and cried very loudly and wept very bitterly. The honourable doctor stood still, and endured it most meekly until it ceased, and after that carried on with his sermon to the end.

In the afternoon he sent for the same creature to come to him where he was, and made her really very welcome. Then she thanked him for his meekness and his charity that he had shown in support of her crying and her weeping that morning in his sermon. The honourable doctor said back to her, 'Margery, I wouldn't speak against you, even if you had cried until evening. And if you wish to come to Norwich you shall be made very welcome and have such a reception as I can make for you.'

Thus God sent her excellent patronage in this worthy doctor to strengthen her against her detractors, worshipped be His name!

Afterwards, at Lent, a good cleric, an Augustinian Friar, preached in his own house at Lynn,* and he had a great audience, the said creature being present at that time. And God, in His goodness, inspired the friar to preach much about His Passion, so expressively and so devoutly that she could not bear it. Then she fell down weeping and crying so bitterly that many of the people were amazed by her, and insulted and cursed her very bitterly, supposing that she could stop her crying if she wanted, inasmuch as the good friar had preached against this, as is written earlier. And then this good man who preached at this time said to the people, 'Friends, be quiet! You really know very little what she is feeling.'

And so the people stopped and were quiet and heard out the sermon with silence and rest of body and soul.

CHAPTER 69

ALSO, one Good Friday at St Margaret's Church, the Prior* of that same place and the same town, Lynn, intended to preach. And he took 'Jesus is dead' as his theme. Then the said creature, all wounded with pity and compassion, cried and wept as if she had seen our Lord dead with her physical eyes. The honourable Prior and doctor of divinity endured her very meekly and held nothing against her.

Another time, Bishop Wakering, the Bishop of Norwich,* preached at Lynn in the said church of St Margaret, and the aforementioned creature cried and wept most noisily during his sermon, and he endured it very meekly and patiently, and so did many an honourable cleric, both regulars and seculars, for there was never a cleric who preached openly against her crying except the Grey Friar, as is written earlier.

So our Lord, in His mercy, just as He had promised the said creature that He should always provide for her, stirring the spirits of two good clerics* who had long and for many years known her conversation and all her perfection, made them strong and bold to speak for His part in excusing the said creature, both in the pulpit and outside it, wherever they heard anything directed against her: they amply strengthened her skills by authoritative quotations of holy scripture, and one of these clerics was a White Friar, a doctor of divinity; the other cleric was a bachelor of canon law, a man well-schooled in scripture.

And then some envious people complained to the Provincial of the White Friars* that the said doctor was too intimate with the said creature, in that he supported her weeping and her crying, and also informed her in questions of scripture, when she would ask any of him. Then he was warned, by virtue of obedience, that he should no longer speak with her, or inform her in scriptural texts, and that was very painful to him because (as he said to some people), he would have rather lost one hundred pounds (if he had had it) than lose communication with her, for it was so spiritual and fruitful.

When her confessor perceived how the worthy doctor was charged by obedience that he should neither speak with nor associate with her, then he (to prevent any such opportunity) warned her too, by virtue of obedience, that she should no longer go to the friars, or speak with the said doctor, or ask him any questions as she had done before. And then her thoughts were very much of sorrow and depression, as she was excluded from much spiritual comfort. She would rather have lost any worldly goods than his communication, for it was, to her, a great increase of virtue.

Then, long afterwards, as she was going down a street she happened to meet with the said doctor, and neither of them spoke a word to each other. And then she had a great crying, with many tears. After, when she came to her meditation, she said in her mind to our Lord Jesus Christ,

'Alas, Lord, why may I have no comfort from this honourable cleric, who has known me for so many years and often strengthened me in your love? Now you, Lord, have taken the anchorite from me—I trust to your mercy—the most special and singular comfort that I ever had on earth, for he always loved me for your love and would never forsake me for anything that anybody could do or say, while he was alive. And Master Alan is banned from me and I from him. Sir Thomas Andrew* and Sir John Amy* have got benefices and are out of town. Master Robert hardly dares speak to me. Now in a way I have no comfort, neither of adult nor of child.'

Our merciful Lord Christ Jesus, answering to her mind, said, 'Daughter, I am more worthy of your soul than the anchorite ever was, and all those whom you have mentioned and all those who may be in this world; I shall comfort you myself, for I would speak to you more often than you would let me. And daughter, I want you to believe that you shall speak to Master Alan again as you have done before.'

And then our Lord sent, by arrangement with the Prior of Lynn, a priest to be the keeper of a chapel of our Lady, called the Gesine,* within the church of St Margaret; this priest* many times heard her confession in the absence of her principal confessor. And to this priest she disclosed all her life, as accurately as she could, from her youth: both her sins, her labours, her vexations, her contemplations, and also her revelations and such grace as God performed in her through His mercy, and so that priest trusted well that God performed very great grace in her.

CHAPTER 70

ONE time, God visited the aforesaid doctor, Master Alan, with a terrible illness so that nobody who saw him believed he would live. Then the said creature was told of his illness. Then she grieved so for him, and especially because she had had a revelation that she should speak with him again as she had before and, if he died of this illness, her feeling would not be true. Therefore she ran into the choir of St Margaret's Church, kneeling down in front of the sacrament and saying in this way, 'Oh, Lord, I ask you, for all the goodness that you have shown to me, and as certainly as you love me, let this worthy cleric never die until I can speak with him, as you have promised that I should.

And you, glorious Queen of Mercy, remember what he was wont to say of you in his sermons. He was wont to say, Lady, that he who had you as a friend was indeed blessed, for when you prayed, all the company of Heaven prayed with you. Now, for the blissful love that you have for your son, let him live until such time that he has leave to speak with me and I with him, for now we are kept apart out of obedience.'

Then she was answered in her soul that he should not die before that time that she had leave to speak with him, and he with her, as they had done years before. And, as our Lord wished, a short time later the worthy cleric recovered and went about hale and hearty, and had permission of his ruler* to speak with the said creature. And she had leave from her confessor to speak with him.

It so happened that the aforesaid doctor was going to dine in town with an honourable woman who had taken the mantle and the ring,* and he sent for the said creature to come and speak with him. She, being really astonished by this, got permission and went to him. When she came into the place where he was, she could not speak for weeping and for joy that she had in our Lord, in that she found her feeling to be true and not deceptive, that he had permission to speak to her and she to him.

Then the honourable doctor said to her, 'Margery, you're welcome to me, for I have been kept from you for long, and now our Lord has sent you here so that I may speak with you, blessed may He be!' There was a dinner of great joy and gladness, much more spiritual than physical, for it was seasoned and savoured with tales of holy scripture. And then he gave the said creature a pair of knives, as a sign that he would stand with her in God's cause, as he had done beforehand.

CHAPTER 71

ONE day, a priest came to the said creature who really trusted in her feelings and in her revelations, but desired to test them at different times, and asked her to pray to our Lord that she might have understanding if the Prior of Lynn, who was the good patron of the said priest, should be transferred or not; just as she felt it, she was to make him a true account of it. She prayed about the aforesaid matter, and when she had an answer to it, she told the priest that the Prior of Lynn, his master, should be called home to Norwich, and another of his brethren* should be sent to Lynn in his place. And indeed so it happened. But he who was sent to Lynn stayed there for just a little while before he was called home to Norwich again, and he who had been Prior of Lynn before went back to Lynn and lived there for about four years until he died.

And in the meantime, the said creature often had a feeling that he who was last called home to Norwich, and stayed just a little while in Lynn, would still be Prior of Lynn again. She would give no credence to this, in that he had been there and then soon been called home again. Then, once as she was going up and down the White Friars' church at Lynn, she felt a wondrously sweet, heavenly scent, so that she thought that she could have lived on it without food or drink, if it had continued. And at that moment our Lord said to her, 'Daughter, by this sweet smell you may know that, in a short time, there shall be a new Prior at Lynn, and that shall be he who was last removed from there.'

And soon afterwards the old Prior died, and then our Lord said to her as she lay in her bed, 'Daughter, as reluctant as you are to believe my promptings, you will yet see him, of whom I showed you before, Prior of Lynn before the end of the week.' And so our Lord repeated this matter to her each day for a week, until she saw that it was indeed so, and then she was really glad and joyful that her feeling was true.

Afterwards, when this honourable man had come to Lynn and had lived there for a short while (and he was a really honourable cleric, a doctor of divinity) he was appointed to go overseas to the King in France, with other clerics too, the worthiest in England. Then a priest who held office under the said Prior came to the foresaid creature and begged her to bear this matter in mind, when God wished to administer His holy communication to her soul, and knew in this matter whether the Prior should go overseas or not. Nevertheless, he himself expected to go, and was all prepared to do so, and with great sadness had said goodbye to his friends, supposing that he would never come back, for he was a very weak man and feeble of complexion. And in the meantime the King died,* and the Prior stayed at home. And so her feeling was true without any deception.

Also, it was said that the Bishop of Winchester* was dead, but nevertheless she had a feeling that he lived. And so it was in truth. And so she had many more feelings than are written down, which our Lord, of His mercy, revealed to her understanding, though she was unworthy by her own merits.

CHAPTER 72

So in the course of time her mind and her thought was so joined to God that she never forgot Him, but continually had Him in mind, and beheld Him in all creatures. And always the more that she increased in love and in devotion the more she increased in sorrow and in contrition, in humility, in meekness, and in the holy dread of our Lord, and in knowledge of her own frailty so that, if she saw a creature being punished or sharply chastised, she would think that she was the more worthy to be chastised than was the creature, because of her unkindness to God. Then she would cry, weep, and sob for her own sin, and for the compassion of the creature that she saw so being punished and sharply chastised.

If she saw a prince, or a prelate, or an honourable statesman or nobleman, whom people worshipped and revered with humility and meekness, then her mind was refreshed in our Lord, thinking about what joy, what bliss, what worship and reverence He had in Heaven amongst His blessed saints, since a mortal man could have such great worship on earth.

And most of all, when she saw the precious sacrament carried around the town with candles and reverence, the people kneeling on their knees, then she had many holy thoughts and meditations, and then often she would cry and roar as though she should burst, for the faith and trust that she had in the precious sacrament.

Also, many people desired to have the said creature with them at the time of their death and to pray for them, because even though they did not love her weeping or her crying during their lifetimes, they desired that she should both weep and cry when they came to die, and this she did. When she saw people being anointed,* she had many holy thoughts, many holy meditations, and, if she saw them dying, she thought that she saw our Lord and sometimes our Lady dying, as our Lord wished to illuminate her spiritual vision of understanding. Then she would cry, weep, and sob really amazingly, as if she had watched our Lord at His death, or our Lady at her death. And she thought in her mind that God took many from this world who would have much preferred to go on living, 'and I, Lord,' she thought, 'would much prefer to come to you, but you have no yearning for me', and such thoughts increased her weeping and her sobbing.

One time, an honourable lady sent for her, in order to converse, and as they were talking together the lady gave to her a kind of worship and praise, and it was very painful to her to be given any praise. Nevertheless, then she offered it up to our Lord, for she desired no praise except only His, with a great cry and many devout tears.

So there was neither respect nor praise, neither love nor libel, neither shame nor spitefulness that could draw her love from God, but, after the saying of St Paul, 'And we know that to them that love God, all things work together unto good',* so it happened with her. Whatsoever she saw or heard, her love and her spiritual affection always increased towards our Lord, blessed may He be, who performed such grace in her for many people's profit.

Another time, another honourable lady (who had a great retinue around her) sent for her, and great respect and great reverence was made to her. When the said creature saw all the lady's retinue around her, and the great respect and reverence made to her, she fell into a great fit of weeping and cried out very mournfully. There was a priest who heard how she cried and how she wept (and he was a man who did not relish spiritual things) and he quickly cursed her, saying to her, 'What the devil is wrong with you? Why are you weeping like this? May God give you sorrow!'

She sat still, and answered not a word. Then the lady took her into a garden alone by themselves and asked her to tell her why she cried so bitterly. And then she, supposing it was expedient to do so, told her part of the reason. Then the lady was most displeased with her priest who had spoken so against her; and the lady loved this creature very well, and desired and asked her to continue to stay with her. But then this creature excused herself and said that she could not agree with the kinds of costumes and the conduct that she saw amongst the lady's retinue.

CHAPTER 73

ON Holy Thursday,* as the said creature went in a procession with other people, she saw in her soul our Lady, St Mary Magdalene, and the Twelve Apostles. And then she watched with her spiritual eye how our Lady took her leave of her blissful son, Christ Jesus, how He kissed her and all His apostles and also His true lover, Mary Magdalene. Then she thought that it was a sorrowful parting yet also a joyful parting. When she beheld this sight in her soul, she fell down in the field amongst the people. She cried, she roared, she wept as though she should burst therewith. She could neither control herself nor govern herself, but she cried and roared so that many people were amazed by her. But she paid no attention to what anybody said or did, for her mind was occupied with our Lord.

During that time she felt many a holy thought that she was never able to feel afterwards. She had forgotten all worldly things and only paid attention to spiritual things. She thought that all her joy had gone. She saw her Lord stepping up into Heaven, yet she could not do without Him on earth. Therefore, she desired to go with Him, for all her joy and all her bliss was in Him, and she knew well that she should never have either joy or bliss until she came to Him. Such holy thoughts and such holy desires caused her to weep, and the people did not know what was wrong with her.

Another time, the said creature saw how, so she thought, our Lady was dying and all the apostles knelt before her, asking for grace.* Then she cried and wept bitterly. The apostles commanded her to stop and be silent. The creature answered to the apostles, 'Would you have me see the mother of God dying and for me not to weep? It cannot be, because I am so full of sorrow that I cannot bear it. I absolutely must cry and weep.'

And then she said in her soul to our Lady, 'Oh, blessed Lady, pray for me to your son that I may come to you and no longer be hindered from you; because, Lady, this is all too great a sorrow, to be both at your son's death and at your death, and not to die with you but still to live alone and have no comfort with me.'

Then our gracious Lady answered to her soul, promising her that she would pray for her to her son, and said, 'Daughter, all these sorrows that you have had for me and for my blessed son shall turn to great joy and bliss for you in eternal Heaven. And do not doubt, daughter, that you shall indeed come to us, and be very welcome when you come. But you cannot come yet, for you shall come in good time enough. And, daughter, rest assured that you shall find in me a very good mother to you, to help you and assist you, as a mother ought to do to her daughter, and purchase for you grace and virtue. And the same pardon that was granted to you previously, it was confirmed on St Nicholas's Day—that is to say, plenary remission*—and it is not only granted to you, but also to all those who believe—and to all those that shall believe until the end of the world—that God loves you, and all those who shall thank God for you. If they will put aside their sin and fully intend not to return to it but are sorry and regretful for what they have done and will do due penance for it, they shall have the same pardon that is granted to you, and that is the whole pardon that is in Jerusalem, as was granted to you when you were at Ramlah'—as is written earlier.

CHAPTER 74

ONE day, the said creature, as she was hearing her mass and turning over in her mind the time of her death, sighing sorrowfully and sorrowing that it was so long delayed, said thus: 'Alas, Lord, how long shall I weep and mourn like this for your love and out of desire for your presence?'

Our Lord answered in her soul and said, 'All these fifteen years.'*

Then she said, 'Oh, Lord, I shall think it's many thousands of years.'

Our Lord answered her, 'Daughter, you must think to yourself about my blessed mother, who lived after me on earth for fifteen years, and also St John the Evangelist, and Mary Magdalene, who loved me very highly.'

'Oh, blissful Lord,' she said, 'I wish I were as worthy to be as sure of your love as Mary Magdalene was.'

Then our Lord said, 'Truly, daughter, I love you as well, and the same peace I gave to her is the same peace that I give to you. For, daughter, no saint in heaven is displeased, even though I love a creature on earth as much as I love them. Therefore, they will not wish otherwise than my wishes.'

Thus our merciful Lord Christ Jesus drew His creature unto His love and to the memory of His Passion, so that she could not endure to see a leper or another sick person, especially if he had any wounds appearing on him. So she cried and so she wept as if she had seen our Lord Jesus Christ with His wounds bleeding. And this she did in the sight of her soul, for through seeing a sick man her mind was entirely transported to our Lord Jesus Christ.

Then she had great mourning and sorrowing for she could not kiss the lepers when she saw them or met them in the streets, for the love of Jesus.* Now she began to love those whom she had hated most before, for there was nothing more hateful and abominable to her, during her period of worldly prosperity, than to see or behold a leper whom now, through our Lord's mercy, she desired to hug and kiss for the love of Jesus, when she had a convenient place and time.

Then she told her confessor how much desire she had to kiss lepers, and he warned her that she should kiss nobody but, if she were going to kiss anyway, she should kiss women. Then she was glad, for she had leave to kiss the sick women, and she went to a place where sick women lived, who were really full of the sickness, and she fell down on her knees in front of them, asking them that she might kiss them on the mouth for the love of Jesus. And so she kissed two sick women there, with many a holy thought and many a devout tear. And when she had kissed them and told them many good words, and stirred them to meekness and patience that they should not grumble about their illness but thank God most highly for it, and they should have great bliss in Heaven through the mercy of our Lord Jesus Christ, then one woman had so many temptations that she did not know how she might best behave herself. She was so harassed by her spiritual enemy that she dared not make the sign of the Cross, or offer any kind of worship to God, out of dread that the Devil should come and kill her. And she was harassed with many foul and horrible thoughts, many more than she could count. And, so she said, she was a virgin. Therefore the said creature went to her many times to comfort her and to pray for her, most especially that God should strengthen her against her enemy, and it is to be believed that He did so, blessed may He be!

CHAPTER 75

As the said creature was in St Margaret's Church to say her devotions, a man came and knelt behind her, wringing his hands and showing signs of great misery. She, perceiving his misery, asked him what was wrong. He said things were going very badly for him, as his wife had recently given birth to a baby and she was out of her mind.

'And, gentle lady,' he said, 'my wife doesn't know me, or any of her neighbours. She roars and cries so, it makes people terribly afraid. She wants both to strike out and bite, and she's had manacles put on her wrists.'

Then she asked the man if he wished her to go with him and see her, and he said, 'Yes, madam, for God's love.'

So she went off with him to see the woman. And when she entered the house, as soon as the sick woman who was out of her wits saw her, she spoke to her seriously and gently and said she was very welcome. And the woman was very glad that she had come and greatly comforted by her presence: 'For', she said, 'you are a really good woman, and I saw many fair angels around you, and therefore, I ask you, do not leave me, for I'm greatly comforted by you.'

And when other people came to her, she cried out and gaped as if she would eat them, and said that she saw many devils around them. She would not willingly allow them to touch her. She roared and cried, during most of both the night and the day, that people would not allow her to live amongst them, as she was so irritating to them. Then she was taken to the furthest end of the town, into a room, so that the people could not hear her crying. And there she was bound, hands and feet, with iron chains, so that she could not strike out at anybody.

And the said creature went to her each day, once or twice at the very least, and while she was with her, she was fairly meek, and heard her speak and converse willingly, without any roaring or crying. And the said creature prayed for this woman every day that God should, if it were His will, restore her to her wits again. And our Lord answered in her soul and said that she would manage very well. Then she was bolder in praying for her recovery than she had been before, and each day, weeping and sorrowing, she prayed for her recovery, until God gave her back her wits and her mind. And then she was brought to church and purified* as other women are, blessed may God be!

It was, as those who knew about it thought, a really great miracle, for he who wrote this book had never before (so he thought) seen a man or woman so far gone as was this woman, so difficult to control or manage, and afterwards he saw her serious and sober enough— may eternal worship and praise be to our Lord for His high mercy and His goodness, who always helps in times of need.

CHAPTER 76

It happened one time that the said creature's husband—a man very much advanced in age, over sixty years old—was coming down from his chamber barefoot and bare-legged, and he slid or somehow missed his footing and fell down to the ground from the stairs, and his head twisted under him and was seriously fractured and bruised, so much so that he had to have five linen plugs in his wound for many days while his head was healing. And as God wished, it was known to some of his neighbours that he had fallen down the stairs, perhaps because of the din and the crashing of his falling. And so they came to him and found him lying with his head twisted under him, only half alive, all splashed with blood, never likely to speak again to a priest or a cleric unless through high grace or a miracle. Then the said creature, his wife, was sent for, and so she came to him. Then he was lifted up and his head was stitched, and he was sick for a long time afterwards, so that people thought that he was going to die.

And then the people said that if he died, his wife deserved to be hanged for his death, insofar as she could have looked after him and she did not. They did not live together, or sleep together, because (as is written beforehand), they both mutually and willingly agreed on both their parts to make a vow to live chastely. And therefore, to avoid any perils, they lived and stayed in different places, where there could be no suspicion about their lack of chastity; for, first, they had lived together after they had made their vow and then the people slandered them and said they employed their lust and their desire as they had before they made their vow. And when they went away on pilgrimage, or to see and speak with other spiritual creatures, many evil people— whose tongues were their own harm, lacking in dread and love of our Lord Jesus Christ—supposed and said that they actually went to the woods, groves, or valleys, to indulge the lust of their bodies where people would not witness it or know about it. Knowing how prone the people were to think evil of them, and desiring to avoid all occasion for it if they possibly could, by their good will and mutual consent, they separated apart as regards their dining and their bedrooms, and went to dine in different places. And this was the reason that she was not with him, and also that she should not be hindered in her contemplation.

And therefore, when he had fallen and was grievously hurt, as was said before, the people said that, if he died, she would have to answer for his death. Then she prayed to our Lord that her husband might live for a year, and that she might be delivered from slander, if it was His pleasure.

Our Lord said to her mind, 'Daughter, you shall have your request, for he shall live, and I have performed a great miracle for you in that he is not dead. And I ask that you take him home and look after him for my love.'

She said, 'No, good Lord, for then I shall not attend to you as I do now.'

'Yes, daughter,' said our Lord, 'you shall have as much of a reward for looking after him and helping him in his need at home as if you were in church to make your prayers. And you have said many times that you would gladly look after me. I ask you now to look after him for the love of me, for he has sometimes fulfilled both your will and my will, and he has made your body freely available to me, so that you could serve me and live chaste and clean, and therefore I wish for you to be free to help him in his need in my name.'

'Oh, Lord,' she said, 'for your mercy, grant me grace to obey your will and fulfil your will, and never let my spiritual enemies have any power to prevent me from fulfilling your will.'

Then she took her husband home with her and looked after him for years afterwards, as long as he lived. She had a great deal of labour with him, for in his last days he turned childish and lost his reason, so that he could not (or else he would not) go to the toilet to relieve himself, but like a child he voided his bowels in his linen as he sat by the fire or at the table, wherever it was, he would spare nowhere. And therefore her labour was much the greater for washing and wringing, and the expenses of keeping a fire, and this impeded her very much from her contemplation so that often she would have hated her labours but she thought to herself how she had, in her youth, had many delectable thoughts, fleshly lusts, and excessive desire for his body. And therefore she was glad to be punished by the same body and took it all the more easily, and served him and helped him, so she thought, as she would have done Christ Himself.

CHAPTER 77

WHEN the said creature had first had her wonderful cryings, one time when she was in spiritual communication with her sovereign Lord Christ Jesus, she said, 'Lord, why will you give me such crying that the people are amazed at me for it? And they say that I am in great peril for, as they say, I am the cause of many people sinning over me. And you know, Lord, that I would wish to give nobody the cause or the occasion to sin if I might, for I would rather, Lord, be in a prison ten fathoms deep for my whole life, crying there and weeping for my sin and for everybody's sins and especially for your love, than that I should give the people occasion to sin wilfully because of me.

'Lord, the world may not allow me to do your will, nor to follow after your directing, and therefore I ask you, if it be your will, to take from me this crying during sermons, so that I do not cry during your holy preaching, and let me have these cryings when I am myself alone, so that I am not excluded from hearing your holy preaching and your holy words, because I cannot endure a greater pain in this world than being excluded from hearing your holy word. And if I were in prison, my greatest pain would be to forgo your holy words and your holy sermons. And, good Lord, if you wish nevertheless that I should cry, I ask you to give it to me alone in my chamber, as much as you wish, and spare me when I am amongst the people, if it pleases you.'

Our merciful Lord Christ Jesus, answering to her mind, said, 'Daughter, do not ask for this. You shall not have your desire in this, although my mother and the saints in Heaven pray for you, for I shall make you obedient to my will, that you will cry whenever I wish, and wherever I wish, both loudly and quietly, for I told you, daughter, that "you are mine and I am yours",* and eternally so you shall be.

'Daughter, you see how the planets are obedient to my will, that sometimes great thunderclaps come and make the people terribly afraid. And sometimes, daughter, you see how I send great lightning bolts that burn down churches and houses. Also sometimes you see that I send great winds that blow down steeples and houses, and trees out of the earth, and do much damage in many places, and yet the wind may not be seen, but it may well be felt.

'And just so, daughter, I proceed with the power of my Godhead; it may not be seen with human eye, and yet it can well be felt in a simple soul in which I like to work grace, as I do in your soul. And, as suddenly as the lightning comes from Heaven, so I suddenly enter into your soul, and illuminate it with the light of grace and of understanding, and set it all on fire with love, and make the fire of love burn inside it, and purge it fully clean from all earthly filth. And sometimes, daughter, I make earthquakes to make the people afraid, so that they should dread me.

'And just so, daughter, have I done with you spiritually and with other chosen souls that shall be saved, for I turn the earth of their hearts upside down and make them terribly afraid, so that they dread that vengeance should fall on them for their sins. And so did you, daughter, when you first turned to me, and it is necessary that young beginners do so, but now, daughter, you have great cause to love me well, for the perfect charity that I give you puts away all dread from you. And though other people set little value on you, I set a higher value on you. As sure as you are of the sun when you see it shining brightly, you are just as sure of the love of God, at all times.

'Also, daughter, you know well that I sometimes send many great rainstorms and heavy showers, and sometimes just small and soft raindrops. And just so I proceed with you, daughter, when it pleases me to speak to you in your soul; I sometimes give you quiet weeping and soft tears for a sign that I love you, and sometimes I give you great cries and roaring in order to make the people afraid at the grace that I put in you, as a token that I wish that my mother's sorrow be known through you, that men and women might have the more compassion for her sorrow that she suffered for me.

'And the third sign is this, daughter, that whatever creature will take as much sorrow for my Passion as you have done many times, and will cease their sins, they shall have the bliss of eternal Heaven. The fourth sign is this: that any creature on earth, even though he may have been the most horrible sinner, he need never fall into despair if he will take example from your way of life and behave somewhat like it, as far as he might.

'Also, daughter, the fifth sign is that I wish you to know in yourself, by the great pain that you feel in your heart when you cry so sorely for my love, that it shall be the cause of why you feel no pain when you leave this world, and also that you shall have the less pain at your death, for you have such great compassion for my flesh that I must need have compassion for your flesh. And therefore, daughter, suffer the people to say what they wish about your crying, for you are in no way the cause of their sin. Daughter, the people sinned over me, and yet I was not the cause of their sin.'

Then she said, 'Oh, Lord, blessed may you be, for I think that you do yourself what you are asking me to do. In Holy Writ, Lord, you ask me to love my enemies,* and I know well that in the whole world there was never such a great enemy to me as I have been to you. Therefore, Lord, even though for your love I would be slain a hundred times

a day (if it were possible) I could still never pay you back for the goodness that you have shown to me.'

Then our Lord answered her and said, 'I ask you, daughter, to give
me nothing but love. You can never please me more than to have me
always in your love, and you shall never, in any penance that you can
do on earth, please me so much as to love me. And, daughter, if you
will be high in Heaven with me, keep me always in mind as much
as you are able and do not forget me while you are dining, but think
always that I am sitting in your heart and know every thought that is
inside it, both good and ill, and that I perceive the slightest thought
and the twinkling of your eye.'*

She said back to our Lord, 'Now, truly, Lord, I wish I could love
you as much as you might make me love you. If it were possible,
I would love you as well as all the saints in Heaven love you, and as
well as all the creatures on earth may love you. And I wish, Lord,
for your love to be laid naked on a hurdle,* and for everybody to be
amazed at me for your love, so it was not a peril to their souls, and
for them to throw slurry and sludge on me, and for me to be dragged
out of town every day of my lifetime, if you were pleased by it and
nobody's soul hindered, your will must be fulfilled and not mine.'

CHAPTER 78

FOR many years, on Palm Sunday,* as this creature was in procession
with other good people in the churchyard, and saw how the priests
performed their observances, how they and the people too knelt to
the sacrament, it seemed to her spiritual sight as though she was at
that time in Jerusalem and saw our Lord in His manhood received by
the people, as He was while He walked here on earth. Then she had
so much sweetness and devotion that she could not bear it, but she
cried, wept, and sobbed very noisily. She had many a holy thought of
our Lord's Passion and beheld Him in her spiritual sight as truly as
if He had been in front of her in her physical sight. Therefore, she
could not stop herself weeping and sobbing, she really had to weep,
to cry, and to sob, when she saw her Saviour suffer such great pains
for her love. Then she would pray for all the people who were alive
on earth, so that they might do worship and reverence to our Lord at
that time and at all times, and so that they might be worthy of hearing

and understanding the holy words and laws of God, and meekly obey and truly fulfil them according to their power.

And it was the custom in the place where she lived to have a sermon on that day, and then, as an honourable doctor of divinity was in the pulpit and said the sermon, he often repeated these words, 'Our Lord Jesus languishes for love.' These words worked so in her mind, when she heard talk of the perfect love that our Lord Jesus Christ had for mankind, and how dearly He redeemed us with His bitter Passion, shedding His heart-blood for our redemption, and He suffered such a shameful death for our salvation, then she might no longer keep the fire of love enclosed within her breast but, whether she wanted to or not, such things which were enclosed within would appear outwardly. And so she cried very loudly and wept and sobbed really bitterly, as though she would burst out of pity and compassion that she had for our Lord's Passion. And sometimes she was all soaked with the effort of crying, it was so loud and violent, and many people were amazed by her and cursed her bluntly, supposing that she pretended to cry.

And soon after our Lord said to her, 'Daughter, this very much pleases me, for the more shame and more spitefulness that you have endured for my love, the more joy shall you have with me in Heaven, and it is appropriate that it should be so.'

Sometimes she heard great sounds and great melodies with her physical ears, and then she thought it was very merry in Heaven and had very powerful languishing and powerful longing towards Heaven with a great deal of quiet mourning. And then many times our Lord Jesus Christ would say to her, 'Daughter, there are some fair people here today, and many of them shall be dead within a year's time', and told her beforehand when a plague shall happen. And indeed she found it as she had felt it beforehand, and that much strengthened her in the love of God.

Our Lord would also say, 'Daughter, they who will not believe in the goodness and the grace that I show towards you in this life, I shall make them know the truth when they are dead and out of this world. Daughter, you have a good charitable zeal in that you wish that everybody should be saved, and I wish so too. And they say that they wish so themselves, but you can see well that they do not wish themselves to be saved, even though they sometimes will hear the word of God, but they will not always act after it, and they will not be sorrowful for their sins, and they will allow anyone else to suffer for them. Nevertheless, daughter, I have ordained you to be a mirror amongst them, to have great sorrow, so that they should take example from you to have some little sorrow in their hearts for their sins, so that through it they might be saved, but they do not like to hear of sorrow or of contrition.

'But, good daughter, you do your duty and pray for them while you are in this world, and you shall have the same prize and reward in Heaven as if all the world was saved by your good will and your prayer. Daughter, I have many times said to you that many thousands of souls shall be saved through your prayers, and some who lie at the point of death shall have grace through your merits and your prayers, for your tears and your prayers are very sweet and most acceptable to me.'

Then she said in her mind to our Lord Jesus Christ, 'Oh, Jesus, may you be blessed eternally, for I have many good reasons to thank you and love you with all my heart, for it seems to me, Lord, that you are all charity, to the profit and health of a man's soul. Oh Lord, I believe that he shall be really wicked that shall be separated from you for eternity: he shall neither wish for good, nor do good, nor desire good. And therefore, Lord, I thank you for all goodness that you have shown to me, a most unworthy wretch.'

And then, on the same Sunday, when the priest took the staff of the cross and struck the church door,* and the door opened for him, and the priest entered with the sacrament and all the people followed into church, then she thought that our Lord spoke to the Devil and opened the gates of Hell, confounding him and all his host, and such grace and goodness He showed to those souls, delivering them from the everlasting prison, in spite of the Devil and all his kind. She had many a holy thought and many a holy desire that she could never speak or rehearse, and her tongue could never express the abundance of grace that she felt, blessed be our Lord in all His gifts.

When they had come into the church and she saw the priests kneeling before the crucifix, and, as they sang, the priest who performed the service that day drew up a cloth in front of the crucifix three times, each time higher than the last, so that the people should see the crucifix, and then her mind was entirely taken out of all worldly things and focused on spiritual things, praying and desiring that she might finally have the full sight of Him in Heaven who is both God and man in one Person. And then afterwards, at the time of Mass, she wept and sobbed most plentifully, and sometimes cried out very fervently too, for she thought that she saw our Lord Christ Jesus as truly in her soul with her spiritual eye as she had seen the crucifix with her physical eye.

CHAPTER 79

THEN she saw, in the sight of her soul, our blissful Lord Christ Jesus coming towards His Passion, and before He went, He knelt down and took His mother's blessing. Then she saw His mother falling down in a swoon before her son, saying to Him, 'Alas, my dear son, how shall I suffer this sorrow and have no joy in the whole world but you alone? Oh, dear son, if you will die anyway, let me die before you, and let me never suffer this day of sorrow, for I may never bear this sorrow that I shall have for your death. I wish, son, that I might suffer death for you, so that you should not die—if mankind's soul could be so saved. Now, dear son, if you have no pity for yourself, take pity on your mother, for you know full well that nobody in the whole world can comfort me except you alone.'

Then our Lord took up His mother in His arms and kissed her very sweetly and said to her, 'Oh, blessed mother, be cheery and comforted, for I have often told you that I must needs suffer death, or otherwise nobody should be saved or ever come to bliss. And mother, it is my Father's will that it is so, and therefore I ask you to let it also be your will, for my death shall turn me to great worship, and you and all mankind to great joy and profit, those who trust in my Passion and act in accordance with it.

'And therefore, blessed mother, you must wait here after me, for in you the faith of Holy Church shall rest, and by your faith Holy Church shall be increased in her faith. And therefore I ask you, mother, stop your sorrowing, for I shall not leave you comfortless. I shall leave John,* my cousin, here with you, to comfort you instead of me; I shall send my holy angels to comfort you on earth; and I myself shall comfort you in your soul, because, mother, you know well that I have promised you the bliss of Heaven and you are sure of that.

'Oh, esteemed mother, what would you wish for better than where I am king you shall be queen, and all the angels and saints shall be obedient to your will? And whatever grace you ask of me, I shall not deny your desire. I shall give you power over the devils, so that they are afraid of you and you not afraid of them. And also, my blessed mother, I have said to you beforehand that I shall come for you myself when you shall pass out of this world, with all my angels and all my saints who are in Heaven, and bring you before my Father with all kinds of music, melody, and joy. And there I shall set you in great peace and eternal rest. And you shall be crowned as Queen of Heaven, as lady of the whole world, and as Empress of Hell. And therefore, my esteemed mother, I ask you, bless me and let me go to do my Father's will, for that is why I came into this world and took flesh and blood of you.'

When the said creature beheld this glorious sight in her soul and saw how He blessed His mother and His mother blessed Him, and then His blessed mother could not speak one more word to Him but fell down to the ground, and so they parted from each other, His mother lying still as though she were dead, then the said creature thought she took our Lord Jesus Christ by the clothes and fell down at His feet, asking Him to bless her, and at that she cried very loudly and wept very bitterly, saying in her mind, 'Oh, Lord, what will become of me? I had much rather that you kill me than let me stay in the world without you, for without you I cannot stay here, Lord.'

Then our Lord answered her, 'Be quiet, daughter, and rest with my mother here and comfort yourself in her, for she who is my own mother must suffer this sorrow. But I shall come back, daughter, to my mother and comfort both her and you, and turn all your sorrow to joy.'

And then she thought our Lord went on His way, and she went to our Lady and said, 'Oh, blessed Lady, get up and let's follow your blessed son as long as we may see Him, so that I can gaze enough on Him before He dies. Oh, dear Lady, how may your heart last, seeing your blissful son seeing all this woe? Lady, I cannot stand it and I'm not His mother!'

Then our Lady answered and said, 'Daughter, you have heard well that it will not be otherwise, and therefore I really must suffer it for my son's love.'

And then she thought that they followed on after our Lord, and saw how He made His prayers to His Father on the Mount of Olives,* and heard the good answer that came from His Father and the good answer that He gave back to His Father.

Then she saw how our Lord went to His disciples and asked them to wake up, His enemies were near. And then a great crowd of people came with many lights, and many armed men with staves, swords and pole-axes, to find our Lord Jesus Christ, our merciful Lord, meek as a lamb, saying to them, 'Whom seek ye?'*

They answered coarsely, 'Jesus of Nazareth.'

Our Lord said back, '*Ego sum*.'*

And then she saw the Jews fall down to the ground,* they could not stay standing out of fear, but then they got straight back up again and searched as they had done before. And our Lord asked, 'Whom seek ye?'*

And they said back, 'Jesus of Nazareth.'

Our Lord answered, 'I am he.'*

And then at once she saw Judas come and kiss our Lord,* and the Jews laid hands upon Him very violently. Then she and our Lady had much sorrow and great pain in seeing the Lamb of Innocence so contemptibly handled and dragged around by His own people to whom He was especially sent. And soon the said creature saw with her spiritual eye the Jews putting a cloth in front of our Lord's eyes, beating Him and buffeting Him about the head, and striking Him in front of His sweet mouth, crying most cruelly at Him: 'Tell us, who is it that struck thee?'*

They did not refrain from spitting in His face in the most shameful ways that they could. And then our Lady and she, her unworthy handmaiden for the time, wept and sighed most bitterly because the Jews behaved so foully and so venomously towards their blissful Lord. And they would not refrain from pulling His blissful ears and tugging at the hair of His beard. And then afterwards she saw them pull off His clothes and strip Him all naked, and then they dragged Him forth in front of them as if He had been the greatest criminal in the whole world. And He went on very meekly in front of them, as naked as the day He was born, towards a stone pillar, and He spoke no word against them, but let them do and say whatever they wished. And there they bound Him to the pillar as tightly as they were able, and they beat Him on His fair white body with rods, with whips, and with scourges.

And then she thought that our Lady wept astonishingly bitterly. And therefore the said creature needed to weep and to cry, when she saw such spiritual sights in her soul as freshly and as truly as if they had been done in her physical sight; and she thought that she and our Lady were always together to see our Lord's pains. She had such spiritual sights every Palm Sunday and every Good Friday, and in many other ways too, many years together. And therefore she cried and wept very bitterly and suffered very much spitefulness and scolding in many a region.

And then our Lord said to her soul, 'Daughter, I suffered these sorrows and many more for your love, and different pains, more than anybody can describe on earth. Therefore, daughter, you have a great reason to love me very well, for I have bought your love very dearly.'

CHAPTER 80

ANOTHER time in her contemplation she saw our Lord Jesus Christ bound to a pillar, and His hands were bound above His head.* And then she saw sixteen men with sixteen scourges, and each scourge had eight spiked, lead balls on the end, and each ball was full of sharp spikes, like the rowels of a spur. And the men with the scourges made an agreement that each of them should give our Lord forty strokes.*

When she saw this pitiful sight, she wept and cried very loudly as if she might burst from sorrow and pain. And when our Lord was all beaten up and scourged, the Jews loosed Him from the pillar and gave Him His cross to bear on His shoulders. And then she thought that she and our Lady went by a different route to meet Him, and when they met Him, they saw Him carrying the heavy cross in great pain; it was so heavy and so gigantic that He could hardly bear it.*

And then our Lady said to Him, 'Oh, my sweet son, let me help you carry that heavy cross.'*

And she was so weak that she could only fall down and swoon and lay as still as a dead woman. Then the creature saw our Lord fall down by His mother and comfort her as best He might, with many sweet words. When she heard the words and saw the compassion that the mother had for the son, and the son for His mother, then she wept, sobbed, and cried as though she should have died out of pity and compassion that she had for that pitiful sight and the holy thoughts that she had in the meantime, which were so subtle and heavenly that she could never describe them afterwards as she had felt them.

Then she went on in contemplation, through the mercy of our

Lord Jesus Christ, to the place where He was nailed to the Cross. And then she saw the Jews, with great violence, tear off from our Lord's precious body a silken cloth, which was so sticky and hardened with blood that it pulled off the skin from His blissful body and made His precious wounds anew, and made the blood run down all over on every side. Then that precious body appeared to her sight as raw as a thing that had just been flayed out of its skin, utterly pitiful and doleful to look at. And so she had a new sorrow and she cried and wept very bitterly.

And then after she saw how the cruel Jews laid His precious body onto the Cross, and then took a long nail, rough and enormous, and set it on His hand, and with great violence and cruelty they drove it through His hand. His blissful mother was watching, with this creature, how His precious body, with all its sinews and veins, shrank and stiffened out of the pain that it suffered and felt, and they sorrowed and mourned and sighed very bitterly.

Then she saw with her spiritual eye how the Jews fastened ropes on His other hand, for the sinews and the veins were shrunken so with pain that they could not reach the hole that had been made for them, and so they dragged on it to make it fit with the hole. And so her pain and her sorrow continually increased. And then they dragged His blissful feet in the same way. And then she thought that in her soul she heard our Lady say to the Jews: 'Alas, you cruel Jews, why are you behaving like this with my sweet son? He never did you any harm! You fill my heart full of sorrow.'

And then she thought the Jews violently answered back to our Lady, and pushed her away from her son. Then the aforesaid creature thought that she cried out at the Jews and said, 'You cursed Jews! Why are you killing my Lord Jesus Christ? Kill me instead and let Him go!'

And then she wept and cried exceptionally bitterly, so that many of the people in the church marvelled at her body. And then she saw them take up the Cross with our Lord's body hanging on it, and made a great noise and a great cry, and lifted it up a certain distance from the ground, and then let the Cross fall down into the mortice. And then our Lord's body shook and shuddered, and all the joints of that blissful body burst and fell apart, and His precious wounds ran with rivers of blood on every side. And so she then had all the more cause for more weeping and sorrowing.

And then she heard our Lord, hanging on the Cross, say these words to His mother: 'Woman, behold thy son, in St John the Evangelist.'*

Then she thought that our Lady fell down and swooned, and St John took her up in his arms and comforted her with sweet words as well as he could or might.

The creature then said to our Lord, as it seemed to her, 'Alas, Lord, you are leaving a grieving mother. What should we do now, and how shall we bear this great sorrow that we shall have for your love?'

And then she heard the two thieves speak to our Lord, and our Lord said to one thief, 'This day thou shalt be with me in Paradise.'*

Then she was glad of that answer and asked our Lord, for His mercy, that He would be as gracious to her soul when she should come to pass out of this world as He was to the thief, for she was worse, she thought, than any thief.

And then she thought that our Lord commended His spirit into His Father's hands* and, that being done, He died. Then she thought she saw our Lady swoon and fall down and lie still as if she were dead. Then the creature thought that she ran all around the place like a madwoman, crying and roaring. And after that she came to our Lady and fell down on her knees in front of her, saying to her, 'I ask you, Lady, cease your sorrowing, for your son's dead and not in pain, as I think you have sorrowed enough. And, Lady, I will sorrow for you, for your sorrow is my sorrow.'

Then she thought she saw Joseph of Arimathea* take our Lord's body down from the Cross and he laid it in front of our Lady on a marble stone.* Our Lady then had a kind of joy, when her dear son was taken down from the Cross and laid on the stone in front of her. And then our blissful Lady bowed down to her son's body and kissed His mouth, and wept so plentifully over His blessed face that she washed the blood off His face with the tears of her eyes. And then the creature thought she heard Mary Magdalene say to our Lady, 'I ask you, Lady, permit me to touch and kiss His feet, because I shall get grace from these.'

Then our Lady gave her and all those who were thereabouts permission to do whatever worship and reverence they wished to that precious body. And then Mary Magdalene took our Lord's feet, and our Lady's sisters* took His hands, the one sister one hand and the other sister another hand, and they wept very bitterly in kissing those hands and those precious feet. And the said creature thought that she kept on running to and fro, like a woman without reason, deeply desiring to have the precious body to herself alone, so that she might weep now in the presence of that precious body, for she thought that she would have died with weeping and mourning for His death, because of the love she had for Him.

And forthwith she saw St John the Evangelist, Joseph of Arimathea, and other friends of our Lord arrive, and they wanted to bury our Lord's body, and asked our Lady if she would allow them to bury that precious body. Our distressed Lady said to them, 'Sirs, you want to take my son's body away from me? I could never look upon Him enough when He lived; I ask you, let me have Him now He is dead, and do not separate asunder me and my son! And if you will in any case bury Him, I ask you to take me with Him, because I cannot live without Him!'

And the creature thought that they asked our Lady so nicely that in the end our Lady let them bury her dear son with great worship and great veneration, as was appropriate for them to do.

CHAPTER 81

WHEN our Lord was buried, our Lady fell down in a swoon as she was coming from the grave, and St John took her in his arms, and Mary Magdalene went on the other side to support and comfort our Lady, in so far as they could or might. Then the said creature, wanting to wait quietly by the grave of our Lord, mourned, wept, and sorrowed with loud cries out of the tenderness and compassion she had for our Lord's death, and for many a lamentable desire that God put into her mind at that time. The people marvelled at her for this, wondering what was wrong with her, for they knew very little about the cause. She thought she would never have gone away from there, but wanted to die right there and be buried with our Lord. After that the creature thought she saw our Lady go homewards again. And as she went, many good women came to her and said, 'Lady, we are so sad that your son is dead and that our people have been so spiteful towards Him.'*

And then our Lady, bowing down her head, thanked them very meekly through her expression and her look, because she could not speak as her heart was so full of grief.

Then the creature thought, when our Lady had come home and was lying down on a bed, then she made for our Lady a nice hot broth* and brought it to her to comfort her, and then our Lady said to her, 'Take it away, daughter. Do not give me any food except my own child.'

The creature replied to her, 'Oh, blessed Lady, you really need to comfort yourself and cease your sorrowing.'

'Oh, daughter, where should I go or where should I live without sorrow? I tell you truly, there was never a woman on earth who had such great cause to sorrow as I have, for there was never a woman in the world who bore a better child, or one who was meeker to its mother, than my son was to me.'

And presently she thought that she heard our Lady crying with a lamentable voice and say, 'John! Where is my son, Jesus Christ?'

And St John answered and said, 'Dear Lady, you well know that He is dead.'

'Oh, John,' she said, 'that is a wretched message to me!'

The creature heard this answer in the understanding of her soul as clearly as she should understand one person talking to another. And at once the creature heard St Peter knocking at the door, and St John asked, 'Who's there?' Peter answered, 'I, sinful Peter, who has forsaken my Lord Jesus Christ.'

St John wanted to have him come in, but Peter would not until our Lady asked him to come in. And then Peter said, 'Lady, I am not worthy to come into your presence', and he was silent outside the door.

Then St John went to our Lady and told her that Peter was so distraught that he dared not come in. Our Lady asked St John to go back quickly to St Peter and ask him to come in to see her. And then the creature, in her spiritual vision, saw St Peter come before our Lady and fall down on his knees with much weeping and sobbing, and say, 'Lady, I beg for your mercy, for I have forsaken your most prized son and my sweet master who loved me very well, and therefore, Lady, I am never worthy to look on Him, or you either, except through your great mercy.'

'Oh, Peter,' said our Lady, 'do not be afraid because, even though you forsook my sweet son, He never forsook you, Peter, and He shall come back and comfort us all really well; for He promised me, Peter, that He would come back on the third day and comfort me. Oh Peter,' said our Lady, 'I shall think of it for a very long time until the day comes that I can see His blessed face!'

Then our Lady lay still on her bed and heard how the friends of Jesus lamented the sorrow that they had. And our Lady always lay quietly, mourning and weeping with a sad countenance, and in the end Mary Magdalene and our Lady's sisters took their leave of our Lady, in order to go and buy ointment so that they could anoint our Lord's body with it.

Then the creature was left alone with our Lady and thought it was a thousand years until the third day came, and on that day she was with our Lady in a chapel* where our Lord Jesus Christ appeared to her and said, '*Salva sancta parens.*'*

And then the creature thought in her soul that our Lady said, 'Are you my sweet son, Jesus?'

And He said, 'Yes, my blessed mother, I am your own son, Jesus.'

Then He took up His blessed mother and kissed her very sweetly. And then the creature thought that she saw our Lady feel and touch all around our Lord's body, and His hands and His feet, to see if there was any soreness or any pain. And she heard our Lord say to His mother, 'Dear mother, my pain has all gone, and now I shall leave forever. And, mother, thus your pain and your sorrow shall be turned into very great joy. Mother, ask whatever you wish and I shall tell you.'

And when He had allowed His mother to ask whatever she wished and had answered her questions, then He said, 'Mother, with your permission I must go and speak with Mary Magdalene.'

Our Lady said, 'This is well done as, son, she has had much sorrow because of your absence. And I ask you, do not be gone long from me.'

These spiritual sights and significations caused the creature to weep, to sob, and to cry exceptionally loudly, so that she could not control herself or restrain herself on Easter Day and on other days when our Lord wished to visit her with His grace, blessed and worshipped may He be!

And then soon after the creature was—during her contemplation—with Mary Magdalene, mourning and attending our Lord at the grave, and she heard and saw how our Lord Jesus Christ appeared to her in the likeness of a gardener, saying, 'Woman, why weepest thou?'*

Mary, not knowing who He was, all enflamed with the fire of love, said back to Him: 'Sir, if thou hast taken Him hence, tell me, and I will take Him away.'*

Then our merciful Lord, having pity and compassion for her, said, 'Mary.'

And with that word she, recognizing our Lord, fell down at His feet and went to kiss His feet, saying, 'Master.'*

Our Lord said to her, 'Do not touch me.'*

Then the creature thought that Mary Magdalene said to our Lord, 'Oh, Lord, I see well that you do not wish that I am as intimate with you as I was before', and looked very sad.

'Yes, Mary,' said our Lord, 'I shall never forsake you, but I shall always be with you, without end.'

And then our Lord said to Mary Magdalene: 'Go to my brethren and Peter and say to them that I am risen.'*

And then the creature thought that Mary went forth with great joy, and she was really astonished that Mary felt joy, for if our Lord had said to her as He had to Mary, she thought that she would never be merry. That was when Mary wished to kiss His feet and He said, 'Do not touch me.' The creature had such despair and sadness in that phrase that whenever she heard it in a sermon, as she did many times, she wept, sorrowed, and cried as if she should die out of the love and desire that she had to be with our Lord.

CHAPTER 82

ON the Feast of the Purification, or Candlemas Day,* when the said creature saw the people with their candles in church, her mind was ravished into watching our Lady offering her blissful son, our Saviour, to the priest Simeon in the Temple, as true to her spiritual understanding as if she had been there in her physical presence to have made an offering with our Lady herself. Then she was so comforted by the contemplation in her soul of watching our Lord Jesus Christ and His blessed mother, and Simeon the priest, and Joseph, and other people who were there when our Lady was purified, and of the heavenly songs that she thought she heard when our blissful Lord was offered up to Simeon, that she could barely carry her own candle up to the priest as other people did at the moment of the offering, but she went staggering all about as if she was a drunken woman, weeping and sobbing so bitterly that she could hardly stand on her feet because of the fervour of love and devotion that God put into her soul through high contemplation. And sometimes she could not stand but rather fell down amongst the people and cried very loudly, so that many people were amazed and astonished at what was wrong with her, as the fervour of the spirit was so severe that the body failed and could not endure it.

She had such holy thoughts and meditations many times when she saw women being purified after childbirth.* She thought in her soul that she saw our Lady being purified, and had high contemplation in watching the women who came to make an offering with the women that were being purified. Her mind was entirely drawn from earthly thoughts and earthly sights, and focused entirely on spiritual sights, which were so delectable and so devout that she could not, in the time of fervour, withstand her weeping, her sobbing, and her crying, and therefore she suffered much derision, many a jibe and many a sneer.

Also, whenever she saw weddings—men and women being joined together according to the Church's law—she immediately received in meditation how our Lady was joined to Joseph, and about the spiritual joining of man's soul to Jesus Christ, praying to our Lord that her love and her affection could be joined to Him only, without end; and that she might have grace to obey Him, love and dread Him, worship and praise Him, and love nothing except that which He loves, and wish for nothing except that for which He wishes, and always to be ready to fulfil His will both night and day without grumbling or unwillingness but with all gladness of spirit. And she had many more holy thoughts than she could ever repeat, for she did not have them from her own studying or her own understanding but from His gift, whose wisdom is incomprehensible to all creatures except those that He chooses and enlightens more or less as He Himself wishes, for His will may not be constrained, it is His own free disposition.

She had these thoughts and these desires with profound tears, sighs, and sobs, and sometimes with very violent crying as God would send it, and sometimes with soft and private tears, without any violence. She could neither weep loudly nor silently except when God would send it to her, for she was sometimes devoid of tears for a day, or sometimes half a day, and had such a great pain for the desire she had for them that she would have given the whole world, if it had been hers, for a few tears, or have suffered very extreme physical pain with which to have obtained them.

And then, when she was thus devoid of tears, she could find neither joy nor comfort in food and drink and conversation, but was always depressed in her expression and countenance until God would send them to her again, and then she was happy enough. And, although it happened that sometimes our Lord withdrew the abundance of tears from her, He still did not withdraw holy thoughts or desires from her for many years together, for her mind and her desire was always towards our Lord. But she thought there was neither savour nor sweetness except when she could weep, for then she thought she might pray.

CHAPTER 83

Two priests who very much trusted in her manner of crying and weeping nevertheless sometimes greatly doubted whether it was fraudulent or not. By reason of the fact that she cried and wept in front of people, they had a secret idea, unbeknown to her, that they would test whether she cried so that people should hear her or not. So one day the priests came to her and asked her if she wanted to go two miles from where she lived, on pilgrimage to a church standing in the fields, a considerable distance from any other building, which was dedicated to the honour of God and St Michael the Archangel.* And she said that she would very willingly go with them.

They took with them a child or two and all went together to the said place. When they had said their prayers for a while, the afore-mentioned creature had so much sweetness and devotion that she might not keep it secret, but burst out in noisy weeping and sobbing, and cried as loud or even louder than she had when she was amongst people at home, and she could not restrain herself from it, even though there was nobody present other than the two priests and a child or two with them.

And then, as they returned home again, they met women with children in their arms, and the aforesaid creature asked if there were any young boys amongst them, and the women said 'no'. Then her mind was so ravished into the childhood of Christ, out of the desire that she had to see Him, that she could no longer bear it, but fell down and wept and cried so bitterly that it was a marvel to her. Then the priests had all the more faith that all was well with her, when they heard her crying in private places as well as in open places, and in the countryside as well as in the town.

Also, there were nuns who wished to get to know the creature and so be stirred all the more to devotion. She was in her church at midnight to hear their matins, and our Lord sent her such high devotion and such high meditation and such spiritual comforts that she was all aflame with the fire of love, which increased so intensely that it burst out with loud voice and great crying, so that our Lord's name was the more magnified amongst His servants, those who were good, meek, and simple souls and would believe the goodness of our Lord Jesus Christ, who gives His grace to whomever He wishes.

And, especially, her crying greatly assisted in the increase of virtue and of merit of those who neither doubt nor lack faith in their petitioning. To those who had little trust and little believed there was perhaps little increase of virtue and of merit. But whether people believed in her crying or not, her grace was never lessened but always increased. And our Lord visited her well and graciously by night and by day, whenever He wished, and however He wished, for she did not lack grace except when she doubted or mistrusted God's goodness, supposing or dreading that it was her spiritual enemy's will to inform her or teach her otherwise than was to her spiritual health.

When she thought like this or consented to any such thoughts through anybody's prompting or through any evil spirit in her mind (that would many times have had her put aside her good intentions, had the mighty hand of our Lord's mercy not withstood his great malice) then she lacked grace and devotion, and all good thoughts and all good memories, until she was, through our Lord Jesus Christ's mercy, compelled to believe steadfastly, without any doubts, that it was God who spoke in her and wished to be magnified in her for His own goodness and for her profit, and for the profit of many others.

And when she believed that it was God and not an evil spirit that gave her so much grace of devotion, contrition, and holy contemplation, then she had so many holy thoughts, holy speeches, and conversations in her soul, teaching her how she should love God, how she should worship Him and serve Him, that she could only ever repeat a few of them; it was so holy and so high that she was ashamed to tell them to any creature, and also it was so high above her physical wits that she could never express them with her physical tongue the way she felt them.* She understood them better in her soul than she could utter them. If one of her confessors came to her when she got up out of her contemplation or else from her meditation, she could tell him many things about the conversation that our Lord communicated to her soul, and in a short time afterwards she had forgotten the main part of it and almost everything.

CHAPTER 84

THE Abbess at Denny (a nunnery)* often sent for the said creature, for her to come and speak with her and with her sisters. The creature thought she would rather not go for another year, as she could scarcely endure the effort. Then, as she was in her meditation and had great sweetness and devotion, our Lord commanded her to go to Denny and comfort the ladies who desired to converse with her, saying to her soul in this way, 'Daughter, proceed to the house of Denny in the name of Jesus, for I wish you to comfort them.'

She was very loath to go, for it was during a time of plague, and she thought that she did not wish to die there for no good reason. Our Lord said back to her mind, 'Daughter, you shall go safely and you shall return safely.'

She went to an honourable burgess's wife, who loved and trusted her very much, and whose husband lay gravely ill, and she told the honourable wife that she should go to Denny. The worthy woman wanted her not to go, and said, 'I wouldn't wish', she said, 'for forty shillings for my husband to die while you're away.'

And she said back to her, 'Even if you gave me a hundred pounds, I wouldn't stay at home.'

For, when she was asked in her soul to go, she did not wish in any way to withstand it, but in spite of anything she would set off, whatever happened. And when she was asked in her soul to stay at home, nothing would make her go out.

And then our Lord told her that the aforesaid burgess should not die. Then she went back to the worthy wife and asked her to be much comforted, for her husband would live and get on really well and he would not die yet. The good wife was really glad and said back to her, 'Now the Gospel truth must be in your mouth.'

Afterwards, the creature wished to hurry off as she had been commanded and, when she came to the waterside, all the boats had gone towards Cambridge* before she had got there. Then she felt really dejected about how she might fulfil our Lord's command. And then she was asked in her soul not to be sad or dejected, as she would be provided for well enough, and she should go safely and come back safely. And indeed so it happened.

Then our Lord gave her a kind of thanks, inasmuch as she—in contemplation and in meditation—had been His mother's maidservant, and had helped to look after Him in His childhood and such like in the time of His death, and said to her, 'Daughter, you shall have as great a prize and as great a reward in Heaven with me for your good service and for the good deeds that you have done in your mind and your meditation, as if you had done the same deeds with your physical wits outwardly. And also, daughter, when you have for yourself and for your husband food and drink or any other thing that is necessary to you, for your spiritual confessors, or for any others that you receive in my name, you shall have the same reward in Heaven as if you had done it to my own person or to my blessed mother, and I shall thank you for it.

'Daughter, you say that "All Good" is a good name for me to be called, and you shall find that name is all good to you. And also, daughter, you say that it is very worthy that I am called "All Love", and you shall find very well that I am all love to you, for I know every thought of your heart. And I know well, daughter, that you have many times thought that, if you had filled many churches with gold nobles you would have given them in my name. And also that you have thought that, if you had enough money, you would have founded many abbeys for my love, for religious men and women to live in, and to have given each of them a hundred pounds a year for being my servants. And you have also, in your mind, wanted to have many priests in the town of Lynn, who could sing and read night and day to serve me, worship me, and praise and thank me for the goodness I have done for you on earth.

'And therefore, daughter, I promised you that you shall have the same prize and reward in Heaven for these good wishes and these good desires as if you had actually done them. Daughter, I know all the thoughts of your heart that you have towards all kinds of men and women, to all lepers, and to all prisoners, and as much money as you would give them each year with which to serve me, and I take it as if it had actually been done. And, daughter, I thank you for the charity that you have to all dissolute men and women, as you pray for them and weep many a tear for them, desiring that I should deliver them from sin and be as gracious to them as I was to Mary Magdalene, and that they might have as great a love to me as Mary Magdalene had. And in this state you would that every one of them should have twenty pounds a year to love me and to praise me.

'And daughter, this great charity that you have towards them in your prayers greatly pleases me. And also, daughter, I thank you for the charity that you have in your prayers when you pray for all the Jews and Saracens, and all heathen people, that they should come to the Christian faith, that my name might be magnified in them, and for the holy tears and weeping that you have wept for them, praying and desiring that if any prayer might bring them to grace or to Christendom, that I shall hear your prayer for them, if it were to be my will.

'Furthermore, daughter, I thank you for the general charity that you have to all the people who are now alive in this world, and to all those who are to come until the world's end, that you would be chopped up as small as meat for the pot for their love, so that by your death I would save them all from damnation if it pleased me, for you often say in your thought that there are people enough in Hell, and that you would like no more people to deserve to come therein.

'And therefore, daughter, for all these good wishes and desires, you shall have my very high prize and reward in Heaven. Believe it very well, and doubt it not a bit, for all these graces are my graces, and I myself work them in you, so you should have all the more reward in Heaven. And I tell you truly, daughter, every good thought and every good desire that you have in your soul is God's speech, even if you occasionally do not hear me speaking to you as I do sometimes to your clear understanding.

'And therefore, daughter, I am like a hidden God in your soul,* and I sometimes revoke your tears and your devotion, so that you should think of yourself as having no goodness in yourself, for all goodness comes from me; and also you should truly be certain what pain it is to renounce me, and how sweet it is to feel me, and so you should be all the more occupied in looking for me again; also, daughter, so that you know what pain other people have, those who want to feel me but may not. For there is many a man on earth who, if he had just one day in his whole life like many of the days you have, he would always love me the better and thank me for that one day. And you, daughter, may not forgo me for one day without great pain. Therefore, daughter, you have great cause to love me very well, for it is not because of any anger, daughter, that I sometimes withdraw the feeling of grace and the fervour of devotion from you, but because you should know very well that you cannot be a hypocrite for any weeping, for any crying, for any sweetness, for any devotion, for any thought of my Passion, or for any other spiritual grace that I give or send to you. For these are not the Devil's gifts, but they are my graces and my gifts, and these are my own special gifts that I give to my own chosen souls, whom I knew without beginning should come to grace and live with me without end.

'For in all other things you can be a hypocrite if you want, that is to say in terms of comprehension, in praying many prayers, in great fasting, in doing great penance outwardly so other people can see it, or in doing great charitable acts with your own hands, or in speaking good words with your own mouth. In all these, daughter, you can be a hypocrite if you wish, and you may also do them well and piously if you yourself wish to.

'Look, daughter, I have given you such a love that you shall be no hypocrite in that love. And, daughter, you shall never waste time whilst you are occupied in that love, because whoever is thinking well cannot be sinning at that moment. And the Devil does not know the holy thoughts that I give you, and nobody on earth knows how well and piously you are occupied with me, and not even you yourself can describe the great grace and goodness that you feel in me. And therefore, daughter, you beguile both the Devil and the world with your holy thoughts, and it is a very great folly in the people of the world to judge your heart, which nobody except God alone can know.

'And therefore, daughter, I tell you truly, you have as great a reason to enjoy and to be merry in your soul as any lady or virgin in this world. My love for you is so great that I cannot withdraw it from you, because, daughter, there is no heart that can think and no tongue that can tell the great love I have for you, and for that I take witness of my blessed mother, of my holy angels, and of all the saints in Heaven, for they all worship me for your love in Heaven. And so shall I be worshipped on earth for your love, daughter, for I wish to have the grace that I have shown to you on earth known to the world, so that the people can be astonished at my goodness and marvel at the great goodness I have shown to you, who have been sinful. And because I have been so gracious and merciful to you, those who are in the world shall not despair, even if they are never so sinful, for they can have mercy and grace if they wish it for themselves.'

CHAPTER 85

ONE time, as the said creature was kneeling in front of an altar of the cross and saying a prayer, her eyelids kept shutting together, as though she were going to sleep.* And in the end she had no choice: she fell into a light slumber, and instantaneously there truly appeared in her sight an angel, all dressed in white as if it were a little child, bearing a huge book in front of him. Then the creature said to the child, or the angel, 'Oh,' she said, 'this is *The Book of Life*.'*

And in the book she saw the Trinity, done in gold. Then she said to the child, 'Where is my name?'

The child answered and said, 'Here is your name, written at the foot of the Trinity', and with that he was gone, she did not know where.

And then at once our Lord Jesus spoke to her and said, 'Daughter, mind that you are now true and steadfast and have good faith, because your name is written in Heaven in the *Book of Life*, and this was an angel who comforted you. And therefore, daughter, you must be very merry, for I am very much occupied, both morning and afternoon, to pull your heart to my heart, as you should keep your mind entirely on me, and that shall most increase your love for God. For, daughter, if you will be drawn after God's advice, you cannot go amiss, for God's advice is to be meek, patient in charity and in chastity.'

Another time, as the creature lay in her contemplation in a chapel dedicated to our Lady, her mind was occupied in the Passion of our Lord Jesus Christ, and she truly thought that she saw our Lord appear in His manhood to her spiritual sight, with His wounds bleeding as freshly as though He had been scourged in front of her. And then she wept and cried with all her bodily might, for if her sorrow had been great before this spiritual vision, it was even greater after than it had been before, and her love was more increased towards our Lord. And then she was really amazed that our Lord had wished to become a man and suffer such grievous pains for her, who was such an unkind creature to Him.

Another time, as she was in the choir of a church dedicated to

St Margaret, in great sweetness and devotion with a great plenty of tears, she asked our Lord Jesus Christ how she might best please Him. And He answered to her soul, saying, 'Daughter, be mindful of your wickedness and think of my goodness.'

Then many times and often she prayed these words: 'Lord, for your great goodness have mercy on all my wickedness, as surely as I was never as wicked as you are good, and never can be, though I would like to, for you are so good that you can never be any better. And therefore it is a great wonder that anybody should ever be separated from you eternally.'

Then, as she lay still in the choir, weeping and mourning for her sins, suddenly she was in a kind of sleep. And at once she saw, with her spiritual eye, our Lord's body lying in front of her, and His head, so she thought, right next to her with His blessed face upwards, the most handsome man that could ever be seen or thought of. And then someone came into her vision with a fine dagger and cut that precious body all along the breast. And at once she wept amazingly bitterly, having more memory, pity, and compassion of the Passion of our Lord Jesus Christ than she had before. And so every day her thought and her love increased to our Lord, blessed may He be, and the more that her love increased, the more was her sorrow for the people's sins.

Another time, the said creature was in a chapel of our Lady, weeping bitterly in the memory of our Lord's Passion and such other graces and goodness as our Lord allotted to her mind, and suddenly, she had no idea how, she was in a kind of sleep. And straightaway, in her soul's sight, she saw our Lord standing right over her, so close that she thought she took His toes in her hand and felt them, and to her touch it was like it was real flesh and bone. And then she thanked God for all of it, for through these spiritual sights her affection was entirely drawn into the manhood of Christ and into the memory of His Passion, until that time that it pleased our Lord to give her comprehension of His incomprehensible Godhead.

As is written beforehand, she had these kinds of visions and feelings soon after her conversion, when she was utterly staunch and committed to serve God with all her heart and all her powers, and she had utterly left the world, and stayed at church all morning and afternoon, and especially at Lent, when she most insistently and with much prayer had permission from her husband to live in chastity and purity, and she did great physical penance before she went to Jerusalem.

But afterwards, when her husband and she had, by mutual consent, made a vow of chastity, as is written beforehand, and she had been at Rome and Jerusalem and suffered much spitefulness and reproof for her weeping and her crying, our Lord in His high mercy pulled her affection into His Godhead, and this was more fervent in love and desire, and more subtle in understanding, than was the manhood. And nevertheless the fire of love increased in her, and her under-standing was more enlightened and her devotion more fervent than it was before, when she had her meditation and her contemplation only in His manhood. She did not still have that manner of behaving in crying as she had before, but it was more subtle and more soft, and more easy for her spirit to bear, and plentiful in tears as it had been before.

Another time, as this creature was in a house of Preaching Friars and inside a chapel of our Lady,* standing in her prayers, her eyelids shut together in a kind of sleep, and suddenly she saw, as she thought, our Lady in the fairest vision she had ever seen, holding a pretty white handkerchief in her hand and saying to her, 'Daughter, do you want to see my son?'

And then at once she saw our Lady holding her blessed son in her hand, and she wrapped Him really gently in the white handkerchief, so that she could see how she did it. The creature then had a new spiritual joy and a new spiritual comfort, which was so marvellous that she could never describe it as she felt it.

CHAPTER 86

ONE time, our Lord spoke to the said creature, when it pleased Him, saying to her spiritual understanding, 'Daughter, for all the times that you have received the blessed sacrament of the altar with many more holy thoughts than you can repeat, for so many times shall you be rewarded in Heaven with new joys and new comforts. And, daughter, in Heaven it shall be known to you how many days you have had of high contemplation through my gifts on earth. And even though it is the case that they are my gifts and my grace that I have given to you, you shall still have the same grace and reward in Heaven as if it were of your own merits, for I have freely given them to you. But I thank you kindly, daughter, for allowing me to work my will in you and that you let me be so intimate with you. For, daughter, there is nothing you might do on earth that might better please me than to allow me to speak to you in your soul, as then you understand my will and I understand your will. And also, daughter, you call for my mother to enter into your soul, and to take me in her arms, and to lay me on her breasts and give me suck.

'Also, daughter, I know the holy thoughts and good desires that you have when you receive me, and the good charity that you have towards me when you receive my precious body into your soul, and also how you call Mary Magdalene into your soul to welcome me, for, daughter, I know well enough what you think. You think that she is worthiest in your soul, and you trust most in her prayers next to my mother, and so you may indeed, daughter, for she is a really good intercessor to me for you in the bliss of Heaven. And sometimes, daughter, you think your soul is so large and so wide that you call all the court of Heaven into your soul in order to welcome me. I know full well, daughter, what you say: "Come, all twelve apostles that were so well beloved of God on earth, and receive your Lord in my soul."

'Also, you pray to Katherine, Margaret, and all holy virgins in order to welcome me in your soul. And then you pray to my blessed Mother, to Mary Magdalene, to all apostles, martyrs, confessors, to Katherine, Margaret, and all holy virgins, that they should adorn your soul's private chamber with many fair flowers and with many sweet spices,* so that I may rest therein. Furthermore, you sometimes think, daughter, that you have a golden cushion, another of red velvet, and a third of white silk, in your soul.* And you think that my Father sits on the golden cushion, as might and power are His prerogative. And you think that I, the Second Person, your love and your joy, sit on the red velvet cushion, as all your thought is on me because I redeemed you so dearly, and you think that you can never repay me the love that I have shown you, even if you were killed a thousand times a day (if that were possible) for my love. Thus you think, daughter, in your soul, that I am worthy to sit on a red cushion, in remembrance of the red blood that I shed for you. Moreover, you think that the Holy Ghost sits on a white cushion, as you think that He is full of love and cleanness, and therefore it is fitting for Him to sit on a white cushion, for He is the giver of all holy thoughts and chastity.

'And I still know well enough, daughter, that you think that you may not worship the Father unless you worship the Son, or that you may not worship the Son unless you worship the Holy Ghost. And, also, you sometimes think, daughter, that the Father is almighty and all-knowing and all grace and goodness, and you think the same of the Son, that He is almighty and all-knowing and all grace and goodness. And you think that the Holy Ghost has the same properties equal to the Father and the Son, proceeding from both of them. Also, you think that each of the three persons in the Trinity has what the other has in their Godhead, and so in your soul you truly believe, daughter, that there are three different persons and one God in substance, and that each knows what the other knows, and each can do what the other can do, and each wants what the other wants. And, daughter, this is a true faith and a correct faith, and you have this faith only of my gift.

'And therefore, daughter, if you will consider this properly, you have a good reason to love me very well and to give to me your entire heart, so that I may entirely rest in it, as I myself wish. For if you will allow me, daughter, to rest in your soul on earth, believe it very well that you shall rest with me in Heaven eternally. And therefore, daughter, do not be surprised, even though you weep bitterly when you receive communion and receive my blessed body in the form of bread, for you pray to me before you receive communion, saying to me in your mind, "As certainly, Lord, as you love me, cleanse me of all sin and give me grace to receive your precious body worthily, with all kinds of worship and reverence."

'And, daughter, rest assured that I hear your prayer, for you can never say a word more to my liking than "as certainly as I love you", for then I fulfil my grace in you and give you many a holy thought, it would be impossible to describe them all.

'And for the great intimacy that I show towards you at that time, you are much the bolder to ask of me grace for yourself, for your husband, and for your children, and you make every Christian man and woman your child in your soul for the time, and would have as much grace for them as for your own children. Also, you ask for mercy for your husband, and you think that you are really beholden to me, that I have given you such a man that will allow you to live chastely, even though he is alive and in good physical health. For a fact, daughter, you think this very truthfully, and therefore you have a great reason to love me very well.

'Daughter, if you knew how many wives there are in this world who want to love me and serve me very well and dutifully, if they could be as free from their husbands as you are from yours, you would see that you really are very much beholden to me. And even though they are kept from their wish and suffer very great pain, therefore they shall have a very great reward in Heaven, as I receive every good will as a deed.

'Sometimes, daughter, I make you have great sorrow especially for your spiritual confessor's sins, so that he should have as complete forgiveness for his sins as you want to have of yours. And sometimes when you receive the precious sacrament, I make you pray for your spiritual confessor in this way: that as many men and women might be converted by his preaching as you would like to be converted by the tears of your eyes, and that my holy words might settle as fast in their hearts as you would have them settle in your heart. And also you asked the same grace for all good men who preach my word on earth, so that they might profit all rational creatures.

'And often, on those days that you receive my precious body, you ask for grace and mercy for all your friends, and for all your enemies that ever shamed or rebuked you, who either scorned you or sneered at you for the grace that I work in you, and for the whole world, old and young, with many tears of bitter weeping and sobbing. You have suffered much shame and many rebukes, and therefore you shall have very great bliss in Heaven.

'Daughter, do not be ashamed to receive my grace when I wish to give it to you, for I shall not be ashamed of you, so that you shall be received into the bliss of Heaven, to be rewarded there for every good thought, for every good word, and for every good deed, and for every day of contemplation, and for all good desires that you have had here in this world with me eternally as my prized darling, as my blessed spouse, and as my holy wife.

'And therefore, daughter, do not be afraid even though the people wonder why you weep so bitterly when you receive me, for rather if they knew what grace I put in you at that time they would be astonished that your heart does not burst apart. And so it should, if I did not measure out that grace myself; but you yourself can see well, daughter, that when you have received me into your soul, you are at peace and quiet and you no longer sob. And the people are really amazed by that, but it need not surprise you, for you know well that

I behave like a husband who is going to wed a wife. At the time he marries her, he thinks that he is sure enough of her, and that no man shall separate them asunder, for then, daughter, they can go to bed with each other without being ashamed or afraid of the people, and they can sleep in peace and quiet if they wish. And thus, daughter, it happens between you and me, for every week, especially on the Sunday, you have great fear and dread in your soul how you can best be sure of my love, and with great reverence and holy dread how you might best receive me for your soul's salvation, with all manner of meekness, humility, and charity, like any lady in this world is occupied in receiving her husband when he comes home and has been long from her.

'My esteemed daughter, I thank you highly for all the sick people you have tended in my name, and for all the goodness and service of any kind that you have done to them, for you shall have the same reward with me in Heaven as though you had looked after my own self when I was here on earth. Also, daughter, I thank you for as many times as you have bathed me, in your soul,* at home in your room, as though I had been present there in my manhood, for I know well, daughter, all the holy thoughts that you have shown to me in your mind. And also, daughter, I thank you for all the times that you have given me and my blessed mother lodging in your bed.

'For these, and for all other good thoughts and good deeds that you have thought in my name and performed for my love, you shall have with me and with my mother, with my holy angels, with my apostles, with my martyrs, confessors, and virgins, and with all my holy saints, all kinds of joy and bliss, lasting for eternity.'

CHAPTER 87

THE said creature lay utterly silently in the church, hearing and understanding this sweet conversation in her soul as clearly as one friend might speak to another. And when she heard the great promises that our Lord Jesus Christ made to her, then she thanked Him with great weeping and sobbing, and with many holy and reverent thoughts, saying in her mind, 'Lord Jesus, blessed must you be, for I never deserved this from you, but I wish I might be in that place where I should never displease you from this time forwards.'

With this kind of thought, and many more than I could ever write down, she worshipped and magnified our Lord Jesus Christ for His holy visitation and His comfort. And in such a manner of visitations and holy contemplations as are written beforehand, though much more subtle and higher beyond comparison than has been written, the said creature continued her life, through the protection of our Saviour Christ Jesus, for more than twenty-five years when this treatise was written, week by week and day by day, unless she were occupied with sick people, or else prevented by some other necessary occupation as was necessary for her or to her fellow Christians. Then it was withdrawn sometimes, for it can only be had in great peaceful-ness of the soul through long exercise.

From this kind of speech and conversation she was made robust and strong in our Lord's love, and made very stable in her faith and increased in meekness and charity and with other good virtues. And she securely and steadfastly believed that it was God who spoke in her soul and not an evil spirit, for in His speech she had the greatest strength and the greatest comfort and the greatest increase of virtue, blessed be God!

At different times, when the creature was so sick that she thought she was going to die, and other people believed the same, it was answered in her soul that she should not die, but that she should live and prosper, and so she did. Sometimes our Lady spoke to her and comforted her in her illness. Sometimes St Peter, or St Paul, some-times St Mary Magdalene, St Katherine, St Margaret, or whichever saint in Heaven that she could think about through God's will and consent, they spoke to the understanding of her soul, and informed her how she should love God and how she should best please Him, and answered to whatever she would ask of them, and she could understand by their manner of conversation which of them it was that spoke to her and comforted her.

Our Lord, in His high mercy, visited her so much and so plen-tifully with His holy speeches and His holy conversation, that she did not know how many hours of the day had passed. She sometimes supposed that five or six hours had passed and it had not even been the space of an hour. It was so sweet and so heartfelt that it happened as if she had been in Heaven. She never thought about how long it took, and she was never weary of it—the time passed, she knew not how. She would have rather served God, if she could have lived long enough, for a hundred years in this manner of living than just one day as she first began.

And often she said to our Lord Jesus, 'Oh, Lord Jesus, since it is so sweet to weep for your love on earth, I really believe that it shall be very joyful to be with you in Heaven. Therefore, Lord, I ask you, let me never have any other joy on earth except mourning and weeping for your love. For I think, Lord, even if I were in Hell, if I could weep there and mourn for your love as I do here, Hell should not bother me, but it would be a kind of Heaven, as your love puts away all kinds of fear of our spiritual enemy, for I would rather be there as long as you wish and please you, than to be in this world and displease you. Therefore, Lord, as you wish, so may it be!'

CHAPTER 88

WHEN this first book was first being written, the said creature was mostly at home in her room with her writer, and said fewer prayers in order to hasten the writing than she had in previous years. And when she came to church to hear her mass, intending to say her matins and other such devotions as she had made before, her heart was drawn away from speaking and was very focused on meditation. She was afraid of our Lord's displeasure, and He said to her soul: 'Do not be afraid, daughter, for however many prayers as you mean to say, I accept them as though you had said them, and likewise the concentration that you put your mind to, in order to have the grace that I have shown you written down, this pleases me very much, as does he who is doing the writing too. For, although you were in the church and both wept together as bitterly as you ever have, you still should not please me more than you are doing with your writing, for, daughter, many people shall be converted to me by this book and they will believe in me.

'Daughter, where is there a better prayer from your own reason than to pray to me with your heart or your thought? Daughter, when you pray through thought, you yourself understand what you ask of me, and you understand too what I say to you, and you understand what I promise you, to you and yours, and to all your spiritual confessors. And as for Master Robert, your confessor,* I have granted you what you desired,* and he should have half your tears and half the good works that I have performed in you. Therefore, he shall truly be rewarded for your weeping, as though he himself had wept. And really believe, daughter, that in the end you shall be very merry in Heaven together, and you shall bless the time that each of you knew the other.

'And, daughter, you shall eternally bless me for having given you so loyal a spiritual confessor for, even though he has sometimes been sharp with you, it has been greatly to your profit, as otherwise you would have had too much of a liking for him personally. And when he was sharp with you, then you ran with all your thoughts to me, saying, "Lord, there's no confidence but in you alone!" And then you cried to me with all your heart, "Lord, for your wounds smart, draw all my love into your heart."* And, daughter, so have I done.

'You often think that I have done a great deal for you, and you think that it is a great miracle that I have drawn all your affection to me, as sometimes you were so attached to some individual person that you thought at that moment that it would be in a way impossible to withdraw your affection from him. And after that you have desired, if it pleased me, that the same person should abandon you for my love, as if he had not supported you, few people would have set any value by you (as it seemed to you). And you thought, if he had abandoned you, it would have been the greatest rebuke that ever came to you, in the people's eyes, and therefore you would have willingly suffered that rebuke for my love, if it had pleased me.

'And so with such doleful thoughts you increased your love towards me and therefore, daughter, I receive your desires as if they had actually been done. And I know full well that you truly love that same person, and I have often said to you that he should be really glad to love you, and that he should believe that it is God who speaks in you and not a devil. Also, daughter, that person has pleased me very much, for he has often in his sermons excused your weeping and your crying, and so has Master Alan* done both too, and therefore they shall have a really great reward in Heaven. Daughter, I have many times told you that I should support your weeping and your crying by sermons and preaching.

'Also, daughter, I tell you that Master Robert, your spiritual confessor, very much pleases me when he asks you to believe that I love you. And I know well that you have great faith in his words, and very well you might, for he will not flatter you. And also, daughter, I am really pleased with him, for he asks you that you should sit still and give your heart to meditation, and think such holy thoughts as God wishes to put in your mind. And I myself have often asked you to do this, and you still will not do so except with much grumbling.

'And I am still not displeased with you because, daughter, I have often said to you that whether you pray with your mouth or think with your heart, whether you read or hear read,* I will be pleased with you. And still, daughter, I tell you, if you wish to believe in me, that act of meditation is the best for you and shall most increase your love for me; and the more intimately that you allow me to be in your soul on earth, the more worthy and right it is that I shall be more intimate with your soul in Heaven. And therefore, daughter, if you do not wish to follow after my advice, follow the counsel of your spiritual confessor, as he asks you to do the same as I ask you.

'Daughter, when your spiritual confessor says to you that you are displeasing God, you really believe him, and then you feel much sorrow and great depression, and you quickly weep until you have gained grace again. And then I often come to you myself and comfort you for, daughter, I may not allow you to have a moment's pain without my having to remedy it. And therefore, daughter, I come to you and make you sure of my love, and tell you with my own mouth that you are as sure of my love as God is God, and that nothing is so sure to you on earth that you may see with your physical eye. And therefore, blessed daughter, love him who loves you and do not forget me, daughter, for I do not forget you, for my merciful eye is always on you. And my merciful mother knows that very well, daughter, for she has often told you so, and many other saints too. And therefore, daughter, you have very great cause to love me very well, and to give me your entire heart with all your affections, for I desire that and nothing else from you. And in return for that I shall give you all my heart. And believe it very well that if you will be obedient to my will, I shall be obedient to your will, daughter.'

CHAPTER 89

ALSO, while the aforesaid creature was occupied in the writing of this treatise, she had many holy tears and much weeping, and often a flaming fire came around her breast, all hot and delicious, and also he who was her writer sometimes could not stop himself from weeping. And meanwhile, when the creature was in church, our Lord Jesus Christ, with His glorious mother and many saints too, came into her soul and thanked her, saying that they were very pleased with the writing of this book. And also she had many times heard the voice of a sweet bird* singing in her ear, and often she heard sweet sounds and melodies that surpassed her capacity to describe them. And she was ill many times during the writing of this treatise, and as soon as she set about the writing of this treatise she was suddenly healthy and fit. And often she was commanded to get herself ready in great haste.

And one time, as she lay at prayer in the church at the time of Advent before Christmas, she thought in her heart that she wished that God in His goodness would make Master Alan say a sermon as well as he could. And as soon as she had thought this, she heard our Sovereign Lord Christ Jesus saying in her soul, 'Daughter, I know full well what you are now thinking of Master Alan, and I tell you truly that he shall preach a really good sermon. And be sure that you staunchly believe the words that he shall preach, as though I were preaching them myself, for they shall be words of great solace and comfort to you for I shall speak in him.'

When she had heard this answer, she went and told it to her confessor and another two priests in whom she had much confidence. And when she had told them of her feelings, she was very sorry, for fear of whether or not he would speak as well as she had felt it, for sometimes revelations are hard to understand. And sometimes things that people believe to be revelations are deceits and illusions and therefore it is not appropriate to give credence too eagerly to every stirring but rather to wait discreetly and test if they are sent from God. Nevertheless, as for the feelings of this creature, it was utterly true, as shown in experience, and her dread and her depression turned into great spiritual comfort and gladness.

Sometimes she was in such a great depression over her feelings, when over many days she did not know how they might be understood, in fear of deceits and illusions, that she thought that she wished her head might be chopped from her body, until God, in His goodness, explained them to her mind. For sometimes that which she understood physically was to be understood spiritually; and the fear that she had of her feelings was the greatest scourge that she had on earth, and especially when she had her first feelings; and that dread made her very meek, for she had no joy in the feeling until she knew through experience whether it was true or not. But may God always be blessed, for He always made her mightier and stronger in His love and in His fear, and gave her increased virtue with perseverance.

Here ends this treatise, for God took to His mercy he who wrote the copy of this book. And even though he did not write clearly or openly in our kind of language, he, in his kind of writing and spelling, made correct sense, the which, through God's help and through the help of herself who experienced all this treatise in feeling and in working, is truly drawn out of that copy into this little book.

BOOK II

CHAPTER 1

AFTER our Sovereign Saviour had taken the person who first wrote the aforesaid treatise to His manifold mercy, and the priest of whom it is written beforehand had copied the same treatise according to his simple understanding, He believed it suitable to the honour of the blissful Trinity that His holy works should be notified and declared to the people, when it pleased Him, to the worship of His holy name. And then he began to write, in the year of our Lord 1438, on the feast of St Vitalis, martyr,* of such grace as our Lord performed in His simple creature during the years that she lived afterwards—not all but some of it, according to her own tongue.

And first here is a notable matter, which is not written in the preceding treatise.* It happened soon after the previously-mentioned creature had forsaken worldly pursuits and was joined in her mind to God, as much as infirmity would allow. The said creature had a son, a tall young man, living with an honourable burgess in Lynn, trading goods and sailing overseas, whom she wished to draw out of the perils of this wretched and unstable world, if her power might have achieved that. Nevertheless she did as much as was in her, and many times when she was able to meet him at leisure she advised him to leave the world and follow Christ, so much so that he fled her company and did not readily want to meet with her.

So one time it happened that the mother met with her son, even though it was then against his will and his intentions. And as she had done beforehand, so again she now spoke to him: that he should flee from the perils of this world and not fix his mind or his business so much upon it as he did. He did not agree but rather answered back sharply, and she, herself moved somewhat with a sharpness of spirit, said, 'Now, since you'll not leave the world on my advice, I order you, at my blessing, at least to keep your body clean from women's company until you take a wife according to the Church's law. And if you don't, I pray that God may chastise you and punish you for it.'

They parted company, and soon afterwards the young man went overseas on business, and then, whether through the evil enticements of other people or the stupidity of his own self-conduct, he fell into the sin of lechery. Soon afterwards his complexion changed, his face filled with spots and pustules as if he were a leper. Then he came back home to Lynn to his master with whom he had been dwelling before-hand. His master put him out of his job, not for any fault he found with him but supposing that he were perhaps a leper, as suggested by his face. The young man told him how his mother had banished him, due to which, he supposed, God so grievously cursed him. Some person, knowing about his complaint and having compassion for his disease, came to his mother, saying she had acted very wickedly, for through her prayers God had taken vengeance on her own child. She, paying little attention to their words, let it pass as if it were of no account until he would come and ask for grace himself.

So in the end, when he could see no other remedy, he came to his mother, telling her about his misconduct, and promising to be obedient to God and to her, and to correct his faults with God's help, eschewing all misconduct from that time on, to the best of his ability. He asked his mother for her blessing, and especially he asked her to pray for him that our Lord, in His high mercy, would forgive him for having trespassed and would take away that severe illness because of which people fled his company and his friendship as if from a leper. For he supposed that through her prayers our Lord sent him that punishment, and therefore he trusted that through her prayers he would be released from it, if she would, of her charity, pray for him.

Then she, having trust in his correction and compassion for his malady, promised, with sharp words of correction, to fulfil his plan if God wished to grant it. When she came to her meditation, not forget-ting the fruit of her womb,* she asked for forgiveness for his sin and for release from the sickness that our Lord had given him, if it were His will, and a profit to his soul. She prayed for so long that he was completely released from the illness and lived for many years after and he had a wife and child, blessed may God be, for he married his wife in Prussia, in Germany.*

When tidings came to his mother from overseas that her son had married, she was really glad and thanked God with all her heart, sup-posing and trusting that he should live clean and chaste, as the law of matrimony demands. After that, when God wished, his wife had a child, a lovely baby girl. Then he sent word to his mother in England of how God had graciously visited him and his wife. His mother, then being in a chapel dedicated to our Lady, thanked God for the grace and goodness that He had shown to her son, and desiring to see them if she might, then it was answered to her mind that she should see them all before she died. She was amazed by this feeling, how it could be just as she felt, inasmuch as they were far overseas and she was on this side of the sea, never intending to go overseas for the rest of her life. Nevertheless, she knew well that nothing was impossible for God. Therefore she trusted it should be so as she had that feeling, when God wished.

CHAPTER 2

A few years after this young man had married, he came home to England to his father and his mother, all transformed in his clothing and his disposition. Before, his clothes were all fashionably cut and his language was all idle chatter; now, he wore no fashionably cut clothes, and his conversation was full of virtue. His mother, astonished by this sudden change, said to him, '*Benedicite*, son, how has this happened to you, that you're so transformed?'

'Mother,' he said, 'I think that through your prayers our Lord has drawn me to Him, and I propose, by the grace of God, to follow your advice more than I did before.'

Then his mother, seeing this marvellous movement on the part of our Lord, thanked God as best she could, paying close attention to her son's conduct out of fear of dissimulation. The longer she watched his self-conduct, the more serious she thought him and the more pious towards our Lord. When she knew it was through the movement of our Lord's mercy, then she was really joyful, thanking God many times for His grace and His goodness.

After that, so he could be more diligent and more occupied in following our Lord's movement, she opened her heart to him, showing him and informing him how our Lord had moved her through His mercy and through what means; and also how much grace He had shown for her, which her son said he was not worthy of hearing.

Then he went on many pilgrimages to Rome and to many other holy places to purchase pardons for himself, returning to his wife and his child as he was bound to do. He told his wife about his mother, so much so that she wished to leave her father and her mother and her own country in order to come to England to see his mother. He was very glad of this and sent word to England to his mother to inform her of his wife's desire, and to know whether his mother would advise him to travel by land or by water, for he placed much trust in his mother's advice, believing it to come from the Holy Ghost.

His mother, when she had a letter from him and knew his desires, went to her prayers to know our Lord's advice and our Lord's will. And as she prayed about the said matter, it was answered to her soul that whether her son travelled by land or by water he would travel in safety. Then she wrote letters to him, saying that whether he travelled by land or by water, he would travel in safety, by God's grace. When he was informed of his mother's advice, he enquired as to when ships should come to England and he hired a ship (or, rather, part of a ship) in which he put his goods, his wife, his child, and himself, intending them all to come to England together.

When they were in the ship, such gales arose that they dared not set sail, and so they came back on land: him, his wife, and their child. Then they left their child in Prussia with their friends, and he and his wife came to England by the overland route to his father and his mother. When they had got there, his mother greatly rejoiced in the Lord that her feeling was true, for she had the feeling in her soul, as is written earlier, that whether they travelled by land or by water they should travel safely. And so it was in deed, blessed may God be!

They came home on the Saturday in good health, and on the next day, that was Sunday, while they were dining at lunch with other good friends, he fell very ill so that he got up from the table and lay down on a bed, and this illness and ailment occupied him for about a month, and then, in good life and true belief, he passed to the mercy of our Lord.* So spiritually and physically it can really be well verified—'He shall travel home in safety'—not only to this mortal land, but also into the land of living people, where death shall never appear.

A short time afterwards, the father of the said person followed the son the way every person must go.

Then still there lived the mother of the said person, of whom this treatise makes especial mention, and she who was his wife, a German woman, living with his mother for a year and a half, until the time that her friends who were in Germany wrote letters to her, desiring to have her home, and encouraged her to return to her own country. And so she, desiring her friends' affection, mentioned her notion to her mother-in-law, asking for her good love and permission, stating to her the desire of her friends that she might return to her own country. And so, with her mother-in-law's consent, she arranged herself to leave as soon as any ships were going to that country. So they enquired about a ship of that same country and her own compatriots were sailing there, and they thought it was excellent that she should sail in their ship rather than with other people.

Then she went to her confessor to be shriven, and while she was in confession, the said creature, her mother-in-law, walked up and down the choir, thinking in her mind, 'Lord, if it were your wish, I would leave my confessor and go overseas with her.'

Our Lord answered to her thought, saying, 'Daughter, I know well that if I requested you to go, you would go at once. Therefore I wish that you speak no word to your confessor about this matter.'

Then she was really glad and merry, trusting that she should not travel overseas, for she had before been in great peril at sea and intended never again to travel by sea by her own will.

When her daughter-in-law had confessed, the good man who was then confessor to both of them came to her and said, 'Who's going to go with your daughter to the seashore until she reaches her ship? It is not right that she should travel so far alone with a young man in a foreign country where neither of them are known', for a foreign man had come for her, and both of them were only slightly known in this country, which is why her confessor had all the more compassion for her.

Then the creature replied, 'Sir, if you will ask it of me, I shall go with her myself until she reaches Ipswich,* where the ship is moored and her own compatriots will escort her across the seas.'

Her confessor said, 'How could you go with her? You recently hurt your foot, and you're not yet fully healed, and also you're an old woman. You can't go!'

'Sir,' she said, 'God, as I trust, shall help me very well.'

Then he asked who should go with her and bring her back home. And she said, 'Sir, there is a hermit, belonging to this church, a young man. I hope that he will, for our Lord's love, go with me and come back with me, if you will give me permission.'

So she had permission to bring her daughter to Ipswich and then come back to Lynn. Thus they set out on their journey during Lent, and when they were five or six miles from Lynn they came upon a church, and so they turned aside to hear Mass. And as they were in church, the foresaid creature desiring tears of devotion was unable to obtain them at that time, but was continually commanded in her heart to go overseas with her daughter. She wanted to put it out of her mind, and it kept on coming back so fast that she could not rest or have peace in her mind, but kept on being tasked and commanded to go overseas. She thought it was a burden to her to take such an effort upon herself, and excused herself to our Lord in her mind, saying, 'Lord, you know well that I have no permission from my spiritual confessor, and I am committed to obedience. Therefore I may not do this without his command and his consent.'

It was answered back in her thought, 'I ask you to go in my name— Jesus—for I am above your spiritual confessor, and I shall excuse you, and guide you and bring you back in safety.'

She still wanted to excuse herself if in any way she could, and therefore she said, 'I am not provided with enough gold or silver to travel with as I ought to be, and even if I were and if I wanted to travel, I know full well that my daughter would rather that I stayed at home, and perhaps the ship's master won't welcome me into their ship to travel with them.'

Our Lord replied, 'If I am with you, who can be against you?* I shall provide for you and get friends to help you. Do as I ask you, and nobody on the ship shall say "no" to you.'

The creature saw there was no other help, but that she must set out at God's commandment. She thought that she would go first to Walsingham* and make an offering in worship of our Lady, and as she was on the way there she heard tell that a friar would be preaching a sermon in a little village a little out of her way. She turned into the church where the friar, a famous man, was saying the sermon and there was a big audience at his sermon. And many times he said these words: 'If God be for us, who can be against us?'* Through these words she was all the more stirred to obey God's will and carry out her intent.

So she set out for Walsingham, and after that to Norwich, with her daughter-in-law and with them the hermit. When they came to Norwich, she met a Grey Friar, an honourable cleric, a doctor of divinity, who had heard of her way of life and her feelings before. The doctor showed her great cheer and conversed with her as he had done previously. She, sighing often, was downcast in her expression and manner. The doctor asked what was wrong with her?

'Sir,' she said, 'when I left Lynn with my confessor's permission,

I intended to guide my daughter to Ipswich, where there is a ship in which she (by God's grace) shall sail to Germany, and then to return home to Lynn as soon as I well might, with a hermit who came with me for the same reason, to escort me back home. And he fully believed that I would do so. Yet, sir, when I was about six miles out of Lynn in a church to say my prayers, I was commanded in my soul that I should go overseas with my daughter, and I know well that she would rather I were at home, and so I would, if I dared. Thus I was guided in my soul, and I can have no rest in my spirit or in my devotions, until I gain consent to do as I was guided in my spirit, and this is very frightening and depressing to me.'

The honourable cleric said to her, 'You shall obey God's will, as I believe that it is the Holy Ghost who speaks in you, and therefore follow the guiding of your spirit in the name of Jesus.'

She was much comforted by his words and took her leave, setting out for the coast with her companions. When they got there, the ship was ready to sail. Then she asked the ship's master if she might sail with them to Germany, and he welcomed her kindly, and those who were on the ship did not even once say 'no'. There was nobody so much against her as her daughter, who ought to have been most in favour of her.

Then she took her leave of the hermit who had come there with her, rewarding him somewhat for his labour and asking him to excuse her to her confessor and to her other friends when he got home to Lynn, for it was not something she knew about or intended when she had left them to have gone overseas ever again while she was alive, 'but,' she said, 'I must obey God's will.'

The hermit parted from her with a sorry countenance and came back home to Lynn, excusing her to her confessor and to other friends, telling them of her sudden and marvellous departure, and how it had not been known to him that they should have gone their separate ways so suddenly. The people who heard about it were utterly astonished and said whatever they wanted. Some said, for the love of her daughter-in-law, that it was womanly spirit and a great folly for her to have put herself, an elderly woman, in peril of the sea, and to go to a foreign country where she had not been before, and without knowing how she should come back again. Some believed it was a great charitable deed, inasmuch as her daughter had earlier left her friends and her country and came with her husband to visit her in this country, that she would now help her daughter come home again to the country that she came from. Others, who knew more about the creature's way of living, supposed and trusted that it was the will and workings of almighty God to the magnifying of His own name.

CHAPTER 3

THE said creature and her companions boarded their ship on the Thursday of Passion Week,* and God sent them a good wind and weather that day and on the Friday but, on the Saturday and on the Palm Sunday too, our Lord, turning His hand as He liked and testing her faith and her patience, both nights sent such storms and gales that they all believed they were going to be shipwrecked. The gales were so dreadful and hideous that they could not control or manage their ship. They knew no better strategy than to commend themselves and their ship to the guidance of our Lord; they put aside their skill and their initiative and let our Lord direct them wherever He wished. The said creature had plenty of sorrow and remorse; she thought she had never had so much before. She cried to our Lord for mercy and protection for her and all her companions. She thought in her mind, 'Oh, Lord, I came here for your love, and you have often promised me that I should never perish either on land or in water or in any storm. The people have condemned me many times, and cursed me, and insulted me for the grace that you have performed in me, as they wished that I should die in misfortune and great distress, and now, Lord, it seems that their condemnations are be realized and I, unworthy wretch that I am, have been deceived by and defrauded of the promise that you have many times made to me, who have always trusted in your mercy and your goodness, unless you swiftly withdraw these gales and show us mercy! Now my enemies may rejoice, and I'll sorrow, if they have their intent and I be deceived. Now, blissful Jesus, think about your manifold mercy and fulfil your promises that you have promised to me! Show that you are honestly God and not an evil spirit that has brought me here into the sea's perils, whose advice I have trusted and followed for many years, and shall do, through your mercy, if you deliver us out of these dreadful perils. Help us and assist us, Lord, before we perish or despair, as we may not long endure this sorrow that we're in without your mercy and your assistance!'

Our merciful Lord, speaking in her mind, blamed her for her fear-fulness, saying, 'What are you scared of? Why are you so afraid? I am as mighty here at sea as I am on the land. Why do you wish to distrust me? All that I have promised you, I shall truly fulfil, and I shall never deceive you. Suffer patiently for a while and trust in my mercy. Do not waver in your faith, for without faith you may not please me. If you would truly trust me and not doubt at all, you may have great comfort in yourself, and might comfort all your companions, whereas now you are all in great fear and despair.'

With this kind of conversation, and some much more high and holy than I could ever write, our Lord comforted His creature, blessed may He be! She prayed to holy saints who conversed with her soul with our Lord's permission, giving her words of great comfort. In the end our Lady came and said, 'Daughter, be comforted. You have always found my tidings to be true, and therefore do not be afraid any longer, for I shall tell you truly that these winds and gales shall soon cease, and you shall have excellent weather.'

And so, blessed may God be, it was shortly afterwards that her ship was driven to the coast of Norway,* and they landed there on Good Friday and waited there over Easter Eve, and Easter Day, and the Monday after Easter. And on that Monday all those who belonged to the ship received communion on board the ship. On Easter Day, the ship's master and the said creature and others (most of the ship's company) went on land and heard their service at the church. After the local custom, the Cross was raised on Easter Day at about noon,* and she had her meditation and her devotion with weeping and sob-bing as well as if she had been at home. God did not withdraw His grace from her, neither in church nor on ship, nor at sea, nor in any place that she went to, for she always had Him in her soul.

When they had received the sacrament on Easter Monday, as is written previously, our Lord sent them a fair wind that brought them out of that country and drove them back to Germany as they wanted. The aforesaid creature found such grace in the ship's master that he organized meat and drink for her and all that was necessary for her as long as she was on board the ship, and he was as tender to her as if she had been his mother. He covered her on board ship with his own clothes, as otherwise she might have died of the cold; she was not as equipped as others were. She went at the bidding of our Lord, and therefore her Master, who asked her to go, provided for her so that she managed like any of her companions, therefore may worship and praise be to our Lord!

CHAPTER 4

THE said creature waited in Gdańsk in Germany* for about five or six weeks, and was warmly welcomed by many people for our Lord's love. There was nobody as against her as her daughter-in-law who, if she had been properly dutiful, was the most compelled and obligated to have comforted her.

Then the creature rejoiced in our Lord that she had such a warm welcome for His love and she intended to stay there for more time. Our Lord, speaking to her thought, commanded her to leave the country. She was then in great sorrow and confusion about how she should do God's bidding, which she wished in no way to resist, and yet she had neither man nor woman to accompany her. She did not want to go by water, though she was easily able to, as she had been afraid of the sea on her way there; and she could not travel easily by land, for there was a war in that region* that she should have to pass. So for one reason and another she was very distressed, not knowing how she might be comforted. She went into a church and made her prayers that our Lord, as He had commanded her to go, should send her help and companions with which she might travel.

Then suddenly a man, coming up to her, asked if she would like to go on pilgrimage to a region far from there, to a place called Wilsnack,* where the precious blood of our Lord Jesus Christ is worshipped, which miraculously came from three consecrated Hosts, the sacrament of the altar—the which three Hosts and precious blood are there to this day, worshipped and held in great reverence, and visited by those from many a country.

Very happily she said that she would go there if she had good company, and if she knew of any honest man who might afterwards bring her to England. And he promised her that he would go on pilgrimage with her to the aforesaid place at his own cost, and then, if she wanted to repay all his own expenses to England, he would come with her until she was at the English coast so that she might have companions from her nation. He organized a boat, a little vessel, in which they would sail towards the holy place. And then she could not get permission to leave that region, as she was an Englishwoman, and so she was very vexed and much hindered before she could get permission from one of the Teutonic Knights of Prussia* to leave there. In the end, through the directing of our Lord, there was a merchant from Lynn who heard about this, and he came to her and comforted her, promising her that he would help her leave, either secretly or openly. And this good man, through great labour, got her permission to go where she wished.

Then she, with the man who had arranged things for her, boarded her vessel, and God sent them a calm wind, the which wind pleased her very well, for there were no waves rising on the water. Her company thought they made no progress and were morose and grumbling. She prayed to our Lord, and He sent them enough wind that they sailed on a great surge and the waves rose very much indeed. Her companions were glad and merry, and she was glum and miserably afraid of the waves. When she looked at them, she was always frightened. Our Lord, speaking to her spirit, asked her to lay down her head, so that she should not see the waves, and she did so. But she kept on being afraid, and for this she was often scolded. And so they sailed on to a place that is called Stralsund.*

(If the names of the place are not written correctly, nobody should be astonished, for she gave more thought to contemplation than place-names, and he who wrote them down had never seen them, and therefore do excuse him.)

CHAPTER 5

WHEN they reached Stralsund, they landed and the said creature went onwards with the aforementioned man towards Wilsnack in great fear and passing many dangers. The man who was her guide was always scared and he kept trying to get away from her. Many times she spoke to him as nicely as she could, asking that he not leave her in these strange regions and in the midst of her enemies, for there was open war* between the English and those regions. Therefore her fear was much the worse, and in the midst of all this our Lord always spoke to her mind: 'Why are you afraid? Nobody shall do any harm to you or to anyone travelling with you. Therefore, comfort your man and tell him that no man shall hurt him or harm him while he is in your company. Daughter, you know well that a woman who has an attractive and handsome man for her husband, if she love him, she will travel with him wherever he wishes. And, daughter, there is nobody so attractive and so handsome and so good as I. Therefore, if you love me, you shall not be afraid to travel with me wherever I will have you go. Daughter, I brought you here, and I shall bring you safely home again to England. Do not doubt it, but believe it very well.'

Such holy conversation and speech in her soul caused her to sob most noisily and weep very plentifully. The more she wept, the more irked was the man accompanying her and the more he concerned himself with getting away from her and leaving her alone. He walked so quickly that she could not keep up with him without great exertion and great discomfort. He said that he was afraid of enemies and thieves, that perhaps they would take her away from him, and beat him and rob him too. She comforted him as well as she could, and said she dared undertake that nobody there should either beat them or rob them or say any wicked words to them.

And soon after their conversation, a man came out of a wood, a tall man with good weapons and dressed as if to fight them (so it seemed to them). Then her man, being very afraid, said to her, 'Look! What do you say now?'

She said, 'Trust in our Lord God and be afraid of nobody.'

The man passed them by, and did not say any wicked words to them, so they continued on towards Wilsnack with great effort. She could not manage such long journeys as could the man, and he had no compassion for her, and would not wait for her. And therefore she struggled as best as she could until she became ill and could go no further. It was a great marvel and miracle that a woman unaccustomed to walking, and also about sixty years of age, should daily endure to keep her pace on her journey with a brisk man travelling vigorously.

On the eve of Corpus Christi* they chanced to come upon a little hostel far from any town, and they could find no bedding there, just a little straw. And the said creature rested there that night, and the next day until it was evening-time again. Our Lord sent lightning, thunder, and rain nearly all the time, so that they dared not venture outside. She was very glad of it, as she was really ill and she knew well that, had it been fair weather, the man travelling with her would not have waited for her, he would have left her. Therefore she thanked

God, who had given him occasion to wait even though it was against his will.

And in the meantime, because of her illness, a wagon was arranged, and thus was she carried onwards to the Holy Blood of Wilsnack with great suffering and great discomfort. As they passed, the local women had compassion and said many times to the aforesaid man that he deserved to be severely blamed because he had worked her so hard. He, wishing to be rid of her, paid no attention to what they said, and never went any the easier on her. So what with good times and with grief, through our Lord's help, she was brought to Wilsnack and saw that precious blood which miraculously came out of the blessed sacrament of the altar.

CHAPTER 6

THEY did not stay long in the said place, but in a short while they went on their way towards Aachen, riding in wagons until they came to a riverside* where there was a great gathering of people, some going towards Aachen and some to other places, amongst whom was a monk, an utterly irresponsible man and of bad conduct, and in his party were young men, merchants.

The monk and the merchants knew the man well who was the said creature's guide and they called him by name, showing him a most warm welcome. When they had crossed the water and travelled by land (the monk with the merchants, and the said creature with her man, all in one party together in wagons), all being very thirsty, they came upon a house of Friars Minor. Then they asked that the said creature would go into the friary and get them some wine. She said, 'Sirs, you'll have to excuse me, for if it were a nunnery I should be ready to go in, but because they are men, I shall not, by your leave, go in.'

So one of the merchants went in and fetched them half a gallon of wine. Then friars came to them and asked them to come and see the blessed sacrament in their church, as it was during the Octave of Corpus Christi,* and it stood on show in a crystal vessel, so that people could see it if they wanted.* The monk and the men went with the friars to see the precious sacrament. The said creature thought she would see it as well as them and she followed after them, as though it were against her will. And when she saw the precious sacrament, our Lord gave her so much sweetness and devotion that she wept and sobbed marvellously bitterly and could not restrain herself from doing so.

The monk (and all her companions too) were angry because she wept so bitterly and when they came back to their wagons they chastised and reproached her, calling her 'hypocrite', and said many a wicked word to her. So to excuse herself she cited scripture at them, these verses from the Psalter: '*Qui seminant in lacrimis*', *et cetera*, '*euntes ibant et flebant*', *et cetera,** and similar ones. Then they were much angrier, and said that she should no longer travel in their company, and convinced her man to abandon her. She meekly and gently asked if they might, for God's love, allow her to travel on in their company, and not leave her all alone where she knew nobody, and nobody knew her, wherever she went. With great prayers and supplications she did travel on with them until they came to a good town, during the Octave of Corpus Christi. And there they said that on absolutely no account should she travel any further with them. He who was her guide and who had promised her that he would take her to England had abandoned her, handing over her gold and other such things as he had of hers in safekeeping, and offered to lend her more gold if she wanted it. She said to him, 'John, I didn't want your gold; I'd rather have had your company in these foreign regions than all the money you've got, and I believe you'd please God more if you'd travel with me as you promised me at Gdańsk than if you went to Rome by your own feet.'

Thus they put her out of their company and let her travel wherever she wished. Then she said to him who had been her guide, 'John, you're abandoning me for no other reason than that I weep when I see the sacrament and when I think about our Lord's Passion. And since I am abandoned because of God, I believe that God shall provide for me and bring me forth as He Himself wishes, for He has never deceived me, blessed may He be!'

So they went on their way and left her there still. The night came upon her, and she was very forlorn because she was alone. She knew nobody with whom she might stay that night or with whom she might travel the next day. Local priests came to her, where she was lodging. They called her 'English tail',* and said many vile words to her, giving her dirty looks and expressions, offering to show her around if she wanted. She was very much afraid for her chastity and was very forlorn.

Then she went to the landlady of the house, asking her if some of her maidservants might sleep with her that night. The landlady allocated two maidservants, who were with her all that night, yet she dared not sleep for fear of being raped. She was awake and praying nearly all night long to be preserved from impurity and to meet with some good company that might help her travel on to Aachen. Suddenly she was commanded in her soul to go to church early the next day, and there she should meet with companions.

Early the next day she paid for her lodgings, enquiring of her hosts if they knew of any party heading towards Aachen. They said 'no.' Taking leave of them, she went to the church to feel and test if her feelings were true or not. When she got there, she saw a group of poor people. Then she went to one of them, enquiring as to where they intended to travel. He said 'To Aachen.' She asked him to allow her to travel in their party.

'Why, madam,' he said, 'haven't you anybody to travel with you?'

'No,' she said, 'my man's left me.'

So she was welcomed into a party of poor people, and when they arrived in any town she bought her food and her companions went about begging. When they were outside the towns, her companions took off their clothes and, sitting naked, picked at themselves. Need compelled her to wait with them and prolong her journey, and to incur many more costs than she would otherwise. The creature was afraid to take off her clothes as did her companions, and therefore she, through mixing with them, got some of their parasites and she was bitten and stung most wickedly both day and night, until God sent her other companions. She kept with her party with great anguish and distress, and much difficulty, until the time that they reached Aachen.

CHAPTER 7

WHEN they reached Aachen, the said creature met with an English monk, who was on the way to Rome. Then she was much comforted, in so far as she had someone she could understand. And so they waited there together for ten or maybe eleven days, in order to see our Lady's smock and other holy relics that were shown on St Margaret's Day.*

And in the meantime, as they waited there, it happened that an honourable woman came from London, a widow with a large retinue with her, to see and worship the holy relics. The said creature came to this worthy woman, complaining that she had no companions to travel home with her to England. The worthy woman granted her all her desires, and ate and drank with her, and made her very welcome indeed.

When St Margaret's Day had come and gone, and they had seen the holy relics, the honourable woman hurried out of Aachen with all her retinue. The said creature, expecting to travel with her and thus cheated out of her intent, was very miserable. She took her leave of the monk who was on the way to Rome, as is written before, and after that she got herself a wagon with other pilgrims and followed after the said honourable woman as quickly as she could, to see if she could overtake her, but it was not to be.

Then she chanced to meet with two men from London going towards London. She asked to travel in their company. They said that if she could bear to go as quickly as them she should be welcome, but they could not be much delayed; nevertheless, they would willingly help her continue with her journey. So she followed behind them with great effort, until they reached a fine town where they met English pilgrims who had come from the court at Rome* and intended to go back to England. She asked them if she might travel with them, and they said abruptly that they would not delay their journey for her, as they had been robbed and had only a little money to get themselves home, for which reason they needed to make a swift journey. And therefore, if she might endure travelling as quickly as they, she should be welcome, but otherwise not.

She saw no other relief than to wait with them as long as she could, and so she left the other two men and waited quietly with these men. Then they went to their dinner and made merry. The said creature looked to one side of her and saw a man lying down and resting on a bench-end. She enquired, 'What man is that?' They said he was a friar, one of their party.

'Why isn't he eating with you?'

'Because we were robbed as well as him, and therefore each man must help himself as best as he can.'

'Well,' she said, 'he shall have part of such money as God sends me.'

She trusted well that our Lord would arrange for them both as was necessary to them. She had him eat and drink and comforted him a great deal. After that they travelled all together in one group. The said creature soon fell behind; she was too elderly and too weak to keep step with them. She ran and skipped as fast as she could until her strength failed.

Then she spoke with the poor friar whom she had tended before, offering to pay his costs until he reached Calais,* if he would wait with her and let her travel with him until they got there, and still give him a reward in addition to his labour. He was very content and consented to her wish. So they let their companions go on, and the two of them followed at a gentle pace, as they could manage. The friar, being terribly thirsty, said to the creature, 'I know these regions well, for I've often gone this way towards Rome, and I know well that there is an inn a little way from here. Let's go there and have a drink.'

She was very pleased and she followed him. When they got there, the landlady of the house, having compassion for the creature's travails, advised that she should take the wagon with other pilgrims and not travel alone with a man. She said that she had intended and fully expected to travel with an honourable woman from London but she had been deceived. By the time that they had rested themselves for a while and chatted with the landlady of the house, a wagon carrying pilgrims came by. The landlady, knowing the pilgrims in the wagon, implored them that this creature might ride with them in their wagon better to speed her journey. They, happily consenting, welcomed her into the wagon, all riding together until it reached a fine town, where the said creature perceived the honourable woman from London, of whom mention was made before.

Then she asked the pilgrims who were in the wagon to excuse her, and let her pay for the time that she had been with them as they pleased, as she would go to an honourable woman from her country whom she had perceived in the town, with whom she had made an agreement when she was in Aachen to travel home with her to England. She made a fond farewell and parted from them.

They rode away, and she went to the honourable woman, expecting to be welcomed with great friendliness. But it was exactly the opposite; she was met with a very abrupt manner and was spoken to most sharply, the honourable woman saying to her, 'Why are you expecting to travel with me? No: I'll have you know that I'll not mix with you.'

The creature was so rebuked that she did not know what to do. She knew nobody there, and nobody knew her. She did not know where to go. She knew neither where the friar was (who should have been her guide) nor whether or not he should travel by that way. She was in great doubt and depression, the greatest (she thought) that she had suffered since she had left England. Nevertheless she trusted in our Lord's promise and waited quietly in the town until God wished to send her some comfort. And when it was nearly evening, she saw the friar coming into the town. She hurried to speak to him, complaining about how she had been deceived and refused by the good woman in whom she had so trusted. The friar said that they should manage as well as God would give them grace, and he comforted her as best as he could, but he said that he would not stay in that town that night, as he knew well that it had dangerous people.

Then they went on together, out of the town, towards evening, with great fear and depression, worrying along the way about where they would be lodged that night. They happened to come to the edge of a wood, busily looking if they might spot a place where they might rest. And as our Lord wished, they saw a house or two, and they made their way there in haste, and a good man was living there with his wife and two children. They did not take anyone in to stay over and they would not receive guests into their lodgings. The said creature saw a heap of bracken in an outhouse, and, with great insistence, she obtained permission to rest herself on the bracken that night. After much persuasion, the friar was laid in a barn, and they thought they were well looked-after as they had a roof over their heads. On the next day, they settled up for their lodgings, taking the route towards Calais, travelling by tiring and dangerous routes in deep sand, over hills, and through valleys, for two days before they got there, suffering great thirst and great penance, for there were few towns and very poor lodgings.

And at night she often had the greatest fear, and perhaps it was from her spiritual enemy, as she was always afraid of being raped or dishonoured. She dared trust no man; whether or not she had reason, she was always afraid. She barely dared to sleep each night, as she expected a man to dishonour her. Therefore not one night did she gladly go to bed, unless she had one or two women with her. For that grace God sent her (for the most part), wherever she went, maidservants who would happily lie down beside her, and that was a great comfort to her. She was so weary and so overcome with effort towards Calais that she thought that her spirit would have departed from her body as she went on her way. Thus with great labour she reached Calais, and the good friar with her, who had behaved very well and honestly towards her for the time that they travelled together. And therefore she gave him such a reward as she could manage, so that he was very pleased and content and they parted from each other.

CHAPTER 8

In Calais this creature was warmly welcomed by various people, both by men and by women, who had never seen her before. There was a good woman who had her home to her house, who washed her thoroughly clean and gave her a new smock and comforted her very much. Other good people had her to eat and to drink. Whilst she was waiting for a ship there for three or four days she met with various persons who had known her before, who spoke nicely to her and talked well with her. They did not give her anything else, these people waiting, like her, for a ship.

She wished to sail with them to Dover;* they would not help her, or let her know what ship they intended to sail in. She enquired and looked out as diligently as she could, and she always knew their intentions one way or another until she had arranged to sail with them, and when she had carried her stuff onto the ship where they were—supposing they should sail away in haste, she did not know how quickly—they arranged for themselves another ship ready to sail. She never knew what the cause was.

Through grace, she, having knowledge of their purpose and of how ready they were to sail, left all her stuff in the vessel she was in and went to the ship they were in, and through our Lord's help she was welcomed onto the ship. And there was the honourable woman from London who had rejected her, as is written before. And so they all sailed together to Dover.

The said creature, perceiving by their expressions and countenances that they had little affection for her personally, prayed to our Lord that He would grant her grace to hold her head up, and preserve her from vomiting from seasickness in their presence, so that she should not cause them to be disgusted. Her wish was fulfilled so that, whilst other people in the ship were vomiting and throwing up violently and filthily she, to the amazement of all of them, could help them and do whatever she wished. And especially the woman from London had the worst of that suffering and illness, and this creature was most busy to help and comfort her for our Lord's love and through charity—she had no other reason!

So on they sailed until they reached Dover, and then each one of that party got himself companions with which to travel, if he wanted them, except for her alone, as she could get no companion to help her. Therefore she made her way towards Canterbury by herself alone, in a sorry and dejected state, for she had neither companions nor did she know the way. She was up early in the morning and came to a poor man's house, knocking at the door. The good poor man, huddled in his clothes, unlaced and unbuttoned, came to the door to know what she wanted. She asked him, if he had any horses, that he might help her to Canterbury, and she should pay him for his labours. He, desiring to do her pleasure in our Lord's name, fulfilled her wish, and led her on to Canterbury.

She had great joy in our Lord, who sent her help and assistance for every need, and thanked Him with many a devout tear, with much sobbing and weeping, in nearly every place that she came into (although it is not written down), on this side of the sea as well as on the other side of the sea, on water and on land, blessed may God be!

CHAPTER 9

From there she went to London, clad in a canvas cloth, like a coarse sackcloth, just as she had when she went overseas. When she reached London, many people knew her well enough; in so far as she was not dressed as she would have wanted, because of shortage of money, she, wishing to go unknown for a time until she might arrange a loan, wore a veil in front of her face. Despite her doing so, some dissolute persons, supposing it was Margery Kempe of Lynn,* said, so she might easily hear these derisive words: 'Oh, you false flesh, you'll eat no good meat!'

She, not answering, carried on as if she had not heard them. The aforesaid words were never of her speaking, neither of God nor of any good man, even though they were attributed to her, and she many times and many places had great derision because of them. They were devised by the Devil, father of lies, favoured, maintained, and born forth on his members, false, envious people, indignant at her virtuous way of life, without power to hinder her except through their false tongues. There was never man nor woman that could ever prove that she had said such words, but they always made other liars their authorities, saying, to excuse themselves, that other people had told them so. In this way were these false words devised through the Devil's suggesting.

Some person, or else persons, deceived by her spiritual enemy, contrived this tale not long after the said creature's conversion, seeing that she, sitting down to dine on a fish-day* at a good man's table, had been served with different fish—such as red herring,* and good pike, and various others—thus she was supposed to have said, as they reported, 'Oh, you false flesh, you'd eat red herring now, but you shall not have your way!'

And at that she put aside the red herring and ate the fine pike. And there were other things like this she was supposed to have said, so they said, and thus it sprung up as a kind of proverb against her, that people said 'False flesh, you shall eat no herring.' And some said the words that are written before, and it was entirely false, but they are still not forgotten. They were repeated in many a place where she was never recognized or known.

She went on to an honourable widow's house in London, where she was nicely received and had a very warm welcome for our Lord's love, and in many places in London she was greatly welcomed in our Lord's name, may God reward them all! There was one honourable woman especially who showed her high charity both in food and drink, and in giving other rewards, in whose place she was dining one time with various persons of various conditions, she being unknown to them and they to her, of which some were from the Cardinal's house* (as she had been told by others), and they had a great feast and got on very well. And when they were having fun, someone repeated the words written above or something like it, that is to say, 'You false flesh, you shall eat none of this good meat.' She was silent and suffered for a good while. They each chattered away to each other, making sport of the imperfection of the person about whom these words were said.

When they had amused themselves with these words, she asked them if they had any knowledge of the person who was supposed to have said these words.

They said, 'No, in truth, but we have heard tell that there is such a false, feigned hypocrite in Lynn who says such words, and, leaving aside common foods, she eats the most delicious and delectable foods that are brought to the table!'

'Look, sirs,' she said, 'you ought to say no worse than you know of, and yet not so much evil as you know of. Nevertheless, here you're saying worse than you know, may God forgive you for it, for I am that very person to whom these words have been attributed, who has often suffered great shame and reproof and I am not guilty of this matter, as I swear by God!'

When they saw her unmoved in this matter, not reproving them whatsoever, desiring their correction in a spirit of charity, they were rebuked by their own honesty, humbling themselves to make amends.

She spoke boldly and strongly wherever she went in London, against swearers, cursers, liars, and other such vicious people, against the elaborate apparel both of men and of women. She did not spare them, she did not flatter them, neither for their gifts nor for their food nor for their drink. Her speaking did a great deal of good to many people. Therefore, when she came into church to her contemplation, our Lord sent her very high devotion, thanking her that she was not afraid to rebuke sin in His name and because she suffered scorns and reproofs for His sake, promising her very much grace in this life and, after this life, to have eternal joy and bliss.

She was so comforted by the sweet conversation of our Lord that she could not control herself or conduct her spirit according to her own will, or according to the discretion of other people, but only according to how our Lord would lead it and control it Himself, in sobbing very extravagantly and weeping most plentifully, for which she suffered a great deal of slander and reproof, especially from the curates and the priests of the London churches. They would not allow her to stay in their churches, and therefore she went from one church to another, so that she would not be tedious to them. Many of the common people magnified God in her, trusting well that it was the goodness of God that performed that high grace in her soul.

CHAPTER 10

FROM London she went to Sheen,* three days before Lammas Day,* in order to purchase her pardon through our Lord's mercy. And when she was in the church at Sheen, she had great devotion and very high contemplation. She had plentiful tears of compunction and of compassion, in memory of the bitter pains and passions which our merciful Lord Jesus Christ suffered in His blessed manhood. Those who saw her weeping and heard her sobbing so violently were seized by great wonder and astonishment as to what was occupying her soul.

A young man who watched her expression and her countenance, moved through the Holy Ghost, went to her when he properly could, alone by himself, with a fervent desire to understand what might be causing her weeping, and he said to her, 'Mother, if it pleases you, I ask you to show me the cause of your weeping, for I have not seen a person with such plentiful tears as you have, and especially I have not before heard any person as violent in their sobbing as you are. And mother, even though I am young, my desire is to please my Lord Jesus Christ and so to follow him as I can and may. And I intend, by the grace of God, to assume the habit of this holy order, and therefore I ask you to be not a stranger towards me. In a motherly and kindly way, show your opinion to me, as I trust in you.'

She, kindly and meekly and with a glad spirit as she thought appropriate, commended him for his intentions and partly showed him the cause of her weeping and sobbing was her great unkindness towards her maker, through which she had many times offended His goodness, and the great abomination of her sins caused her to sob and weep. Also, the great, excellent charity of her Redeemer—by whom, through the virtue of suffering His Passion and shedding His precious blood, she was redeemed from everlasting pain, trusting to inherit joy and bliss—moved her to sob and weep, and this was no surprise. She told him many good words of spiritual comfort, through which he was stirred to great virtue, and afterwards he ate and drank with her for the time that she was there and was very glad to be in her company.

Lammas Day was the principal day of pardon and, as the said creature went into the church in Sheen, she caught sight of the hermit who led her from Lynn when she went towards the coast with her daughter-in-law, as is written before. Then with great joy of spirit she introduced herself into his presence, welcoming him with all the powers of her soul, saying to him, 'Oh, Reginald,* you are welcome! I trust our Lord sent you here, for now I hope, as you led me out of Lynn, you shall bring me back home to Lynn!'

The hermit looked at her with a cold expression and a frowning countenance, neither willing nor intending to bring her home to

Lynn as she wished. He, answering most coldly, said, 'I'll have you know that your confessor has forsaken you, because you went overseas and wouldn't tell him anything about it. You took your leave to bring your daughter to the coast; you asked for no further leave. None of your friends knew of your scheme; therefore I suppose you shall find but little friendship when you get home. I ask you, take your companions where you can, because I was blamed for your faults when last I escorted you; I want no more of this!'

She spoke nicely and prayed for God's love that he would not be displeased, for those who loved her for God before she left would love her for God when she came home. She offered to cover all his costs on the way homewards. So in the end he, consenting, brought her back to London and then home to Lynn, to the high worship of God and to the great merit of both their souls.

When she had come home to Lynn, she humbled herself in front of her confessor. He gave her very sharp words, for she owed him her obedience and had taken on such a journey without his knowledge. Therefore he was all the more angry with her, but our Lord helped her so that she had as good love from him and other friends as she had before, worshipped be God! Amen.*

*

THIS creature, as discussed beforehand, for many years used to begin her prayers in this way: first, when she got to church, kneeling in front of the sacrament in worship of the blessed Trinity (Father, Son, and Holy Ghost: one God and three Persons), and of that glorious Virgin, Queen of Mercy, our Lady St Mary, and of the Twelve Apostles, she said this holy hymn, '*Veni creator spiritus*',* with all the verses belonging to it, so that God would enlighten her soul, as He did His apostles on Pentecost Day, and endow her with the gifts of the Holy Ghost, so that she might have grace to understand His will and perform it in action, and so that she might have grace to withstand the temptations of her spiritual enemies and eschew all kinds of sins and wickedness. When she had said '*Veni creator spiritus*' with its verses, she spoke in the following way:

'I take the Holy Ghost as witness, our Lady, St Mary, the mother of God, the whole holy court of Heaven, and all my spiritual confessors here on earth that, even if it were possible for me to have knowledge and understanding of the secrets of God through the telling of any devil of hell, I would not want it.

'And as surely as I would not want to know, hear, see, feel, or understand in my soul in this life more than is God's will that I should know, as surely God must help me in all my thoughts, and in all my speeches, eating and drinking, sleeping and waking.

'As surely as it is neither my will nor my intention to worship any false devil as my God, nor any false faith, nor to have any false belief, as surely I defy the Devil, and all his false advice, and all that I have ever done, said, or thought, following the Devil's advice, believing it to have been God's counsel and inspiration of the Holy Ghost.

'If it has not been so, God, who sees and knows the secrets of all people's hearts, have mercy on me for it and grant me, in this life, a well of tears springing plentifully, with which I may wash away my sins through your mercy and your goodness.

'And, Lord, for your high mercy, all the tears that may increase my love to you and intensify my merit in Heaven, and help and profit my fellow-Christians' souls, dead or alive, visit me with them here on earth!

'Good Lord, spare the eyes in my head no more than you did the blood in your body which you shed plentifully for mankind's sinful soul, and grant me so much pain and sorrow in this world that I am not hindered from your bliss and from beholding your glorious face when I shall pass away.

'As for my crying, my sobbing, and my weeping, Lord God almighty, as surely as you know what scorn, what shames, what spitefulness, and what reproofs I have had because of it and, as surely as it is not in my power to weep either loudly or quietly, for devotion or sweetness, but only through the gift of the Holy Ghost, so surely, Lord, excuse me, so the whole world knows and trusts that it is your work and your gift, for the magnifying of your name and the increasing of other people's love to you, Jesus.

'And I pray to you, Sovereign Lord Christ Jesus, that as many people are converted by my crying and my weeping as have scorned me for it, or shall scorn me until the end of the world, and many more, if it is your wish. And, as regards any earthly man's love, as surely as I would have no love other than God, to love above all things and all other creatures for God and in God, just so surely quench all fleshly lust in me, and in all those in whom I have beheld your blissful body. And give us your holy fear in our hearts for your stinging wounds.

'Lord, make my spiritual confessors fear you in me and love you in me, and make everyone in the whole world have the more sorrow for their own sins, for the sorrow that you have given me for other people's sins. Good Jesus, make my will your will, and your will my will, so that I may have no will but your will only.

'Now, good Lord Christ Jesus, I cry to you for mercy for all the estates that are in Holy Church, for the Pope and all his cardinals, for all archbishops and bishops, and for the whole order of priesthood, for all men and women religious, and especially those who busy themselves saving and defending the faith of Holy Church. Lord, in your mercy bless them and grant them victory over all their enemies, and back them in all that they do to your worship; for all who are in grace at this time, God send them perseverance until the end of their lives, and make me worthy to be able to partake in their prayers, and them in mine, and each of us the other's.

'I cry you mercy, blissful Lord, for the King of England* and for all Christian kings, and for all lords and ladies in this world. God, place them in such governance so that they may most please you and be lords and ladies eternally in Heaven. I cry you mercy, Lord, for the rich people in this world who have your goods in their control; give them grace to spend them to your pleasure. I cry you mercy, Lord, for Jews, and Saracens, and all heathen people. Good

Lord, remember that there is many a saint in Heaven who was once a heathen on earth, and thus do you spread your mercy to those who are on earth.

'Lord, you say yourself that nobody shall come to you without you, that nobody shall be drawn to you unless you draw them.* And therefore, Lord, if there is anybody who is not drawn, I pray you draw him to you. You have drawn me, Lord, and I never deserved to be drawn, but according to your great mercy you have drawn me. If the whole world knew my wickedness as you do, it should marvel at the great goodness that you have shown me. I wish that the whole world was worthy to thank you for me, and, as you have made unworthy creatures worthy, so make the whole world worthy to thank you and praise you.

'I cry you mercy, Lord, for all false heretics and for all misbelievers, for all dishonest tithe-payers, thieves, adulterers and all loose women, and for all those who live roguishly. Lord, for your mercy, have mercy on them, if it is your will, and bring them out of this misconduct all the sooner for my prayers.

'I cry you mercy, Lord, for all those who are tempted and vexed by their spiritual enemies, that you, in your mercy, give them grace to withstand their temptations and deliver them from them when it is most to your pleasure.

'I cry you mercy, Lord, for all my spiritual confessors, that you vouchsafe to spread as much grace in their souls as I wish that you might in mine.

'I cry you mercy, Lord, for all my children, spiritually and physically, and for all the people in this world, that you make their sins over to me in true contrition as if they were my own sins, and forgive them as I wish that you forgive me.

'I cry you mercy, Lord, for all my friends and all my enemies, especially for all those who are sick, for all lepers, for all bedridden men and women, for all who are in prison, and for all creatures who have said either good or evil about me in this world, or shall do until the world's end. Have mercy upon them, and be as gracious to their souls as I wish you to be to mine.

'And those that have said anything evil about me, for your high mercy, forgive them for it; and those that spoke well, I pray you, Lord, to reward them, for it is through their charity and not through my merits; for, although you allowed the whole world to avenge you on me and to hate me because I have displeased you, you did me no wrong.

'I cry you mercy, Lord, for all the souls that are in the pains of Purgatory, waiting there for your mercy and the prayers of Holy Church as surely, Lord, as they are your own chosen souls. Be as gracious to them as I would wish you to be to me if my soul were in the same pain that they are in.

'Lord Christ Jesus, I thank you for all health and all wealth, for all riches and all poverty, for sickness and all scorn, for all spitefulness, and all wrongs, and for all the different tribulations that have happened and shall happen to me as long as I live. I thank you highly that you wished to let me suffer any pain in this world in remission of my sins and in increasing my merit in Heaven. As surely as I have great cause to thank you, hear my prayers; for although I had as many hearts and souls enclosed in my soul as God knew from without beginning how many should live eternally in Heaven, and as many drops of water, fresh and salty, that there are, and chips of gravel, stones small and great, grasses growing on earth, kernels of corn, fish, fowl, beasts, and leaves upon trees when there is the greatest plenty, feathers of bird or fur of beast, seeds that grow in the earth, or weeds, or flowers, on land, or in water when most grow, and as many creatures as there have been on earth, and are now, and shall be, and might be through your power, and as there are stars and angels in your sight, or other kinds of good that grow on earth, and each were a soul as holy as ever was our Lady St Mary who bore Jesus our Saviour, and if it were possible that each could think and speak all such great reverence and worship as ever did our Lady St Mary here on earth and now does in Heaven and shall do eternally, I might well think in my heart and speak it with my mouth at this time in worship of the Trinity and of all the court of Heaven, to the great dishonour and disgrace of Satan who fell from God's face, and of all his wicked spirits, that all these hearts and souls could neither ever thank God nor fully praise Him, neither bless Him fully nor worship Him, neither love Him fully nor fully give acclaim, praise, and reverence to Him as He would be worthy to have the great mercy that he has shown to me on earth. That I cannot and may not do.

'I pray my Lady, who is alone the Mother of God, the well of grace, flower and fairest of all women that God ever made on earth, the worthiest in His sight, the most loved, the most dear to Him and prized by Him; the worthiest to be heard by God, and the highest that has deserved it in this life, benign Lady, meek Lady, charitable Lady, with all the reverence that is in Heaven with all your holy saints, I pray you, Lady, offer thanks and praise to the blissful Trinity for my love, asking mercy and grace for me and for all my spiritual confessors, and perseverance until the end of our lives in that life in which we may most please God.

'I bless my God in my soul and all of you who are in Heaven. Blessed may God be in you all, and all of you in God. Blessed are you, Lord, for all your mercies that you have shown to all who are in Heaven and on earth. And especially, I bless you, Lord, for Mary Magdalene, for Mary the Egyptian, for St Paul, and for St Augustine.* And as you have shown mercy to them, so show me your mercy and to all those who ask your mercy of heart. The peace and rest you have bequeathed to your disciples and to your lovers, may you bequeath the same peace and rest to me on earth and eternally in Heaven.

'Remember, Lord, the woman who was taken in adultery* and brought in front of you, and as you drove away all her enemies from her and she stood alone by you, so truly may you drive away all my enemies, both physical and spiritual, from me, so that I may stand alone by you, and make my soul dead to all the joys of this world, and alive to and eager for high contemplation in God.

'Remember, Lord, Lazarus,* who lay for four days dead in his grave and, as I have been in that holy place* where your body was alive and dead and crucified for mankind's sin, and there Lazarus was raised from death to life, as surely, Lord, if any man or woman were dead right now of mortal sin, if any prayer might help them, hear my prayers for them and make them live eternally.

'Many thanks, Lord, for all those sins from which you have kept me, which I have not done, and many thanks, Lord, for all the sorrow that you have given me for those that I have done, for these graces and all other graces which are necessary to me and to all the creatures on earth.

'And for all those that have faith and trust, or shall have faith and trust, in my prayers until the world's end, such grace as they desire, spiritually and physically, to the profit of their souls, I pray you, Lord, grant them for the abundance of your mercy. Amen.'

*Jhesu mercy quod Salthows.**

EXPLANATORY NOTES

ABBREVIATIONS

BMK   *The Book of Margery Kempe*, ed. Sanford Brown Meech and Hope Emily Allen, EETS o.s. 212 (London, 1940)

BMKA   *The Book of Margery Kempe: An Annotated Edition*, ed. Barry Windeatt (Cambridge, 2004)

CBMK   *A Companion to the Book of Margery Kempe*, ed. John H. Arnold and Katherine J. Lewis (Cambridge, 2004)

CCKJ   Denys Pringle, *Churches of the Crusader Kingdom of Jerusalem*, 4 vols. (Cambridge, 1993–2009)

EAN   Ann Nichols, *The Early Art of Norfolk: A Subject List of Extant and Lost Art Including Items Relevant to Early Drama* (Kalamazoo, MI, 2002)

EETS   Early English Text Society [o.s. = original series, s.s. = supplementary series]

IE   *Index Exemplorum*, ed. Frederic Tubach (Helsinki, 1971)

LSRev   Birgitta of Sweden, *Life and Selected Revelations*, ed. and trans. Marguerite Tjader Harris and Albert Ryle Kezel (Mahwah, NJ, 1990)

ODNB   *The Oxford Dictionary of National Biography*, via oxforddnb.com

3 *Liber Montis Gracie . . . Mount Grace*: this ownership inscription refers to the Carthusian priory of Mount Grace (Yorkshire). It appears on one of the introductory binding pages of the manuscript, not on the first page of the text itself. This inscription allows us to locate the unique surviving manuscript of Kempe's *Book* in a later fifteenth-century monastic community.

In the name of Jesus Christ: the sacred monogram, 'IHC' from the Greek name for Jesus (IHΣ), appears throughout the manuscript. This reflects a special devotion to the Holy Name; on this distinctive late medieval cult, see Rob Lutton, 'Love this Name that is IHC: vernacular prayers, hymns and lyrics to the Holy Name of Jesus in pre-Reformation England', in Elisabeth Salter and Helen Wicker, eds., *Vernacularity in England in Wales* (Turnhout, 2011), 115–41.

His handiwork and His creature: throughout the *Book* Kempe is referred to, in the third person, as a 'creature', emphasizing that she is a thing created by God's 'handiwork'. The word 'creature' was used frequently to describe mankind in fifteenth-century religious texts; as the fifteenth-century Wycliffite tract *The Lantern of Light* urges, 'Preach the gospel to each creature, that is, to each person!'

4 *Through the inspiration . . . happen afterwards*: Kempe's gift of prophecy appears throughout the *Book*, although female prophecy was a contentious

issue. Kempe's contemporary, Eleanor Cobham (*c.*1400–52), the Duchess of Gloucester, was convicted for necromancy in 1441 having consulted astrologers in order to foresee the future; Cobham died in prison. See Diane Watt, *Secretaries of God: Female Prophecy in Late Medieval and Early Modern England* (Cambridge, 1997).

Then this creature . . . spiritual enemies: a concern with the discernment of spirits, false prophecy, and diabolical inspiration runs through the *Book*.

anchorites: Kempe visited Julian of Norwich, one of the most famous anchorites of medieval England (see p. 41), at her anchorhold at St Julian's, Norwich. Anchorites and recluses were by no means rare at this time and indeed the Lynn Carmelites had an anchoress of a similar background to Kempe: Joanna Catfield, who came from a prominent merchant family of the town's elite class (William Liddle, *The Virtue of Place in Late Medieval Lynn*, unpublished PhD thesis, Queen's University Belfast (2013), 191).

5 *Germany*: the Middle English word '*Dewchlond*' could mean anywhere in Germanic Europe, from present-day Belgium to Lithuania. Kempe's son moves to Prussia (p. 202) and Kempe herself visits Gdańsk (p. 210) and Stralsund (p. 211), attesting to the close links between Lynn and the Baltic. Moreover, Kempe's book is notably influenced by northern European religious women, not least St Bridget (whose order was based at Vadstena in southern Sweden), Marie d'Oignies (d. 1213; of the Flemish city of Liège), and Dorothea of Montau (d. 1394; she lived in a cell at Marienwerder (now Kwidzyn), near Gdańsk). Many readers have surmised that the man mentioned here might be Kempe's son, as the account mirrors what we later learn about Kempe and her son, although the identity of this scribe has not been conclusively established.

6 *mend his pen*: i.e. to sharpen his stylus or quill.

spectacles: this paragraph is concerned with favouring spiritual vision over physical vision and continues the theme of the correct discernment of spirits. Eyeglasses became common in Europe from the late thirteenth century; for instance, some 1,151 pairs of spectacles were imported to England from Europe through the Port of London in the summer of 1384 alone. See further John Dreyfus, 'The invention of spectacles and the advent of printing', *The Library*, sixth series, 10 (1988), 93–106; p. 101.

quire: a constituent booklet of a medieval book; usually a sheet of vellum folded to make eight pages.

7 *White Friar*: probably the Carmelite Alan of Lynn, on whom see note to p. 24.

And so he began to write . . . information of this creature: this can be dated precisely to 23 July 1436, the day after St Mary Magdalene's feast day on 22 July (for Kempe's relationship to Mary Magdalene see pp. 70, 156). 23 July was also a particularly auspicious date, for it was the feast of the death of St Bridget. Thus the *Book of Margery Kempe* is structured in such a way as to take the figures of the Magdalene (representing repentant female sinners, the renunciation of the world, and proximity to Christ and the Crucifixion) and St Bridget (embodying noble female sanctity and mystical vision) as its framework and its point of departure.

11 *she had something . . . her whole life*: the nature of this secret is not clearly revealed in the course of the *Book*. The sin may plausibly have been connected to marriage, lust, and temptation—topics which very much concern Kempe—but may equally have been connected to something spiritual, possibly an error in religious behaviour.

in good health . . . merciful enough: confession was normally thought to be essential, but the Lollards believed that confession to a priest was unnecessary, as it sufficed to confess to God in one's heart, not through speech. Kempe's devil, therefore, here takes on the aspect of a fifteenth-century heretic.

12 *'Daughter . . . never forsook you?'*: this foreshadows Mary's interview with St Peter, p. 175, in which she says 'even though you forsook my sweet son, He never forsook you, Peter, and He shall come back and comfort us all really well'.

13 *gold piping on her headdress*: immoderate headgear was often the subject of preachers' and clerics' satires of female worldly vanity. The Suffolk monk and poet John Lydgate (1370–1449) wrote a satirical poem, known as *Horns Away*, on this subject, arguing that pointed and adorned hats were 'contrary to femininity', worn only by 'arch wives, eager in their violence'.

dagged with tippets: slashed at the edges into points, with long, narrow pieces of cloth attached; dagging allowed a lining in a different colour or fabric to show through.

town of N.: here, early on in the *Book*, the name of the town of Lynn is concealed. This may accord with Kempe's desire (p. 6) that the *Book* should not be read during her lifetime, although the concealment is not kept up throughout the *Book*.

Guild of the Trinity: the most important and prestigious of Lynn's guilds, the Guild of the Trinity was central to Lynn's local government, charity, and religious rituals. In 1421, the Guildhall, adjacent to St Margaret's Church, was damaged in the fire that engulfed Lynn (see p. 146). In 1423, work on a magnificent new hall was commenced; the hall, with its arched beamed roof and impressive window, survives today within Lynn's Town Hall. On the social context of medieval guilds, see Gervase Rosser, 'Going to the fraternity feast: commensality and communal relations in late medieval England', *Journal of British Studies* 33 (1994), 430–46.

began to brew: a common occupation amongst medieval women; see Judith Bennett, *Ale, Beer, and Brewsters in England: Women's Work in a Changing World 1300–1600* (Oxford, 1999). Kempe's husband is recorded in the Lynn records as a brewer, and her family was also involved in importing wine.

14 *Eve of Corpus Christi*: i.e. some time in May or June, the Wednesday after Trinity Sunday.

15 *she heard the sound . . . been in Paradise*: the harmonious sound of Heaven and Paradise was a common motif; Kempe had almost certainly seen, at St Margaret's, Lynn, the imposing funeral brass (of Robert Braunche and his wives, *c*.1364) featuring angel musicians playing an organ, a psaltery, rebecs, and recorders (*EAN* 293–7). Richard Rolle, with whose writings Kempe or her scribe was certainly familiar, describes in his *Fire of Love* how he heard a symphony of harmony as the sound of Heaven. On the devotional importance to mysticism of sound and music, see Beth Williamson, 'Sensory experience and medieval devotion: sound and vision, invisibility and silence', *Speculum* 88 (2013), 1–44.

conjugal debt: the right, enshrined in medieval canon law, of both a husband and wife to sexual intercourse within marriage. See Dyan Elliott, *Spiritual Marriage: Sexual Abstinence in Medieval Wedlock* (Princeton, 1993), 132–94 (pp. 227–8 on Kempe, whose 'revulsion to sex was focused on the [conjugal] debt alone and, even after her conversion, she continued to be attracted to other men').

16 *that sin . . . the Book*: Kempe's special sin, the nature of which remains unclear. See p. 11.

haircloth from a kiln: i.e. a piece of fabric made from coarse horsehair.

18 *evensong on the Eve of St Margaret's Day*: 19 July. This is a significant date for Kempe, not least because St Margaret was the dedicatee of Kempe's church, the main church in medieval Lynn. The evensong service, in which the liturgy was usually sung chorally, picks up the theme of heavenly music introduced in the previous chapter. St Margaret of Antioch— who was tortured when she refused a pagan governor of Antioch who tried to woo her—was the patron saint of childbirth. Her cult was very popular in medieval East Anglia, where she was usually represented fighting with or emerging from a dragon.

St Margaret's Church: founded in 1101, this was the parish church of Lynn. It is also the site of the chapel of the Guild of the Holy Trinity (to which both Kempe and her father belonged), behind a fifteenth-century wooden screen on the north side of the chancel. The church, much modified, still stands.

paternoster: the Lord's Prayer, said in Latin.

permitted time and permitted for her: the Christian faithful were required to abstain from sex at certain times: the major feast days, Advent and Lent, during menstruation and pregnancy, and before receiving communion. See Elliott, *Spiritual Marriage*, 10, 195–7.

hacked . . . for the pot: this foreshadows Kempe's own desire to be made into mincemeat (pp. 129, 183). The phrase echoes Michaes [Micah] 3: 3, 'Who have eaten the flesh of my people, and have flayed their skin from off them? And have broken, and chopped their bones as for the kettle, and as flesh in the midst of the pot?' This kind of phrase was evidently proverbial in fifteenth-century England; a lyric, 'Jankyn, the clerical seducer', describes the foolish lover Jankyn singing 'a hundred notes at a time, | Yet he chopped them smaller | than vegetables for the pot'.

19 *chapel of St John*: dedicated to St John the Baptist, and used by the guild of young clerks, this was one of several now-vanished chapels within St Margaret's Church.

twinkling of an eye: an appropriate biblical allusion, from 1 Corinthians 15: 51–2, 'Behold, I tell you a mystery. We shall all indeed rise again: but we shall not all be changed. In a moment, in the twinkling of an eye, at the last trumpet: for the trumpet shall sound, and the dead shall rise again incorruptible: and we shall be changed.'

contrition: a technical religious term for complete remorse for one's sins (from Latin *contritus*, 'pounded to pieces' by guilt).

20 *eating meat*: later in the *Book*, during her trip to Palestine *c.*1413, Kempe says that she has not eaten meat for some four years, suggesting that this conversation with Jesus took place around 1409.

my flesh . . . the sacrament of the altar: medieval Christianity held that the bread and wine of the Eucharist contained the 'real presence' of the body and blood of Christ; see Miri Rubin, *Corpus Christi: The Eucharist in Late Medieval Culture* (Cambridge, 1991).

stock-fish: hard, cured, air-dried cod, a medieval staple food.

Preaching Friars: that is, the recluse attached to the Dominican priory, then situated in the east of Lynn. The recluse visited by Kempe reappears several times in her *Book* as a loyal supporter—as confessor, intimate, prophet, and a fervent believer in Kempe's visions.

you are sucking even at Christ's breast: whilst Kempe generally depicts Christ as a handsome man, here she uses the language of maternal nurturing. This is far from unprecedented and, indeed, Julian of Norwich described Jesus as 'mother'; see Caroline Walker Bynum, *Holy Feast, Holy Fast: The Religious Significance of Food to Medieval Women* (New York, 1987), 270.

pledge: the sense is of a guarantee of, or deposit on, entry to Heaven.

21 *St Anne*: the mother of Mary, grandmother of Jesus. In medieval art she is often depicted teaching her daughter to read. St Anne was very popular in medieval East Anglia and her cult was widely practised there, including at Lynn, where she was the patron saint of a guild.

St John was born: the encounter between Mary and Elizabeth and the birth of St John the Baptist is taken from Luke 1: 39–60.

22 *on the twelfth day*: Epiphany; the twelve days are not mentioned in the Gospels but the date was fixed, from the early Christian period, on 6 January.

to leave the region of Bethlehem for Egypt: Matthew 2: 8–13.

languish in love: Canticles 2: 5 ('Stay me up with flowers, compass me about with apples: because I languish with love') and Canticles 5: 8 ('I adjure you, O daughters of Jerusalem, if you find my beloved, that you tell him that I languish with love'), phrases often alluded to by medieval mystical writers.

Trinity: a ubiquitous symbol in medieval England, comprising the First Person (the Father), the Second Person (the Son, Jesus Christ), and the Third Person (the Holy Spirit or Holy Ghost); the merchants' guild at Lynn, to which Kempe's family belonged, was dedicated to the Trinity.

23 *lay down*: Kempe is repeatedly represented as lying down to pray (see pp. 20, 39, 49).

Master N.: as the town of Lynn is earlier called N. but is then revealed, so too the identity of this man, Kempe's confessor Robert Springold (*fl.* 1436), parish priest at St Margaret's, Lynn, is at first obscured and then revealed. See p. 126; Anthony Goodman, *Margery Kempe and her World* (Harlow, 2002), 90–2.

slay your husband: it is not clear if the intended meaning is that God will kill Mr Kempe or if God will slay Kempe's sexual desire; a later medieval annotator understood the latter, and added the words 'the fleshly lust in' after the word 'slay'. In Chapter 11, John Kempe himself connects having sex with having his head cut off and his wife reminds him that she had told him he would be suddenly killed (p. 26).

24 *Wednesday of Easter Week*: Easter Sunday in 1413 was on 23 April, so this day, the Wednesday of the week following Holy Week, was 26 April 1413.

book: presumably a devotional book, such as a book of hours or a psalter. Such books usually contained pictures as well as the Latin text of prayers.

John of Wereham: a Lynn mercer (a dealer in fabrics) and member of the Guild of St Giles and St Julian (*BMK* 372). The village of Wereham (Norfolk) is about 14 miles from Lynn.

Master Alan, a White Friar: the Cambridge-educated Carmelite friar and theologian, Alan of Lynn (1347/8–1432). Most of his writings do not survive; much of his work was concerned with making indices to the works of Church Fathers and theologians and included an index to the revelations of St Bridget of Sweden. See Richard Copsey, 'Lynn, Alan (1347/8–1432)', *ODNB*. Alan of Lynn reappears in the *Book* at several points as a close advisor to Kempe; see pp. 124, 152, 194.

25 *I am in you, and you in me*: John 14: 20. The phrase is repeated later, at p. 79.

York: the main city of northern England and the second largest city in the country, after London. York is some 130 miles from Lynn.

Midsummer's Eve: 23 June 1413. In the Middle Ages, Midsummer's Eve was also known as St John's Eve (the following day is the Feast Day of St John the Baptist) and was one of the four 'quarter days', on which accounts were settled and rents were due. As Corpus Christi Day occurred on 22 June 1413, many scholars have suggested that the Kempes would have seen the famous York Corpus Christi mystery plays.

26 *Now, good sir . . . my wish*: referring back to p. 23 (see note thereto), this
conversation suggests that Kempe hoped that her husband's sexual appe-
tite would be killed off, rather than that he himself would be killed.

haircloth or chain-mail: i.e. worn next to the skin in penance.

Bridlington: a town on the Yorkshire coast, about 43 miles from York. The
shrine of St John of Bridlington (*c.*1320–79) was located here. St John had
been sainted in Kempe's lifetime; he took a vow of chastity at the age of
12, later studied at Oxford, and became an Augustinian prior in Yorkshire.
Known in his lifetime for charity and humility, miracles were reported
after his death at his tomb and, in 1401, Pope Boniface IX canonized him.
See Michael J. Curley, 'John of Bridlington [St John of Bridlington, John
Thwing] (*c.*1320–1379)', *ODNB*.

27 *I'll repay your debts . . . Jerusalem*: Kempe's father died at around this time
(*BMK* 361) and it is possible that a legacy allowed Kempe to make this
promise to her husband.

28 *despair*: i.e. in lacking hope, a part of the sin of pride; Kempe's struggles
with despair are described earlier (p. 18).

external office: the Lollards inveighed against the keeping of external
offices by the clergy; according to the Lollards, all curates '[should] be
fully excused of temporal office and occupy them with their cure and
nothing else' (sixth conclusion of the Lollards, 1395).

29 *Canterbury*: pre-eminent English religious city, and, through the site of
the shrine of St Thomas Becket, frequently visited by pilgrims. Kempe
was visiting Christ Church, the Benedictine abbey attached to what is
now Canterbury Cathedral, the site of Becket's shrine and the tomb of the
recently-deceased Henry IV.

an old monk . . . a rich man: this was probably John Kynton (d. 1416), treasurer to Joanne of Navarre (1368–1437), queen of England, second consort
of Henry IV. Kynton became a monk at Christ Church, Canterbury, in
1408 (*BMK* 270).

30 *false Lollard*: the first accusation against Kempe of following the Lollard
heresy. On the church's pursuit of Lollards, see Ian Forrest, *The Detection
of Heresy in Late Medieval England* (Oxford, 2005). See too note to p. 37.

31 *ardour of love*: here, in the margin of the manuscript (fo. 14v), is written
'R. Medlay v. was wont so to say', referring to Richard Methley (1450/51–
1527/8), Carthusian monk and mystic of Mount Grace (the priory which
owned the manuscript). Methley's works survive in unique copies in three
manuscripts; these writings deal with aspects of contemplation, and translations of the mystical works, *The Cloud of Unknowing* and Marguerite
Porete's *Mirror of Simple Souls*. Methley is referred to several times in the
annotations to Kempe's *Book* (e.g. p. 64). See further Michael Sargent,
'Methley [Furth], Richard (1450/51–1527/8)', *ODNB*.

Godhead: divinity, the divine personality.

a pillar of Holy Church: the manuscript here (fo. 15r) includes a marginal picture of a pillar with a trefoil—a three-pointed leaf, representing the Trinity—springing from it. The pillar at once represents stability (God as Kempe's 'supporter', Kempe as a 'foundation' of the Church) and martyrdom (the pillar on which Christ suffered during His Passion).

bound to a stake . . . sharp axe, for God's love: this image recalls saintly martyrdoms; in church art it was common for decapitated saints (such as Denis, Edmund, Oswald, Osyth, Paul) to be represented carrying their own heads.

written upon my hands and my feet: adapting Isaiah 49: 16, 'Behold, I have graven thee in my hands: thy walls are always before my eyes.'

32 *a hidden God*: Isaiah 45: 15 ('Verily thou art a hidden God, the God of Israel the saviour'); the hidden God (*deus absconditus*), a God unknowable to the human mind, was a favourite image of medieval mystics.

"For whosoever shall . . . my sister, and mother": Mark 3: 35.

33 *two years before she went*: this is then *c.*1411. Kempe left for Jerusalem in 1413 and visited Santiago de Compostela in 1417.

white and of no other colour: white clothes would have been a sign of virginity, virtue, or chastity (see Mary Erler, 'Margery Kempe's white clothes', *Medium Ævum* 62 (1993), 78–83). The elect are described as being dressed in white clothes in Matthew 28: 3 ('raiment as snow'); Apocalypse 3: 4 ('they shall walk with me in white, because they are worthy'); 4: 4 ('four and twenty ancients sitting, clothed in white garments'). Kempe may have known of the 'Bianchi', pious penitent men and women who in the summer of 1399 marched in procession from Genoa. They observed fasts, listened to sermons, visited churches, and, famously, wore white robes. See further Daniel E. Bornstein, *The Bianchi of 1399: Popular Devotion in Late Medieval Italy* (Ithaca, 1993).

34 *Bishop of Lincoln, who was called Philip*: Philip Repingdon, Bishop of Lincoln 1405–19. He had studied in Leicester and at Oxford, and had preached in favour of Wycliffite views. Under pressure, he recanted in 1382; in 1393 he was elected abbot of Leicester; from 1400 to 1403 he was chancellor of Oxford University, and around this time he became close to Henry IV. He was appointed bishop of Lincoln in 1405 and, in general, he was a church reformer with a profound commitment to helping the poor. See Simon Forde, 'Repyndon [Repington, Repingdon], Philip (*c.*1345–1424)', *ODNB*.

35 *the mantle and the ring*: the signs of a vow of chastity. These trappings were usually available only to widows, hence Bishop Repingdon's disquiet.

And the Bishop . . . very welcome: here the narrative briefly moves into describing 'us', rather than 'they', as if Kempe is dictating the account herself.

36 *the children of Israel . . . leave with it*: Exodus 12: 35–6, 'And the children

of Israel did as Moses had commanded: and they asked of the Egyptians vessels of silver and gold, and very much raiment. | And the Lord gave favour to the people in the sight of the Egyptians, so that they lent unto them: and they stripped the Egyptians.'

36 *Archbishop of Canterbury—Arundel*: Thomas Arundel (1353–1414); a key administrator of early Lancastrian England, Arundel was an aristocratic scholar, a political operator in affairs of both church and state, and a staunch opponent of the Lollards. Born into the Fitzalan family on his father's side and the English royal family on his mother's, Arundel was made bishop of Ely at the astonishingly young age of 20; he became Archbishop of Canterbury in 1397. From 1401 Arundel's attention was fixed on eliminating heresy, and he oversaw the institution of the burning of heretics, and the interrogation and trials of Lollards such as William Sawtry, William Thorp, John Badby, and Sir John Oldcastle. See Jonathan Hughes, 'Arundel [Fitzalan], Thomas (1353–1414)', *ODNB*.

twenty-six shillings and eight pence: for comparison, in 1413 the slightly larger sum of 28s. 4½d. was enough for the East Anglian gentlewoman Alice Brian to buy thirty white loaves, three black loaves, wine, ale, eighty red and white herring, half a salt-fish, one stock-fish, and hay and oats for six horses (*The Household Book of Dame Alice de Bryene*, ed. Vincent B. Redstone, trans. M. K. Dale (Ipswich, 1931), 51).

Lambeth . . . at that time: Lambeth Palace, the archbishops' residence since *c.*1200, 2 miles west upriver from London and across the river from Westminster, on the south bank of the Thames.

37 *Smithfield . . . burn you with*: adjacent to St Bartholomew's Priory, just outside the north-west extent of medieval London's city walls, Smithfield was the site of many important and gruesome executions. In Kempe's day, William Sawtry (d. 1401), a heretic formerly of Lynn, was burned there (tied to a post, set in a barrel), as was the Worcester Lollard John Badby (d. 1410). The lady's 'faggot' would have been a bundle of kindling for the fire.

receive communion every Sunday: most laypeople confessed once a year and only to their parish priest.

38 *(Read the twenty-first chapter first, and then this chapter after that)*: Chapter 21 (p. 47) describes Kempe's pregnancy, whereas Chapter 17 starts with Kempe having a baby.

Vicar of St Stephen's: he is later identified as Richard of Caister (see p. 94), vicar 1402–20. St Stephen's Church is a large church in central Norwich, on Rampant Horse Street, where, in the fifteenth century, the city's horse market met. The church was rebuilt in the early sixteenth century.

39 *black clothing*: Kempe's black clothing has not received as much attention as her white attire, and it does not seem to have provoked the same hostile reaction. Black clothing would have been a sign of mourning (as in Chaucer's poem *The Book of Duchess* (*c.*1370), featuring a mourning man in

black) but could also be a sign of chastity (Erler, 'Margery Kempe's white clothes', 79).

Benedicite!: a common interjection, 'bless us!', 'bless you!', or 'bless my soul!'

Second Person of the Trinity: the Son, Jesus Christ.

Hilton's book . . . Incendium Amoris: four key works of late medieval mysticism, all of which were widely read in medieval England. These are *The Scale of Perfection* by Walter Hilton (*c.*1343–96), the *Liber Celestis* or *Revelations* of St Bridget of Sweden (d. 1373), the *Stimulus Amoris* or *Pricking of Love* by the Pseudo-Bonaventura but often attributed to Hilton, and the *Incendium Amoris* or *Fire of Love* by Richard Rolle (d. 1349). These works are mentioned again (p. 130).

40 *and so he did as she . . .*: in the manuscript (fo. 20r) the end of the sentence has been lost due to damage.

William Southfield: Carmelite friar (d. 1414); the evangelical polemicist and historian John Bale (1495–1563) gives a detailed account of Southfield's visions and prayerfulness (*BMK* 374–5). According to Bale, Southfield was a native of Norwich, 'a simple man, but endowed with incredible devotion'.

41 *He will not . . . falseness and fakery*: paraphrasing Wisdom 1: 4–5.

He asks of us . . . a good will: echoing Psalm 50: 19, 'A sacrifice to God is an afflicted spirit: a contrite and humbled heart, O God, thou wilt not despise.'

"My spirit shall . . . who fears my words": paraphrasing Isaiah 66: 2, 'But to whom shall I have respect, but to him that is poor and little, and of a contrite spirit, and that trembleth at my words?'

Dame Julian: of Norwich (1342–*c.*1416), anchoress and mystical author. She was a recluse at the parish church of St Julian, Norwich (from which she might have taken her name; it is possible, however, that her name was simply 'Juliana', 'Gillian'). She wrote two versions of her *Revelations of Divine Love*, reflections on sixteen visions of the crucified Christ. Julian's spirituality, emphasizing penance, tears, contemplation, mystical contemplation, and worldly rejection, has much in common with Kempe's. See Santha Bhattacharji, 'Julian of Norwich (1342–*c.*1416)', *ODNB*.

42 *temple of the Holy Ghost*: 1 Corinthians 6: 19.

And a double-minded . . . all his ways: James 1: 8.

He who is always doubting . . . Lord's gifts: James 1: 6–7.

St Paul . . . lamentations and unspeakable groaning: Romans 8: 26, 'For we know not what we should pray for as ought; but the Spirit himself asketh for us with unspeakable groaning.'

as Jerome says . . . pains of Hell: St Jerome (d. 420), theologian and Doctor of the Church. This quotation cannot be directly traced to Jerome's known writings; Jerome appears to Kempe in Rome (p. 91).

42 *seat of God*: Romans 14: 10; 2 Corinthians 5: 10.

Patience is necessary . . . preserve your soul: paraphrasing Luke 21: 19, 'In your patience you shall possess your souls'.

43 *confessor in your absence*: i.e. Robert Springold, see p. 23.

44 *blacksmith with a file*: echoing Isaiah 44: 12, 'The smith hath wrought with his file, with coals, and with hammers he hath formed it, and hath wrought with the strength of his arm.' Bridget of Sweden likened Christ to a goldsmith (*Liber Celestis*, ed. Roger Ellis, EETS o.s. 297 (Oxford, 1987), 149–50).

One time beforehand . . . to the widow: this section appears to be out of order; the 'widow' suggests that it follows the subsequent chapter, which describes Kempe's dealings with more than one widow. In the manuscript (fo. 22v), a capital 'C' in the margin suggests that a scribe or reader may have felt that this was a new chapter, or perhaps wished to mark the abrupt transition.

45 *Purgatory*: in medieval theology, an antechamber to Heaven in which those en route to Heaven were purged of their sins through purification or punishment. A soul's time in Purgatory could be reduced by performing pious deeds during life (for example, undertaking a pilgrimage or giving alms) or by prayers offered by the living for souls imprisoned in Purgatory.

46 *My daughter, Bridget . . . in this way*: this section of the *Book* shows Kempe's profound imitation of (and competition towards) St Bridget of Sweden. The incident with the dove-like sacrament echoes a vision Bridget had at mass, when she saw a lamb in the Host. 'Ocular communion'—receiving the sacrament by gazing on it—became quite widespread in the later Middle Ages; see Suzannah Biernoff, *Sight and Embodiment in the Middle Ages* (New York, 2002), ch. 6; see also p. 213, on the monstrance.

earthquake: whilst no earthquake is subsequently mentioned, earthquakes do appear frequently in medieval miracle stories. One such story describes an earthquake in front of a heretics' church when the Devil leaves it (*IE* 1060). In another, an earthquake is felt in Tyre, which causes Saladin to refuse to attack the city (*IE* 1848).

47 *die in their sin*: to die without contrition or last rites meant that a soul would go to Hell, rather than Heaven via Purgatory.

At the time: this section is evidently out of chronological order, as it must have taken place before Kempe agreed to live chastely with her husband.

48 *Mary Magdalene . . . St Paul*: three holy, repentant sinners. Mary Magdalene is named in the Gospels as one of the women healed by Christ 'of evil spirits and infirmities' and from whom 'seven devils were gone forth' (Luke 8: 3); she was identified as the woman named Mary who left aside her household tasks to sit at Jesus' feet ('Mary was she that anointed the Lord with ointment, and wiped his feet with her hair: whose brother

Lazarus was sick', John 11: 2). In the Middle Ages, Mary Magdalene was the patron saint of repentant sinners and of the contemplative life, thus being singularly appropriate for Kempe at this point. St Mary the Egyptian was a teenage prostitute in fifth-century Alexandria; she joined a pilgrimage to Jerusalem out of curiosity. She was held back from entering the Church of the Holy Sepulchre by an invisible force and thus miraculously converted. She was instructed by an icon of the Virgin to retire to the desert, where she lived a contemplative and devout life. St Paul the Apostle (d. *c*.65) is invoked here because of his status as a famous convert: he had witnessed and approved of the stoning of St Stephen (Acts 22: 20) and persecuted Christians.

50 *anointed for death*: i.e. received extreme unction, often called the last rites, a sacrament in medieval Christianity, in which the dying person was prepared for their passage into eternal life and, if they had been unable to perform the sacrament of penance, their sins were forgiven.

St Barbara: virgin martyr. According to her legend, Barbara became a Christian and lived as a hermit. In the Middle Ages, she was often paired with St Margaret and was known for her devotion to the Trinity, for her forbearance in imprisonment, and for guaranteeing that those facing sudden or violent deaths would receive the sacrament of extreme unction. Like Margaret and Katherine, Barbara was one of the Fourteen Holy Helpers, favourite saints of late medieval women's devotions.

51 *an offering of a mass-penny*: a common, and cheap, way of paying for a name to be entered onto a roll of those to be prayed for after death.

52 *who read and expounded Scripture*: the word in Middle English is *lyster* (from the French, *lector*), usually used to indicate a clerk whose duties were to read and expound Scripture, or a Preaching Friar. The word was also used to describe any 'reader' of books, i.e. someone who, like Kempe, listened to reading.

54 *breviary*: a portable breviary or portiforium, probably containing the daily 'Divine Office', psalms and other readings to be recited each day.

55 *Pentney Abbey*: Pentney Priory (Norfolk), Augustinian Priory, founded *c*.1130. Pentney is about 8 miles south-east of Lynn. It was dissolved in 1537, and little but the gatehouse remains.

56 *It happened . . . already cited*: the arrangement of St Margaret's, Lynn, is being described here. St Margaret's had two chapels-of-ease, dedicated to St James and St Nicholas. The controversy dated back to the time of Margery's childhood, when her father had opposed the 1379 attempt to gain further sacramental privileges for the chapel of St Nicholas at Lynn. The issue reappeared in 1426 and 1431, when the communities of St James and St Nicholas appealed to the Pope for greater privileges. Goodman, *Margery Kempe*, 83–4.

a bull from the papal Court: a charter issued by or authorized by a pope; in Kempe's time, issued by the papal Chancery court.

56 *the Prior*: at this point, John Dereham; Goodman, *Margery Kempe*, 51, 79.

Alnwick: William Alnwick (d. 1449), Bishop of Norwich and Lincoln, well known for his prosecution of heretics. These included Margery Baxter of Martham (Norfolk), an active Lollard in the late 1420s whose 'formidable', 'eccentric', and 'intriguing' personality and whose devotional poses have some similarities to Kempe's. See Rosemary C. E. Hayes, 'Alnwick, William (d. 1449)', *ODNB*; on Baxter, see Norman P. Tanner, 'Lollard women (*act. c.*1390–*c.*1520)', *ODNB*.

57 *bushel of nobles*: a bushel was a common medieval measurement for corn, seeds, fruit, and so on; here it is being used to suggest a large amount. A noble is a gold coin (see Note on Money).

When the time came: i.e. mid or late 1413.

58 *Master Robert*: i.e. Robert Springold (see note to p. 23).

offering at the Trinity: that is, at the high altar of the Cathedral of the Holy Trinity, Norwich. Lynn was in the diocese of Norwich.

Yarmouth: now Great Yarmouth (Norfolk), a shipping and fishing town on the Norfolk coast, about 60 miles east of Lynn. Kempe probably made her offering at the grand minster church of St Nicholas in Yarmouth, where there was an unusual altar and chapel dedicated to Our Lady of Ardenbourg (*EAN* 114). This recalled a shrine to the Virgin at Ardenbourg in Flanders, to which Edward III (1312–77) had made a pilgrimage. Eamon Duffy, *The Stripping of the Altars*, rev. edn. (New Haven, 1994), 166, suggests the Yarmouth shrine was established after the Battle of Sluys/ L'Ecluse (1340) as a thanksgiving gesture by the Yarmouth men who had fought under Edward III and returned home safely.

Zierikzee: a town in Zeeland (now The Netherlands), not far from Middelburg; the crossing to Zierikzee was one of the shortest from Norfolk to the Continent.

59 *Constance*: the city of Konstanz, a major centre for medieval travellers as it had the only nearby crossing of the River Rhine. In 1414–18 the Council of Constance took place there, during which Jan Hus (a Bohemian religious reformer connected to the English Lollards) was burned at the stake. Kempe's visit was probably just before the Council, which is not reported here.

shaggy sackcloth: the Middle English *gelle* (from *gil*, a female ferret), suggesting a badger- or ferret-hair garment, which would have been coarse. Kempe's outfit seems to have been a parody of the sackcloth of biblical mourning and, in particular, makes a mockery of Kempe's piety (cf. Joel 1: 8, 'Lament like a virgin girded with sackcloth for the husband of her youth'; Apocalypse 6: 12, 'And I saw, when he had opened the sixth seal, and behold there was a great earthquake, and the sun became black as sackcloth of hair . . .').

61 *twenty pounds . . . sixteen pounds*: this would have been a significant amount

of money, presumably enough to cover Kempe's expenses for the duration of her long pilgrimage. In 1419, £20 15s. 6d. was enough for the household of the East Anglian gentlewoman Alice Brian to pay for a pipe of red wine from London, carriage for it to be brought to Colchester, two pipes and a hogshead of red wine and a hogshead and a quart of white wine from Ipswich, four carters' expenses to carry the wine from Ipswich, two small barrels of malmsey and rumney from London, and twelve quarters of wheat bought from the rector of Stansted (*Household Book of Alice de Bryene*, ed. Redstone, 119).

William Weaver: this man has not been identified in other historical records. The name is not an unusual one.

62 *And every day . . . before our Lord*: a reference to the biblical story about a woman who was to be stoned for committing adultery, prompting Jesus to say, 'He that is without sin among you, let him first cast a stone at her' (John 8: 7).

Bologna the Rich: in Middle English, the *Book* calls it '*Boleyn de Grace*', a version of the nickname '*Bologna la Grassa*', Bologna the Fat (in the sense of rich or fertile). Wealthy and progressive, Bologna, 100 miles south-west of Venice, was a culturally sophisticated university city.

63 *a ship in which to sail*: the *Book* tells us little about the practicalities of the journey from Venice to Jerusalem. Pilgrims sailed in galleys, usually with stops at ports on the Dalmatian coast such as Zara (Zadar), Curzola (Korčula), and Ragusa (Dubrovnik) and on the Greek islands of Corfu, Rhodes, and/or Crete, to the port of Jaffa. Here they were registered by local Mameluk officials and were required to carry a letter of safe-conduct. Pilgrims stayed in basic accommodations in either Jaffa or more usually Ramlah (Kempe mentions this town on pp. 70, 158). By the time Kempe visited the Holy Land, the Latin Christian pilgrimage industry was largely subcontracted to Franciscans, who operated the hostels in Ramlah.

until they could see Jerusalem: it was customary for pilgrims to travel via Mount Joy (now Nabi Samwil, Palestine), 6 miles north-west of Jerusalem. From here they gained their first view of the city. The village also holds the tomb of the prophet Samuel.

64 *the city of Heaven*: the apocalyptic Heavenly City, 'the holy city, the new Jerusalem, coming down out of heaven from God' (Apocalypse 21: 2, 21: 10).

the Temple in Jerusalem: the *Book* describes the Church of the Holy Sepulchre, the site of Christ's grave and one of the holiest places in Christianity. The *Book* makes a not uncommon mistake in referring to the Church as the Temple; there was a separate Temple of our Lord (the Temple Mount, with the Dome of the Rock and al-Aqsa mosque), held to be the site of Abraham's binding of Isaac and the First and Second Jewish Temples. In the fifteenth century, the Dome of the Rock had been re-consecrated according to the Islamic rite.

64 *they were let in . . . next day at evensong*: it was customary for pilgrims to spend the night in vigil, locked inside the Church of the Holy Sepulchre.

friars: the Franciscan friars of the *Custodiae Terrae Sanctae* (the Custody of the Holy Land) shared the Church of the Holy Sepulchre with other Christian denominations (Greeks, Armenians, Copts, and so on) but were the only Latin (Western) Christian group represented there.

Mount of Calvary: the Latin Calvary (located above the Greek Calvary) is inside the Church of the Holy Sepulchre; pilgrims were able to touch the bedrock of the 'Mount'—a small outcrop—housed in a richly-decorated chapel.

St John: St John the Evangelist (St John the Apostle), often represented as present at the Crucifixion.

this was the first cry that she ever cried in any contemplation: Calvary is an appropriate site for the beginning of Kempe's contemplative crying, as part of her *imitatio Christi*, recalling Christ's final cry at the moment of death at Calvary (Matthew 27: 50: 'And Jesus again crying with a loud voice, yielded up the ghost'). At Calvary, Bridget of Sweden also had a vision of Christ's Passion that caused her to weep (*LSRev*, 187–8).

it made her really weak . . . our Lord's Passion: a marginal note in the manuscript (fo. 33v) refers to Richard Methley and John Norton, mystics of Mount Grace (see note to p. 31; also *BMKA* 164); these men also suffered physical 'weakness' during contemplation of the Passion.

66 *dove-cote*: Canticles 2: 14, 'My dove in the clefts of the rock, in the hollow places of the wall, shew me thy face, let thy voice sound in my ears.'

the grisly and grievous wound . . . blood and water: following John 19: 34, 'one of the soldiers with a spear opened his side, and immediately there came out blood and water'. On this iconography, see Flora Lewis, 'The wound in Christ's side and the Instruments of the Passion: gendered experience and response', in Jane H. M. Taylor and Lesley Smith, eds., *Women and the Book: Assessing the Visual Evidence* (London, 1996), 204–29.

fire of love: this phrase connects Kempe with other mystical authorities, not least Richard Rolle, who wrote a treatise called *The Fire of Love*. At an earlier date, Jacques de Vitry (d. 1240) had repeatedly described the 'fire of love' in his life of the mystic Marie d'Oignies, which was known to Kempe and/or her scribe. See Margot H. King, ed. and trans., *Two Lives of Marie d'Oignies*, 4th edn. (Toronto, 1998), 58, 64.

67 *the grave where our Lord was buried*: the Holy Sepulchre itself (or Aedicule), in the rotunda of the Church of the Holy Sepulchre. In Kempe's time, it took the form of a house with columns and an ornate cupola. See Colin Morris, *The Sepulchre of Christ and the Medieval West* (Oxford, 2005), 321–7.

where our Lord was nailed to the Cross: the Chapel of the Nailing of the Cross, a Franciscan chapel adjacent to the Calvary chapel inside the Church of the Holy Sepulchre.

a marble stone: the Slab of Anointing or Unction, at the Church's entrance, a Crusader-era pilgrimage site, where Christ's body was said to have been prepared for burial.

she received communion on the Mount of Calvary: see note to p. 64.

she swooned . . . He fell down too: this seems to be a tour of the sites of the *via dolorosa*, only then becoming defined as a set route from Geth-semane at the foot of the Mount of Olives through the eastern side of Jerusalem and on to the Church of the Holy Sepulchre. The site where Mary swooned was the Church of St Mary of the Spasm, a Crusader-era church almost certainly in ruins at the time of Kempe's visit. *CCKJ* 3. 320–2.

Mount Zion: a hill, just outside the city walls, to the south-west of the old city of Jerusalem. In 1333, King Robert of Naples bought the site and established a Franciscan community there; subsequent papal bulls and arrangements with the Mameluk rulers of Palestine ensured that, until their expulsion in 1552, the Franciscans became the Roman Catho-lic custodians of all the Christian holy sites. The Franciscans of Mount Zion effectively controlled the Latin pilgrimage industry in Jerusalem and Bethlehem.

our Lord washed . . . Last Supper with His disciples: the traditional site of the Last Supper (John 13: 1–17; Acts 1: 13), the Cenacle or Coenaculum on Mount Zion held a Crusader-era chapel that can still be visited.

plenary remission from sin: complete forgiveness for one's sins; travelling to the holy sites of Jerusalem was one of the most spiritually profitable exer-cises one could do; sins were forgiven and time in Purgatory was reduced. Christ tells Bridget of Sweden in her account that by going to Jerusalem 'you are entirely cleansed of all your sin . . . and for your travails and your devotion, some of your friends that were in Purgatory are delivered and gone to Heaven' (translated from Bridget of Sweden, *Liber Celestis*, ed. Ellis, 479).

68 *where the Holy Cross was buried*: the Chapel of St Helena, underneath but entered via the Church of the Holy Sepulchre.

the place where the apostles received the Holy Ghost: the Cenacle or 'Upper Room' (Acts 2: 1–6); see note to p. 67.

the place where our Lady was buried: the Crusader-era Franciscan Church of the Tomb of the Virgin, in the Kidron Valley adjacent to Gethsemane (*CCKJ* 3. 286–306).

Bethlehem: approximately 6 miles by foot south from the Church of the Holy Sepulchre. Originally built by Constantine in the fourth century but rebuilt as a Byzantine basilica in 565 CE, the Church of the Nativity was held to be the site of Jesus' birth and the medieval grotto chapels can still be visited. A Franciscan presence was established in Bethlehem by 1347 and subsequently the Sultan gave the Franciscans control of the chapels and shrines within the Church of the Nativity.

68 *crib where our lord was born*: in the cave chapel, underneath the Church of the Nativity, which can still be visited today.

69 *River Jordan*: a pilgrimage site on account of traditions of baptism, the river is about 26 miles east of Jerusalem through the desert and 6 miles south of Jericho.

Mount Quarantine: a Crusader-era community of hermits near Jericho that had, by Kempe's time, become a Greek and Georgian establishment, al-Quarantul (*CCKJ* 1. 252–4). The biblical account referred to is Matthew 4: 2, Mark 1: 13, Luke 4: 2.

70 *the place where St John the Baptist was born*: Ein Kerem (Israel), the Church of the Franciscan Monastery of St John (*CCKJ* 1. 30–8), 5 miles west of Jerusalem.

Bethany, where Mary and Martha lived: a pilgrimage site (now al-Eizariya (Palestine)), a short distance east of Jerusalem, at the top of the Mount of Olives.

Lazarus: the story of Lazarus is given in John 11. The modern Church of St Lazarus at Bethany (al-Eizariya) sits on the site of the medieval pilgrimage church. In Kempe's time, a mosque was situated here and she would have seen the ruins of the Crusader-era church.

our blessed Lord . . . in the morning: the Chapel of the Apparition, a Franciscan chapel adjacent to the rotunda of the Church of the Holy Sepulchre.

Mary, why weepest thou?: John 20: 15.

wishing that she might stay with them: visitors to Jerusalem who were in religious orders were put up with the Franciscans on Mount Zion, whereas lay pilgrims usually lodged at the Mauristan near the Church of the Holy Sepulchre. The invitation here thus suggests the friars' acceptance of Kempe's religiosity.

Ramlah: founded in the eighth century, Ramlah, about 8 miles inland from Jaffa, was a major stopping-off point for pilgrims to Jerusalem. It was here that most pilgrims spent their first nights in the Holy Land in a hostel.

to purchase more pardons for herself: i.e. to purchase more time out of Purgatory after death and thereby proceed more quickly to Heaven.

as if you were physically present there: in fifteenth-century Europe, 'virtual pilgrimage' was becoming widely practised. The mental and spiritual 'exercise' of pilgrimage was re-created in liturgical, spatial, and visual forms, which allowed people to visualize themselves in the Holy Land and reap the same spiritual benefits as if they had physically been there. See Kathryn Rudy, *Virtual Pilgrimages in the Convent: Imagining Jerusalem in the Late Middle Ages* (Turnhout, 2011).

72 *an image in it made in our Lord's likeness*: such an object might have taken the form of a painted icon, a crucifix, or a small altarpiece, but here, as the text goes on to explain, it seems to be an ivory or wooden statue or doll

(see p. 134 for Kempe's encounter with a pietà, and p. 167 for her encounter with a crucifix). On portable images of Christ see Christiane Klapisch-Zuber, 'Holy dolls: play and piety in Florence in the Quattrocento', in *Women, Family, and Ritual in Renaissance Italy*, trans. Lydia Cochrane (Chicago, 1985), 310–29; Ulinka Rublack, 'Female spirituality and the infant Jesus in late medieval Dominican convents', *Gender and History* 6 (1994), 37–57, who describes the doll which once belonged to Margaretha Ebner (d. 1351), whose spirituality may have influenced Kempe's.

'Jhesus est amor meus': i.e. 'Jesus is my love.' Meech and Allen give further examples of beads bearing the same inscription (*BMK* 297) and, as Windeatt (*BMKA* 178) notes, the motto is somewhat similar to that of St Bridget's Order of the Holy Saviour (*'Amor meus crucifixus est'*). For Bridget of Sweden (*Liber Celestis*, ed. Ellis, 247) the finger-ring represented the soul. In a story in the *Gesta Romanorum*, a popular medieval collection of preachers' stories, the round finger-ring is a symbol of faith, 'that ought to be round, without forgetfulness'; it goes on to say that 'he who has the ring of true faith shall have the love of God and of angels'.

73 *the measurement of Christ's grave*: it was common for medieval pilgrims to bring back candles, images, or ribbons, often bought at Venice, bearing the measure of Christ's grave and body. William Wey's fifteenth-century chapel at Edington (Wiltshire), which held various models and relics of Jerusalem, included, made in planks, the length of Christ's grave, with the height and width of the door, the length of Christ's foot, and the depth and circumference of the mortice in which the Cross was placed (William Wey, *The Itineraries*, ed. Francis Davey (Oxford, 2010), 224).

'Bone Cristian, prey pur me!': apparently an attempt to record the woman's Italian, 'Good Christian, pray for me!' (probably something like *'Buona cristiana, preghi per me!'*).

Friar Minor: the Perugian town of Assisi was the home of the Franciscan movement; St Francis (d. 1226) founded the order in the town in 1209. Franciscan monks dedicated themselves to poverty and were responsible for developing the medieval culture of *imitatio Christi* and, as custodians of the holy sites in Palestine, were closely involved in the kinds of pilgrimage undertaken by Kempe.

our Lady's veil: a famous relic at the thirteenth-century basilica of San Francesco d'Assisi, where Kempe would have seen the upper and lower churches richly decorated with frescoes by Cimabue, Giotto, and others. As Windeatt (*BMKA* 180) notes, the story that Mary had swaddled the infant Christ in her veil appears in Bonaventure's *Meditations on the Life of Christ*, known to Kempe.

Lammas Day: 1/2 August, probably 1414. Kempe would have known Lammas (the feast of St Peter) as the English festival of the wheat harvest, and she later receives a Lammas Day indulgence at Syon Abbey in England (p. 222). The 'huge pardon' referred to is the 'Portiuncula indulgence', a plenary indulgence that could only be gained on Lammas Day at the Portiuncula chapel at Santa Maria degli Angeli (where Francis founded his Order) about 2 miles from Assisi. See Alastair Minnis, 'Reclaiming the pardoners', *Journal of Medieval and Early Modern Studies* 33 (2003), 312–34.

74 *Margaret Florentine*: this person has not been identified. As elsewhere, Kempe looks upon her friend to validate and confirm her devotions.

Knights of Rhodes: Knights Hospitaller. Originating as an organization for Jerusalem pilgrims, founded *c*.1048, the Knights Hospitaller became a wealthy fraternity and paramilitary organization; following the loss of the crusader kingdoms, it was headquartered on the island of Rhodes.

the hospital of St Thomas of Canterbury in Rome: known as the English Hospice, it was founded in the form known to Kempe, as the Hospital of the Most Holy Trinity and St Thomas of Canterbury, in 1362, endowed by the gift of John and Alice Shepherd, English expatriates in Rome. The English College in Rome, on the Via di Monserrato, occupies the site of the Hospice today. See *The English Hospice in Rome* (Exeter, 1962).

a church opposite the Hospital: i.e. Santa Caterina della Rota, rebuilt in the sixteenth and eighteenth centuries.

75 *Confiteor*: 'I confess', the opening words of the penitential rite.

St John the Evangelist: St John could be invoked by women who were not able to confess to an earthly confessor.

'Benedicite': a common interjection, 'bless us!', 'bless you!', or 'bless my soul!'

'Dominus': Lord.

well of tears: Jeremiah 9: 1, 'Who will give water to my head, and a fountain of tears to my eyes?' The phrase is repeated (pp. 91, 128, 225).

76 *proverb*: not a literary proverb; possibly influenced by religious stories about having seats in Heaven and Hell reserved. In one such story, twin brothers enter a monastery; one is sinful, the other good. The good brother has a vision of a chair prepared for him in Heaven and another for his brother in Hell (*IE* 4215; see too 4214, 4216, 4217).

Church of St John Lateran: the basilica of San Giovanni in Laterano, the cathedral of the Diocese of Rome and official seat of the Pope in his role as Bishop of Rome. Originally dedicated in 324 CE, the building seen by Kempe had been rebuilt in the 1360s after a catastrophic fire. St Bridget had also visited this church as part of a sequence of visits to shrines around Italy.

79 *Apostles' Church in Rome*: the church of Santi Apostoli. Shortly after the time of Kempe's visit the church was comprehensively rebuilt by Pope Martin V.

St Lateran's Day: 9 November, probably 1414; the feast of the dedication of the basilica of San Giovanni in Laterano.

80 *my wedded wife . . . for poorer*: the echoes of the modern marriage service

can be seen here; characteristically, the Godhead's marriage to Margery takes the form of a late medieval English wedding service. The fifteenth-century *York Manual* gives the man's vows thus: 'I take you N. to my wedded wife, to have and to hold, from this day forward, for better for worse, for richer for poorer, for fairer for fouler, in sickness and in health, til death us depart, if Holy Church will ordain it, and thereto I plight you my troth.' See Kenneth W. Stevenson, *Nuptial Blessing: A Study of Christian Marriage Rites* (Oxford, 1983), 78–80.

81 *you have many angels around you . . . no evil man can harm you*: Psalm 90: 11, 'For he hath given his angels charge over thee; to keep thee in all thy ways.'

'Benedictus qui venit in nomine Domini': Matthew 21: 9, 'Blessed is He that cometh in the name of the Lord.'

flame of the fire of love: Richard Rolle's account of the fire of love in his heart can be seen as a model for Kempe's; his *Fire of Love* begins with a description of how 'I felt my heart grow warm and truly, not in my imagination, as if it burned with a palpable fire.' In the manuscript of Kempe's book, a picture of the flames of the fire of love has been drawn in the margin (fo. 43v).

83 *I must be intimate . . . lie in your bed with you*: such erotic imagery, ultimately taken from the biblical book of Canticles and Bernard of Clairvaux's influential interpretation of it, is relatively common in medieval mysticism. See Introduction, p. xxv.

a pair of bellows: bellows could be both godly and diabolical in medieval symbolism, which perhaps explains Kempe's apprehension. In Chaucer's 'Parson's Tale' (I. 351), the devil's bellows blow 'the fire of fleshly concupiscence' into mankind. Bridget of Sweden describes how 'a bishop who loves the world is like a bellows full of wind' (*Liber Celestis*, ed. Ellis, 206–7). However, biblically, the bellows are a symbol of godly industry (Jeremiah 6: 29), and the English religious writer Reginald Peacock (*c*.1395–*c*.1461) wrote in his *Donet* that devout reading can be like the bellows that 'blow and puff up the fire of devotion into the soul . . . banishing away the cold of undevotion and uncharity'.

dove: the Christian symbol of peace and love, often representing the Holy Spirit (Canticles 2: 14, 6: 8; Matthew 3: 16; Mark 1: 10; Luke 3: 22; John 1: 32). See too p. 66, for the imagery of the dove-cote.

redbreast: i.e. a robin; in medieval imagery, a symbol of Christ's Passion, the robin was said to have plucked a thorn from Christ's crown on the way to Calvary; the drops of blood stained the robin's breast red.

84 *a little before Christmas*: probably 1414.

Wenceslas: given in Middle English as '*Wenslawe*', this likely translates the German name *Wenzel* or Bohemian *Václav*. The cult of the saint of this name was not practised in medieval England, but was widespread in continental Europe.

85 *And so He did*: this comes to pass in Chapter 44.

St Marcellus's church in Rome: the church of San Marcello al Corso. The ancient church seen by Kempe was destroyed by fire in 1519.

86 *'Margerya . . . madam'*: the scribe records this in broken English and a kind of French or Italian, a rudimentary conversation between foreigners; the question seems to be 'Is Margery in poverty?' and the answer 'yes, great poverty' (*'grande pauvreté'*, *'grande povertà'*).

87 *Hospital of St Thomas*: i.e. the English Hospice; see note to p. 74.

St Bridget's maidservant in Rome: the canonization documents of St Bridget and her daughter Katherine state that Bridget had three serving maids in Rome, one Swedish, one Norwegian, and one Italian (*BMK* 304). Archbishop Gregersson (d. 1383), in his *Life* of St Bridget, states that Bridget 'always had honest women in her retinue who served her' (*Liber Celestis*, ed. Ellis, 1).

the room in which St Bridget died: the saint's death chamber, much altered but with its fourteenth-century ceiling and the relic of St Bridget's tablecover on which she died, survives at the Casa di Santa Brigida in Rome's Piazza Farnese, just a few metres from the site of the English Hospice.

she knelt . . . on what day she should die: Archbishop Gregersson, who wrote the life of St Bridget of Sweden in order that she be canonized as a saint, records how St Bridget received a vision at Arras of 'how she should travel to Rome and to Jerusalem, and how she should pass out of this world' (*Liber Celestis*, ed. Ellis, 2; also *LSRev*, 26–7).

one of St Bridget's days: the feast of Bridget's canonization and translation was 8 October; her saint day was 23 July.

88 *the saint was to be worshipped more than she was at that time*: these events took place during the canonization of St Bridget in Rome, and this clause indicates that Kempe sees Bridget as a worthy recipient of canonization.

Stations of Rome: a pilgrimage route around various churches and holy sites in Rome; guides like the Middle English poem *The Stations of Rome* and John Capgrave of Lynn's *Solace of Pilgrims* provided pilgrimage itineraries and guides to the relics and indulgences associated with each 'station'.

91 *This woman has sown . . . came here*: Matthew 13: 37–8, 'He that soweth the good seed, is the Son of Man | And the field, is the world. And the good seed are the children of the kingdom. And the cockle, are the children of the wicked one.'

St Jerome: Jerome (d. 420), Church Father, best known for his translation of the Bible in the Vulgate Latin; buried at the basilica of Santa Maria Maggiore, Rome. Medieval traditions held that his body was miraculously transferred from Bethlehem, where he died, to Rome. The church seen by Kempe was essentially a fifth-century basilica with a twelfth-century façade.

St Laurence: the basilica of San Lorenzo fuori le Mura, Rome. The building seen by Kempe was largely built in the thirteenth century with frescoes of the lives of saints Stephen and Laurence; much of the church as seen by Kempe survives, although it was reconstructed after a bombing raid in 1943. This church is in fact about 1½ miles from S Maria Maggiore.

When Easter, or Passover, had come and gone: the year is probably 1415.

92 *St Peter's Church*: the basilica of San Pietro in Vaticano; Kempe would have seen the fourth-century church, held to have been built on the burial site of St Peter. The enormous and opulent building that stands today was built in the sixteenth and seventeenth centuries.

Middelburg: a commercial port in Zeeland (now part of Holland), on the south-western coast, facing England.

the Sunday: by tracing back from Kempe's visit to Norwich on Trinity Sunday (Chapter 44), this can probably be dated to 12 May 1415.

93 *the next day*: probably Saturday, 18 May 1415.

94 *when she had left England*: i.e. Kempe's offering at Norwich in Chapter 26 (p. 58).

Master Richard Caister: Richard of Caister (d. 1420), priest and theologian. A native of Norfolk and a noted preacher, Caister was said to have written numerous religious books and, after his death, a local cult developed around him. The only surviving piece of his writing seems to be the widely-copied and elegant lyric celebrating Christ's Passion which shows particular devotion to Christ's wounds. The first stanza of this lyric reads

> JESU, Lord, that madest me,
> And with Thy blessed blood has bought,
> Forgive that I have grieved Thee
> With word, with will, and eke with thought.

See further Norman P. Tanner, 'Caistor, Richard (d. 1420)', *ODNB*.

an anchorite . . . Chapel in the Fields: this refers to the College of St Mary in the Fields, founded in the thirteenth century, which lay in countryside to the south-west of the city. Norman P. Tanner, *The Church in Late Medieval Norwich, 1370–1532* (Toronto, 1984), 199, shows how there were certainly anchorites there in the fifteenth century, including one called 'Sir Thomas', although the sources are very sketchy. The anchorite was probably Thomas Brackley (d. *c.*1417), an anchorite (possibly of Brackley, Northamptonshire) who had influential patrons in Norwich (see *BMK* 307). Tanner (pp. 198–203) details the numerous hermits and anchorites in and around Norwich in the period 1370–1549.

Sir Edward: a Sir Edward Hunt is mentioned in the will of Thomas Brackley (see previous note). 'Sir' and 'Master' were not necessarily technical academic or religious titles, but were used merely as honorifics to suggest authority.

95 *Trinity Sunday*: the first Sunday after Pentecost; probably 26 May 1415.

96 *extreme unction*: one of the sacraments, the anointing of the sick was an essential preparation for death through appealing to Christ to pardon the ill person's sins of the body. See John Mirk, *Instructions for Parish Priests*, ed. G. Kristensson (Lund, 1974), 164, 170–4.

   visit Santiago: i.e. visit the shrine of St James [Iago] at Santiago de Compostela in northern Spain, one of the pre-eminent pilgrimage sites in medieval Europe. See p. 101 for Kempe's visit.

   twisted her body: a note in the manuscript (fo. 51v) says 'so did prior Norton in his excesses', referring to John Norton (d. 1522), Prior of Mount Grace, the monastery that owned the Kempe manuscript. See p. 3.

97 *I shall go . . . wherever you go*: echoing Ruth's words to Naomi, 'whithersoever thou shalt go, I will go' (Ruth 1: 16).

   Bristol: a major seaport in the west of England, made rich by trade with French, Icelandic, Irish, and Spanish ports.

   Wednesday in Whit Week: probably 26 May 1417 (working backwards from the reference to Henry V's French expedition of 1417).

   detained and requisitioned for the King: in spring and early summer 1417 Henry V had requisitioned shipping, ordering vessels to assemble at Southampton to prepare for an invasion of France. See Christopher Allmand, *Henry V* (London, 1992), 113.

98 *"Father, forgive them, for they know not what they do"*: Luke 23: 34.

   Corpus Christi Day: 10 June 1417, celebrating the body and blood of Christ in the Eucharist. In medieval England, the festival was often celebrated with religious drama as well as the kinds of procession described by Kempe. See Rubin, *Corpus Christi*.

   Newcastle: probably Newcastle-under-Lyme (Staffordshire), a major market town with several thriving religious houses, rather than the far distant Newcastle-upon-Tyne (Northumberland). Marshall accompanies Kempe back from Spain to the Midlands (to Leicester, about 60 miles from Newcastle-under-Lyme) but not north to York, towards Newcastle-upon-Tyne.

   Thomas Marshall: Marshall has not been positively identified; the name is not an unusual one.

99 *Bishop of Worcester*: Thomas Peverell (d. 1419), Bishop of Worcester (1407–19). Peverell was almost certainly from the same area of Norfolk as Kempe: his first recorded ecclesiastical position is as a member of the Carmelite friary at Lynn in 1377 (this helps explain how he knows about her background in their subsequent conversation). The assumption of the bishopric was the zenith of Peverell's career; see *ODNB*, 'Thomas Peverel [Peverell]'.

   lodged three miles away from Bristol: the bishops of Worcester owned a palace at Henbury (Gloucestershire), where Peverell was to die. Now in a suburb of Bristol, the palace was ruined during the Reformation and, in the eighteenth century, Blaise Castle was built over it. The gatehouse of the medieval bishops' palace remains.

modishly striped and cut: the Middle English '*al-to-raggyd and al-to-daggyd*' suggests that the clothes are slashed to reveal colourful linings and cut to points. See p. 99 for Kempe's objections to similar fashions.

100 '*Sir*': Kempe's language becomes noticeably polite here; she addresses the Bishop with the respectful '*you*' form, whereas he uses the intimate '*thou*' form to her.

101 *fourteen days*: Kempe gives no details of her stay in Santiago. For a clear account of the kinds of pilgrim rituals she might have experienced, see Kathleen Ashley and Marilyn Deegan, *Being a Pilgrim: Art and Ritual on the Medieval Routes to Santiago* (Farnham, 2009), 222–42.

Blood of Hailes: a celebrated relic, a phial said to contain Christ's blood, which was a popular pilgrimage destination; it was held by the now-ruined Hailes Abbey, a wealthy Cistercian house in rural Gloucestershire, just over 50 miles from Bristol. During the Reformation, Henry VIII's commissioners declared that the blood was that of a duck, renewed regularly (see Alexandra Walsham, 'Skeletons in the cupboard: relics after the English Reformation', *Past and Present* 206 (2010), 121–43).

Leicester: a large and important Midlands town. From Hailes to Leicester is a journey of some 63 miles.

fire of love: cf. pp. 31, 66.

Mayor: the Mayor of Leicester at the time would have been one John Arnesby (*BMK* 310).

102 *St Katherine*: one of Kempe's favourite saints (see pp. 40, 49, 188). The *Golden Legend* describes how St Katherine was stripped naked, tormented with scorpions and then put in a dark prison for twelve days without food and, in this prison cell, was visited by angels who tended her wounds and filled the cell with light.

Lollard: the Middle English word ascribed to the Mayor, *loller*, could mean both Lollard (or Wycliffite heretic) and lazy vagabond, literally, somebody who lolls about; on the history of this term see Paul Strohm, *Theory and the Premodern Text* (Minneapolis, 2000), 20–2. It is clear that the Mayor objects to Kempe on the ground of her misleading the people in religious belief and suspects her of heterodox thinking.

Boston: a town in Lincolnshire, on the other side of the Wash estuary from Lynn, some 30 miles away.

Steward of Leicester: this man has not been identified.

103 *Wisbech*: the inland port-town of Wisbech (Cambridgeshire) is 13 miles south-west of Lynn and 60 miles east of Leicester.

104 *Guildhall*: a fourteenth-century timber-framed hall, on Guildhall Lane in the centre of Leicester and adjacent to the modern cathedral. Originally

the meeting-place of the Leicester Corpus Christi guild, the Guildhall seems to have been functioning as the town hall for the Leicester Corporation at the time Kempe was in the city. The building, on Guildhall Lane, can be visited today.

104 *Church of All Hallows at Leicester*: All Saints Highcross Street, a Norman church (now decommissioned) on the northern side of the city.

Abbot of Leicester: at this point, the abbot was Richard Rothley. See Goodman, *Margery Kempe*, 128.

Dean of Leicester: the identity of this man is not clear.

blessed sacrament of the altar . . . believed in it: the status and efficacy of the sacrament of the Eucharist was one of the key issues around which Wycliffite and Lollard controversies were fought. See Anne Hudson, *The Premature Reformation: Wycliffite Texts and Lollard History* (Oxford, 1988), 281–90.

105 *ordinary bread*: Kempe is here referring to the distinction between 'substance' and 'accident': according to orthodox belief, the bread was merely a non-essential attribute (the 'accident') of the Eucharist, the 'substance' of which was the actual, living body and blood of Christ.

fourteen children: Kempe's only reference to her offspring, apart from the references to her son.

vengeance on the cities . . . see: Genesis 18: 21, referring to God's destruction of Sodom and Gomorrah (Genesis 18–19).

106 *Abbey at Leicester*: the Augustinian priory of St Mary de Pratis, a very wealthy and influential institution to the north of the medieval city. Ruins of the monastic precincts can still be seen.

107 *aforementioned son*: i.e. Thomas Marshall.

Patrick: possibly one John Patryk or Patrick of Melton Mowbray; see Goodman, *Margery Kempe*, 149, 252–3.

Melton Mowbray: a Leicestershire market-town, 15 miles north-east of Leicester.

a staff like Moses' rod: presumably a souvenir, a kind of walking-stick memento of Moses' rod (Exodus 9–10, Numbers 20: 9). Kempe is likely to have seen the relic of Aaron's rod, with which it was sometimes conflated, at San Giovanni in Laterano at Rome. John Capgrave of Lynn, in his *Solace of Pilgrims* (ed. C. A. Mills (London, 1911), 73), noted that the church held 'the ark of the Old Testament with the Tablets of the Law, the rod that flowered, and the golden vessel with manna in it'.

109 *Our Lady's Eve*: this could be one of several festivals: of the Purification or the Assumption of the Virgin, but fasting was customary for the Nativity of the Virgin; this can then be dated to 7 September 1417.

a church in York: this is the Benedictine cathedral church of York Minster, as revealed in the pages that follow.

Children of the monastery: a school at York Minster to educate choristers can be traced back as far as the sixth century; see Nicholas Orme, *Medieval Schools* (New Haven, 2006), 266–87.

110 *Crescite et multiplicamini*: God's command 'increase and multiply' (Genesis 1: 22; repeated Genesis 1: 28, 8: 17, 9: 1, 9: 7). Lollard debates on sexual continence may provide a pressing context for the cleric's interrogation of Kempe here, though, as elsewhere in the *Book*, the episode merely allows Kempe to give an orthodox reply to her detractors.

Master John Acomb: d. 1427, rector of St Margaret's Walmgate, York, and canon prebendary at York Minster. Jonathan Hughes, *Pastors and Visionaries: Religious and Secular Life in Late Medieval Yorkshire* (Cambridge, 1988), 239, describes Acomb as a member of a 'Cambridge circle of northerners who were students of contemplative literature'.

Sir John Kendal: d. 1427, a vicar choral of York Minster (Hughes, *Pastors and Visionaries*, 205).

Chapter House: effectively the courtroom and meeting place of the Minster's canons, the Chapter House can still be visited today, on the north side of the building.

111 *the shrine of St William*: St William of York (d. 1154), William Fitzherbert, Archbishop of York. He was possibly poisoned and, following his burial at York, miracles were reported. His cult became very popular in northern England in the fourteenth and fifteenth centuries, focused on his shrine behind the high altar of York Minster.

an affidavit from your husband: i.e. a letter from Kempe's husband giving her permission to go on pilgrimage.

Cawood: formerly the site of the palace of the archbishops of York; by foot, 10 miles south of York.

112 *Archbishop of York*: at this time, the Archbishop was Henry Bowet (Archbishop 1407–23). Bowet was from a Cumbrian gentry family; he studied at Cambridge and served at the papal court. Following Henry IV's rise to power, Bowet was a member of the king's inner circle and a stern prosecutor of heresy. See T. F. Tout, rev. J. J. N. Palmer, 'Bowet, Henry (d. 1423)', *ODNB*.

114 *rudely*: the Archbishop uses the disrespectful and familiar form '*thou*', whilst Kempe replies with the more formal '*you*'.

my confessor: Kempe is referring here to St John of Bridlington (d. 1379), an Augustinian prior who worked miracles. He took a vow of chastity at the age of 12 and was well known as a model of piety. A commentary on his prophecies, written by John Ergome (*fl.* 1364), circulated during his lifetime and miracles were worked at his tomb soon after his death. Kempe's Lynn contemporary John Capgrave wrote a Latin account of John of Bridlington's miracles. See Michael J. Curley, 'John of Bridlington [St John of Bridlington, John Thwing] (*c.*1320–1379)', *ODNB*. Bridlington's confessor, William Sleightholme, is mentioned in the next chapter. See note to p. 117.

115 *"Blessed is the womb . . . gave thee suck"*: Luke 11: 27.

"Yea rather, blessed are they who hear the word of God, and keep it": Luke 11: 28.

no woman should preach: 1 Corinthians 14: 34, 'Let women keep silence in the churches: for it is not permitted them to speak, but to subject, as also the law saith.' On Lollard women and their involvement in scriptural teaching, see Claire Cross, '"Great reasoners in scripture": the activities of women Lollards', in Dawn Baker, ed., *Medieval Women* (Oxford, 1978), 359–80.

old man: a stock figure of medieval preachers' exemplary tales, usually signifying wisdom, memory, and divinity. Chaucer uses a similar figure in his 'Pardoner's Tale'.

117 *her confessor (who was named Sleightholme) at Bridlington*: William Sleightholme (d. 1420), canon of Bridlington and family confessor of the aristocratic and powerful Neville family of Raby (Durham) (Hughes, *Pastors and Visionaries*, 303). Sleightholme's name no doubt comes from the hamlet of that name, about 15 miles from Raby.

Hull: Hull (Kingston-upon-Hull), a port town on the Humber estuary, a principal port for trade with Scandinavia and the Baltic.

Hessle: Hessle is a town on the north bank of the Humber estuary, 5 miles west of Hull; medieval Hessle was a small village where ferries across the Humber landed. It is now the terminal point of the Humber Bridge.

Duke of Bedford's yeomen: the Duke of Bedford at this time was John (1389–1435), the third son of Henry IV; see Jenny Stratford, 'John [John of Lancaster], duke of Bedford (1389–1435)', *ODNB*. John was devout and orthodox, and a dogged persecutor of Joan of Arc.

118 *Beverley*: a town 10 miles north of Hessle, and a major pilgrimage centre on account of the shrine of St John of Beverley (see p. 26). The town was wealthy in the Middle Ages from the import and export of wool, cloth, and tannery products, and one of the larger English towns in Kempe's day.

119 *Chapter House*: at Beverley Minster, the large gothic parish church which housed the shrine of St John of Beverley. The Chapter House is no longer standing.

120 *a perfect woman*: Matthew 5: 48, 'Be you therefore perfect, as also your Heavenly Father is perfect.'

Cobham's daughter . . . around the region: the reference is to Sir John Oldcastle, Lord Cobham (d. 1417). At this time, Cobham was on the run from the authorities, having been declared a heretic in 1413 and imprisoned. He escaped from the Tower of London later that year and was not recaptured until the winter of 1417; he attempted, in league with Lollards, to make an armed rebellion against Henry V. On 14 December 1417 he was hanged and burnt under the orders of the Duke of Bedford (see p. 117 for his role in Kempe's persecution). The allegation made by the officers is that Kempe is distributing Cobham's Lollard literature around Yorkshire.

she had not been in Jerusalem . . . in truth: Lollards were opposed to pilgrimage on the grounds that to make offerings to what the Lollards' Twelve Conclusions called 'blind roods and deaf images of wood and stone' was a kind of idolatry. Therefore the guards seek to deny Kempe's pilgrimages in order to present her as a Lollard.

121 *to his bedside*: this detail reflects Archbishop Bowet's advanced age at the time; he was probably born before the mid-1340s (T. F. Tout, rev. J. J. N. Palmer, 'Bowet, Henry (d. 1423)', *ODNB*).

Suffragan: identified as John Rickinghall (*c*.1355–1429), later Bishop of Chichester. He was probably from Suffolk and during the 1420s was the Duke of Bedford's confessor. See Christopher Whittick, 'Rickinghall [Rickinghale], John, *c*.1355–1429', *ODNB*.

you were at my Lady Westmoreland's: Joan Beaufort, Lady Westmoreland (d. 1440), daughter of John of Gaunt, wife of Ralph Neville, first Earl of Westmoreland. See Anthony Tuck, 'Beaufort, Joan, countess of Westmorland (1379?–1440)', *ODNB*. Hughes, *Pastors and Visionaries*, 100–1, describes the Neville family's support of the cult of St John of Bridlington and surmises that Beaufort had hosted Kempe at Raby Castle (Durham), some 86 miles north-west of Bridlington.

Lady Greystoke: Elizabeth, Lady Greystoke (d. 1434). (Lord Greystoke at this time was John de Greystoke, 4th Baron (1389–1436).)

123 *to the River Humber*: the boundary of the Archbishop of York's diocese. A distance of 9 miles by foot from Beverley.

"Take no thought . . . speaketh in you": Matthew 10: 19–20.

124 *West Lynn*: the western settlement across the River Great Ouse from the main town of Lynn; it was connected by ferry with Lynn although it was, by this point, separate from the borough of Lynn and had its own parish church.

London: from West Lynn to London is a journey of some 99 miles.

Archbishop of Canterbury: Henry Chichele (*c*.1362–1443), Archbishop of Canterbury 1414–43; Chichele continued and extended the Church's attack on Lollardy, allowing bishops to try such cases themselves. See Jeremy Catto, 'Chichele, Henry (*c*.1362–1443)', *ODNB*.

Ely: Ely is 28 miles from Lynn.

a thoughtless man . . . many more occasions: this story is glaringly similar to one reported in the canonization documents of St Bridget of Sweden: 'Once when she was passing through a narrow street, a nobleman whom she had called to account threw his dirty wash basin water down on her head. She calmly went on, thanking God for this insult to increase her humility' (*LSRev*, 10).

126 *Prior's Chapel at Lynn*: a chapel in the south choir aisle of St Margaret's church. St Margaret's was a parish church but also had a priory attached to it; the chancel was maintained by the priory, apart from the Guild of the Holy Trinity's own chapel.

time of removing: the day on which it was customary for people to move house.

Thomas Hevingham: little is known about him, other than that he was Prior of Lynn and sympathetic to Kempe's piety (*BMK* 369).

127 *sepulchre*: an Easter sepulchre, a common feature of late medieval English churches. They were usually decorated with scenes of Christ's Passion and Resurrection. At Easter, the crucifix and Eucharist were placed in the Easter Sepulchre, candles were lit around it, and the bringing out of the Host from the Sepulchre formed a kind of dramatic tableau of Christ's resurrection.

as has been written before: one of the signs of the text's complicated process of composition: this has not, in fact, been stated previously!

128 *ask whatever you will, and you shall have it*: alluding to John 16: 24 ('Ask, and you shall receive'), as noted by one of the medieval annotators in the margins.

well of tears . . . constrain you: see note to p. 75.

129 *as meat for the pot*: see note to p. 18.

taken the anchorite away from me: as reported in Chapter 5.

many days after this answer: we discover in the following lines that this priest was with Kempe for seven or eight years before Kempe travelled to Norwich, probably in 1420, to pray for him during a spell of illness. Therefore the priest seems to have come to Lynn about 1412–13.

130 *our Lord . . . wept thereupon*: Luke 19: 41. In the medieval Jerusalem visited by Kempe, there was a church (now a twentieth-century building on top of an early medieval chapel) of Dominus Flevit ('the Lord wept') which commemorated this episode. Kempe would undoubtedly have been familiar with the traditions of this pilgrimage site on the Mount of Olives.

she, Jerusalem: the gendering of Jerusalem as female is conventional, deriving from the biblical representation of the city as a beautiful woman (e.g. Apocalypse 21: 2).

When she had gone: one of the points at which the narrator does not use Kempe's eyewitness account, but rather a more 'novelistic' voice, reconstructing the conversation between the priest and his mother.

the Bible . . . other such books: a conventional late medieval library of mystical and devotional bestsellers, repeating the books mentioned in Chapter 17 with the addition of a glossed Latin bible.

133 *where the good vicar is buried*: referring to Richard of Caister (see p. 94), who died on 29 March 1420. He quickly became a local saint. See Norman P. Tanner, 'Caistor, Richard (d. 1420)', *ODNB*.

134 *a pretty image . . . called a 'pity'*: a pietà, usually a painted image or sculpture of the seated Virgin with the dead Christ lying in her lap.

a friar: a note in the margin of the manuscript later on records the name 'Melton'. William Melton was a Franciscan friar and noted preacher (see Goodman, *Margery Kempe*, 86). We cannot be sure that the friar described by Kempe was Melton, as the annotator's reliability cannot be guaranteed.

135 *a chapel of St James at Lynn*: a twelfth-century chapel of ease near St Margaret's church. Now demolished, only a few ruins remain.

136 *a worshipful doctor of divinity . . . many years' standing*: this would then seem to be Master Alan of Lynn and Robert Springold.

137 *St James's Day*: 25 July; the year is probably in the early 1420s.

138 *Marie d'Oignies*: the Flemish holy woman Marie d'Oignies (d. 1213) whose life was a major source for Kempe's book. Born to a wealthy family, Marie was a devout child who rarely mixed with others. At 14, her parents married her to a local youth, John, but Marie punished her own body with extreme ascetic deeds. John was converted to Marie's 'holy plan' of living chaste, which caused their relatives to hold Marie in contempt. Marie fasted, made pilgrimages, and was visited with tears ('when she tried to restrain the intensity of the flowing river, then a greater intensity wondrously sprang forth' (*Two Lives*, ed. King, 55). Marie wore a rough hairshirt and 'a white woollen tunic . . . without the addition of any fur or any puffery' (*Two Lives*, ed. King, 72). She retired to the monastery at Oignies near Lille and predicted that she would die there; she was celebrated as a holy woman and did indeed die, aged 36, at Oignies.

he: it is not clear which author is being referred to here; Marie's *Vita* was written down by her confessor, Jacques de Vitry (*c.*1170–1240), and was then multiply translated and reformatted: for instance, there was a Middle English translation, a supplement to the life by Thomas of Cantimpré, and Jacques' life of Marie was also excerpted by Vincent of Beauvais in his hugely widespread *Speculum historiale* and in the preachers' story collection, the *Alphabet of Tales*.

'Bonus es . . . in te': this quotation does not correspond directly with Jacques de Vitry's *Life* of Marie, but suggests that Kempe's confessor was familiar with a Latin rather than Middle English version of Marie's legend. The story is similar to that given in Jacques de Vitry's account: one day, before Good Friday, a priest 'softly but firmly exhorted her to pray in silence and to restrain her tears'. Marie slipped outside, quietly, as she was asked. But another time, at Mass, the same priest burst into floods of tears, so much so that he was 'drenched with his tears and the book and the altar cloths were dripping as well' (*Two Lives*, ed. King, 55).

139 *Prick of Love*: probably a Middle English translation of the *Stimulus Amoris* or *Pricking of Love*, a popular mystical prose treatise which originated in thirteenth-century Italy but was adapted in translation.

Et capitulo . . . ut supra: 'And a chapter from the *Stimulus Amoris* [*Pricking of Love*] and a chapter as above'; again, this suggests the Latin original from which Kempe's scribe translated this. On these texts, see Roger Ellis, 'Margery Kempe's scribe and the miraculous books', in Helen Phillips, ed., *Langland, the Mystics, and the Mediaeval English Religious Tradition* (Woodbridge, 1990), 161–75.

139 *Richard of Hampole . . . Incendio Amoris*: the *Fire of Love* by Richard Rolle. By Kempe's time, Rolle had become perhaps the pre-eminent mystical author, and was certainly the most widely-read vernacular religious writer, with nearly 500 surviving manuscripts of his work. See Jonathan Hughes, 'Rolle, Richard (1305x10–1349)', *ODNB*.

Elizabeth . . . treatise: the visions attributed to St Elizabeth of Hungary (1207–31), a Hungarian princess who devoted herself to austerity and charity. She became a popular figure in fifteenth-century England, with her *Revelations* translated into Middle English some time before the 1430s. See Alexandra Barratt, 'Margery Kempe and the king's daughter of Hungary', in Sandra J. McEntire, ed., *Margery Kempe: A Book of Essays* (New York, 1992), 189–201.

140 *Gesine*: from the French *gesine*, 'childbed', named after an image of the Nativity housed in the chapel at the east end of St Margaret's church (*BMK* 324, 329).

142 *You once made me . . . good deeds*: see Chapter 8, p. 23.

143 *I must love . . . as my own self*: Matthew 22: 39, 'Thou shalt love thy neighbour as thyself' (as Matthew 19: 19, Mark 12: 33, Mark 12: 31, Luke 10: 27, Romans 13: 9, Galatians 5: 14, James 2: 8).

145 *"Jesus is my love"*: identical to the inscription on her ring (p. 72).

'Lord, for all your wounds smart . . . into your heart': a rhyming refrain, with the sound of a lyric, which recurs on p. 194.

146 *there happened to be a great fire in Bishop's Lynn*: 23 January 1421; the present Guildhall was built in the aftermath of this fire.

149 *Master Constance*: Thomas Constance, mentioned in 1423 as belonging to the Dominican house at Norwich (*BMK* 327).

I've read about a holy woman . . . but rather comforted her: the story is from the life of Marie d'Oignies; see p. 138.

150 *his own house at Lynn*: the Augustinian friary at Lynn, founded by the late thirteenth century. Remains of its walls can still be seen.

the Prior: at this point, Thomas Hevingham. See Chapter 57, p. 126.

151 *Bishop Wakering, the Bishop of Norwich*: John Wakering (d. 1425) became Bishop of Norwich in 1416. Wakering was Henry V's delegate at the Council of Constance and, from 1422, served on the council of regency of Henry VI. See R. G. Davies, 'Wakering, John (d. 1425)', *ODNB*.

two good clerics: once again, the text keeps anonymous two identities it has already disclosed—these clerics are Alan of Lynn and Robert Springold.

Provincial of the White Friars: the head of the Carmelites in England. At this point, the Provincial of the English Carmelites was Thomas Netter (*c*.1370–1430), a learned man and an energetic prosecutor of Lollards. Three books survive that were part of Netter's gift to the London Carmelites (see Anne Hudson, 'Netter [Walden], Thomas, *c*.1370–1430', *ODNB*).

152 *Thomas Andrew*: rector of the parish church of St Peter Hungate, Norwich (*BMK* 328).

John Amy: at this point, probably the vicar of Appleton, about 9 miles east of Lynn (*BMK* 328–9).

Gesine: see note to p. 140.

this priest: it is not clear who Kempe means by this.

153 *his ruler*: i.e. the Provincial, Thomas Netter, mentioned earlier (p. 151).

taken the mantle and the ring: i.e. a widow who had taken a vow of chastity; see too p. 35.

154 *the Prior of Lynn . . . another of his brethren*: i.e. Thomas Hevingham and John Dereham.

the King died: Henry V died on 31 August 1422.

Bishop of Winchester: Henry Beaufort (1375?–1447), also known as 'The Cardinal of England', illegitimate son of John of Gaunt, Bishop of Winchester, Lancastrian statesman, and cardinal. Towards the end of Henry V's reign, Beaufort had fallen from favour but, upon the king's death, he manoeuvred successfully for a role in Henry VI's minority regime. See G. L. Harriss, 'Beaufort, Henry [*called* the Cardinal of England] (1375?–1447)', *ODNB*.

155 *anointed*: i.e. given the sacrament of the last rites.

156 *'And we know . . . together unto good'*: Romans 8: 28.

Holy Thursday: i.e. Maundy Thursday, marked with penance to signify the day on which Christ was betrayed by Judas and arrested. As with the Palm Sunday vision (Chapter 78), Kempe's vision makes her an observer of the biblical events marked by the festival.

157 *our Lady was dying . . . asking for grace*: the Death of the Virgin was a staple subject of medieval devotion, even though it does not appear in the Canonical Gospels. Kempe had seen the twelfth-century tomb-shrine of the Virgin at the foot of the Mount of Olives in Jerusalem (see note to p. 68).

same pardon . . . plenary remission: this passage seems to recall the pardon Kempe received on her return from Jerusalem, although it includes details—including the reference to St Nicholas' Day, apparently at Ramlah—not mentioned in the original account (Chapter 30, p. 158). 'Plenary remission' means a full pardon from sins.

158 *fifteen years*: St Bridget says that the Virgin died fifteen years after the Crucifixion (*LSRev*, 207).

kiss the lepers . . . love of Jesus: intimacy with lepers was a standard sign of

devotion amongst some of Kempe's favourite religious figures: St Francis
of Assisi, Marie d'Oignies, and St Catherine of Siena all cared for lepers,
as did Bridget of Sweden. See Julie Orlemanski, 'How to kiss a leper',
postmedieval 3 (2012), 142–57.

160 *purified*: the ritual of churching; see p. 178.

163 *"you are mine and I am yours"*: echoing Canticles 2: 16, 'My beloved to me,
and I to him'; Canticles 6: 2, 'I to my beloved, and my beloved to me.'

164 *to love my enemies*: Matthew 5: 44; Luke 6: 27; Luke 6: 35.

165 *twinkling of your eye*: 1 Corinthians 15: 52, 'In a moment, in the twinkling
of an eye, at the last trumpet: for the trumpeter shall sound, and the dead
shall rise again incorruptible: and we shall be changed.'

naked on a hurdle: recalling a fifteenth-century punishment for criminals,
whereby the hurdle was used as a kind of sledge on which criminals were
taken to be executed. For example, the fifteenth-century *London Chronicle*
records how Sir John Mortimer (executed 1424) was 'laid on a hurdle and
drawn through the city of London to Tyburn and there hanged, beheaded'.

Palm Sunday: by the late Middle Ages, Palm Sunday processions had
become highly elaborate affairs. Duffy, *The Stripping of the Altars*, 23–7,
gives a summary of the Palm Sunday procession according to the late
medieval Sarum rite. It was a multimedia event, including palms, a painted
cross, processions through the churchyard, a special shrine in which relics
and the sacrament were displayed, children's role-playing, gospel reading, the singing of anthems by the congregation, and the strewing of
flowers and unconsecrated hosts. The procession culminated, as the *Book*
describes (p. 167), with a dramatic unveiling: a cloth hung over the crucifix
in the church was drawn off, probably using pulleys, to reveal the crucified
Christ. As Claire Sponsler notes, these aspects of Kempe's piety seem to
be 'directly influenced by contemporary drama' (*CBMK* 137).

167 *the staff of the cross and struck the church door*: a widespread practice, sym-
bolizing Christ's descent to the Harrowing of Hell and the opening of
Hell's gates or doors.

168 *John*: St John the Baptist, frequently represented with Mary.

169 *on the Mount of Olives*: Matthew 26: 30, 'And a hymn being said, they went
out unto Mount Olivet.'

170 *'Whom seek ye?'*: John 18: 4.

'Ego sum': 'I am he'; John 18: 5.

she saw the Jews fall down to the ground: John 18: 6.

'Whom seek ye?': John 18: 7.

'I am he': John 18: 8.

Judas come and kiss our Lord: Matthew 26: 49, Mark 14: 45.

who is it that struck thee?: the account of the blindfold and the Jews' question is taken from Luke 14: 65.

171 *Christ bound to a pillar, and His hands were bound above His head*: Kempe would have seen the relic of this pillar at the Church of the Holy Sepulchre in Jerusalem. She may well have seen the magnificent Despenser Retable (*c.*1382) at Norwich Cathedral, which shows Christ in an identical pose, bound to a pillar, his wrists bound above his head (*EAN* 81–2).

forty strokes: cf. Deuteronomy 25: 3, stipulating that the wicked could receive a maximum of forty stripes.

it was so heavy . . . bear it: in Nicholas Love's translation of the *Meditation on the Life of Christ*, Christ's exhaustion at carrying the cross is richly evoked: 'he was . . . so overcome with labour and weariness that he could no longer carry that heavy cross, he laid it down . . .' (Nicholas Love, *The Mirror of the Blessed Life of Christ*, ed. Michael Sargent (Exeter, 2004), 172).

let me help you carry that heavy cross: in the Wakefield play of the Scourging of Christ, Mary likewise offers to help her son carry the heavy cross (*The Towneley Plays*, ed. Martin Stevens and A. C. Cawley, EETS s.s. 13 (Oxford, 1974), 282).

173 *'Woman, behold thy son, in St John the Evangelist'*: paraphrasing John 19: 26.

'This day thou shalt be with me in Paradise': Luke 23: 43.

into His Father's hands: Luke 23: 46, 'Father, into thy hands I commend my spirit. And saying this, he gave up the ghost.'

Joseph of Arimathea: a disciple of Jesus (Matthew 27: 57) who obtained permission from Pilate to take down Jesus' body (John 19: 38).

a marble stone: the 'Slab of Unction' at the entrance to the Church of the Holy Sepulchre; see note to p. 67.

our Lady's sisters: the 'Three Marys', following John 19: 25 ('Now there stood by the cross of Jesus, his mother, and his mother's sister, Mary of Cleophas, and Mary Magdalen').

174 *we are so sad . . . spiteful towards him*: based on the lamenting women of Jerusalem in Luke 23: 28, to whom Jesus said 'Daughters of Jerusalem, weep not over me; but weep for yourselves, and for your children.'

175 *a nice hot broth*: the Middle English word used, '*cawdel*', suggests a hot spiced wine or ale beverage. Gail McMurray Gibson writes, 'it would not be surprising if the fragmentary fifteenth-century recipe (ground sugar and cinnamon are amongst its ingredients) that appears on the verso of the last folio [fo. 124v] of the Kempe manuscript was intended to be the recipe for Margery's wine caudle, a kind of spiritual chicken soup' (*The Theatre of Devotion: East Anglian Drama and Society in the Late Middle Ages* (Chicago, 1989), 51).

176 *in a chapel*: Kempe possibly recalls here the Chapel of the Apparition in the Church of the Holy Sepulchre, Jerusalem. This chapel, extant by the eleventh century and adjacent to the Church's Calvary chapels, commemorates Christ's appearance to His mother.

176 *'Salva sancta parens'*: literally, 'Hail, holy mother'; a liturgical rather than biblical citation, these are the opening words of the Mass of our Lady.

'Woman, why weepest thou?': John 20: 15.

'Sir, if thou hast taken Him hence, tell me, and I will take Him away': John 20: 15.

177 *Mary . . . Master*: John 20: 16.

'Do not touch me': John 20: 17.

'Go to my brethren . . . I am risen': paraphrasing John 20: 17.

Feast of the Purification, or Candlemas Day: 2 February, a major festival in the medieval Christian year. The holiday celebrated the ritual purification of the Virgin and the presentation of Jesus at the Temple (Luke 2: 22–40), and was marked by parishioners offering candles and pennies to the priest.

178 *purified after childbirth*: essentially a thanksgiving ceremony. Medieval women were 'churched' in imitation of the Virgin; they appeared at church, typically forty days after the birth, and this was usually the woman's first communion after giving birth.

179 *dedicated to . . . God and St Michael the Archangel*: St Michael's, Mintlyn, a now-deserted village 3 miles to the east of Lynn; the church is now ruined.

180 *she could never express them . . . felt them*: mystical writing often returns to the impossibility of describing God through language (see similar statements at pp. 4, 81, 132, 171) and this was an important feature of negative mysticism (describing what God is not, rather than what God is). For example, the author of *The Cloud of Unknowing* writes how 'I dare not take upon myself with my blundering, earthly tongue to speak of what belongs solely to God' (*The Cloud of Unknowing*, ed. C. Wolters (Harmondsworth, 1978), 86).

181 *Denny (a nunnery)*: a nunnery 6 miles north of Cambridge; formerly a Templar house, it was re-founded as a Franciscan monastery in 1327 by Marie, Countess of Pembroke. The abbess who sent for Kempe was probably either Agnes Bernard (abbess *c.*1413–19) or Margery Milley (abbess *c.*1419–31).

towards Cambridge: the River Great Ouse runs from Lynn through Ely towards Cambridge; travel by waterway would have been routine in fifteenth-century East Anglia.

183 *I am like a hidden God in your soul*: see note to p. 32, on the image of the hidden God.

185 *as though she were going to sleep*: this chapter features several episodes involving Kempe in sleep-like states, possibly recalling Canticles 5: 2, 'I sleep, and my heart watcheth'. In *The Book of Privy Counselling*, mystical experience is compared to sleep, 'This work can be likened to a "sleep"' (*The Cloud of Unknowing*, ed. Wolters, 179).

The Book of Life: in Christian thought, God's book in which is recorded the name of every person destined for Heaven (after Apocalypse 17: 8, 20:

12–15, 22: 19). The episode is related to one in Bridget of Sweden (*Liber Celestis*, ed. Ellis, 99), 'those who savour my words and those who hope greatly that "My name is written in the *Book of Life*", they support my words' (my translation). A further vision (*Liber Celestis*, ed. Ellis, 331–2) describes Christ's book with two leaves, one of mercy and one of righteousness. Several episodes in Kempe's *Book* feature books as miraculous or divine objects that authorize her spirituality.

187 *house of Preaching Friars . . . chapel of our Lady*: the Dominican house to the east of Lynn, founded by the 1250s (and referred to on p. 20), demolished in the sixteenth century and the ruins cleared in the nineteenth century.

188 *many fair flowers and with many sweet spices*: another echo of Canticles 5, implicitly casting Kempe as bride of Christ ('I am come into my garden, O my sister, my spouse, I have gathered my myrrh, with my aromatical spices'). At the same time, Kempe imagines herself here as a *vièrge ouvrante* (a sculpture of the Virgin that opened up to reveal scenes of the lives of Christ and Mary), opening to receive the Trinity inside her.

golden cushion . . . in your soul: a cushion is a mark of authority in medieval heraldry, but the image of God as three cushions has no known direct source, although it is in keeping with the domesticity and materiality of Kempe's religion. It may be influenced by late medieval texts and images of the Christian heart as a well-furnished house (see Jeffrey Hamburger, *Nuns as Artists: The Visual Culture of a Medieval Convent* (Berkeley and Los Angeles, 1997), 151–7).

191 *bathed me, in your soul*: the reference to Kempe 'bathing' Christ may refer to her visions of His childhood, or to her bathing Him with her tears, and is another characteristically domestic image.

193 *Master Robert, your confessor*: Robert Springold, see pp. 126, 151.

what you desired: i.e. Kempe's request (p. 23) that 'Master N.' (clearly here Robert Springold) be given half the 'credit' for all Kempe's good works and prayers; the other half to be spread amongst her friends and enemies. Springold lived until at least 1436 (*BMK* 368–9).

194 *"Lord, for your wounds smart . . . into your heart"*: see note to p. 145.

Master Alan: Alan of Lynn; see pp. 24, 152.

195 *whether you read or hear read*: this line may suggest that Kempe had some ability to read, or is perhaps intended to ward off Kempe's detractors who felt that she was not learned enough to assume religious authority.

196 *the voice of a sweet bird*: the solace of birdsong is a common medieval literary motif. See C. M. Woolgar, *The Senses in Late Medieval England* (New Haven, 2006), 68–9.

201 *St Vitalis, martyr*: 28 April 1438. Shortly before this, Kempe had been admitted to the Holy Trinity guild at Lynn. St Vitalis of Ravenna's cult was popular in Italy and Dalmatia; his feast was recorded in English martyrologies but was not widely celebrated in England.

201 *the preceding treatise*: it is clear from the opening sentences of Book II that it was conceived as being somewhat separate from Book I, and it seems that Book I, for a period, stood alone as a 'finished' treatise.

202 *fruit of her womb*: a biblical idiom (Genesis 30: 2, Deuteronomy 28: 4, Psalms 126: 3, etc.) and famous particularly from Gabriel's address to the Virgin: 'Blessed art thou among women, and blessed is the fruit of thy womb' (Luke 1: 42). Kempe thus suggests that her care for her son is imitative of the Virgin's care for her son, as described at length in Book I.

   in Prussia, in Germany: as described on p. 5, Lynn had a close relationship with the Baltic, and the Burnham and Kempe families are recorded as being involved in this trade.

204 *he passed to the mercy of our Lord*: the death of Kempe's son, John, can probably be dated to the second half of 1431; recent research by Sebastian Sobecki has shown that John Kempe Jr was still alive in July 1431 and the *Book* later says that the daughter-in-law stayed with Kempe for eighteen months prior to Kempe's trip to Aachen, which probably took place in summer 1433.

205 *Ipswich*: port town in Suffolk, approximately 63 miles south-east of Lynn.

206 *'If I am with you, who can be against you?'*: Romans 8: 31.

   Walsingham: after Canterbury, probably the pre-eminent pilgrimage site in medieval England; Walsingham (Norfolk) is about 24 miles east of Lynn. The village contained the Priory of Our Lady and the miraculous 'Holy House', a replica of the house at Nazareth in which the Annunciation took place. See Stella A. Singer, 'Walsingham's local genius: Norfolk's "newe Nazareth"', in Dominic Janes and Gary Waller, eds., *Walsingham in Literature and Culture from the Middle Ages to Modernity* (Farnham, 2010), 23–35.

   'If God be for us, who can be against us?': repeating the quotation from Romans 8: 31 as spoken by Jesus to Kempe.

208 *Thursday of Passion Week*: i.e. the Thursday after Passion Sunday. Kempe's trip to Aachen (can securely be dated to 1433, so the date on which she sailed would have been 2 April 1433.

209 *Norway*: at this time (1433), Norway was part of what is now known as the 'Kalmar Union' with Denmark and Sweden, all ruled by the same monarch. When Kempe visited, the countries were ruled by Eric III or Eric of Pomerania, whose wife was from the English royal family (Philippa of Lancaster, the daughter of Henry IV of England).

   the Cross was raised . . . noon: the *Book* notes the difference in the Norwegian custom, as in England it was considered necessary for the Host and the Cross to be removed from the Easter Sepulchre early on Easter morning. See Pamela Sheingorn, *The Easter Sepulchre in England* (Kalamazoo, MI, 1987), 29.

210 *Gdańsk in Germany*: now in Poland, this port was one of the major entrepots

of the Teutonic Order and had close trading links with both Lynn and London.

a war in that region: the area around Gdańsk had been conquered by the Teutonic Order in 1308 and many years of war followed between the Teutonic Order and Poland and, later, the Hussite armies (which were connected with the English Lollards); in 1433, during Kempe's visit, the city council of Gdańsk needed to consider defensive measures against the invading Hussites. See David Wallace, *Strong Women: Life, Text, and Territory, 1347–1645* (Oxford, 2011), 113–15.

Wilsnack: the pilgrimage town of Bad Wilsnack is 335 miles from Gdańsk by foot. On the history and meaning of the Wilsnack cult, see Caroline Walker Bynum, *Wonderful Blood: Theology and Practice in Late Medieval Northern Germany and Beyond* (Philadelphia, 2007).

211 *Teutonic Knights of Prussia*: at this point, the Teutonic Order (whose state covered inland areas of the Baltic) was at war with the Hussites, who were to some extent influenced by and perceived to be in league with the England Lollards. Moreover, there were frequent trade disputes between the Hanseatic port and English traders. See Goodman, *Margery Kempe*, 19, 253; Wallace, *Strong Women*, 113–20.

Stralsund: a wealthy Baltic trading port, about 300 miles west by sea from Gdańsk. Around 1389, Kempe's husband John was imprisoned as a result of a Stralsund merchant's lawsuit. At this time, Kempe was importing stock-fish, beer, cloth, wool, and timber from the Baltic ports. See Goodman, *Margery Kempe*, 65.

open war: this is an exaggeration, but probably refers to one of the frequent trade disputes between the Hanseatic and English ports. In 1415 the Hanseatic ports had accused Lynn merchants of trading illegally in Norway whilst in 1428 Lynn merchants complained at the town's Guildhall that they had been forced to flee Norway by ships threatening them (Goodman, *Margery Kempe*, 19). See too note to p. 210.

212 *On the eve of Corpus Christi*: 10 June, probably 1433.

213 *Aachen . . . a riverside*: the foot journey from Wilsnack to Aachen is about 530 miles; the river mentioned here is likely the Rhine, which Kempe would probably have encountered in the region of what is now Leverkusen and Düsseldorf. Kempe did not visit the nearby popular pilgrimage destination of Cologne (Köln), probably choosing Aachen instead because of the relics which were on display only every seven years. Thus Kempe's trip to Aachen can be dated to 1433, when the relics were shown.

the Octave of Corpus Christi: the festival period of eight days, which began with the Feast of Corpus Christi itself (i.e. 11–19 June 1433).

so that people could see it if they wanted: medieval churches usually had an elaborate monstrance, a portable precious holder in which the Host was placed in order to be shown to the congregation. In an act of 'ocular communion', the gazing on the shown Host could sometimes be a proxy for the taking of the Host.

214 *Qui seminant . . . et cetera*: Psalm 126: 5–7, 'They that sow in tears shall reap in joy | Going they went and wept, casting their seeds, | But coming they shall come with joyfulness, carrying their sheaves.'

'English tail': this insult refers to a European and Scottish jibe, according to which the English were alleged to have tails (see Ardis Butterfield, *The Familiar Enemy: Chaucer, Language, and Nation in the Hundred Years Wars* (Oxford, 2009), 124–9). In Middle English one word for a tail is *stert*, and this is what Kempe alleges the German priests called her (*'Englisch sterte'*). However, there may have been a misunderstanding: possibly in German they called her *'sterzer'* (vagabond) or *'stört'* ([she is] annoying, disrupting). See further Klaus Bitterling, 'Margery Kempe, an English sterte in Germany', *Notes & Queries* 43 (1996), 21–2.

215 *our Lady's smock . . . St Margaret's Day*: the relic was believed to have been the smock worn by the Virgin at the Nativity. This was one of the important relics at Aachen, housed in a lavish reliquary in the Carolingian cathedral. At this point in the manuscript (fo. 115r) a red smock has been drawn in the margin.

216 *the court at Rome*: the papal *curia*, essentially the Pope's court and cabinet to which Latin Christians throughout the world could appeal.

217 *Calais*: the port on the northern coast of France, closest to the English coast. At this point (from 1347 to 1558), Calais was a territorial possession of England. Calais is 202 miles west of Aachen.

219 *Dover*: the port on the southern coast of England, from where the crossing to France is shortest (about 21 miles).

220 *Margery Kempe of Lynn*: the only time Kempe's surname is used in the *Book*.

221 *fish-day*: Kempe observes the conventional Friday fasting from meat. Strict Christians would abstain from meat on Wednesdays and Fridays, and during Lent, Advent, and Pentecost.

red herring: a strongly smoked fish (such as a kipper), that turns pinky-red in brine. Here, red herring is a cheaper, less fine dish than the pike, so the proverb refers to someone who declines something cheap only to reach for a finer delicacy. The modern idiom of 'red herring' as a distraction from the main question does not seem to have been current in Kempe's day.

the Cardinal's house: referring to the household of Cardinal Beaufort. See note to p. 121.

222 *Sheen*: the location of both Sheen Priory, a Carthusian monastery (founded 1414), and the Bridgettine house of Syon Abbey (founded 1415). Both were established by Henry V as a major devotional and architectural scheme. Sheen is 10 miles west of London.

Lammas Day: 1 August (presumably 1434). Kempe would have received the Lammas Day indulgence at Syon Abbey; this was one of several indulgences available there. See G. J. Aungier, *The History and Antiquities of Syon Monastery* (London, 1840), 421–6.

223 *Reginald*: the identity of this person has not been established.

224 *Amen*: this is evidently the end of Book II. In the manuscript, the rest of the folio is left blank, and the next section, describing Kempe's extended prayers, begins on the reverse. Whilst Book II is clearly written in the voice of Kempe's narrator, the prayers that follow give the appearance of being composed by Kempe herself.

225 *'Veni creator spiritus'*: 'Come creator Spirit', a Latin Pentecost hymn sung at solemn events, including coronations and ordinations.

226 *King of England*: probably Henry VI (king from 1421). Whilst it is not clear when these prayers were composed, they must date from after Kempe's trip to Jerusalem as they refer to her tears.

227 *nobody . . . unless you draw them*: John 6: 44: 'No man can come to me, except the Father, who hath sent me, draw him.'

229 *Mary Magdalene . . . St Augustine*: four penitents. The first three have appeared earlier in the *Book* (see p. 48).

the woman who was taken in adultery: a famous parable (John 7: 53–8: 11), describing Jesus' discussion with the Pharisees about whether or not an adulterous woman should be stoned.

Lazarus: John 11: 1–12, 17.

that holy place: i.e. the Church of the Holy Sepulchre, Jerusalem.

Jhesu mercy quod Salthows: a conventional thanksgiving on the part of the scribe: 'Thanks be to Jesus! says Salthouse.' Written in the scribe's hand, this closing inscription suggests a Norfolk man (Salthouse is a village, on the north Norfolk coast, some 35 miles north-east of Lynn; the family name Salthouse was known in fifteenth-century Lynn (*BMK*, p. xxxiii)). Another manuscript (Cambridge, University Library Ii.4.12, Geoffrey of Monmouth, *History of the Kings of Britain*, a manuscript certainly owned in the fourteenth century by the library of the Benedictine cathedral priory at Norwich) contains the name 'Richard Salthouse' ('Ric*hard*us Salthow*us*', fo. iir). The lettering of this signature is very similar to that used in the manuscript of *The Book of Margery Kempe*. Richard Salthouse (*fl.* 1443, d. before 1487) entered the priory at Norwich as a monk in 1443 and occupied various roles there, as hostiller, cellarer, and infirmarer, chamberlain, and gardener (see Joan Greatrex, *Biographical Register of the English Cathedral Priories of the Province of Canterbury c.1066 to 1540* (Oxford, 1997), 554). In the 1480s Salthouse was prior of St Leonard's, a dependent cell of Norwich Cathedral. If the similarity of the two signatures is accepted, it is thus possible that the surviving manuscript of *The Book of Margery Kempe* was copied at Norwich by this Richard Salthouse.

GLOSSARY OF OFFICES
AND INSTITUTIONS

The range of different offices and institutions encountered by Kempe can be unfamiliar to a modern reader. There are subtle but important differences between the kinds of roles described; the following list aims to differentiate between them.

alderman a senior civic officer, junior to mayor

anchoress a female *anchorite*

anchorite a recluse, normally enclosed in a cell. From the Latin *anachorita*, one who withdraws, retires, retreats.

bachelor a man who has taken the lowest degree at university

Black Friar a member of the *Dominican* order of friars

burgess a town citizen with full rights and privileges, often used to describe craftsmen and merchants; a member of a local governing body, elected from amongst the townsmen

canon a clergyman living under ecclesiastical law

Carmelites an order of friars, founded in the twelfth century, dedicated to contemplation

Carthusians an order of monks, founded by St Bruno of Cologne in 1084, dedicated to eremitical withdrawal and a life of prayer

doctor of divinity a scholar of theology, a man who has taken the highest degree at university

Dominicans an order of friars, founded by St Dominic (d. 1221), dedicated to preaching

Franciscans an order of friars, founded by St Francis of Assisi (d. 1226), dedicated to charity and penitence

Friars Minor the *Franciscan* order

Grey Friar a member of the *Franciscan* order of friars

legate a church official invested with papal authority

master of divinity a junior scholar of theology, a man who has taken a master's degree

Preaching Friars the *Dominican* order

steward a town official, usually presiding over local courts; in church, a principal office or administrator

suffragan a diocesan bishop, subordinate to an archbishop

vicar a parish priest or an official of a cathedral

White Friar a member of the *Carmelite* order of friars

yeoman a free-born attendant in a noble household; a senior household official

INDEX

References to Margery Kempe (MK), God, Jesus Christ, and the Virgin Mary are not included here, as these figures appear throughout the *Book*.

Index